Frederick Forsyth is the author of ten bestselling novels: *The Day of the Jackal*, *The Odessa File*, *The Dogs of War*, *The Devil's Alternative*, *The Fourth Protocol*, *The Negotiator*, *The Deceiver*, *The Fist of God*, *Icon* and *Avenger*. His other works include *The Biafra Story*, *The Shepherd*; two short story collections, *No Comebacks*, and *The Veteran*; and a sequel to *The Phantom of the Opera*, *The Phantom of Manhattan*. He has also compiled an anthology of flying tales, *Great Flying Stories*, which includes stories by Sir Arthur Conan Doyle, Roald Dahl, Len Deighton and H.G. Wells. He lives in Hertfordshire, England.

www.rbooks.co.uk

THE AFGHAN

Frederick Forsyth

CORGI BOOKS

TRANSWORLD PUBLISHERS
61-63 Uxbridge Road, London W5 5SA
a division of The Random House Group Ltd
www.rbooks.co.uk

THE AFGHAN
A CORGI BOOK: 9780552155045

First published in Great Britain
in 2006 by Bantam Press
a division of Transworld Publishers
Corgi edition published 2007

Addresses for Random House Group Ltd companies
outside the UK can be found at: www.randomhouse.co.uk
The Random House Group Ltd Reg. No. 954009

The Random House Group Ltd makes every effort to ensure that
the papers used in its books are made from trees that have been
legally sourced from well-managed and credibly certified forests.
Our paper procurement policy can be found at:
www.randomhouse.co.uk/paper.htm

Typeset in 11/13.5pt Palatino by
Falcon Oast Graphic Art Ltd.

Printed and bound in Great Britain by
Cox & Wyman Ltd, Reading, Berkshire.

2 4 6 8 10 9 7 5 3 1

Once again, for Sandy,

PART ONE

Stingray

CHAPTER ONE

If the young *Talib* bodyguard had known that making the cellphone call would kill him, he would not have done it. But he did not know, so he did and it did.

On 7 July 2005 four suicide bombers let off their haversack bombs in Central London. They killed fifty-two commuters and injured about seven hundred, leaving at least one hundred crippled for life.

Three of the four were British born and raised but of Pakistani immigrant parentage. The fourth was a Jamaican by birth, British by naturalization and had converted to Islam. He and one other were still teenagers; the third was twenty-two and the group leader thirty. All had been radicalized, or brainwashed into extreme fanaticism, not abroad but right in the heart of England after attending extremist mosques and listening to similar preachers.

Within twenty-four hours of the explosion they had been identified and traced to various residences in and around the northern city of Leeds; indeed all had spoken with varying strengths of Yorkshire accent. The leader was a special-needs teacher called Mohammad Siddique Khan.

During the scouring of their homes and possessions the police discovered a small treasure trove that they chose not to reveal. There were four receipts showing that one of the senior two had bought cellphones of the buy-use-and-throw variety, tri-band versions usable almost anywhere in the world, and each containing a pre-paid SIM card worth about twenty pounds sterling. The phones had all been bought for cash and all were missing. But the police traced their numbers and 'red-flagged' them all in case they ever came on stream.

It was also discovered that Siddique Khan and his closest intimate in the group, a young Punjabi called Shehzad Tanweer, had visited Pakistan the previous November and spent three months there. No trace was found of whom they had seen but weeks after the explosions the Arab TV station Al-Jazeera broadcast a defiant video made by Siddique Khan as he planned his death and it was clear this video had been made during that visit to Islamabad.

It was not until September 2006 that it also became clear that one of the bombers took one of the 'lily-white' untraceable cellphones with him and presented it to his Al-Qaeda organizer/instructor. (The British police had already established that none of the bombers had the technical skill to create the bombs themselves without instruction and help.)

Whoever this AQ high-up was, he seems to have passed on the gift as a token of respect to a member of the elite inner committee grouped around the person of Osama bin Laden in his invisible hideaway in the bleak mountains of South Waziristan that run along the Pakistani/Afghan border west of Peshawar. It would have been given for emergency purposes only, because all AQ operatives are extremely wary of cellphones, but the donor could not have known at the time that the British fanatic would be stupid enough to leave the receipt lying around his desk in Leeds.

There are four divisions to Bin Laden's inner committee. They deal with operations, financing, propaganda and doctrine. Each branch has a chieftain and only Bin Laden and his co-leader

Ayman al-Zawahiri outrank them. By September 2006 the chief organizer of finance for the entire terror group was Zawahiri's fellow Egyptian Tewfik al-Qur.

For reasons which became plain later, he was under deep disguise in the Pakistani city of Peshawar on 15 September, not departing on an extensive and dangerous tour outside the mountain redoubt, but returning from one. He was waiting for the arrival of the guide who would take him back into the Waziri peaks and into the presence of the Sheikh himself.

To protect him in his brief stay in Peshawar he had been assigned four local zealots belonging to the Taliban movement. As befits men who originate in the North-western Mountains, the chain of fierce tribal districts that runs along this ungovernable frontier, they were technically Pakistanis but tribally Waziris. They spoke Pashto rather than Urdu and their loyalties were to the Pashtun people of whom the Waziris are a sub-branch.

All were raised from the gutter in a *madrassah* or Koranic boarding school of extreme orientation, adhering to the Wahhabi sect of Islam, the harshest and most intolerant of all. They had no knowledge of, or skill in, anything other than reciting the Koran and were thus, like teeming millions of *madrassah*-raised youths, virtually unemployable. But given a task to do by their clan chief, they would die for it. That September they had been charged with protecting the middle-aged Egyptian who spoke Nilotic Arabic but had enough Pashto to get by. One of the four youths was Abdelahi and his pride and joy was his cellphone. Unfortunately its battery was flat because he had forgotten to recharge it.

It was after the midday hour. Too dangerous to emerge to go to the local mosque for prayers; Al-Qur had said his orisons along with his bodyguards in their top-floor apartment. Then he had eaten sparingly and retired for a short rest.

Abdelahi's brother lived several hundred miles to the west in the equally fundamentalist city of Quetta and their mother had been ill. He wished to enquire after her so he tried to get through on his cellphone. Whatever he wished to say would be unremarkable, just a few of the trillions of words of 'chatter' that pass through the ether of all five continents every day. But his phone would not work. One of his companions pointed out the absence of black bars in the battery window and explained about charging. Then Abdelahi saw the spare phone lying on the Egyptian's attaché case in the sitting room.

It was fully charged. Seeing no harm, he dialled his brother's number and heard the rhythmic ringing tone far away in Quetta. And in an underground rabbit warren of connecting rooms in Islamabad that constitute the listening department of Pakistan's Counter-Terrorism Centre, a small red light began to pulse.

Many who live in it regard Hampshire as England's prettiest county. On its south coast, facing the waters of the Channel, it contains the huge maritime port of Southampton and the naval dockyard of Portsmouth. Its administrative centre is the historic city of Winchester, dominated by its cathedral almost a thousand years old.

At the very heart of the county, away from all the motorways and even the main roads, lies the quiet valley of the River Meon, a gentle chalk stream along whose banks lie villages and townlets that date back to the Saxons.

One single A-class road runs through from south to north but the rest of the valley is a network of winding lanes edged with overhanging trees, hedges and meadows. This is farm country the way it used to be, with few fields larger than ten acres and even fewer farms larger than five hundred. Most of the farmhouses are of ancient beam, brick and tile and some of these are served by clusters of barns of great size, antiquity and beauty.

The man who perched at the apex of one such

14

barn had a panorama of the Meon valley and a bird's eye view of his nearest village, Meonstoke, barely a mile away. At the time, several zones to the east, that Abdelahi made the last phone call of his life, the roof-climber wiped some sweat off his forehead and resumed his task of carefully removing the claypeg tiles that had been placed there hundreds of years earlier.

He should have had a team of expert roofers, and they should have clad the whole barn in scaffolding. It would have been faster and safer to do the job that way, but much more expensive. And that was the problem. The man with the claw hammer was an ex-soldier, retired after his twenty-five-year career, and he had used up most of his bounty to buy his dream: a place in the country to call home at last. Hence the barn with ten acres and a track to the nearest lane and then to the village.

But soldiers are not always shrewd with money and the conversion of the medieval barn into a country house and a snug home had produced estimates from professional companies that specialize in such projects that took his breath away. Hence the decision, whatever time it took, to do it himself.

The spot was idyllic enough. In his mind's eye he could see the roof restored to its former leak-proof glory, with nine-tenths of the original and unbroken tiles retained and the other ten per cent bought from a yard selling the artefacts of old demolished buildings. The rafters of the hammerbeam roof were still as sound as the day they were hacked from the oak tree, but the cross-battens would have to come off to be replaced over good modern roofing felt.

He could imagine the sitting room, kitchen, study and hall he would make far below him where dust now smothered the last old hay bales. He knew he would need professionals for the electrics and the plumbing, but he had already signed on at Southampton Technical College for night courses in bricklaying, plastering, carpentry and glazing.

One day there would be a flagstoned patio and a kitchen garden; the track would be a gravelled drive and sheep would graze the old orchard. Each night, camping in the paddock as nature favoured him with a balmy late summer heat wave, he went over the figures and reckoned that with patience and a lot of hard work he could just survive on his modest budget.

He was forty-four, olive-skinned, black-haired and -eyed, lean and very hard of physique. And he had had enough. Enough of deserts and jungles, enough of malaria and leeches, enough of freezing cold and shivering nights, enough of garbage food and pain-racked limbs.

He would get a job locally, find a Labrador or a couple of Jack Russells and maybe even a woman to share his life.

The man on the roof removed another dozen tiles, kept the ten whole ones, threw down the fragments of the broken ones, and in Islamabad the red light pulsed.

Many think that with a pre-paid SIM card in a cellphone all future billing is cancelled out. That is true for the purchaser and user but not for the service provider. Unless the phone is used only within the confines of the transmitting area where it was bought, there is still a settling-up to be accomplished, but between the cellphone companies, and their computers do it.

As Abdelahi's call was taken by his brother in Quetta, he began to use time on the radio mast situated just outside Peshawar. This belongs to Paktel. So the Paktel computer began to search for the original vendor of the cellphone in England; its intent was to say, electronically, 'One of your customers is using my time and airspace, so you owe me.' But the Pakistani CTC had for years required both Paktel and its rival Mobitel to patch through every call emitted or received by their networks to the CTC listening room. And, alerted by the British, the CTC had inserted British software into its eavesdropping

17

computers with an intercept suite for certain numbers. One of these had suddenly gone active.

The young Pashto-speaking Pakistani army sergeant monitoring the console hit a button and his superior officer came on the line. He listened for several seconds, then asked: 'What is he saying?'

The sergeant listened and replied: 'Something about the speaker's mother. He seems to be speaking to his brother.'

'From where?'

Another check. 'The Peshawar transmitter.'

There was no need to ask the sergeant any more. The entire call would automatically be recorded for later study. The immediate task was to locate the sender. The CTC major on duty that day had little doubt this would not be possible in one short phone call. Surely the fool would not spend long on the line?

From his desk high above the cellars the major pressed three buttons and by speed-dial a phone trilled in the office of the CTC Head of Station in Peshawar.

Years earlier, and certainly before the event now known as 9/11, the destruction of the World Trade Center on 11 September 2001, the Pakistani Inter-Services Intelligence Department, always known as the ISI, had been deeply infiltrated by fundamentalist Muslims of the Pakistani army.

That was its problem and the reason for its complete unreliability in the struggle against the Taliban and their guests Al-Qaeda.

But Pakistan's President General Musharraf had had little choice but to listen to the USA's strongly worded 'advice' to clean his house. Part of that programme had been the steady transfer of extremist officers out of ISI and back to normal military duties; the other part had been the creation inside ISI of the elite Counter-Terrorism Centre, staffed by a new breed of young officers who had no truck with Islamist terrorism, no matter how devout they might be. Colonel Abdul Razak, formerly a tank commander, was one such. He commanded the CTC in Peshawar and he took the call at half past two.

He listened attentively to his colleague in the national capital, then asked: 'How long?'

'About three minutes, so far.'

Colonel Razak had the good fortune to have an office just eight hundred yards from the Paktel mast, within the radius – a thousand yards or less – normally needed for his direction-finder to work efficiently. With two technicians he raced to the flat roof of the office block to start the D/F sweeps of the city that would seek to pin the source of the signal to a smaller and ever smaller area.

In Islamabad the listening sergeant told his superior: 'The conversation has finished.'

'Damn,' said the major. 'Three minutes and forty-four seconds. Still, one could hardly have expected more.'

'But he doesn't appear to have switched off,' said the sergeant.

In a top-floor apartment in the Old Town of Peshawar Abdelahi had made his second mistake. Hearing the Egyptian emerging from his private room, he had hastily ended his call to his brother and shoved the cellphone under a nearby cushion. But he forgot to turn it off. Half a mile away Colonel Razak's sweepers came closer and closer.

Both Britain's Secret Intelligence Service (SIS) and America's Central Intelligence Agency (CIA) have big operations in Pakistan, for obvious reasons. It is one of the principal war zones in the current struggle against terrorism. Part of the strength of the western alliance, right back to 1945, has been the ability of the two agencies to work together.

There have been spats, especially over the rash of British traitors starting with Philby, Burgess and Maclean in 1951. Then the Americans became aware they too had a whole rogues' gallery of traitors working for Moscow and the inter-agency sniping stopped. The end of the Cold War in 1991 led to the asinine presumption among politicians on both sides of the Atlantic that peace had come at last and come to stay. That was precisely the moment that the new Cold War, silent and hidden in the depths of Islam, was having its birth pangs.

After 9/11 there was no more rivalry and even the traditional horse-trading ended. The rule became: if we have it, you guys had better share it. And vice versa. Contributions to the common struggle come from a patchwork quilt of other foreign agencies but nothing matches the closeness of the Anglosphere information-gatherers.

Colonel Razak knew both the Heads of Station in his own city. On personal terms he was closer to the SIS man, Brian O'Dowd, and the rogue cellphone was originally a British discovery. So it was O'Dowd he rang with the news when he came down from the roof.

At that moment Mr Al-Qur went to the bathroom and Abdelahi reached under the cushion for the cellphone to put it back on top of the attaché case where he had found it. With a start of guilt, he realized it was still 'on' so he switched it off at once. He was thinking of battery wastage, not interception. Anyway, he was too late by eight seconds. The direction-finder had done its job.

'What do you mean, you've found it?' asked O'Dowd. His day had suddenly become Christmas and several birthdays rolled into one.

'No question, Brian. The call came from a top-floor apartment of a five-storey building in the Old Quarter. Two of my undercover people are slipping down there to have a look and work out the approaches.'

'When are you going in?'

'Just after dark. I'd like to make it three a.m., but the risk is too big. They might fly the coop . . .'

Colonel Razak had been to Camberley Staff College in England on a one-year Commonwealth-sponsored course and was proud of his command of idiom.

'Can I come?'

'Would you like to?'

'Is the Pope Catholic?' said the Irishman.

Razak laughed out loud. He enjoyed the banter.

'As a believer in the one true God I would not know,' he said. 'All right. My office at six. But it is mufti. And I mean our mufti.'

He meant there would not only be no uniforms but no western suits either. In the Old Town, and especially in the Qissa Khawani Bazaar, only the shalwar kameez assembly of loose trousers and long shirt would pass unnoticed. Or the robes and turbans of the mountain clans. And that also applied to O'Dowd.

The British agent was there just before six, with

his black and black-windowed Toyota Land Cruiser. A British Land-Rover might have been more patriotic, but the Toyota was the preferred vehicle of local fundamentalists and would pass unnoticed. He also brought a bottle of the whisky known as Chivas Regal. It was Abdul Razak's favourite tipple. He had once chided his Pakistani friend on his taste for the alcoholic tincture from Scotland.

'I regard myself as a good Muslim but not an obsessive one,' said Razak. 'I do not touch pork, but see no harm in dancing or a good cigar. To ban these is Taliban fanaticism which I do not share. As for the grape, or even the grain, wine was widely drunk during the first four Caliphates and if, one day in Paradise, I am chided by a higher authority than you, then I shall beg the all-merciful Allah for forgiveness. In the meantime, give me a top-up.'

It was perhaps strange that a tank corps officer should have made such an excellent policeman, but such was Abdul Razak. He was thirty-six, married with two children and educated. He also embodied a capacity for lateral thought, for quiet subtlety and the tactics of the mongoose facing the cobra rather than the charging elephant. He wanted to take the apartment at the top of the block of flats without a raging fire-fight, if he could. Hence his approach was quiet and stealthy.

Peshawar is a most ancient city and no part is older than the Qissa Khawani Bazaar. Here caravans travelling the Great Trunk Road through the towering and intimidating Khyber Pass into Afghanistan have paused to refresh men and camels for many centuries. And like any good bazaar the Qissa Khawani has always provided for man's basic needs: blankets, shawls, carpets, brass artefacts, copper bowls, food and drink. It still does.

It is multi-ethnic and multilingual. The accustomed eye can spot the turbans of Afridis, Waziris, Ghilzai and Pakistanis from nearby, contrasting with the chitral caps from further north and the fur-trimmed winter hats of Tajiks and Uzbeks.

In this maze of narrow streets and lanes where a man can lose any pursuer are the shops and food stalls of the clock bazaar, basket bazaar, money-changers, bird market and the bazaar of the storytellers. In imperial days the British called Peshawar the Piccadilly of Central Asia.

The apartment identified by the D/F sweeper as the source of the phone call was in one of those tall, narrow buildings with intricately carved balconies and shutters; it was four floors above a carpet warehouse in a lane wide enough for only one car. Because of the heat in summer, all these buildings have flat roofs where tenants may catch a breath of cool night air, and open stair-wells leading up from the street below. Colonel Razak led his team quietly and on foot.

He sent four men, all in tribal clothes, up to the roof of a building four houses down the street from the target. They emerged on to the roof and calmly walked from roof to roof until they reached the final building. Here they waited for their signal. The colonel led six men up the stairs from the street. All had machine pistols under their robes save the point man, a heavily muscled Punjabi who bore the rammer.

When they were all lined up in the stairwell the colonel nodded to the point man who drew back the rammer and shattered the lock. The door sprang inwards and the team went inside at the run. Three of the men on the roof came straight down the access stairs; the fourth remained aloft in case anyone tried to escape upwards.

When Brian O'Dowd tried to recall it later, it all appeared extremely fast and blurred. That was the impression the occupants received as well.

The attack squad had no idea how many men would be inside or what they would find. It could have been a small army; it could have been a family sipping tiffin. They did not even know the layout of the apartment; architects' plans may be filed in London or New York, but not in the

Qissa Khawani Bazaar. All they knew was that a call had been made from a red-flagged cellphone.

In fact they found four young men watching TV. For two seconds the attack group feared they might have raided a perfectly innocent household. Then they registered that all the young men were heavily bearded, all were mountain men and one, the fastest to react, was reaching beneath his robes for a gun. His name was Abdelahi and he died with four bullets from a Heckler & Koch MP5 through the chest. The other three were smothered and held down before they could fight. Colonel Razak had been very clear; he wanted them alive if possible.

The presence of the fifth man was announced by a crash from the bedroom. The Punjabi had dropped his rammer but his shoulder was enough. The door came down and two CTC hard men went in, followed by Colonel Razak. In the middle of the room they found a middle-aged Arab, his eyes wide and round with fear or hatred. He stooped to try to gather up the laptop computer he had hurled to the terracotta tiles in an effort to destroy it; then he realized there was no time, turned and ran for the window which was wide open. Colonel Razak screamed: 'Grab him,' but the Pakistani missed his grip. The Egyptian had been caught naked to the waist because of the heat, and his skin was slick with sweat. He did not even pause for the balustrade but went straight over and crashed to the cobbles forty feet below. Bystanders gathered round the body within seconds but the AQ financier gurgled twice and died.

The building and street had become a chaos of shouting and running figures. Using his mobile phone the colonel called up the fifty uniformed soldiers he had positioned in the black-windowed vans four streets away. They came racing down the alley to restore order, if that is what even more chaos can be called. But they served their purpose; they sealed the apartment block. In time Abdul Razak would want to inter-view every neighbour and above all the landlord, the carpet-seller at street level.

The corpse on the street was surrounded by the army and blanketed. A stretcher would appear. The dead man would be carried away to the morgue of Peshawar General Hospital. Still no one had the faintest idea who he was. All that was clear was that he had preferred death to the tender attention of the Americans at Bagram camp up in Afghanistan where he would surely have been horse-traded by Islamabad with the CIA Station Chief in Pakistan.

Colonel Razak turned back from the balcony. The three prisoners were handcuffed and hooded. There would have to be an armed escort to get them out of here; this was 'fundo' territory. The tribal street would not be on his side. With the prisoners and the body gone, he would spend hours scouring the flat for every last clue about the man with the red-flagged cellphone.

Brian O'Dowd had been asked to wait on the stairs during the raid. He was now in the bedroom holding the damaged Toshiba laptop. Both knew this would almost certainly be the crown jewel. All the passports, all the cellphones, any scrap of paper however insignificant, all the prisoners and all the neighbours – the lot would be taken to a safe place and wrung dry for anything they could yield. But first the laptop . . .

The dead Egyptian had been optimistic if he thought denting the frame of the Toshiba would destroy its golden harvest. Even seeking to erase the files within it would not work. There were wizards over in Britain and the USA who would painstakingly strip out the hard disk and peel away the surface chatter to uncover every word the Toshiba had ever ingested.

'Pity about Whoever-he-was,' said the SIS agent.

Razak grunted. The choice he had made was logical. Hang on for days and the man could have disappeared. Spend hours snooping around the building and his agents would have been spotted; the bird would still have flown. So he had gone in hard and fast and for five extra seconds he would have had the mysterious suicide in handcuffs. He would prepare a statement for the public that an unknown criminal had died in a fall while resisting arrest. Until the corpse was identified. If he turned out to be an AQ high-up the Americans would insist on an all-singing, all-dancing press conference to claim the triumph. He still had no idea how high up Tewfik al-Qur had really been.

'You'll be pinned down here for a while,' said O'Dowd. 'Can I do you the favour of seeing the laptop safely back to your HQ?'

Fortunately Abdul Razak possessed a wry humour. In his work it was a saving grace. In the covert world only humour keeps a man sane. It was the word 'safely' that he enjoyed.

'That would be most kind of you,' he said. 'I'll give you a four-man escort back to your vehicle. Just in case. When this is all over we must share the immoral bottle you brought over this evening.'

Clutching the precious cargo to his chest, flanked fore and aft, and on each side, by Pakistani soldiers, the SIS man was brought back to his Land Cruiser. The technology he needed was already in the back and at the wheel, protecting machinery and vehicle, was his driver, a fiercely loyal Sikh.

They drove to a spot outside Peshawar where O'Dowd hooked up the Toshiba to his own bigger and more powerful Tecra; and the Tecra opened a line in cyberspace to the British Government Communication Headquarters at Cheltenham, deep in the Cotswold hills of England.

O'Dowd knew how to work it, but he was still hazy about the sheer magic (to a layman) of cyber-technology. Within a few seconds, across thousands of miles of space, Cheltenham had acquired the entire contents of the Toshiba's hard disk. It had gutted the laptop as efficiently as a spider drains the juices of a captured fly.

The Head of Station drove the laptop to CTC headquarters and delivered it into safe hands. Before he reached the CTC office block Cheltenham had shared the treasure with America's National Security Agency at Fort Meade, Maryland. It was pitch black in Peshawar, dusk in the Cotswolds and mid-afternoon in Maryland. It mattered not. Inside GCHQ and NSA the sun never shines; there is no night and no day.

In both sprawling complexes of buildings set in rustic countryside the listening goes on from pole to pole and all points between. The trillions of words spoken by the human race every day in five hundred languages and more than a thousand dialects are heard, culled, winnowed, sorted, rejected, retained and, if interesting, studied and traced.

Even that is just the start. Both agencies encode and decrypt in hundreds of codes and each has special divisions dedicated to file recovery and the unearthing of cyber-crime. As the planet rolled on into another day and another night, the two agencies began to strip down the measures Al-Qur thought had obliterated his private files. The experts found the limbo files and exposed the slack spaces.

The process has been compared to the work of a skilled restorer of paintings. With immense care the outer layers of grime or later paint are eased off the original canvas to reveal the hidden work beneath. Mr Al-Qur's Toshiba began to reveal document after document that he thought had been wiped away or overpainted.

Brian O'Dowd had of course alerted his own colleague and superior, the Head of Station in Islamabad, before even accompanying Colonel Razak on the raid. The senior SIS man had informed his 'cousin' the CIA Station Chief. Both men were waiting avidly for news. In Peshawar there would be no sleeping.

Colonel Razak returned from the bazaar at midnight with his treasure trove in several bags. The three surviving bodyguards were lodged in cells in the basement of his own building. He would certainly not entrust them to the common jail. Escape or assisted suicide would be almost a formality. Islamabad now had their names and was no doubt haggling with the US Embassy, which contained the CIA station. The colonel suspected they would end up in Bagram for months of interrogation even though he suspected they did not even know the name of the man they had been guarding.

The telltale cellphone from Leeds, England, had been found and identified. It was slowly becoming clear the foolish Abdelahi had only borrowed it without permission. He was on a slab in the morgue with four bullets in the chest but an untouched face. The man who had been next door had a smashed head but the city's best facial surgeon was trying to put it back together. When he had done his best a photo was taken. An hour later Colonel Razak rang O'Dowd with ill-concealed excitement. Like all counter-terrorist agencies collaborating in the struggle against Islamist terror groups, the CTC of Pakistan has a huge gallery of photos of suspects.

It means nothing that Pakistan is a long way from Egypt. AQ terrorists stem from at least forty nationalities and double that number of ethnic groups. And they travel. Razak had spent the night flashing his gallery of faces from his computer to a big plasma screen in his office and he kept coming back to one face.

It was already plain from the captured passports, eleven of them, all forged and all of superb quality, that the Egyptian had been travelling and for this he had clearly changed his appearance. And yet this one face – that of a man who could pass unnoticed in a bank's boardroom in the West, but who was consumed by hatred for everything and everyone not of his own twisted faith – seemed to have something in common with the shattered head on the marble slab.

Razak caught O'Dowd over breakfast, which he was sharing with his American CIA colleague in Peshawar. Both men left their scrambled eggs and raced over to CTC headquarters. They too stared at the face and compared it with the photo from the morgue. If only it could be true . . . And both men had one priority: to tell Head Office about the stunning discovery they had made. The body on the slab was none other than Tewfik al-Qur, the senior banker of Al-Qaeda himself.

In mid-morning a Pakistani army helicopter came to take it all away. The prisoners, shackled and hooded, went. Two dead bodies and the boxes of evidence recovered from the apartment. Thanks were profuse but Peshawar is an outstation; the centre of gravity was moving, and moving fast. In fact it had already arrived in Maryland.

In the aftermath of the disaster now known simply as 9/11 one thing became clear and no one seriously denied it. The evidence not simply that something was going on, but pretty much what was going on, was there all the time. It was there as intelligence is almost always there; not in one beautiful gift-wrapped package but in dribs and drabs, scattered all over. Seven or eight of the USA's nineteen primary intel-gathering or law-enforcement agencies had the bits. But they never talked to each other.

Since 9/11 there has been a huge shake-up. There are now the six principals to whom everything has to be revealed at an early stage. Four are politicians: the President, Vice-President and the Secretaries of Defense and State. One of the two professionals is chairman of the National Security Committee, Steve Hadley, who oversees the Department of Homeland Security and the nineteen agencies. But the other is the top of the pile: the Director of National Intelligence, John Negroponte.

The CIA is still the primary outside-the-USA intel-gathering body but the Director of Central Intelligence is no longer the lone ranger he used to be. Everyone reports upwards and the three watchwords are: collate, collate, collate. Among the giants the National Security Agency at Fort Meade is still the biggest, in budget and personnel, and the most secret. It alone retains no links to the public or media. It works in darkness but it listens to everything, decrypts everything, translates everything and analyses everything. But so impenetrable is some of the stuff overheard, recorded, downloaded, translated and studied that it also uses an 'out of house' committee of experts. One of these is the Koran committee.

As the treasure from Peshawar came in, electronically or physically, other agencies also went to work. Identification of the dead man was vital and the task went to the FBI. Within twenty-four hours the Bureau reported it was certain. The man who went over the Peshawar balcony was indeed the principal finance-gatherer for Al-Qaeda and one of the rare intimates of OBL himself. The connection had been through Ayman al-Zawahiri, his fellow-Egyptian. It was he who had spotted and headhunted the fanatical banker.

The State Department took the passports. There were a stunning eleven of them. Two had never been used but nine showed entry and exit stamps all over Europe and the Middle East. To no one's surprise six of them were Belgian, all in different names and all completely genuine, except the details inside.

For the global intelligence community Belgium has long been the leaky bucket. Since 1990 a staggering nineteen thousand Belgian 'blank' passports have been reported stolen – and that is according to the Belgian government itself. In fact they were simply sold by civil servants on the take. Forty-five were from the Belgian Consulate in Strasbourg, France, and twenty from the Belgian Embassy in The Hague, Holland. The two used by the Moroccan assassins of anti-Taliban resistance fighter Ahmad Shah Massoud were from the latter. So was one of the six used by Al-Qur. The other five were assumed to be from the still-missing 18,935.

The Federal Aviation Administration, using its contacts and huge leverage across the world of international aviation, checked out plane tickets and passenger lists. It was tiresome but entry and exit stamps pretty much pinpointed the flights to be checked.

Slowly but surely it began to come together. Tewfik al-Qur had seemingly been charged to raise large sums of untraceable money to make unexplained purchases. There was no evidence he had made any himself, so the only logical deduction was that he had put others in funds to make the purchases themselves. The US authorities would have given their eye teeth to learn precisely whom he had seen. These names, they guessed, would have rolled up an entire covert network across Europe and the Middle East. The one notable target country the Egyptian had not visited was the USA.

It was at Fort Meade that the train of revelation finally hit the buffer. Seventy-three documents had been downloaded from the Toshiba recovered in the apartment at Peshawar. Some were just airline timetables and the flights listed on them that Al-Qur had actually taken were now known. Some were public-domain financial reports that had seemingly interested the financier so that he had noted them for later perusal. But they gave nothing away.

Most were in English, some in French or German. It was known Al-Qur spoke all three languages fluently, apart from his native Arabic. The captured bodyguards, up in Bagram air base and singing happily, had revealed the man spoke halting Pashto, indicating he must have spent some time in Afghanistan, though the West had no trace of when or where.

It was the Arabic texts that caused the unease. Because Fort Meade is basically a vast army base it comes under the Department of Defense. The commanding officer of the NSA is always a four-star general. It was in the office of this soldier that the chief of the Arabic translation department asked for an interview.

The NSA's preoccupation with Arabic had been increasing steadily during the nineties as Islamist terrorism, apart from the constant interest evoked by the Israel–Palestine situation, began to grow. It leapt to prominence with the attempt by Ramzi Yousef on the World Trade Center towers with a truck bomb in 1993. But after 9/11 it became a question of: 'Every single word in that language, we want to know.' So the Arabic department is huge and involves thousands of translators, most of them Arabs by birth and education with a smattering of non-Arab scholars.

Arabic is not just one language. Apart from the classical Arabic of the Koran and academia, it is spoken by half a billion people but in at least fifty different dialects and accents. If the speech is fast, accented, using local idiom and the quality is bad, it will usually need a translator from the same area as the speaker to be certain of catching every meaning and nuance.

More, it is often a flowery language, using a great deal of imagery, flattery, exaggeration, simile and metaphor. Added to that, it can be very elliptical, with meanings inferred rather than openly stated. It is quite different from one-meaning-only English.

'We have focused on the two last documents,' said the head of the Arabic translation department. 'They seem to be from different hands. We believe one may well be from Ayman al-Zawahiri himself and the other from Al-Qur. The first seems to have the word patterns of Al-Zawahiri as taken from his previous speeches and videos. Of course, with sound we could be positive to one hundred per cent.

'The reply seems to be from Al-Qur but we have no text on record of how he writes in Arabic. As a banker he mainly spoke and wrote in English.

'But both documents have repeated references to the Koran and passages therein. They are invoking Allah's blessing on something. Now, I have many scholars of Arabic, but the language and subtle meanings contained in the Koran are special, written fourteen hundred years ago. I think we should call on the Koran Committee to take a look.'

The commanding general nodded.

'OK, professor, you got it.' He glanced up at his ADC. 'Get hold of our Koran scholars, Harry. Fly them in. No delays, no excuses.'

CHAPTER TWO

There were four men in the Koran committee, three Americans and a British academic. All were professors, none were Arabs but all had spent their lives steeped in the study of the Koran and its thousands of attendant scholarly commentaries.

One was resident at Columbia University, New York, and following the order from Fort Meade a military helicopter was despatched to bring him to the NSA. Two were with the Rand Corporation and the Brookings Institution respectively, both in Washington, DC. Army staff cars were detached to collect them.

The fourth and youngest was Dr Terry Martin, on secondment to Georgetown University, Washington, DC, from the School of Oriental and

African Studies, London. Part of London University, SOAS enjoys a worldwide reputation for Arabic scholarship.

In terms of the study of matters Arabic the Englishman had had a head start. He was born and raised in Iraq, the son of an accountant with a major oil company operating there. His father had deliberately not sent him to the Anglo-American school but to a private academy that schooled the sons of the elite of Iraqi society. By the time he was ten he could, linguistically at least, pass for an Arab boy among the others. Only his pink face and tufty ginger hair made sure he could never *completely* pass for an Arab.

Born in 1965, he was in his eleventh year when Mr Martin senior decided to leave Iraq and return to the safety of the UK. The Ba'ath Party was back in power, but that power truly resided not with President Bakr but with his Vice-President, who was carrying out a ruthless pogrom of his political enemies, real and imagined.

The Martins had already lived through tumultuous times since the balmy days of the fifties when the boy King Feisal was on the throne. They had seen the massacre of the young King and his pro-western premier Nuri Said, the equally gory murder on camera in the TV studio of his successor General Kassem and the first arrival of the brutal Ba'ath Party. That in turn had been toppled, then returned to power in 1968. For seven years Martin senior watched the growing power of the psychotic Vice-President Saddam Hussein and in 1975 decided it was time to leave.

He had obtained a good post with Burmah Oil in London thanks to a kind word from a certain Denis Thatcher whose wife Margaret had just become leader of the Conservative Party. His elder son, Mike, was thirteen and ready for a British boarding school. All four of them, the father, Mrs Martin, Mike and Terry, were back in the UK by Christmas.

Terry's brilliant brain had already been noted. He walked through exams for boys two and even three years his senior as a knife through butter. It was presumed, as it turned out almost rightly, that a series of scholarships and bursaries would carry him through senior school and Oxford or Cambridge. But he wanted to continue with Arabic studies. While still at school he had applied to SOAS, attending the spring interview in 1983, joining as an undergraduate that same autumn, studying History of the Middle East.

He walked through a first class degree in three years and then put in three more for his doctorate, specializing in the Koran and the first four Caliphates. He took a sabbatical year to continue Koranic studies at the famed Al-Azhar Institute in Cairo and on his return was offered a lectureship at the young age of twenty-five, a signal honour because when it comes to matters Arabic SOAS is one of the toughest schools in the world. He was promoted to a readership at the age of thirty-four, earmarked for a professorship by forty. He was forty-one the afternoon the NSA came seeking his advice, spending a year as a visiting professor at Georgetown because that same spring of 2006 his life had fallen apart.

The emissary from Fort Meade found him in a lecture hall concluding a talk on the teachings of the Koran as relevant to the contemporary age.

It was plain from the wings of the stage that his students liked him. The hall was packed. He made his lectures feel like a long and civilized conversation between equals, seldom referring to notes, jacket off, pacing up and down, his short, plump body radiating enthusiasm to impart and share scholarship, to give serious attention to any point raised from the floor, never putting a student down for lack of knowledge, talking in layman's language, keeping the body of the lecture short with plenty of time for student questions. He had reached that point when the spook from Fort Meade appeared in the wings.

A red plaid shirt in the fifth row raised a hand.

'You said you disagreed with the use of the term "fundamentalist" to refer to the philosophy of the terrorists. Why?'

Given the blizzard of publicity concerning matters Arabic, Islamic and Koranic that had swept across America since 9/11, every question session swerved quickly from theoretical learning to the onslaught on the West that had occupied so much of the previous ten years.

'Because it is a misnomer,' said the professor. 'The very word implies "back to basics". But the planters of bombs in trains, malls and buses are not going back to the basics of Islam. They are writing their own new script, then arguing retroactively, seeking to find Koranic passages that justify their war.

'There are fundamentalists in all religions. Christian monks in a closed order, sworn to poverty, self-denial, chastity, obedience – these are fundamentalists. Ascetics exist in all religions but they do not advocate indiscriminate mass murder of men, women and children. That is the key phrase. Judge all religions and all sects within those religions by that phrase and you will see that to wish to return to the basic teachings is not terrorism, for in no religion, including Islam, do the basic teachings advocate mass murder.'

In the wings the man from Fort Meade tried to

attract Dr Martin's attention. The professor glanced sideways and noted the young man with the short-barbered hair, button-down shirt and dark suit. He had 'government' written all over him. He tapped the watch on his wrist. Martin nodded.

'Then what would you call the terrorists of today? Jihadists?'

It was an earnest young woman further back. From her face Dr Martin judged her parents must have come from the Middle East: India, Pakistan, Iran perhaps. But she did not wear the hejab scarf over the head to indicate strict Muslim.

'Even jihad is the wrong word. Of course jihad exists, but it has rules. Either it is a personal struggle within oneself to become a better Muslim, but in that case it is completely non-aggressive. Or it means true holy war, armed struggle in the defence of Islam. That's what the terrorists claim they are about. But they choose to airbrush the rules out of the text.

'For one thing true jihad can only be declared by a legitimate Koranic authority of proven and accepted repute. Bin Laden and his acolytes are notorious for their lack of scholarship. Even if the West had indeed attacked, hurt, damaged, humiliated and demeaned Islam and thus all Muslims, there are still rules and the Koran is absolutely specific on these.

'It is forbidden to attack and kill those who have offered no offence and done nothing to hurt you. It is forbidden to kill women and children. It is forbidden to take hostages and it is forbidden to mistreat, torture or kill prisoners. The AQ terrorists and their followers do all four on a daily basis. And let us not forget that they have killed far more fellow-Muslims than Christians or Jews.'

'Then what do you call their campaign?'

The man in the wings was becoming agitated. A full general had given him an order. He did not wish to be the last to report back.

'I would term them the New Jihadis, because they have invented an unholy war outside the laws of Holy Koran and thus of true Islam. True jihad is not savage, but what they practise is. Last question, I am afraid.'

There was a gathering of books and notes. A hand shot up at the front. Freckles, white T-shirt advertising a student rock group.

'All the bombers claim to be martyrs. How do they justify this?'

'Badly,' said Dr Martin, 'because they have been duped, well educated though some of them are. It is perfectly feasible to die a *shahid*, or martyr, fighting for Islam in a truly declared jihad. But again there are rules and these are quite specific in the Koran. The warrior must not die by his own hand even though he has volunteered for a no-return mission. He must not know the time and place of his own death.

'Suicides do exactly that. Yet suicide is specifically forbidden. In his lifetime Muhammad absolutely refused to bless the body of a suicide even though the man had ended his own life to avoid the crippling agony of his disease. Those who commit mass murder of innocents and commit suicide are destined for hell, not paradise. The false preachers and imams who trick them down this road will join them there. And now, I fear, we must rejoin the world of Georgetown and hamburgers. Thank you for your attention.'

They gave him a standing ovation and, pink with embarrassment, he took his jacket and walked into the wings.

'Sorry to interrupt, professor,' said the man from Fort Meade, 'but the brass need the Koran Committee back at the Fort. The car is outside.'

'In a hurry?'

'Yesterday, sir. There's a flap on.'

'Any ideas?' asked Martin.

'No, sir.'

Of course. Need to know. The unshakeable rule. If you do not need to know, to do your job, they are not going to tell you. Martin's curiosity would have to wait. The car was the usual dark sedan with the telltale aerial on the roof. It needed to be in touch with base all the time. The driver was a corporal, but even though Fort Meade is an army base the man was in plain clothes, not uniform. No need to advertise either.

Dr Martin climbed into the back while the driver held the door open. His escort took the front passenger seat and they began to drive through the early evening traffic out to the Baltimore highway.

Far to the east the man converting his own barn into a retirement home stretched out by the camp fire in the orchard. He was perfectly happy like that. If he could sleep in rocks and snow drifts he could certainly sleep on the soft grass beneath the apple trees.

Camp-fire fuel was absolutely no problem. He had enough rotten old planks to last a lifetime. His billycan sizzled above the red embers and he prepared a welcome mug of steaming tea. Fancy drinks are fine in their way but after a hard day's work a soldier's reward is a mug of piping hot tea.

He had in fact taken the afternoon off from his lofty task up on the roof and walked into Meonstoke to visit the general store and buy provisions for the weekend.

It was clear everyone knew that he had bought

the barn and was trying to restore it himself. That went down well. Rich Londoners with a cheque book to flash and a lust to play the squire were greeted with politeness up front but a shrug behind their back. But the dark-haired single man who lived in a tent in his own orchard while he did the manual work himself was, so ran the growing belief in the village, a good sort.

According to the postman he seemed to receive little mail save a few official-looking buff envelopes, and even these he asked to be delivered to the Buck's Head public house to save the postman the haul up the long, muddy track; a gesture appreciated by the postman. The letters were addressed to 'Colonel' but he never mentioned that when he bought a drink at the bar or a newspaper or food at the store. Just smiled and was very polite. The locals' growing appreciation of the man was, however, tinged with curiosity. So many 'incomers' were brash and forward. Who was he, and where had he come from, and why had he chosen to settle in Meonstoke?

That afternoon, on his ramble through the village, he had visited the ancient church of St Andrew, and met and fallen into conversation with the Rector, Reverend Jim Foley.

The ex-soldier was beginning to think he would enjoy life where he had decided to settle.

He could pedal his rugged mountain bike down to Droxford on the Southampton road to buy straight-from-the-garden food in the produce market. He could explore the myriad lanes he could see from his roof and sample ale in the old beamed pubs they would reveal.

But in two days he would attend Sunday matins at St Andrew's and, in the quiet gloom of the ancient stone, he would pray, as he often did.

He would ask for forgiveness of the God in whom he devoutly believed for all the men he had killed and for the rest of their immortal souls. He would ask for eternal rest for all the comrades he had seen die beside him; he would give thanks that he had never killed women or children nor any who came in peace, and he would pray that one day he too could expiate his sins and enter into the Kingdom.

Then he would come back to the hillside and resume his labours. There were only another thousand tiles to go.

Vast as is the National Security Agency's complex of buildings, it is only a tiny fraction of Fort Meade, one of the largest military bases in the USA. Situated four miles east of the Interstate 95 and halfway between Washington and Baltimore, the base is home to around ten thousand military staff and twenty-five thousand civilian employees. It is a city in itself and has all the habitual facilities of a small city. The 'spook' part is tucked away in one corner inside a rigidly guarded security zone that Dr Martin had never visited before.

The sedan bearing him glided through the sprawling base with no let or hindrance until it came to the zone. At the main gate passes were examined, and faces peered through the windows at the British academic as his guide up front vouched for him. Half a mile later the car drew up at a side door of the huge main block and Dr Martin and his escort entered. There was a desk guarded by army personnel. More checks; some phoning; thumbs placed on keypads; iris recognition; final admission.

After what seemed like another marathon of corridors they came to an anonymous door. The escort knocked and went in. Dr Martin found himself at last among faces he knew and recognized: friends, colleagues and fellow members of the Koran Committee.

Like so many government-service conference rooms, it was anonymous and functional. There were no windows but air conditioning kept the atmosphere fresh. There were a circular table and padded upright chairs; on one wall hung a screen, presumably for displays and graphics should they be needed; small tables stood to the side with coffee urns and trays of food for the insatiable American stomach.

The hosts were clearly two non-academic intelligence officers; they introduced themselves with give-nothing-away courtesy. One was the Deputy Director of the NSA, sent to attend by the general himself. The other was a senior officer from Homeland Security in Washington.

And there were the four academics, including Dr Martin. They all knew each other. Before agreeing to be co-opted on to the no-name, no-publicity committee of experts steeped in one book and one religion, they had known each other vicariously from their published works and personally from seminars, lectures and conferences. The world of such intense Koranic study is not large.

Terry Martin greeted Doctors Ludwig Schramme from Columbia, New York, Ben Jolley from Rand and 'Harry' Harrison from Brookings, who certainly had a different first name but was always known as Harry. The oldest and therefore the presumed senior was Ben Jolley, a great bearded bear of a man who promptly and despite pursed lips from the Deputy Director produced and lit up a fearsome briar pipe on which he drew happily, once it was going like an autumn bonfire. The Westinghouse extraction technology above their heads did its best and almost succeeded, but was clearly going to need a complete servicing.

The Deputy Director cut straight to the heart of the reason for the convocation of the scholars. He distributed copies of two documents, one file to each man. These were the Arabic originals as teased out of the AQ financier's laptop, and translations by the in-house Arabic division. The four men went straight to the Arabic versions and read in silence. Dr Jolley puffed; the man from Homeland Security winced. The four finished more or less at the same time.

Then they read the English translations to see what had been missed and why. Jolley looked up at the two intelligence officers.

'Well?'

'Well . . . what, professor?'

'What,' asked the Arabist, 'is the problem that has brought us all here?'

The Deputy Director leaned over and tapped a portion of the English translation.

'The problem is that. There. What does it mean? What are they talking about?'

All four of them had spotted the Koranic reference in the Arabic text. They had no need of translation. Each had seen the phrase many times and studied its possible various meanings. But that had been in scholarly texts. This was in modern letters. Three references in one of the letters, a single reference in the other.

'Al-Isra? It must be a code of some kind. It refers to an episode in the life of the Prophet Muhammad.'

'Then forgive our ignorance,' said the man from Homeland. 'What is Al-Isra?'

'You explain, Terry,' said Dr Jolley.

'Well, gentlemen,' said Terry Martin, 'it refers to a revelation in the life of the Prophet. To this day scholars argue as to whether he experienced a genuinely divine miracle or whether it was simply an out-of-body experience.

'Briefly, he was asleep one night a year before his emigration from his birthplace of Mecca to Medina when he had a dream. Or a hallucination. Or a divine miracle. For brevity let me say "dream" and stick with it.

'In his dream he was transported from the depths of modern Saudi Arabia across deserts and mountains to the city of Jerusalem, then a city holy only to Christians and Jews.'

'Date? In our calendar?'

'Around six hundred and twenty-two AD.'

'Then what happened?'

'The Archangel Gabriel, mounted on a winged horse, took Muhammad up through the seven heavens and finally into the presence of Almighty God himself, who instructed him in all the prayer rituals required of a True Believer. These he memorized and later dictated to a scribe as what became an integral part of the six thousand, six hundred and sixty-six. These verses became and remain the basis of Islam.'

The other three professors nodded in agreement.

'And they believe that?' asked the Deputy Director.

'Let us not be too patronizing,' Harry Harrison interrupted sharply. 'In the New Testament we are told that Jesus Christ fasted in the wilderness for forty days and forty nights and then confronted and rebuffed the Devil himself. After that period alone with no food, a man would surely be hallucinating. But for Christian true believers that is Holy Scripture and not to be doubted.'

'All right, my apologies. So Al-Isra is the meeting with the archangel?'

'No way,' said Jolley. 'Al-Isra is the journey itself. A magical journey. A divine journey, undertaken on the instructions of Allah himself.'

'It has been called,' Dr Schramme cut in, 'a journey through the darkness to great enlightenment . . .'

He was quoting from an ancient commentary. The other three knew it well and nodded.

'So what would a modern Muslim and a senior operative in Al-Qaeda mean by it?'

This was the first time the academics had been given an inkling as to the source of the documents. Not an intercept, but a capture.

'Was it fiercely guarded?' asked Harrison.

'Two men died trying to prevent us seeing it.'

'Ah, well, yes. Understandable.' Dr Jolley was studying his pipe with great attention. The other three looked down. 'I fear it can be nothing but a reference to some kind of project, some operation. And not a small one.'

'Something big?' asked the man from Homeland Security.

'Gentlemen, devout Muslims, not to say fanatical ones, do not regard Al-Isra lightly. For them it was something that changed the world. If they have code-named something Al-Isra, they intend that it should be huge.'

'And no indication what it might be?'

Dr Jolley looked round the table. His three colleagues shrugged.

'Not a hint. Both the writers call down divine blessings on their project but that is all. That said, I think I can speak for us all in suggesting you find out what it refers to. Whatever else, they would never give the title Al-Isra to a mere satchel bomb, a devastated nightclub or a wrecked commuter bus.'

No one had been taking notes. There was no need. Every word had been recorded. This was, after all, the building known in the trade as 'the Puzzle Palace'.

Both professional intelligence officers would have the transcripts within an hour and would spend the night preparing their joint report. That report would leave the building before dawn, sealed and couriered with armed guard, and it would go high. Very high; as high as it gets in the USA, which is the White House.

Terry Martin shared a limousine with Ben Jolley on the ride back to Washington. It was bigger than the sedan in which he had come, with a partition between front and rear compartments. Through the glass they could see the backs of two heads: the driver and their youthful escorting officer.

The gruff old American thoughtfully kept his pipe in his pocket and stared out at the passing scenery, a sea of the russet and gold of autumn leaves. The younger British man stared the other way and also lapsed into reverie.

In all his life he had only really loved four people and he had lost three of them in the past ten months. At the start of the year his parents, who had had their two sons in their thirties and were both over seventy, had died almost together. Prostate cancer had taken his father and his mother was simply too broken-hearted to want to go on. She wrote a moving letter to each of her sons, took a bottle of sleeping tablets in a piping hot bath, fell asleep and, in her own words, 'went to join Daddy'.

Terry Martin was devastated, but survived by leaning on the strength of two men, the other two he loved more than himself. One was his partner of fourteen years, the tall, handsome stockbroker with whom he shared his life. And then on one wild March night there had been the drunken driver going crazily fast; and the crunch of metal hitting a human body; and the body on the slab; and the awful funeral with Gordon's parents stiffly disapproving of his open tears.

He had seriously contemplated ending his own by now miserable life, but his elder brother Mike seemed to sense his thoughts, moved in with him for a week and talked him through the crisis.

He had hero-worshipped his brother since they were boys in Iraq and through their years at the British public school at Haileybury outside the market town of Hertford.

Mike had always been everything he was not. Dark to his fair, lean to his plump, hard to his soft, fast to his slow, brave to his frightened. Sitting in the limousine gliding through Maryland he let his thoughts return to that final rugby match against Tonbridge with which Mike had ended his five years at Haileybury.

When the two teams came off the field Terry

was standing by the roped passageway, grinning. Mike reached out and ruffled his hair.

'Well,' he said, 'we did it, bro.'

Terry had been seized by gut-wrenching fear when the moment came to tell his brother that he now knew he was gay. The older man, by then an officer in the Paras and just back from combat in the Falklands, thought about it for a moment, cracked his mocking grin and handed back the final line by Joe E. Brown in *Some Like it Hot*.

'Well, nobody's perfect.'

From that moment Terry's hero-worship of his elder brother knew no limits.

In Maryland the sun set. In the same time zone it was setting over Cuba and on the south-western peninsula known as Guantanamo a man spread his prayer mat, turned to the east, knelt and began his prayers. Outside the cell a GI watched impassively. He had seen it all before, many times, but his instructions were never, ever, to let his watchfulness slip.

The man who prayed had been in the jail, formerly Camp X-Ray, now Camp Delta, and in the media usually 'Gitmo' as short for Guantanamo Bay, for nearly five years. He had been through the early brutalities and privations without a cry or a scream. He had tolerated the scores of humiliations of his body and his faith without a sound, but when he stared at his tormentors even they could read the implacable hatred in the black eyes above the black beard, so he was beaten the more. But he never broke.

In the stick-and-carrot days when inmates were encouraged to denounce their fellows in exchange for favours, he remained silent and earned no better treatment. Seeing this, others had denounced him in exchange for concessions, but as the denunciations were complete inventions, he had neither denied nor confirmed them.

In the room full of files kept by the interrogators as proof of their expertise, there was much about the man who prayed that night, but almost nothing from him. He had civilly answered questions put to him years earlier by one of the interrogators who had decided on a humane approach. That was how a passable record of his life existed at all.

But the problem was still the same. None of the interrogators had ever understood a word of his native language and had always relied on the interpreters, or 'terps', who accompanied them everywhere. But the terps had an agenda too. They also received favours for interesting revelations, so they had a motive to make them up.

After four years the man at prayer was dubbed

'non-cooperative', which simply meant unbreakable. In 2005 he had been transferred across the Gulf to the new Camp Echo, a locked-down permanent isolation unit. Here the cells were smaller, with white walls and exercise only at night. For a year the man had not seen the sun.

No family clamoured for him; no government sought news of him; no lawyer filed papers for him. Detainees around him became deranged and were taken away for therapy. He just stayed silent and read his Koran. Outside, the guards changed while he prayed.

'Goddam Arab,' said the man coming off duty. His replacement shook his head.

'He's not Arab,' he said. 'He's an Afghan.'

'So, what do you think of our problem, Terry?'

It was Ben Jolley, out of his daydream, staring at Martin across the rear of the limo.

'Doesn't sound good, does it?' Terry Martin replied. 'Did you see the faces of our two spook friends? They knew we were only confirming what they had suspected, but they were definitely not happy when we left.'

'No other verdict, though. They have to discover what it is, this Al-Isra operation.'

'But how?'

'Well, I've been around spooks for a long time. Been advising as best I can on matters of the

Mid-East since the Six Day War. They have a lot of ways: sources on the inside, turned agents, eavesdropping, file-recovery, over-flying; and the computers help a lot, cross-referencing data in minutes that used to take weeks. I guess they'll figure it out and stop it somehow. Don't forget we have come on a hell of a long way since Gary Powers was shot down over Sverdlovsk in nineteen sixty, or the U2 took those photos of the Cuba missiles in sixty-two. Guess before you were born, right?' He chuckled chestily at his own antiquity as Terry Martin nodded.

'Maybe they have someone right inside Al-Qaeda,' Martin suggested.

'Doubt it,' said the older man. 'Anyone that high up would have given us the location of the leadership by now and we'd have taken them down with smart bombs.'

'Well, maybe they could slip someone inside Al-Qaeda to find out and report back.'

Again the older man shook his head, this time with total conviction.

'Come on, Terry, we both know that's impossible. A native-born Arab would quite possibly be turned and work against us. As for a non-Arab, forget it. We both know all Arabs come from extended families, clans, tribes. One enquiry of the family or clan and the impostor would be exposed.

'So he would have to be CV-perfect. Add to that he would have to look the part, speak the part and, most important, pray the part. One syllable wrong in all those prayers and the fanatics would spot it. They recite five times a day and never miss a beat.'

'True,' said Martin, knowing his case was hopeless but enjoying the fantasy. 'But one could learn the Koranic passages and invent an untraceable family.'

'Forget it, Terry. No Westerner can pass for an Arab among Arabs.'

'My brother can,' said Dr Martin. In seconds, if he could have bitten off his own tongue, he would have. But it was all right. Dr Jolley grunted, dropped the subject and studied the early outskirts of Washington. Neither head in the front, beyond the glass, moved an inch. Martin let out a sigh of relief. Any mike in the car must be turned off.

He was wrong.

CHAPTER THREE

The Fort Meade report on the deliberations of the Koran Committee was ready by dawn of that Saturday and destroyed several planned weekends. One of those roused during the Saturday night at his home in Old Alexandria was Marek Gumienny, Deputy Director (Operations) at the CIA. He was bidden to report straight to his office without being told why.

The 'why' was on his desk when he got there. It was not even dawn over Washington but the first indications of the coming sun pinked the distant hills of Prince George's County where the Patuxent River flows down to join the Chesapeake.

Marek Gumienny's office was one of the few on the sixth and top floor of the big, oblong building among the cluster that forms the headquarters of the CIA and is known simply as Langley. It had recently been redubbed the Old Building to distinguish it from the mirror-image New Building that housed the expanding agency since 9/11.

In the hierarchy of the CIA, the Director of Central Intelligence has traditionally been a political appointment but the real muscle are habitually the two Deputy Directors. Ops handles the actual intelligence-gathering while the DD (Intelligence) covers the collation and analysis of the incoming harvest to turn raw information into a meaningful picture.

Just below these two are the Directors of Counter-Intelligence (to keep the agency free from penetration and in-house traitors) and Counter-Terrorism (increasingly becoming the boiler room as the agency's war swerved from the old USSR to the new threats out of the Middle East).

DDOs, since the start of the Cold War in about 1945, had always been Soviet experts with the Sov. Division and SE (Satellites and Eastern Europe), making the running for an ambitious career officer. Marek Gumienny was the first Arabist to be appointed DDO. As a young agent he had spent years in the Middle East, mastered two of its languages (Arabic and Farsi, the language of Iran) and knew its culture.

Even in this twenty-four-hours-a-day building,

pre-dawn on a Sunday is not an easy time to rustle up piping hot and aromatic black coffee, the way he liked it, so he brewed his own. While it perked Gumienny started on the package on his desk, which contained the slim, wax-sealed file.

He knew what to expect. Fort Meade may have handled the file-recovery, translation and analysis, but it was the CIA, in collaboration with the British and Pakistan's CTC over in Peshawar, who had made the capture. The CIA's stations in Peshawar and Islamabad had filed copious reports to keep their boss in the picture.

The file contained all the documents down-loaded from the AQ financier's computer, but the two letters, taking up three pages, were the stars. The DDO spoke fast and fluent street Arabic, but reading script is always harder so he repeatedly referred to the translations.

He read the report of the Koran Committee, prepared jointly by the two intelligence officers at the meeting, but it offered him no surprises. To him it was clear the references to Al-Isra, the magical journey of the Prophet through the night, could only be the code for some kind of important project.

That project now had to have a name in-house for the American intelligence community. It could not be Al-Isra; that alone would betray to others what they had found out. He checked with file-cryptography for a name to describe in future how he and all his colleagues would call the Al-Qaeda project, whatever it was.

Code names come out of a computer by a process known as random selection, the aim being to give nothing away. The CIA naming process that month was using fish; the computer chose Stingray, so Project Stingray it became.

The last sheet in the file had been added during Saturday night. It was brief and short. It came from the hand of a man who disliked wasting words, one of the six principals, the Director of National Intelligence. Clearly the file out of Fort Meade had gone straight to the National Security Committee (Steve Hadley), to the DNI and to the White House. Marek Gumienny imagined there would have been lights burning late in the Oval Office.

The final sheet was on the DNI's personal headed paper. It said in capital letters:

WHAT IS AL-ISRA?
IS IT NUCLEAR, BIOLOGICAL, CHEMICAL,
    CONVENTIONAL?
FIND OUT WHAT, WHEN AND WHERE.
TIMESCALE: NOW
RESTRAINTS: NONE
POWERS: ABSOLUTE
    JOHN NEGROPONTE

There was a scrawled signature. There are nineteen primary intelligence-gathering and archive-storing agencies in the USA. The letter in Marek Gumienny's hand gave him authority over them all. He ran his eye back to the top of the sheet. It was addressed to him personally. There was a tap on the door.

A young GS15 stood there with yet another delivery. General Service is simply a salary scale, a 15 means a very junior staffer. Gumienny gave the young man an encouraging smile; he had clearly never been this high up the building before. Gumienny held out his hand, signed the clipboard to confirm receipt and waited until he was alone again.

The new file was a courtesy from the colleagues at Fort Meade. It was a transcript of a conversation held by two of the Koran eggheads in the car on the way back to Washington. One of them was British. It was his last line that some-one at Fort Meade had underlined with a brace of question marks in red ink.

During his time in the Middle East Marek Gumienny had had much to do with the British and, unlike some of his fellow countrymen who had been trying to cope with the hellhole of Iraq for three years, he was not too proud to admit the CIA's closest allies in what Kipling once called the Great Game were a repository of much arcane knowledge of the badlands between the Jordan River and the Hindu Kush.

For a century and a half, either as soldiers or administrators of the old empire, or as eccentric explorers, the British had been trudging over desert, mountain range and goat-pen in the zone that had now become the intelligence time bomb of the world. The British code-named the CIA 'the Cousins' or 'the Company'; the Americans called the London-based Secret Intelligence Service 'the Friends' or 'the Firm'. For Marek Gumienny one of those friends was a man he had shared good times, not-so-good times and downright dangerous times with when they were both field agents. Now he was pinned to a desk in Langley and Steve Hill had been pulled out of the field and elevated to Controller Middle East at the Firm's Vauxhall Cross headquarters.

Gumienny decided a conference would do no harm and might yield some good. There was no security problem. The Brits, he knew, would have just about everything he had. They too had transmitted the guts of the laptop from Peshawar to their own listening and cryptography HQ at Cheltenham. They too would have printed out its contents. They too would have analysed the strange references to the Koran contained in the coded letters.

What Marek Gumienny had that was probably

not with London was the bizarre remark by a British academic in the back of a car in the middle of Maryland. He punched up a number on the console on his desk. Central switchboards are fine up to a point, but modern technology has meant any senior executive can be connected faster by speed-dial on his personal satphone.

A number rang in a modest commuter house in Surrey, just outside London. Eight a.m. in Langley, one p.m. in London; the house was about to sit down to a roast beef lunch. A voice answered at the third ring. Steve Hill had enjoyed his golf and was about to enjoy his beef.

'Hello?'

'Steve? Marek.'

'My dear chap, where are you? Over here by any chance?'

'No, I'm at my desk. Can we go to secure?'

'Sure. Give me two minutes . . .' And in the background: 'Darling, hold the roast.' The phone went down.

At the next call the voice from England was slightly tinny but uninterceptable.

'Am I to understand that something has hit the ventilation system close to your ear?' asked Hill.

'All over my nice clean shirt,' admitted Gumienny. 'I guess you have much the same stuff as I have out of Peshawar?'

'I expect so. I finished reading it yesterday. I was wondering when you would call.'

'I have something you may not have, Steve. We have a visiting professor over here from London. He made a chance remark Friday evening. I'll cut to the chase. Do you know a man called Martin?'

'Martin who?'

'No, that's his surname. His brother over here is called Dr Terry Martin. Does it ring a bell?'

Steve Hill had dropped all banter. He sat holding the phone and staring into space. Oh yes, he knew the Martin brother. Back in the first Gulf War of 1990/91 he had been one of the control team in Saudi Arabia when the academic's brother had slipped into Baghdad and lived there as a humble gardener under the noses of Saddam's secret police while transmitting back priceless intelligence from a source inside the dictator's cabinet.

'Could do,' he conceded. 'Why?'

'I think we should talk,' said the American. 'Face to face. I could fly over. I have the Grumman.'

'When do you want to come over?'

'Tonight. I can sleep on the plane. Be in London for breakfast.'

'OK. I'll arrange it with Northolt.'

'Oh, and Steve, while I'm flying could you get out the full file on this man Martin? I'll explain when I see you.'

West of London, on the road to Oxford, lies the Royal Air Force base of Northolt. For a couple of years after World War II it was actually London's civil airport as Heathrow was hastily constructed. Then it relapsed into a role as a secondary airfield and finally a field for private and executive jets. But because it remains an RAF property, flights in and out can be fixed to take place in complete security without the usual formalities.

The CIA has its own very private airfield near Langley and a small fleet of executive jets. Marek Gumienny's all-powerful piece of authority paper secured him the Grumman V, on which he slept in perfect comfort on the flight over. Steve Hill was at Northolt to meet him.

He took his guest not to the green and sandstone ziggurat at Vauxhall Cross on the south bank of the Thames by Vauxhall Bridge, home of the SIS, but to the much quieter Cliveden Hotel, formerly a private mansion, set inside its own estate not thirty miles from the airport. He had reserved a small conference suite with room service and privacy.

There he read the analysis of the American Koran Committee, which was remarkably similar to the analysis from Cheltenham, and the transcript of the conversation in the back of the car.

'Damn fool,' he muttered when he reached the end. 'The other Arabist was right. It can't be done. It's not just the lingo, it's all the other tests. No stranger, no foreigner could ever pass them.'

'So, given my orders from the All-High, what would you suggest?'

'Pick up an AQ insider and sweat it out of him,' said Hill.

'Steve, if we had the faintest idea of the location of anyone that high in Al-Qaeda, we'd take them as a matter of course. We don't have any such target in our sights as of now.'

'Wait and watch. Someone will use the phrase again.'

'My people have to presume that if Al-Isra is to be the next spectacular it will be the USA that is the target. Waiting for a miracle that may not happen will not pacify Washington. Besides, AQ must know by now we got the laptop. Chances are they will never use that phrase again, except person to person.'

'Well,' said Hill, 'we could put it about in places they would hear it that we have it all and are closing in. They would discontinue, cut and run.'

'Maybe, maybe not. But we'd never know. We'd still be in limbo, never knowing whether Project Stingray had been terminated or not. And if not? And if it works? Like my boss says: is it nuclear, biochemical, conventional? Where and when? Can your man Martin really pass for an Arab among Arabs? Is he really that good?'

'He used to be,' grunted Hill and passed over a file. 'See for yourself.'

The file was an inch thick, in standard buff manila, and fronted simply with the words: 'COLONEL MIKE MARTIN'.

The Martin boys' maternal grandfather had been a tea-planter at Darjeeling, India, between the two world wars. While there he had done something almost unheard of. He had married an Indian girl.

The world of the British tea-planters was small, remote and snooty. Brides were brought out from England or found among the daughters of the officer class of the Raj. The boys had seen pictures of their grandfather, Terence Granger, tall, pink-faced, blond-moustached, pipe in mouth and gun in hand, standing over a shot tiger.

And there were pictures of Miss Indira Bohse, gentle, loving and very beautiful. When Terence Granger would not be dissuaded the tea company, rather than create an alternative scandal by firing him, hit on a solution. They posted the young couple to the wilds of Assam, up on the Burmese border.

If it was supposed to be a punishment, it did

not work. Granger and his new bride loved the life up there: a wild, ravined countryside teeming with game and tigers. And there Susan was born in 1930. By 1943 war had rolled towards Assam, the Japanese advancing through Burma to the border. Terence Granger, though old enough to avoid the army, insisted on volunteering and in 1945 died crossing the River Irrawaddy.

With a tiny widow's pension from the company, Indira Granger went the only place she could, back into her own culture. Two years later came more trouble; India was being partitioned for independence. Ali Jinnah insisted on his Muslim Pakistan to the north, Pandit Nehru settled for mainly Hindu India to the south. Waves of refugees rolled north and south and violent fighting broke out.

Fearing for her daughter's safety Mrs Granger sent Susan to stay with her late husband's younger brother, a very proper architect of Haslemere, Surrey. Six months later the mother died in the rioting.

Susan Granger came at seventeen to the land of her fathers, which she had never seen. She spent a year at a girls' school and three as a nurse at Farnham General Hospital. At twenty-one, the youngest age allowed, she applied to be a stewardess with the British Overseas Airways Corporation. She was drop-dead beautiful, with tumbling chestnut hair, her father's blue eyes and the skin of an English girl with a honey-gold suntan.

BOAC put her on the London–Bombay route because of her fluent Hindi. The route then was long and slow: London to Rome to Cairo to Basra to Bahrain to Karachi and finally Bombay. No crew could make it all the way; the first crew-change and stopover was at Basra, southern Iraq. There, at the country club in 1951, she met oil company accountant Nigel Martin. They married in 1952.

There was a ten-year wait until the birth of the first son, Mike, and three more years to second son Terry. But the two boys were like chalk and cheese.

Marek Gumienny stared at the photo in the file. Not a suntan but a naturally saturnine complexion, black hair and dark eyes. He realized the genes of the grandmother had jumped a generation to the grandson; he was not even remotely like his brother the academic in Georgetown, whose pink face and ginger hair came from his father.

He recalled the objections of Dr Ben Jolley. Any infiltrator with a chance of getting away with it inside Al-Qaeda would have to look the part and speak the part. Gumienny skipped through the rest of the boyhood.

They had both gone in succession to the Anglo-Iraqi school and learned also from their *dada*, or nanny, the gentle plump Fatima from up country, who would go back to the tribe once she had saved enough wages to find a proper young man for a husband.

There was a reference that could only have come from an interview with Terry Martin: the older boy in his white Iraqi dishdash, racing about the lawn of the house in Saadun suburb, Baghdad, and his father's delighted Iraqi guests laughing with pleasure and shouting, 'But, Nigel, he's more like one of us.'

More like one of us, thought Marek Gumienny, more like one of them. Two points down of Ben Jolley's four: he looked the part and could pass for an Arab in Arabic. Surely with intensive schooling he could master the prayer rituals?

The CIA man read a bit more. Vice-President Saddam Hussein had started nationalizing the foreign-owned oil companies, and that included Anglo-Iraq Petroleum in 1972. Nigel Martin had stuck it out three more years before bringing the whole family home in 1975. The boy Mike was thirteen, ready to go to senior school at Haileybury. Marek Gumienny needed a break and a coffee.

'He could do it, you know,' he said when he came back from the toilet. 'With enough training and back-up he really could. Where is he now?'

'Apart from two stints working for us when we borrowed him, he spent his military career between the Paras and the Special Forces. Retired last year after completing his twenty-five. And no, it wouldn't work.'

'Why not, Steve? He has it all.'

'Except the background. The parentage, the extended family, the birthplace. You don't just walk into Al-Qaeda except as a youthful volunteer for a suicide mission; a low-level low-life; a gopher. Anyone who would have the trust to get near the gold-standard project in preparation would have to have years behind him. That's the killer, Marek, and it remains the killer. Unless . . .'

He drifted off into a reverie, then shook his head.

'Unless what?' asked the American.

'No, it's not on the table,' said Hill.

'Indulge me.'

'I was thinking of a ringer. A man whose place he could take. A doppelgänger. But that's flawed too. If the real object were still alive, AQ would have him in their ranks. If he were dead, they'd know that too. So no dice.'

'It's a long file,' said Marek Gumienny. 'Can I take it with me?'

'It's a copy, of course. Eyes only?'

'You have my word, ole buddy. My eyes only. And my personal safe. Or the incinerator.'

The DD Ops flew back to Langley but a few days later he phoned again. Steve Hill took the call at his desk in Vauxhall Cross.

'I think I should fly back,' the DDO said without preamble. Both men knew that by then the British Prime Minister in Downing Street had given his friend in the White House his word on total cooperation from the British side on tracking down Project Stingray.

'No problem, Marek. Do you have a breakthrough?' Privately Steve Hill was intrigued. With modern technology there is nothing that cannot be passed from the CIA to the SIS in complete secrecy and a matter of seconds. So why fly?

'The ringer,' said Gumienny. 'I think I have him. Ten years younger but looks older. Height and build. Same dark face. An AQ veteran.'

'Sounds fine. But how come he's not with the bad guys?'

'Because he's with us. He's in Guantanamo. Has been for five years.'

'He's an Arab?' Hill was surprised; he ought to have known about a high-ranking AQ Arab in Gitmo these past five years.

'No, he's an Afghan. Name of Izmat Khan. I'm on my way.'

* * *

Terry Martin was still sleepless a week after his meeting at Fort Meade. That stupid remark. Why could he not keep his mouth shut? Why did he have to brag about his brother? Supposing Ben Jolley had said something? Washington was one big, gossiping village, after all. Seven days after the remark in the back of the limousine he rang his brother.

Mike Martin was lifting the last clutch of unbroken tiles off his precious roof. At last he could start on the laying of the roofing felt and the battens to keep it down. Within a week he could be waterproof. He heard the tinkling of Lillibulero from his mobile phone. It was in the pocket of his jerkin which was hanging from a nail nearby. He inched across the now dangerously frail rafters to reach it. The screen said it was his brother in Washington.

'Hi, Terry.'

'Mike, it's me.' He could still not work out how people he was ringing already knew who he was. 'I've done something stupid and I want to ask your pardon. About a week ago I shot my mouth off.'

'Great. What did you say?'

'Never mind. Look, if ever you get a visitation from any men in suits – you know who I mean – you are to tell them to piss off. What I said was stupid. If anyone visits—'

From his eagle's nest Mike Martin could see the charcoal-grey Jaguar nosing slowly up the track that led from the lane to the barn.

'It's OK, bro,' he said gently, 'I think they're here.'

The two spymasters sat on folding camp chairs and Mike Martin on the bole of a tree that was about to be chainsawed into bits for camp-fire timber. Martin listened to the 'pitch' from the American and cocked an eyebrow at Steve Hill.

'Your call, Mike. Our government has pledged the White House total cooperation on whatever they want or need, but that stops short of pressuring anyone to go on a no-return mission.'

'And would this one fit that category?'

'We don't think so,' Marek Gumienny interjected. 'If we could even discover the name and whereabouts of one single AQ operative who would know what is going down here, we'd pull you out and do the rest. Just listening to the scuttlebutt might do the trick.'

'But, passing off . . . I don't think I could pass for an Arab any more. In Baghdad fifteen years ago I made myself invisible by being a humble gardener living in a shack. There was no question of surviving an interrogation by the Mukhabarat. This time you'd be looking at intensive questioning. Why would someone who has been in American hands for five years not have become a turncoat?'

'Sure, we figure they would question you. But with luck the questioner would be a high-ranker brought in for the job. At which point you break out and finger the man for us. We'll be standing right by, barely yards away.'

'This' – Martin tapped the file on the man in the Guantanamo cell – 'is an Afghan. Ex-Taliban. That means Pashtun. I never got to be fluent in Pashto. I'd be spotted by the first Afghan on the plot.'

'There would be months of tutorials, Mike,' said Steve Hill. 'No way you go until you feel you are ready. Not even then if you don't think it will work. And you would be staying well away from Afghanistan. The good news about Afghan fundos is that they hardly ever appear outside their own manor. Do you think you could talk poor Arabic with the accent of a Pashtun of limited education?'

Mike Martin nodded.

'Possibly. And if the towelheads bring in an Afghan who really knew this guy?'

There was silence from the other two men. If that happened, everyone round the fire knew it would be the end.

As the two spymasters stared at their feet rather than explain what would happen to an agent unmasked at the heart of Al-Qaeda, Martin flipped open the file on his lap. What he saw caused him to freeze.

The face was five years older, lined by suffering and looking ten years more than his calendar age. But it was still the boy from the mountains, the near-corpse at Qala-i-Jangi.

'I know this man,' he said quietly. 'His name is Izmat Khan.'

The American stared at him open-mouthed.

'How the hell can you know him? He's been cooped up at Gitmo since he was captured five years ago.'

'I know, but many years before that we fought the Russians in the Tora Bora.'

The men from London and Washington recalled the Martin file. Of course, that year in Afghanistan helping the Mujahidin in their struggle against Soviet occupation. It was a long shot, but not unfeasible that the men had met. For ten minutes they asked him about Izmat Khan to see what else he could add. Martin handed the file back.

'What is he like now, Izmat Khan? How has he changed in five years with your people at Camp Delta?'

The American from Langley shrugged.

'He's tough, Mike. Very, very hard. He arrived with a bad head wound and double concussion.

Injured during capture. At first our medics thought he was maybe . . . well . . . a bit simple. Backward. Turned out he was just totally disoriented. The concussion and the journey. This was early December two thousand and one, just after Nine/Eleven. Treatment was . . . how shall I put it . . . not gentle. Then it seemed nature took its course and he recovered enough for questioning.'

'And what did he tell you?'

'Not very much. Just his résumé. Resisted all third degree and all offers. Just stares at us and what the grunts see in those black eyes is not brotherly love. That is why he is in lock-down. But from others we understand he has passable Arabic, learned inside Afghanistan and before that from years in a *madrassah* rote-learning the Koran. And two British-born AQ volunteers who were in there with him and have been released say he now has some halting English which they taught him.'

Martin glanced sharply at Steve Hill.

'They'd have to be picked up and kept in quarantine,' he said. Hill nodded.

'Of course. It can be arranged.'

Marek Gumienny rose and wandered round the barn as Martin studied the file. Martin stared into the fire and deep in the embers saw a bleak and bare hillside far away. Two men, a cluster of rocks and the Soviet Hind helicopter gunship swinging to the attack. A whisper from the turbaned boy: 'Are we going to die, Angleez?' Gumienny came back, squatted on the ground and poked the fire. The image went up in a cloud of sparks.

'Quite a project you have taken on here, Mike. I'd have thought this was a job for a crew of professionals. You doing it all yourself?'

'As much as I can. For the first time in twenty-five years I have the time.'

'But not the dough, eh?'

Martin shrugged. 'There are scores of security companies out there if I want a job. Iraq alone has spawned more professional bodyguards than one can count, and still more are wanted. They make more in a week working for your guys in the Sunni Triangle than they made in half a year as soldiers.'

'But that would mean back to the dust, the sand, the danger, the too-early death. Didn't you retire from that?'

'And what are you offering? A vacation with AQ in the Florida Keys?'

Marek Gumienny had the grace to laugh.

'Americans are accused of many things, Mike, but not often of being ungenerous to those who have helped them. I am thinking of a consultancy at, say, two hundred thousand dollars a year for five years. Paid abroad, no need to disturb the taxman. No need actually to show up for work. No need to go into harm's way ever again.'

Mike Martin's thoughts flitted to a scene in his all-time favourite film. T. E. Lawrence has offered Auda Abu Tayi money to join him in the attack on Aqaba. He recalled the great reply: Auda will not ride to Aqaba for the British gold, he will ride to Aqaba because it pleases him. He stood up.

'Steve, I want my home shrouded in tarpaulins from top to bottom. When I come back I want it just the way I left it.'

The Controller Middle East nodded. 'Done,' he said.

'I'll get my kit. There's not much of it. Enough to fill the boot, no more.'

And so the western strike-back against Project Stingray was agreed under apple trees in a Hampshire orchard. Two days later a computer by random selection dubbed it Operation Crowbar.

If challenged, Mike Martin would never have been able to defend himself. But in all the briefings he later gave them about the Afghan who had once been his friend, there was one detail he kept to himself.

Perhaps he thought that need-to-know was a

two-way street. Perhaps he thought the detail too unimportant. It had to do with a muttered conversation in the shadows of a cave hospital run by Arabs at a place called Jaji.

PART TWO

Warriors

CHAPTER FOUR

The decision in the Hampshire orchard led to a blizzard of decision-making from the two spymasters. To start with, sanction and approval had to be sought from both men's political masters.

This was easier said than done because Mike Martin's first condition was that no more than one dozen people should ever know what Operation Crowbar was about. His concern was completely understood.

If fifty people know anything that interesting, one will eventually spill the beans. Not intentionally, not viciously, not even mischievously; but inevitably.

Those who have ever been in deep cover in a lethal situation know that to trust in one's own tradecraft never to make a mistake and be caught is nerve-racking enough. To hope that one will never be given away by some utterly unforeseeable fluke is constantly stressful. But the ultimate nightmare is to know that capture and the long, agonizing death to follow was all caused by some fool in a bar boasting to his girlfriend and being overheard – that is the worst fear of all. So Martin's condition was acceded to at once.

In Washington John Negroponte agreed with Marek Gumienny that he alone would be the repository, and gave the go-ahead. Steve Hill dined at his club with one man in the British government and secured the same result. That made four.

But Gumienny and Hill knew they could not personally be on the case twenty-four hours a day. Each needed an executive officer for the day-to-day running. Marek Gumienny appointed a rising Arabist in the CIA's Counter-Terrorism Division: Michael McDonald dropped everything, explained to his family that he had to work in the UK for a while, and flew east as Marek Gumienny returned home.

Steve Hill picked his own deputy on the Middle East Desk, Gordon Phillips. Before they parted company the two principals agreed that every aspect of Crowbar would have a plausible cover story so that no one below the top ten would really know that a western agent was going to be slipped inside Al-Qaeda.

Both Langley and Vauxhall Cross were told that the two men about to go missing were simply on a career-improving sabbatical of academic study and would be away from their desks for about six months.

Steve Hill introduced the two men who would now be working together and told them what Crowbar was going to try to do. Both McDonald and Phillips went very silent. Hill had installed them both not in offices in the headquarters building by the Thames, but in a safe house, one of several retained by the Firm, out in the countryside.

When they had unpacked and convened in the drawing room he tossed them both a thick file.

'Finding an ops HQ starts tomorrow,' he said. 'You have twenty-four hours to commit this to memory. This is the man who is going to go in. You will work with him until that day, and for him after that. This' – he tossed on to the coffee table a thinner file – 'is the man he is going to replace. Clearly we know much less. But that is everything the US interrogators have been able to secure from him in hundreds of hours of inter-rogations at Gitmo. Learn this also.'

When he was gone the two younger men asked for a large pot of coffee from the household staff and started to read.

* * *

It was during a visit to the Farnborough Air Show in the summer of 1977 when he was fifteen that the schoolboy Mike Martin fell in love. His father and younger brother were with him, fascinated by the fighters and bombers, aerobatic fliers and first-viewing prototypes. For Mike the high point was the visit of the Red Devils, the stunt team from the Parachute Regiment, free-falling from tiny specks in the sky to swoop to earth in their harnesses right in the heart of the tiny landing zone. That was when he knew what it was he wanted to do.

He wrote a personal letter to the Paras during his last summer term at Haileybury, in 1980, and was offered an interview at the Regimental Depot at Aldershot for the same September. He arrived and stared at the old Dakota out of which his predecessors had once dropped to try to capture the bridge at Arnhem, until the sergeant escorting the group of five ex-schoolboys led them to the interview room.

He was regarded by his school (and the Paras always checked) as a moderate scholar but a superb athlete. That suited the Paras just fine. He was accepted, and began training at the end of October, a gruelling twenty-two weeks that would bring the survivors to April 1981.

There were four weeks of square-bashing,

basic weapons handling, fieldcraft and physical fitness; then two more of the same plus first aid, signals and study of precautions against NBC (nuclear, bacteriological and chemical warfare).

The seventh week was for more fitness training, getting harder all the time; but not as bad as weeks eight and nine: endurance marches through the Brecon range in Wales in midwinter, where fit men have died of exposure, hypothermia and exhaustion. The numbers began to thin out.

Week ten saw the course at Hythe, Kent, for shooting on the range where Martin, just turned nineteen, was rated a marksman. Eleven and twelve were 'test' weeks – just running up and down sandy hills carrying tree trunks in the mud, rain and freezing hail.

'Test weeks?' muttered Phillips. 'What the hell has the rest been?'

After test weeks the remaining young men got their coveted red beret before three more weeks in the Brecons for defence exercises, patrolling and 'live firing'. By then, late January, the Brecons were utterly bleak and freezing. The men slept rough and wet, without fires.

Sixteen to nineteen covered what Mike Martin had come for: the parachute course at RAF Abingdon, where a few more dropped out and not just from the aircraft. At the end came the 'wings parade' when the wings of a paratrooper were finally pinned on. That night the old 101 club at Aldershot saw another riotous party.

There were two more weeks devoted to a field exercise called 'last fence' and some polishing-up of parade-ground skills; week twenty-two saw Pass-Out Parade, when proud parents could finally view their spotty youths amazingly transformed into soldiers.

Private Mike Martin had long been earmarked as POM – potential officer material – and in April 1981 went to join the new short course at the Royal Military Academy, Sandhurst, passing out in December as a Second Lieutenant. If he thought glory awaited him, he was entirely mistaken.

There are three battalions in the Parachute Regiment and Martin was assigned to Three Para, which happened to be Aldershot in penguin mode.

For three years out of every nine, or one tour out of three, each battalion is off parachuting and used as ordinary lorry-born infantry. Paras hate penguin mode.

Martin, as a platoon commander, was assigned to Recruit Platoon, putting newcomers through the same miseries he had endured. He might have remained there for the rest of Three Para's tour as penguins but for a faraway gentleman called Leopoldo Galtieri. On 2 April 1982, the

Argentine dictator invaded the Falkland Islands. Three Para was told to kit up and get ready to move out.

Within a week, driven by the implacable Margaret Thatcher, a British task force was steaming south in a collection of vessels, bound for the far end of the Atlantic where a southern winter, with its roaring seas and driving rain, was waiting for them.

The journey south was on the liner *Canberra* with a first stop at Ascension Island, a bleak button of a place lashed by constant wind. Here there was a pause as, far away, the last diplomatic efforts were pursued to persuade Galtieri to evacuate or Margaret Thatcher to back off. Neither could dream of agreeing and surviving in office. The *Canberra* sailed on, shadowing the expedition's two aircraft carrier, *Hermes* and *Invincible*.

When it became clear that invasion was inevitable, Martin and his team were 'cross-decked' by helicopter from *Canberra* to a landing craft. Gone were the civilized conditions of the liner. The same wild and stormy night that Martin and his men cross-decked in Sea King helicopters, another Sea King went down and sank, taking with her nineteen of the Special Air Service Regiment, the biggest one-night loss the SAS has ever taken.

Martin took his thirty men ashore with the rest

of Three Para at the landing ground of San Carlos Water. It was miles from the main island's capital at Port Stanley, but for that reason it was unopposed. Without a pause the Paras and the Marines began the gruelling forced march through the mud and rain east to the capital.

They carried everything in Bergen rucksacks so heavy it was like carrying another man. The appearance of an Argentine Skyhawk meant diving into the slime, but in the main the 'Argies' were after the ships offshore, not the men in the mud below. If the ships could be sunk, the men on shore were finished.

The real enemies were the cold, the constant freezing rain, the exhausting 'tab' across a landscape that could not support a single tree. Until Mount Longdon.

Pausing below the hills, Three Para set themselves up in a lonely farm called Estancia House and prepared to do what their country had sent them seven thousand miles to do. It was the night of 11/12 June.

It was supposed to be a silent night attack and remained so until Corporal Milne stepped on a mine. After that it became noisy. The Argie machine guns opened up and flares lit the hills and the valley as daylight. Three Para could either run back to cover or into the fire and take

Longdon. They took Longdon, with twenty-three dead and over forty injured.

It was the first time, as bullets tore through the air around his head and men fell beside him, that Mike Martin experienced that strange, brassy taste on the tongue that is the flavour of fear.

But nothing touched him. Of his own platoon of thirty, including one sergeant and three corporals, six were dead and nine injured.

The Argentine soldiers who had held the ridge were forced recruits, lads from the sunny pampas – the sons of the well-off could avoid military service – and wanted to go home, out of the rain, cold and mud. They had quit their bunkers and foxholes and were heading back to shelter in Port Stanley.

At dawn Mike Martin stood atop Wireless Ridge, looked east to the town and rising sun, and rediscovered the God of his fathers whom he had neglected for many years. He prayed his thanks and vowed never to forget again.

At the time the ten-year-old Mike Martin was capering round his father's garden at Saadun, Baghdad, to the delight of the Iraqi guests, a boy was being born a thousand miles away.

West of the road from Pakistani Peshawar to

Afghan Jalalabad lies the range of the Spin Ghar, the White Mountains, dominated by the towering Tora Bora.

These mountains, seen from afar, are like a great barrier between the two countries, bleak and cold, always tipped with snow and in winter wholly covered.

The Spin Ghar lies inside Afghanistan with the Safed Koh range on the Pakistani side. Running down to the rich plains around Jalalabad are myriad streams that carry the snow-melt and rain off the Spin Ghar, and these form many upland valleys where small patches of land may be planted, orchards raised and flocks of sheep and goats grazed.

Life is harsh and with the life-support system being so sparse the communities of the valleys are small and scattered. The people bred up here are the ones the old British Empire knew and feared, calling them the Pathans, now Pashtun. Back then they fought from behind their rocky fastness with long, brass-bound muskets called the jezail, with which each man was accurate as a modern sniper.

Rudyard Kipling, the poet of the old Raj, evoked the deadliness of the mountain men against subalterns expensively educated in England in just four lines:

> A scrimmage in a border station—
> A canter down some dark defile—
> Two thousand pounds of education
> Drops to a ten-rupee jezail . . .

In 1972 there was a hamlet in one of these upland valleys called Maloko-zai; like all these hamlets, it was named after a long-dead warrior founder. There were five walled compounds in the settlement, each the home of one extended family of about twenty persons. The village headman was Nuri Khan and it was in his compound and round his fire that the men gathered on a summer evening to sip hot, unmilked and sugarless tea.

As with all the compounds, the walls were where the residences and livestock pens were built, so that all faced inwards. The fire of mulberry logs blazed as the sun dropped far to the west and darkness clothed the mountains, bringing chill even in high summer.

From the women's quarters the cries were muted, but if one was especially loud the men would cease their jovial conversation and wait to see if news would arrive. The wife of Nuri Khan was bearing her fourth child and her husband prayed that Allah would grant him a second son. It was only right that a man should have sons to take care of the flocks when young and defend the compound when they had become men. Nuri Khan had a boy of eight and two daughters.

The darkness was complete and only the flames lit the hawk-nosed faces and black beards when a midwife came scurrying from the shadows. She whispered in the ear of the father and his mahogany face broke into a flashing smile.

'*Allahu akhbar!* I have a son,' he cried. His male relatives and neighbours rose as one and the air crackled and roared with the sound of their rifles exploding upwards into the night sky. There was much embracing and congratulations and thanks to all-merciful Allah who had granted his servant a son.

'How will you call him?' asked a herdsman from a nearby compound.

'I shall call him Izmat after my own grand-father, may his soul rest in eternal peace,' said Nuri Khan. And so it was when an imam came to the hamlet a few days later for the naming and the circumcision.

There was nothing unusual about the raising of the child. When he could toddle he toddled, and when he could run he ran furiously. Like most farm boys he wanted to do the things the older boys did, and by five was entrusted to help drive the flocks up to the high pastures in summer and watch over them while the women cut forage for the winter.

He yearned to be out of the house of the women and it was the proudest day of his life thus far when he was at last allowed to join the men round the fire and listen to stories of how the Pashtun had defeated the red-coated Angleez in these mountains only a hundred and fifty years ago, told as if it were only yesterday.

His father was the richest man in the village in the only way a man could be rich: in cows, sheep and goats. These, along with relentless caring and hard work, provided meat, milk and hides. Patches of corn yielded porridge and bread; fruit and nut-oil came from the prolific mulberry and walnut orchards.

There was no need to leave the village, so for the first eight years of his life Izmat Khan did not. The five families shared the small mosque, and joined each other for communal worship on Fridays. Izmat's father was devout but not fundamentalist and certainly not fanatical.

Beyond this mountain existence, Afghanistan called itself the Democratic Republic, or DRA, but as so often this was a misnomer. The government was Communist and heavily supported by the USSR. In terms of religion, this was an oddity, because the people of the wild interior were traditionally devout Muslims for whom atheism was godlessness and therefore unacceptable.

But equally traditionally the Afghans of the

cities were moderate and tolerant – the fanaticism would be imposed on them later. Women were educated, few covered their faces, singing and dancing was not only allowed but commonplace and the feared secret police pursued those suspected of political opposition, not religious laxity.

The hamlet of Maloko-zai had two links with the outside world. One was the occasional party of Kuchi nomads passing through with a mule-train of contraband, avoiding the Great Trunk Road through the Khyber Pass with its patrols and border guards, seeking the track to the town of Parachinar across in Pakistan. They would have news of the plains and the cities, of the government in faraway Kabul and the world beyond the valleys. And there was also the radio, a treasured relic that squawked and screeched but then uttered words they could understand. This was the BBC's Pashto service, bringing the Pashtun a non-Communist version of the world. It was a peaceful boyhood. Then came the Russians.

It mattered not much to the village of Maloko-zai who was right or wrong. They neither knew nor cared that their Communist president had displeased his mentors in Moscow because he could not control his bailiwick. It mattered only that an entire Soviet army had rolled across the

Amu Darya river from Soviet Uzbekistan, roared through the Salang Pass and taken Kabul. It was not (yet) about Islam versus atheism; it was an insult.

Izmat Khan's education had been very basic. He had learned the Koranic verses necessary for prayer, even though they were in a language called Arabic and he could not understand them. The local imam was not resident; indeed it was Nuri Khan who led the prayers; he had taught the boys of the village the rudiments of reading and writing, but only in Pashto. It was Izmat's father who had taught him the rules of the Pukhtunwali, the code by which a Pashtun must live. Honour, hospitality, the necessity of vendetta to avenge insult: these were the rules of the code. And Moscow had insulted them.

It was in the mountains that the Resistance began and they called themselves warriors of God, Mujahidin. But first the mountain men needed a conference, a *shura*, to decide what to do and who would lead them.

They knew nothing of the Cold War, but they were told they now had powerful friends, the enemies of the USSR. That made perfect sense. He who is the enemy of my enemy ... First among these was Pakistan, lying right next door and ruled by a fundamentalist dictator, General Zia-ul-Haq. Despite the religious difference, he was allied with the Christian power called America, and her friends, the Angleez, the one-time enemy.

Mike Martin had tasted action and knew he enjoyed it. He did a tour in Northern Ireland, operating against the IRA, but the conditions were miserable and, though the danger of a sniper's bullet in the back was constant, the patrols were boring. He looked around and in spring 1986 applied for selection to the SAS.

Quite a proportion of the SAS comes from the Paras because their training and combat roles are similar, but the SAS claims their tests are harder. Martin's papers went through the Regiment's records office at Hereford where his fluent Arabic was noted with interest and he was invited to a selection course.

The SAS claims they take very fit men and then start to work on them. Martin did the standard 'initial' selection course of six weeks among others drawn from the Paras, infantry, cavalry, armour, artillery and even engineers. Of the other 'crack' units, the Special Boat Service draw their recruits mainly from the Marines.

It is a simple course based on a single precept. On the first day a smiling sergeant instructor told them all: 'On this course, we don't try to train you. We try to kill you.'

They did, too. Only ten per cent of applicants pass the 'initial'. It saves time later. Martin passed. Then came continuation training: jungle training in Belize, and one extra month back in England devoted to resistance to interrogation. 'Resistance' means trying to stay silent while some extremely unpleasant practices are inflicted. The good news is that both the Regiment and the volunteer have the right every hour to insist on an RTU – return to unit.

Martin started in the late summer of 1986 with 22 SAS as a troop commander with the rank of captain. He opted for 'A' Squadron, the free-fallers, a natural choice for a Para to pick.

If the Paras had no use for his Arabic, the SAS did, for it has a long and intimate relationship with the Arab world. It was formed in the Western Desert in 1941 and its empathy with the sands of Arabia has never left it.

It has the jokey reputation of being the only army unit that actually makes a profit – not quite true, but close. SAS men are the world's most sought-after bodyguards and trainers of body-guards. Throughout Arabia the sultans and emirs have always sought a team from the SAS to train their own personal guards, and they pay hand-somely for it. Martin's first assignment was with the Saudi National Guard in Riyadh when, in summer 1987, he was called home.

'I don't like this sort of thing,' said the CO in his office at Stirling Lines, the Regiment's Hereford HQ. 'No, I bloody well don't. But Vauxhall wants to borrow you. He was referring to a green and sandstone building on the south bank of the Thames in London called Vauxhall Cross. He meant the SIS – the Firm.'

He had used the occasionally friendly phrase reserved by fighting soldiers for intelligence people.

'Haven't they got their own Arabic speakers?' asked Martin.

'Oh, yes, desks full of them. But this isn't just a question of speaking it. And it's not really Arabia. They want someone to go behind the Soviet lines in Afghanistan and work with the Resistance, the Mujahidin.'

The military dictator of Pakistan had decreed that no serving soldier of a western power was to be allowed to penetrate into Afghanistan via Pakistan. He did not say so, but his own ISI military intelligence much enjoyed administering the American aid pouring in the direction of the 'Muj' and he further had no wish to see a serving American or British soldier, infiltrated via Pakistan, captured by the Russians and paraded around.

But halfway through the Soviet occupation the British had decided the man to back was not the Pakistani choice Gulbuddin Hekmatyar, but the Tajik Shah Massoud, who was not skulking in Europe or Pakistan but doing real damage to the occupiers. The trouble was bringing that aid to him. His territory was up in the north.

Securing good guides from the Muj units near the Khyber Pass was not a problem. As in the time of the Raj, a few pieces of gold go a long way. There is an aphorism that you cannot buy the loyalty of an Afghan, but you can always rent it.

'The key word at every stage, Captain,' they told him at SIS headquarters, which back then was at Century House near the Elephant and Castle, 'is deniability. That is why you actually have to – just a technicality – resign from the army. Of course, the moment you come back' – they were nice enough to say 'when', not 'if' – 'you will be completely reinstated.'

Mike Martin knew perfectly well that the SAS already had within its ranks the ultra-secret Revolutionary Warfare Wing whose task was to stir up as much trouble for Communist regimes worldwide as they could handle. He mentioned this.

'This is even more covert,' said the mandarin. 'We call this unit Unicorn, because it doesn't exist. There are never more than twelve and at the moment only four men in it. We really need someone to slip into Afghanistan through the

Khyber Pass, secure a local guide and be brought north to the Panjshir Valley where Shah Massoud operates.'

'Bringing gifts?' asked Martin. The smooth one made a helpless gesture.

'Only tokens, I am afraid. A question of what a man can carry. But later we might move to mule-trains and a lot more kit, if Massoud will send his own guides south to the border. It's a question of first contact, don't you see.'

'And the gift?'

'Snuff. He likes our snuff. Oh, and two Blowpipe surface-to-air tubes with missiles. He is much troubled by air attacks. You'd have to teach his people how to use them. I reckon you'd be away six months from this autumn. How do you feel about it?'

Before the invasion was half a year old it was clear that the Afghans would still not do one thing that had always been impossible for them: unite. After weeks of arguing in Peshawar and Islamabad, with the Pakistani army insisting it would not distribute American funds and weapons to any but the resisters accredited to them, the number of rival Resistance groups was reduced to seven. Each had a political leader and a war commander. These were the Peshawar Seven.

Only one was not Pashtun: Professor Rabbani and his charismatic war leader Ahmad Shah Massoud, both Tajiks from the far north. Of the other six, three were soon nicknamed the 'Gucci commanders' because they rarely if ever entered occupied Afghanistan, preferring to wear western dress in safety abroad.

Of the remaining three, two, Sayyaf and Hekmatyar, were fanatical supporters of the Muslim Brotherhood of ultra-Islam. Hekmatyar was so cruel and vindictive that by the end of the Soviet occupation he had executed more Afghans than killed Russians.

The one who tribally controlled the province of Nangarhar where Izmat Khan had been born was the Mullah Maulvi Younis Khalès. He was a scholar and preacher, but he had a twinkle in his eye that spoke of kindness, as opposed to the cruelty of Hekmatyar who loathed him.

Although the oldest of the seven at more than sixty, Younis Khalès, over much of the next ten years, made forays into occupied Afghanistan to lead his men personally. When he was not there his war commander was Abdul Haq.

By 1980 the war had come to the valleys of the Spin Ghar. The Soviets were streaming through Jalalabad below the mountains and their air force had started punitive raids on mountain villages. Nuri Khan had sworn allegiance to Younis

Khalès as his warlord and been granted the right to form his own *lashkar* or fighting yeomanry.

He could shelter much of the animal wealth of his village in the natural caves that riddled the White Mountains and his people could shelter in them too, when the air raids came. But he decided it was time for the women and children to cross the border to seek refuge in Pakistan.

The small convoy would of course need a male chaperone for the journey and the stay at Peshawar, however long that would last. As *mahram* he appointed his own father, over sixty and stiff of limb. Donkeys and mules were secured for the journey.

Fighting back his tears at the shame of being sent out like a child, eight-year-old Izmat Khan was embraced by his father and brother, took the bridle of the mule bearing his mother, and turned towards the high peaks and Pakistan. It would be seven years before he returned from exile and when he came it would be to fight the Russians with cold ferocity.

To legitimize themselves in the eyes of the world, it had been agreed the warlords would each form a political party. That of Younis Khalès was called Hizb-i-Islami and everyone under his rule had to join it. Outside Peshawar a rash of tented cities had sprung up under the auspices of something called the United Nations, though

Izmat Khan had never heard of it. The UN had agreed that each warlord, now masquerading as leader of a political party, should have a separate refugee camp, and no one should be admitted who was not a member of the appropriate party.

There was another organization handing out food and blankets. Its insignia was a stumpy red cross. Izmat Khan had never seen one of those either but he was familiar with hot soup and after the arduous crossing of the mountains was glad to drink his fill. There was one more condition required of inhabitants of the camps and those benefiting from the largesse of the West, funnelled through the United Nations and General Zia-ul-Haq: boys should be educated at the Koranic school, or *madrassah*, in each refugee camp. This would be their only education. They would not learn maths or science, history or geography. They would just learn endlessly to recite the verses of the Koran. For the rest, they would only learn about war.

The imams of these *madrassah*s were in the main provided, salaried and funded by Saudi Arabia and many were Saudis. They brought with them the only version of Islam permitted in Saudi Arabia: Wahhabism, the harshest and most intolerant creed within Islam. Thus within sight of the sign of the cross dispensing food and medications, a whole generation of young

Afghans was about to be brainwashed into fanaticism.

Nuri Khan visited his family as often as he could, two or three times a year, leaving his *lashkar* in the hands of his elder son. But it was a harsh journey and Nuri Khan looked older each time. In 1987 when he arrived he looked lined and drawn. Izmat's elder brother had been killed ushering others towards the safety of the caves during a bombing raid. Izmat was fifteen and his chest nearly burst with pride when his father bade him return, join the resistance and become Mujahid.

There was much weeping from the women, of course, and mumbling from the grandfather who would not survive another winter on the plain outside Peshawar. Then Nuri Khan, his remaining son and the eight men he had brought with him to see their families turned west to cross the peaks into Nangarhar Province and the war.

The boy who came back was different and the landscape he found was shattered. In all the valleys hardly a stone bothy was standing. The Sukhoi fighter-bombers and the Hind helicopter gunships had devastated the valleys in the mountains from the Panjshir to the north, where Shah Massoud had his fighting zone, down to Paktia and the Shinkay Range. The people of the plains could be controlled or intimidated by the Afghan army or by the Khad, the secret police taught and stiffened by the Soviet KGB.

But the people of the mountains and those from the plains and cities who chose to join them were intractable and, as it later turned out, unconquerable. Despite air cover, which the British had never had, the Soviets were experiencing something like the fate of the British column cut to pieces on the suicidal march from Kabul to Jalalabad.

The roads were not safe from ambush, the mountains unapproachable save by air. And the deployment in Muj hands of the American Stinger missile since September 1986 had forced the Soviets to fly higher – too high for their firepower to be accurate – or risk being hit. The Soviet losses were relentlessly mounting, with further manpower reductions due to wounds and disease, and even in a controlled society like the USSR morale was dropping like a falcon on the stoop.

It was a savagely cruel war. Few prisoners were ever taken and the quickly dead were the lucky ones. The mountain clans especially hated the Russian fliers; if taken alive, they could be pegged out in the sun with a small cut in the stomach wall so the entrails would burst out and fry in the sun until death brought release. Or they could be given over to the women and their skinning knives.

The Soviet response was to bomb, rocket and strafe anything that moved: man, woman, child or animal. They seeded the mountains with untold millions of air-dropped mines, which eventually created a nation of crutches and prosthetic limbs. Before it was over there would be a million Afghans dead, a million crippled and five million refugees.

Izmat Khan knew all about guns from his time in the refugee camp, and the favourite was of course the Kalashnikov – the infamous AK-47. It was a supreme irony that this Soviet weapon, the favourite assault rifle of every dissident move-ment and terrorist in the world, was now being used against them. But the Americans were pro-viding them for a reason; every Afghan could replenish his ammunition from the packs on a dead Russian, which saved carrying compatible ammunition across the mountains.

Assault rifle apart, the weapon of choice was the rocket-propelled grenade, the RPG, simple, easy to use, easy to reload and deadly at short to medium range. This too was provided by the West.

Izmat Khan was big for fifteen, desperately trying to grow a fuzz round the chin, and the mountains soon made him as hard as he had ever been. Witnesses have seen the Pashtun mountain men moving like wild goats through their own terrain, legs seemingly immune from exhaustion, breathing unlaboured when others are gasping for breath.

He had been back home for a year when his father summoned him. There was a stranger with him; face burned dark from the sun, black-bearded, wearing a grey woollen shalwar kameez over stout hiking boots and a sleeveless jerkin. On the ground behind him stood the biggest backpack the boy had ever seen and two tubes wrapped in sheepskin. On his head was a Pashtun turban.

'This man is a guest and a friend,' said Nuri Khan. 'He has come to help us and fight with us. He has to take his tubes to Shah Massoud in the Panjshir, and you will guide him there.'

CHAPTER FIVE

The young Pashtun stared at the stranger. he did not seem to have understood what Nuri Khan had said.

'Is he Afghan?' he asked.

'No, he is Angleez.'

Izmat Khan was staggered. This was the old enemy. More, he was what the imam in the *madrassah* had condemned with constant venom. He must be *kafir*, an unbeliever, a Nasrani, a Christian, destined to burn for all eternity in hell. And he was to escort this man over a hundred miles of mountainside to a great valley in the north? To spend days and nights in his company? Yet his father was a good man, a good Muslim, and he had called him friend. How could this be?

The Englishman tapped his forefingers lightly on his chest near the heart.

'*Salaam aleikhem*, Izmat Khan,' he said. The father spoke no Arabic even though there were now many Arab volunteers further down the mountain range. The Arabs kept themselves to themselves, always digging, so there was no cause to mix with them and learn any of their language. But Izmat had read the Koran over and over again; it was written in Arabic only; and his imam had spoken only his native Saudi Arabic. Izmat had a good working knowledge.

'*Aleikhem as-salaam*,' he acknowledged. 'How do you call yourself?'

'Mike,' said the man.

'Ma-ick.' Izmat tried it. Strange name.

'Good, let us take tea,' said his father. They were sheltering in a cave mouth about ten miles from the wreckage of their hamlet. Further inside the cave a small fire glowed, too far inside to let a visible plume of smoke emerge to attract a Soviet aircraft.

'We will sleep here tonight. In the morning you will go north. I go south to join Abdul Haq. There will be another operation against the Jalalabad to Kandahar road.'

They chewed on goat and nibbled rice cakes. Then they slept. Before dawn the two heading north were roused and left. Their journey led them through a maze of linking valleys where there would be some shelter. But between the valleys were mountain ridges and the sides of the mountains were steep slopes covered in rock and shale with little or no cover. It would be wise to scale these by moonlight and stay in the valleys by day.

Bad luck struck them on the second day out. To speed the rate of march they had left night-camp before dawn and just after first light found themselves forced to cross a large expanse of rock and shale to find the cover of the next spine of hills. To wait would have meant waiting all day until nightfall. Izmat Khan urged that they cross in daylight. Halfway across the mountainside they heard the growl of the gunship engines.

Both man and boy dived for the ground and lay motionless – but not in time. Over the crest ahead, menacing as a deadly dragonfly, came the Soviet Mil Mi-24D, known simply as the Hind. One of the pilots must have seen a flicker of movement or perhaps the glint of metal down there on the rock field, for the Hind turned from its course and headed towards them. The roar of the two Isotov engines grew in their ears, as did the unmistakable tacka-tacka-tacka of the main rotor blades.

With his head buried in his forearms, Mike Martin risked a quick glance. There was no doubt they had been spotted. The two Soviet pilots, sitting in their tandem seats with the second above and behind the first, were staring straight at him as the Hind went into attack mode. To be caught in the open without cover by a helicopter gunship is every footsoldier's nightmare. He glanced round. One hundred yards away was a single group of boulders; not as high as a man's head but just enough to shelter behind. With a yell to the Afghan boy he was up and running, leaving his 100-lb Bergen rucksack where it was but carrying one of the two tubes that had so intrigued his guide.

He heard the running feet of the boy behind him, the roaring of his own blood in his ears and the matching snarl of the diving Hind. He would never have made the dash had he not seen some-thing about the gunship that gave a flicker of hope. Its rocket pods were empty and it carried no under-slung bombs. He gulped at the thin air and hoped his guess was right. It was.

Pilot Simonov and his co-pilot Grigoriev had been on a dawn patrol to harass a narrow valley where agents had reported that Muj were hiding out. They had dropped their bombs from altitude, then gone in lower to blast the rocky cleft with rockets. A number of goats had pelted from the crack in the mountains, indicating there had indeed been human life sheltering in there.

Simonov had shredded the beasts with his 30-mm cannon, using up most of the shells.

He had gone back to a safe altitude and was heading home to the Soviet base outside Jalalabad when Grigoriev had spotted a tiny movement on the mountainside below and to the port side. When he saw the figures start to run he flicked his cannon to 'fire' mode and dived. The two running figures far below were heading for a cluster of rocks. Simonov steadied the Hind at two thousand feet, watched the two figures hurl themselves into the rock cluster and fired. The twin barrels of the GSH cannon shuddered as the shells poured out, then stopped. Simonov swore as his ammunition ran out. He had used his cannon shells on goats, and here were Muj to kill and he had none left. He lifted the nose and turned in a wide arc to avoid the mountain crest and the Hind clattered out over the valley.

Martin and Izmat Khan crouched behind their pitiable cluster of rocks. The Afghan boy watched as the Angleez rapidly opened his sheepskin case and extracted a short tube. He was vaguely aware that someone had punched him in the right thigh, but there was no pain. Just numbness.

What the SAS man was assembling as fast as his fingers would work was one of the two Blowpipe missiles he was trying to bring to Shah

122

Massoud in the Panjshir. It was not as good as the American Stinger, but more basic, lighter and simpler.

Some surface-to-air missiles are guided to target by a ground-based radar 'fix'. Others carry their own tiny radar set in the nose. Others emit their own infra-red beam. These are the beam-riders. Others are heat-seekers, whose nose cones 'smell' the heat of the aircraft's own engines and home towards it. Blowpipe was much more basic than that; it was styled 'command to line of sight', or CLOS; and it meant the firer had to stand there and guide the rocket all the way to target by sending radio signals from a tiny control stick to the movable fins in the rocket's head.

The disadvantage of the Blowpipe was always that to ask a man to stay still in the face of an attacking gunship was to ensure a lot of dead operators. Martin pushed the two-stage missile into the launching tube, fired up the battery and the gyro, squinted through the sight and found the Hind coming straight back at him. He steadied the image in the sights and fired. With a whoosh of blazing gases the rocket left the tube on his shoulder and headed blindly into the sky. Being completely non-automatic, it now required his control to rise or drop, turn left or right. He estimated the range at 1,400 yards and closing fast. Simonov opened fire with his chain gun.

In the nose of the Hind the four barrels hurling out a curtain of finger-sized machine-gun bullets began to turn. Then the Soviet pilot saw the tiny flickering flame of the Blowpipe coming towards him. It became a question of nerve.

Bullets tore into the rocks, blowing away chunks of stone in all directions. It lasted two seconds but at two thousand rounds per minute some seventy bullets hit the rocks before Simonov tried to evade and the bullet stream swept to one side.

It is proven that in a no-thought instinctive emergency a man will normally pull left. That is why driving on the left of the road, though confined to very few countries, is actually safer. A panicking driver pulls off the road into the meadow rather than into a head-on collision. Simonov panicked and slewed the Hind to its left.

The Blowpipe had jettisoned its first stage and was going supersonic. Martin tweaked the trajectory to his right just before Simonov swerved. It was a good guess. As it turned out the Hind exposed its belly and the warhead slammed into it. It was only just under five pounds in weight and the Hind is immensely strong. But even that size of warhead at a thousand mph is a terrific punch. It cracked the base armour, entered and exploded.

Drenched with sweat on the icy mountainside Martin saw the beast lurch with the impact, start to stream smoke and plunge towards the valley floor far below.

When it impacted in the river bed the noise stopped. There was a silent peony of flame as the two Russians died, then a plume of dark smoke. That alone would bring attention from the Russians at Jalalabad. Harsh and long though the journey might be overland, it was only a few minutes for a Sukhoi ground-attack fighter.

'Let's go,' he said in Arabic to his guide. The boy tried to rise but could not. Then Martin saw the smudge of blood on the side of his thigh. Without a word he put down the reusable Blowpipe launch tube, went for his Bergen and brought it back.

He used his K-Bar knife to slit the trouser leg of the shalwar kameez. The hole was neat and small but it looked deep. If it came from one of the cannon shells, then it was only a fragment of casing, or maybe a splinter of rock, but he did not know how near the femoral artery it might be. He had trained at Hereford Accident and Emergency ward and his first-aid knowledge was good; but the side of an Afghan mountain with the Russians coming was no place for complex surgery.

'Are we going to die, Angleez?' asked the boy.

'*Inshallah*, not today, Izmat Khan. Not today,' he said. He faced a bad quandary. He needed his Bergen and everything in it. He could either carry the Bergen or the boy, but not both.

'Do you know this mountain?' he asked as he rummaged for shell dressings.

'Of course,' said the Afghan.

'Then I must come back with another guide. You must tell him where to come. I will bury the bag and the rockets.'

He opened a flat steel box and took out a hypodermic syringe. The white-faced boy watched him.

So be it, thought Izmat Khan. If the infidel wishes to torture me, let him. I will utter no sound.

The Angleez pushed the needle into his thigh. Izmat Khan made no sound. Seconds later, as the morphine took effect, the agony in his thigh began to diminish. Encouraged, he tried to rise. The Englishman had produced a small, foldable trenching tool and was digging a furrow in the shale among the rocks. When he had done he covered his Bergen and the two rocket tubes with stones until nothing could be seen. But he had memorized the shape of the cairn. If he could only be brought back to this mountainside he could recover all his kit.

The boy protested that he could walk, but

Martin simply hoisted him over one shoulder and began to march. Being all skin and bone, muscle and sinew, the Afghan weighed no more than the Bergen at about a hundred pounds. Still, heading upwards into ever thinner air and against gravity was not an option. Martin followed a course sideways across the scree and slowly downwards to the valley. It turned out to be a wise choice.

Downed Soviet aircraft always attracted Pashtun eager to strip the wreck for whatever might be of use or value. The plume of smoke had not yet been spotted by the Soviets, and Simonov's last transmission had been a final scream on which no one could get a bearing. But the smoke had attracted a small party of Muj from another valley. They saw each other a thousand feet above the valley floor.

Izmat Khan explained what had happened. The mountain men broke into delighted grins and started slapping the SAS man on the back. He insisted his guide needed help and not just a bowl of tea in some *chai-khana* in the hills. He needed transportation and a surgical hospital. One of the Muj knew a man with a mule, only two valleys away. He went to get him. It took until nightfall. Martin administered a second shot of morphine.

With a fresh guide and Izmat Khan on a mule

at last they marched through the night, just three of them, until in the dawn they came to the southern side of the Spin Ghar and the guide stopped. He pointed ahead.

'Jaji,' he said. 'Arabs.'

He also wanted his mule back. Martin carried the boy the last two miles. Jaji was a complex of five hundred caves and the so-called Afghan–Arabs had been working on them for three years, broadening, deepening, excavating, and equipping them into a major guerrilla base. Though Martin did not know it, inside the complex were barracks, a mosque, a library of religious texts, kitchens, stores and a fully equipped surgical hospital.

As he approached Martin was intercepted by the outer ring of guards. It was clear what he was doing; he had a wounded man on his back. The guards discussed among themselves what to do with the pair and Martin recognized the Arabic of North Africa. They were interrupted by the arrival of a senior man who spoke like a Saudi. Martin understood everything but thought it unwise to utter a word. With sign language he indicated his friend needed emergency surgery. The Saudi nodded, beckoned and led the way.

Izmat Khan was operated on within an hour. A vicious fragment of cannon casing was extracted from the leg.

Martin waited until the lad woke up. He squatted, local-style, in the shadows at the corner of the ward and no one took him for anything other than a Pashtun mountain man who had brought in his friend.

An hour later two men entered the ward. One was very tall, youthful, bearded. He wore a camouflage combat jacket over Arab robes and a white headdress. The other was short, tubby, also no more than mid-thirties, with a button nose and round glasses perched on the end of it. He wore a surgical smock. After examining two of their own number the pair came to the Afghan. The tall man spoke in Saudi Arabic.

'And how is our young Afghan fighter feeling?'

'*Inshallah*, I am much better, Sheikh.' Izmat spoke back in Arabic and gave the older man a title of reverence. The tall man was pleased. He smiled.

'Ah, you speak Arabic, and still so young.'

'I was seven years in a *madrassah* at Peshawar. I returned last year to fight.'

'And whom do you fight for, my son?'

'I fight for Afghanistan,' said the boy. Something like a cloud passed across the features of the Saudi. The Afghan realized he might not have said what was wanted.

'And I also fight for Allah, Sheikh,' he added.

The cloud cleared and the gentle smile came back. The Saudi leaned forward and patted the youth on the shoulder.

'The day will come when Afghanistan will no longer have need of you, but the all-merciful Allah will always have need of a warrior like you. Now, how is our young friend's wound healing?' He addressed the question to the Pickwickian doctor.

'Let us see,' said the doctor and peeled back the dressing. The wound was clean, bruised round the edges but closed by six stitches and uninfected. He tutted his satisfaction and re-dressed the suture.

'You will be walking in a week,' said Dr Ayman al-Zawahiri. Then he and Osama bin Laden left the ward. No one took any notice of the sweat-stained Muj squatting in the corner with his head on his knees as if asleep.

Martin rose and crossed to the youth on the bed.

'I must go,' he said. 'The Arabs will look after you. I will seek to find your father and ask for a fresh guide. Go with Allah, my friend.'

'Be careful, Ma-ick,' said the boy. 'These Arabs are not like us. You are *kafir*, unbeliever. They are like the imam in my *madrassah*. They hate all infidel.'

'Then I would be grateful if you would

130

not tell them who I am,' said the Englishman.

Izmat Khan closed his eyes. He would die under torment rather than betray his new friend. It was the code. When he opened his eyes the Angleez was gone. He heard later the man had reached Shah Massoud in the Panjshir, but he never saw him again.

After his six months behind the Soviet lines in Afghanistan Mike Martin made it home via Pakistan unspotted and with fluent Pashto added to his armoury. He was sent on leave, remustered into the army and, being still in service with the SAS, was posted to Northern Ireland again in autumn 1988. But this time it was different.

The SAS were the men who really terrified the IRA and to kill – or better still capture alive, torture and kill – what they called a Sassman was the IRA's greatest dream. Mike Martin found himself working with the 14th Intelligence Company, known as 'the Detachment' or 'the Det'.

These were the watchers, the trackers, the eavesdroppers. Their job was to be so stealthy as never to be seen, but to find out where the IRA killers would strike next. To do this they performed some remarkable feats.

IRA leaders' houses were penetrated via the

roof tiles and bugged from the attic downwards. Bugs were placed in dead IRA men's coffins for it was the habit of the godfathers to hold conferences while pretending to pay their respects to the casket. Long-range cameras caught images of moving mouths and lip-readers deciphered the words. Rifle-mikes recorded conversations through closed windows. When the Det had a real gem, they passed it to the hard men.

The rules of engagement were strict. The IRA men had to fire first and they had to fire at the SAS. If they threw down their guns at the challenge, they had to be taken prisoner. Before firing, both the SAS and Paras had to be immensely careful. It is a recent tradition of British politicians and lawyers that Britain's enemies have civil rights but her soldiers do not.

Notwithstanding, in the eighteen months Martin spent as an SAS captain in Ulster he participated in the dark-of-night ambushes. In each a party of armed IRA men was caught by surprise and challenged. Each time they were foolish enough to draw and point weapons. Each time it was the Royal Ulster Constabulary who found the bodies in the morning.

But it was in the second shootout that Martin took his bullet. He was lucky. It was a flesh wound in the left bicep but enough to see him flown home and sent for convalescence at

Headley Court, Leatherhead. That was where he met the nurse, Lucinda, who was to become his wife after a brief courtship.

Reverting to the Paras in the spring of 1990 Mike Martin was posted to the Ministry of Defence in Whitehall, London. Having set up home in a rented cottage near Chobham so that Lucinda could continue her career, Martin found himself for the first time a commuter in a dark suit on the morning train to London. He ranked as a Staff Officer Three and worked in the office of MOSP, the Military Operations, Special Projects Unit. Once again it was to be a foreign aggressor who would get him out of there.

On 2 August that year Saddam Hussein of Iraq invaded neighbouring Kuwait. Once again Margaret Thatcher would have none of it and US President George Bush, senior, concurred. Within a week plans were in furious preparation to create a multi-national coalition to counter-invade and free the oil-rich mini-state.

Even though the MOSP office was at full stretch the reach and influence of the Secret Intelligence Service was enough to trace him and 'suggest' he join a few of the 'friends' for lunch.

Lunch was in a discreet club in St James's and his hosts were two senior men from the Firm. Also at the table was a Jordanian-born, British-naturalized analyst brought in from GCQH at

Cheltenham. His job there was to listen to and analyse eavesdropped radio chatter inside the Arab world. But his role at the lunch table was different.

He conversed with Mike Martin in rapid Arabic and Martin replied. Finally the analyst nodded at the two spooks from Century House.

'I've never heard anything like it,' he remarked. 'With that face and voice, he can pass.'

With that he left the table, clearly having performed his function.

'We would be so damnably grateful,' said the senior mandarin, 'if you would go into Kuwait and see what is going on there.'

'What about the army?' asked Martin.

'I think they will see our point of view,' murmured the other.

The army grumbled again but let him go. Weeks later, passing himself off as a Bedouin camel drover, Martin slipped over the Saudi border into Iraqi-occupied Kuwait. On the plod north to Kuwait City he passed several Iraqi patrols but they took no notice of the bearded nomad leading two camels to market. The Bedouin are so determinedly non-political that they have for millennia watched the invaders sweep hither and thither through Arabia and never intervened. So the invaders have mostly let them be.

In several weeks inside Kuwait Martin

contacted and assisted the fledgling Kuwaiti resistance, taught them the tricks of the trade, plotted the Iraqi positions, strong points and weaknesses, and then came out again.

His second incursion during the Gulf War was into Iraq itself. He went over the Saudi border in the west and simply caught an Iraqi bus heading for Baghdad. His cover was a simple peasant clutching a wicker basket of hens.

Back in a city he knew intimately well, he took a position as a gardener in a wealthy villa, living in a shack at the end of the garden. His mission was to act as message collector and on-passer; for this he had a small, foldable, parabolic dish aerial whose 'blitz' messages were uninterceptable by the Iraqi secret police but which could reach Riyadh.

One of the best-kept secrets of that war was that the Firm had a source, an 'asset' high in Saddam's government. Martin never met him; he just picked up the messages at pre-agreed dead-letter boxes, or 'drops', and sent them to Saudi Arabia where the American-led Coalition HQ was both mystified and appreciative. Saddam capitulated on 26 February 1991, and Mike Martin came out, only to be very nearly shot by the French Foreign Legion as he came through the border in the dark.

* * *

On the morning of 15 February 1989 General Boris Gromov, commander of the Soviet 40th Army, the army of occupation of Afghanistan, walked alone back across the Friendship Bridge over the Amu Darya river into Soviet Uzbekistan. His entire army had preceded him. The war was over.

The euphoria did not last long. The USSR's own Vietnam had ended in disaster. Her restive European satellites were becoming openly mutinous and her economy was disintegrating. By November the Berliners had torn down the Wall and the Soviet empire simply fell apart.

In Afghanistan the Soviets had left behind a government which most analysts predicted would last no time as the victorious warlords formed a stable government and took over. But the pundits were wrong. The government of President Najibullah, the whisky-appreciating Afghan the Soviets had abandoned in Kabul, hung on for two reasons. One was that the Afghan army was simply stronger than any other force in the country, backed as it was by the Khad secret police, and was able to control the cities and thus the bulk of the population.

More to the point, the warlords simply disintegrated into a mêlée of snarling, grabbing, feuding, self-serving opportunists, who far from uniting to form a stable government did the reverse: they created a civil war.

None of this affected Izmat Khan. With his father still head of the family, although stiff and old before his time, and with the help of neighbours, he helped rebuild the hamlet of Maloko-zai. Stone by stone and rock by rock, they cleared the rubble left by the bombs and rockets and remade the family compound by the mulberry and pomegranate trees.

With his leg fully healed he had returned to the war and taken command of his father's *lashkar* in all but name and the men had followed him for he had been blooded. When peace came, his guerrilla group seized a huge cache of weapons the Soviets could not be bothered to carry home.

These they took over the Spin Ghar to Parachinar in Pakistan, a town that is virtually nothing but an arms bazaar. There they traded the Soviet leftovers for cows, goats and sheep to restart the flocks.

If life had been hard before, starting over was even harder, but he enjoyed the labour and the sense of triumph that Maloko-zai would live again. A man must have roots, and his were here. At twenty he both uttered the call and led the prayers at the village mosque on a Friday.

The Kuchi nomads passing through brought grim tales from the plains. The army of the Democratic Republic of Afghanistan, loyal to Najibullah, still held the cities, but the warlords infested the countryside and they and their men behaved like brigands. Tolls were arbitrarily set up on main roads and travellers were stripped of their money and goods or badly beaten.

Pakistan, in the form of its ISI Directorate, was backing Hekmatyar to become controller of all Afghanistan and in areas he ruled utter terror existed. All those who had formed the Peshawar Seven to fight the Soviets were now at each other's throats and the people groaned. From being heroes the Muj were now seen as tyrants. Izmat Khan thanked the merciful Allah that he was spared the misery of the plains.

With the end of the war the Arabs had almost all gone from the mountains and their precious caves. The one who by the end had become their uncrowned leader, the tall Saudi from the cave-hospital, was also gone. Some five hundred Arabs had stayed behind but they were not popular; they were scattered far and wide and living like beggars.

When he was twenty Izmat Khan was visiting a neighbouring valley when he saw a girl wash-ing the family clothes in the stream. She failed to hear his horse because of the sound of the running water and before she could draw the end of her hejab across her face he had made eye contact. She fled in alarm and embarrass-ment. But he had seen that she was beautiful.

Izmat did what any young man would do. He consulted his mother. She was delighted and soon two aunts had joined with her in happy conspiracy to find the girl and persuade Nuri Khan to contact the father to arrange a union. Her name was Maryam and the wedding took place in the late spring of 1993.

Of course it was in the open air, which was full of blossom being blown off the walnut trees. There was a feast and the bride came from her village on a decorated horse. There was playing of the flutes and *attan* dancing under the trees but of course only for the men. With his *madrassah* training Izmat protested at the singing and dancing, but his father was rejuvenated and overruled him. So for a day Izmat rejected his strict Wahhabi training and he too danced in the meadow and the eyes of his bride followed him everywhere.

The delay between the first glimpse by the stream and the marriage was necessary both to arrange the details of the dowry and to build a new house for the newly-weds inside the Khan compound. It was here that he took his bride when night had fallen and the exhausted villagers returned home, and his mother forty yards away nodded in satisfaction when a single cry in the night told her that her daughter-in-law had become a woman. Three months later it was clear she would bear a child in the snows of February.

As Maryam carried Izmat's child the Arabs came back. The tall Saudi who led them was not among them; he was somewhere far away called Sudan. But he sent a great deal of money and by paying tribute to the warlords was able to set up training camps. Here, at Khalid ibn Walid, al-Farouk, Sadeek, Khaldan, Jihad Wal and Darunta, the thousands of new volunteers from across the Arabic-speaking world came to train for war.

But what war? So far as Izmat Khan could see, they took no sides in the civil war among the tribal satraps, so who were they training to fight? He learned that it was all because the tall one, whom his followers called the Sheikh, had declared jihad against his own government in Saudi Arabia and against the West.

But Izmat Khan had no quarrel with the West. The West had helped defeat the Soviets with arms and money, and the only *kafir* he had ever met had saved his life. It was not his holy war, not his jihad, he decided. His concern was for his country, which was descending into madness.

CHAPTER SIX

The parachute regiment accepted Mike Martin back and asked no questions because that was what it was told to do, but he was already acquiring a reputation as a bit of an oddity. Two unexplained absences from duty inside four years, each for six months, caused raised eyebrows over breakfast in any military unit. For 1992 he was sent to the Staff College at Camberley and thence back to the Ministry, but as a major.

This time it was to the Directorate of Military Operations again, but as a Staff Officer Two in Department Three, the Balkans. The war was still raging, the Serbs under Milosevic were dominant and the world was sickened by the massacres known as ethnic cleansing. Chafing at the lack of any chance of action, he spent two years commuting in a dark suit from the suburbs to London.

Officers who have served in the SAS can return for a second tour, but only on invitation. Mike Martin got his call from Hereford at the end of 1994. It was the Christmas present he had been hoping for. But it did not please Lucinda.

There had been no baby; there were two careers heading in different directions. Lucinda had been offered a big promotion; she called it the chance of a lifetime, but it meant going to work in the Midlands. The marriage was under strain and Mike Martin's orders were to command B Squadron, 22 SAS, and take them covertly to Bosnia. Ostensibly they would be part of the United Nations's UNPROFOR peace-keeping mission. In fact they would hunt down and snatch war criminals. He was not allowed to tell Lucinda the details, only that he was leaving again.

It was the final straw. She presumed it was a transfer back to Arabia and she quite properly put to him an ultimatum: you can have the Paras, the SAS and your bloody desert, or you can come to Birmingham and have a marriage. He thought it over and chose the desert.

Outside the seclusion of the high valleys of the White Mountains Izmat Khan's old party leader

Younis Khalès died and the Hizb-i-Islami party was then wholly in the control of Hekmatyar, whose reputation for cruelty Izmat loathed.

By the time his baby was born in February 1994 President Najibullah had fallen but was alive, confined to a UN guest house in Kabul. He had supposedly been succeeded by Professor Rabbani, but Rabbani was a Tajik and therefore not acceptable to the Pashtun. Outside Kabul, only the warlords ruled their domains, but the real master was chaos and anarchy.

Yet something else was happening too. After the Soviet war thousands of young Afghans had gone back to the Pakistani *madrassahs* to complete their education. Others, too young to have fought at all, went over the border to achieve an education, any education. What they got was years of Wahhabi brainwashing. Now they were coming back, but they were different from Izmat Khan.

Because the old Younis Khalès, though ultra-devout, had possessed some residual moderation in him, his *madrassahs* in the refugee camps had taught Islam with a hint of temperance. Others concentrated only on the ultra-aggressive passages from the Verses of the Sword to be found in the Holy Koran. And old Nuri Khan, though devout also, was humane and saw no harm in singing, dancing, sports and some tolerance of others.

The returnees were ill educated, having been taught by barely literate imams. They knew nothing of life, of women (most lived and died virgins) or even of their own tribal cultures as Izmat had learned from his father. Apart from the Koran, they knew only one thing: war. Most came from the deep south where the Islam practised had always been of the most strict variants in all Afghanistan.

In the summer of 1994 Izmat Khan and a cousin left the upland valley for Jalalabad. It was a short visit but long enough to witness the savage massacre inflicted by the followers of Hekmatyar on a village that had finally refused to pay him any more tribute money. The two travellers found the menfolk tortured and slain, the women beaten, the village torched. Izmat Khan was disgusted. In Jalalabad he learned what he had seen was quite commonplace.

Then something happened in the deep south. Since the fall of any semblance of a central government the old official Afghan army had simply reassigned itself to the local warlord who paid the best. Outside Kandahar some soldiers took two teenage girls back to their camp and gang-raped them.

The preacher from the village they had raided, who also ran his own religious school, went to the army camp with thirty students and sixteen rifles. Against the odds they trounced the soldiers and hanged the commandant from the barrel of a tank gun. The priest was called Muhammad Omar, or Mullah Omar. He had lost his right eye in battle.

The news spread. Others appealed to him for help. He and his group swelled in numbers and responded to the appeals. They took no money, they raped no women, they stole no crops, they asked no reward. They became local heroes. By December 1994, twelve thousand had joined them, adopting this mullah's black turban. They called themselves the students. In Pashto 'student' is *talib*, and the plural is the Taliban. From village vigilantes they became a movement and when they captured the city of Kandahar an alternative government.

Pakistan, through its forever-plotting ISI, had been trying to topple the Tajik Rabbani in Kabul by backing Hekmatyar, but he failed repeatedly. As the ISI was deeply infiltrated by ultra-orthodox Muslims, Pakistan switched support to the Taliban. With Kandahar the new movement inherited a huge cache of arms, plus tanks, armoured cars, trucks, guns, six MiG 21 ex-Soviet fighters and six heavy helicopters. They began to sweep north. In 1995 Izmat Khan embraced his wife, kissed his baby farewell and then came down from the mountains to join them.

Later, on the floor of a cell in Cuba, he would recall that the days on the upland farm with his wife and child had been the happiest days of his life. He was twenty-three.

Too late he learned there was a dark side to the Taliban. In Kandahar, even though the Pashtun had been devout before, they were subjected to the harshest regimen the world of Islam has ever seen.

All girls' schools were closed at once. Women were forbidden to leave the house save in the company of a male relative. The all-enveloping burka robe was decreed at all times; the clacking of female sandals on tiles was decreed forbidden as being too sexy.

All singing, dancing, the playing of music, sports and kite-flying, a national pastime, was forbidden. Prayers were to be said the required five times a day. Beards on men were compulsory. The enforcers in their black turbans were often teenage fanatics, taught only the Verses of the Sword, cruelty and war. From being liberators they became the new tyrants, but their advance was unstoppable. Their mission was to destroy the rule of the warlords, and as these were loathed by the people, the people acquiesced to the new strictness. At least there was law, order, no more corruption, no more rape, no more crime; just fanatical orthodoxy.

Mullah Omar was a warrior-priest but nothing else. Having started his revolution by hanging a rapist from a gun barrel he withdrew into seclusion in his southern fortress, Kandahar. His followers were like something out of the Middle Ages, and among the many things they could not recognize was fear. They worshipped the one-eyed Mullah behind his walls and before the Taliban fell eighty thousand would die for him. Far away in Sudan the tall Saudi who controlled the twenty thousand Arabs now based in Afghanistan watched and waited.

Izmat Khan joined a *lashkar* of men drawn from his own province, Nangarhar. He was quickly respected because he was mature, had fought the Russians and been wounded.

The Taliban army was not a real army; it had no commanding general, no general staff, no officer corps, no ranks and no infrastructure. Each *lashkar* was semi-independent under its tribal leader who often held sway through personality and courage in combat, plus religious devotion. Like the original Muslim warriors of the first Caliphates they swept their enemies aside with fanatical courage, which gave rise to a reputation for invincibility, so much so that opponents often capitulated without a shot fired. When they finally ran into real soldiers, the forces of the charismatic Tajik Shah Massoud, they took unspeakable losses. They had no medical corps so their wounded simply died by the roadside. But still they came on.

At the gates of Kabul they negotiated with Massoud but he refused to accept their terms and withdrew to his own northern mountains whence he had fought and defied the Russians. So began the next civil war, between the Taliban and the Northern Alliance of Massoud the Tajik and Dostum the Uzbek. It was 1996. Only Pakistan (who had organized it) and Saudi Arabia (who paid for it) recognized the new weird government of Afghanistan.

For Izmat Khan the die was cast. His old ally Shah Massoud was now his enemy. Far to the south an aeroplane landed. It brought back the tall Saudi who had spoken to him eight years earlier in a cave at Jaji and the chubby doctor who had pulled a chunk of Soviet steel from his leg. Both men paid immediate obeisance to Mullah Omar, paying huge tribute in money and equipment and thus securing his lifelong loyalty.

After Kabul there was a pause in the war. Almost the first act of the Taliban in Kabul was to drag the toppled ex-president Najibullah from his house arrest, torture, mutilate and execute him before hanging his corpse from a lamp-post. That set the tenor of the rule to come. Izmat Khan had no taste for cruelty for its own sake. He had fought hard enough in the conquest of his country to rise from volunteer to commander of his own *lashkar*, and this in turn grew as word of his leadership spread until it became one of the four divisions in the Taliban army. Then he asked to be allowed to go back to his native Nangarhar and was made Provincial Governor. Based in Jalalabad, he could visit his family, wife and baby.

He had never heard of Nairobi or Dar es Salaam. He had never heard of anyone called William Jefferson Clinton. He had indeed heard much of a group now based in his country called Al-Qaeda and knew that its adherents had declared global jihad against all unbelievers and especially the West and most of all against a place called America. But it was not his jihad.

He was fighting the Northern Alliance to unite his homeland once and for all and the Alliance had been beaten back to two small and obscure enclaves. One was a group of resistants of the Hazara tribe bottled up in the mountains of Dara-i-Suf and the other was Massoud himself in the impregnable Panjshir Valley and the north-eastern corner called Badakshan.

On 7 August 1998 bombs exploded outside the American embassies in two African capitals. He knew nothing of this. Listening to foreign radio was now banned, and he obeyed. On 20 August

America launched seventy Tomahawk cruise missiles at Afghanistan. They came from the two missile cruisers *Cowpen* and *Shiloh* in the Red Sea and from the destroyers *Briscoe*, *Elliot*, *Hayler* and *Milius*, plus the submarine *Columbia*, all in the Arabian Gulf south of Pakistan.

They were aimed at the training camps of Al-Qaeda, and the caves of the Tora Bora. Among those that went astray was one that entered the mouth of a natural and empty cave high in the mountain above Maloko-zai. The detonation deep inside the cave split the mountain and an entire face peeled away. Ten million tons of rock crashed into the valley below.

When Izmat Khan reached the mountain there was nothing to recognize. The entire valley had been buried. There was no stream any more, no farm, no orchards, no stock pens, no mosque, no stables, no compounds. His entire family and all his neighbours were gone. His parents, uncles, aunts, sisters, wife and child were dead beneath millions of tons of granite rubble. There was nowhere to dig and nothing to dig for. He had become a man with no roots, no relatives, no clan.

In the dying August sun he knelt on the shale high above where his dead family lay, turned west towards Mecca, bowed his head to the ground and prayed. But it was a different prayer this time; it was a mighty oath, a sworn vendetta, a personal jihad unto death and it was against the people who had done this. He declared war on America.

A week later he had resigned his governorship and gone back to the front. For three years he fought the Northern Alliance. While he had been away the tactically brilliant Massoud had counter-attacked and again caused huge losses to the less competent Taliban. There had been massacres at Mazar-i-Sharif where after the native Hazara had risen in revolt and killed six hundred Taliban the avenging Taliban had gone back and butchered over two thousand civilians.

The Dayton Agreement had been signed; technically the Bosnian war was over. But what had been left behind was nightmarish. Muslim Bosnia had been the main theatre of war, even though the Bosnians, Serbs and Croats had all been involved. It had been the bloodiest conflict in Europe since the Second World War.

The Croats and the Serbs, far and away the better armed, had inflicted most of the brutalities. A thoroughly and rightly ashamed Europe set up a war crimes tribunal at The Hague in Holland and waited for the first indictments. The problem was, the guilty ones were not about to come forward with their hands up. Milosevic would offer no help at all; indeed, he was preparing fresh miseries for another Muslim province, that of Kosovo.

Part of Bosnia, the exclusively Serbian third, had declared itself the Serb Republic and most of the war criminals were hiding within it. This was the task: find them, identify them, snatch them and bring them out to stand trial. Living mainly in the fields and forests, the SAS spent 1997 hunting down what they called the PIFWICs – persons indicted for war crimes.

By 1998 Mike Martin was back in the UK and back in the Paras, a Lieutenant Colonel and instructor at Staff College, Camberley. The following year he was made Commanding Officer First Battalion, known as One Para. The NATO allies had again intervened in the Balkans, this time a little more speedily than before, and again to prevent a massacre big enough to cause the media to use the over-employed word of genocide.

Intelligence had convinced both the British and American governments that Milosevic intended to 'cleanse' the rebellious province of Kosovo and to do it thoroughly. The medium would be the expulsion of most of its 1.8 million citizens westwards into neighbouring Albania. Under the NATO banner the allies gave Milosevic an ultimatum. He ignored it and columns of weeping and destitute Kosovans were driven through the mountain passes into Albania.

The NATO response was no invasion on the ground but bombing raids which lasted seventy-eight days and wrecked both Kosovo and Serbian Yugoslavia itself. With his country in ruins Milosevic finally conceded and NATO moved into Kosovo to try to govern the wreckage. The man in charge was a lifelong Para, General Mike Jackson, and One Para went with him.

That would probably have been Mike Martin's last 'action' posting had it not been for the West Side Boys.

On 9 September 2001 news flashed through the Taliban army that had the soldiers roaring *Allahu akhbar*, God is Great, over and over again. The air above Izmat Khan's camp outside Bamiyan crackled with the shots fired in a delirium of joy. Someone had assassinated Ahmad Shah Massoud. Their enemy was dead. The man whose charisma had held together the cause of the useless Rabbani, whose cleverness as a guerrilla fighter had caused the Soviets to revere him and whose generalship had carved Taliban forces to pieces, was no more.

In fact he had been assassinated by two suicide

bombers, ultra-fanatical Moroccans pretending to be journalists with stolen Belgian passports, and sent by Osama bin Laden as a favour to his friend Mullah Omar. The Saudi had not thought of the ploy; it was the far cleverer Egyptian Ayman al-Zawahiri who realized that if Al-Qaeda did this favour for Omar, the one-eyed mullah could never expel them for what was going to happen next.

On the eleventh four airliners were hijacked over the American east coast. Within ninety minutes two had destroyed the World Trade Center in Manhattan, one had devastated the Pentagon and the fourth, since its rebellious passengers invaded the flight deck to rip the hijackers from the controls, had crashed in a field.

Within days the identity and inspiration of the nineteen hijackers had been established; within a few more days the new American President had given Mullah Omar a flat ultimatum: yield up the ringleaders or take the consequences. Because of Massoud, Omar could not capitulate. It was the code.

In the West African hellhole of Sierra Leone, a long period of civil war and barbarism had left the once-rich former British colony a vista of chaos, banditry, filth, disease, poverty and hacked-off limbs. Years earlier the British had decided to intervene and the UN had been prevailed upon to ship in fifteen thousand troops who, broadly, just sat in their barracks in the capital, Freetown. The jungle beyond the city limits was regarded as simply too dangerous for the UN force. Only the in-country element of the British army was under national command and was prepared to go there, so it was they alone who patrolled the back country.

In late August 2000 a patrol of eleven men from the Royal Irish Rangers were lured off the main road and down a track to the village which acted as the headquarters of a rebel band calling themselves the West Side Boys. They were, in effect, out-of-control psychopaths. They were relentlessly drunk on pure-alcohol native hooch; they rubbed their gums with cocaine or cut their arms to rub the dope into the cuts and get a faster 'hit'. The horrors they had inflicted on the peasantry over a wide area were unspeakable; but there were four hundred of them and they were armed to the teeth. The Rangers were quickly captured and held hostage.

Mike Martin, after a stint in Kosovo, had brought One Para to Freetown where they were based at Waterloo Camp. After complex negotiations five of the Rangers were ransomed but the remaining six seemed destined to be chopped up.

In London the Chief of Defence Staff, Sir Charles Guthrie, gave the word: go in there by force and get them out.

The task force was forty-eight SAS men, twenty-four from the SBS and ninety from One Para. Ten SAS men in jungle camouflage were dropped in a week before the attack and lived unseen in the jungle round the bandit village, watching and listening. Everything the West Side Boys said and did was overheard by the SAS men in the bush a few yards away and reported back. That was how the British knew there was no further hope of a peaceful exfiltration.

Mike Martin went in with the second wave after an unlucky rebel mortar had injured six including the commander of the first wave who had to be evacuated without ceremony.

The village – or in fact twin villages of Gberi Bana and Magbeni – straddled a slimy and stinking river called Rokel Creek. The seventy-two special forces took Gberi Bana where the hostages were located, rescued them all and fought off a series of manic counter-attacks. The ninety Paras took Magbeni. There were, at dawn, about two hundred West Side Boys in each.

Six prisoners were taken, trussed and brought back to Freetown. A few of them escaped into the jungle. No attempt was made to count the bodies, either in the wreck of the two villages or the surrounding jungle, but no one ever disputed a figure of three hundred dead.

The SAS and the Paras took twelve injured and one SAS man, Brad Tinnion, died of his wounds. Mike Martin, having lost the CO of his first wave, arrived in the second Chinook and led the final wipe-out of Magbeni. It was old-fashioned fighting, point-blank range and hand to hand. On the south side of the Rokel Creek the Paras had lost their radio to the same mortar blast that hit the attack leader. So the circling helicopters overhead could not report on the fall of their own mortar shells and the jungle was too thick to see them drop.

Eventually the Paras just charged, blood pumping, screaming and swearing until the West Side Boys, happy to torture peasants and prisoners, fled, died, fled again and died until there were none left.

It was twelve months later almost to the day that Martin was back in London when lunch was interrupted by those unbelievable images on the TV screen of fully loaded and fuelled airliners flying straight into the Twin Towers. A week later it was plain the USA would have to go into Afghanistan in pursuit of those responsible, with or without the agreement of the Kabul government.

London at once agreed that it would provide

whatever was needed from its own resources and the immediate requirements were air-to-air refuelling tankers and special forces. The SIS Head of Station in Islamabad said he would also need all the help he could get.

That was a matter for Vauxhall Cross, but the Defence Attaché in Islamabad also asked for help. Mike Martin was taken from his desk at Para HQ Aldershot and found himself on the next flight to Islamabad as Special Forces Liaison Officer.

He arrived four weeks after the destruction of the World Trade Center and the day the first allied attacks went in.

CHAPTER SEVEN

Izmat Khan was still commanding in the north, on the Badakhshan front, when the bombs rained on Kabul. As the world studied Kabul and diversionary tactics in the south, the US Special Forces slipped into Badakhshan to help General Fahim who had taken over Massoud's army. This was where the real fighting would be; the rest was window dressing for the media. The key would be Northern Alliance ground forces and American air power.

Without ever taking off, Afghanistan's puny air force was vaporized. Its tanks and artillery, if they could be spotted, were 'taken out'. The Uzbek, Rashid Dostum, who had spent years in safety across the border, was persuaded to come back and open a second front in the north-west to match Fahim's front in the north-east. And in November the great break-out began. The key was target-marking, the technology that has quietly revolutionized warfare since the first Gulf War of 1991.

Hidden, invisible among the allied forces, Special Forces specialists squint through long-range binoculars to identify the enemy's dug-in positions, guns, tanks, ammunition dumps, reserves, supplies and command bunkers. Each is marked or 'painted' with an infra-red dot from a shoulder-held projector. Via radio an air strike is called up.

In the destruction of the Taliban army facing the Northern Alliance these strikes either came from far away in the south where US Navy carriers hovered off the coast, or with A-10 tank-busters flying out of well-rewarded Uzbekistan. Unit by unit, with bombs and rockets that could not miss as they followed the infra-red beam, the Taliban army was blown away and the Tajiks charged in triumph.

Izmat Khan retreated and retreated as position after position was devastated and lost. The Taliban army of the north began with over thirty thousand soldiers, but were losing a thousand a day. There was no medication, no evacuation, no doctors. The wounded said their prayers and died like flies. They screamed *Allahu akhbar* and charged into walls of bullets.

The original volunteers for the Taliban army had long been used up. Few were left. Taliban recruiting squads had pressed tens of thousands more into the ranks, but many did not want to fight. The true fanatics were dwindling away. And still Izmat Khan had to pull them back, each time convinced that, being in the forefront of every combat, he could not last another day. By 18 November they had reached the town of Kunduz.

By a fluke of history Kunduz is a small enclave of Gilzai southerners, all Pashtun, in a sea of Tajiks and Hazaras. Thus the Taliban army could take refuge there. And it was there they agreed to surrender.

Among Afghans there is nothing dishonourable in a negotiated surrender and, once agreed, its terms are always honoured. The entire Taliban army surrendered to General Fahim and, to the rage of the US advisers, Fahim accepted.

Inside the Taliban were two non-Afghan groups. There were six hundred Arabs, all devoted to Osama bin Laden, who had sent them there. Well over three thousand Arabs had already died and the American attitude was that they would not weep salt tears if the rest went to Allah as well.

There were also about two thousand Pakistanis

who were clearly going to be a thundering embarrassment to Islamabad if they were discovered. The Pakistani ruler, General Musharraf, had been left in not a shred of doubt after 9/11 that he had a choice: become a dedicated ally of the USA with billions and billions of dollars in aid; or continue to support (via the ISI) the Taliban and thus bin Laden and pay the direct consequences. He chose the USA.

But the ISI still had a small army of agents inside Afghanistan and the Pakistani volunteers fighting with the Taliban would not stint on revealing the encouragement they had once been given to go north. Over three nights a secret air bridge exfiltrated most of them back to Pakistan.

In another covert deal some four thousand prisoners were sold – for varying sums according to desirability – to the USA and Russia. The Russians wanted any Chechens and (as a favour to Tashkent) any anti-Tashkent Uzbeks.

The original army that surrendered was over fourteen thousand strong but their numbers were coming down. Finally the Northern Alliance announced to the world media, streaming north to cover the real war story, that it had only eight thousand prisoners.

Then it was decided to hand over a further five thousand to the Uzbek commander, General Dostum. He wished to take them far to the west, to Sheberghan inside his own territory. They were packed into steel freight containers without food or water and so compressed they could only stand, straining upwards for the air pocket above their heads. Somewhere on the road west it was agreed to give them air holes. This was done with heavy machine guns that went on firing until the screaming stopped.

Of the remaining 3,015 the Arabs were selected out. They came from every part of the Muslim world: there were Saudis, Yemenis, Moroccans, Algerians, Egyptians, Jordanians and Syrians. The ultra-radical Uzbeks had been shipped back to the tender mercies of Tashkent and most of the Chechens also, but a few had managed to remain. Through the campaign the Chechens had earned the reputation of being the most ferocious, cruel and suicidal of all.

The balance of 2,400 remained behind in Tajik hands and have not been heard of since. Izmat Khan was spoken to by one of the selectors in Arabic. He replied in Arabic and was thought to be an Arab for that reason. He bore no badges of rank, was filthy, matted, hungry and exhausted. When he was pushed in a certain direction he was too tired to protest. Thus he ended up one of the six Afghans in the group destined to be sent west to Mazar-e-Sharif and into the hands of Dostum and his Uzbeks. By this time the western media were watching and the prisoners were given a guarantee of safe conduct by the newly arrived United Nations.

Trucks were found from somewhere and the six hundred were loaded aboard for the journey west along the pitted track to Mazar. But their final destination would not be the city itself but a huge prison fortress ten miles further west.

So they came to the mouth of hell, but it was called the fort of Qala-i-Jangi.

The conquest of Afghanistan, if measured from the first bomb to the fall of Kabul to the Northern Alliance, took about fifty days, but special forces from both allied countries were operational inside Afghanistan well before that. Mike Martin yearned to go with them but the British High Commission in Islamabad was adamant it needed him on the spot to liaise with the Pakistani army brass.

Until Bagram. This vast ex-Soviet air base north of Kabul was clearly going to be a major allied base during the eventual occupation. Taliban aircraft based there were gutted wrecks and the control tower was a ruin. But the sheer size of the runway, the numerous huge hangars and the living quarters where the Soviet garrison had once lived were all restorable with time and money.

It was captured in the third week of November and a team of Special Boat Squadron men moved in to stake the British claim. Mike Martin used the news as a first-rate excuse to hitch a lift from the Americans at Rawalpindi airfield to go and have a look at the place, as he put it.

It was bleak and comfortless but the SBS had 'liberated' a hangar all of their own before the Americans took the lot and were hunkered down at the back, as far from the icy wind as possible.

Soldiers have a remarkable talent for making a kind of home out of the weirdest places and the special forces are the aces because they seem to find themselves in places weirder than most. The SBS unit of twenty had gone foraging with their long-base Land-Rovers and seized a series of steel freight containers which had been dragged inside.

With drums, planks and a bit of ingenuity these were being turned into billets with beds, sofas, tables, electric lights and, supremely important, a power point to plug in the kettle and brew up mugs of tea.

It was on the morning of 26 November that the unit CO told his men: 'There seems to be something going on at a place called Qala-i-Jangi, east of Mazar. Some prisoners appear to have risen in revolt, taken their guards' weapons, and are putting up a fight. I think we should have a look.'

Six Marines were chosen and two Land-Rovers allocated and fuelled. As they were about to leave, Martin asked: 'Mind if I tag along? You might be able to use an interpreter.'

The CO of the small SBS unit was a Marine captain. Martin was a Para colonel. There was no objection. Martin boarded the second vehicle beside the driver. Behind him two Marines crouched over the .50-calibre M2 machine gun. They headed north on the six-hour drive, through the Salang Pass to the northern plains, the city of Mazar and the fort of Qala-i-Jangi.

The exact incident that triggered the massacre of the prisoners at Qala-i-Jangi was disputed at the time and will remain so. But there are compelling clues.

The western media, never shy of getting something completely wrong, persistently called the prisoners Taliban. They were the opposite. They were, in fact, with the exception of the six Afghans included by accident, the defeated army of Al-Qaeda. As such, they had come to Afghanistan specifically to pursue jihad, to fight and to die. What were trucked west from Kunduz were the six hundred most dangerous men in Asia.

What met them at Qala were one hundred partly trained Uzbeks under a desperately incompetent commander. Rashid Dostum himself

166

was away; in charge was his deputy Sayid Kamel.

Among the six hundred were about sixty of three non-Arab categories. There were Chechens who, suspecting back at Kunduz that to be selected for shipment to the Russians was a recipe for death, avoided the cull. There were anti-Tashkent Uzbeks who had also worked out that only a miserable death awaited them back in Uzbekistan and hidden themselves. And there were Pakistanis who, wrongly, avoided repatriation to Pakistan where they would have been set free.

The rest were Arabs. They were, unlike many of the Taliban left behind at Kunduz, volunteers, not pressed men. They were all ultra-fanatical. They had all been through the AQ training camps; they knew how to fight with ferocity and skill. And they had little desire to live. All they asked of Allah was the chance to take a few westerners or friends of westerners with them and thus to die *shahid*, or martyr.

The fort of Qala is not constructed as a western fort. It is a huge, ten-acre compound containing open spaces, trees and one-storey buildings. The whole space is enclosed by a fifty-foot wall, but each side is sloped so that a climber can scramble up the ramp and peer over the parapet at the top.

This thick wall plays host to a labyrinth of barracks, stores and passages with, beneath them, another maze of tunnels and cellars. The Uzbeks had only captured it ten days earlier and seemed not to know that there was a Taliban armoury and magazine stored at the southern end. That was where they shooed the prisoners.

At Kunduz the captives had been relieved of their rifles and RPGs, but no one did a body search. Had they been frisked the captors would have realized almost every man had a grenade or two hidden inside his robes. That was how they arrived in the motorcade at Qala.

The first hint came on the Saturday night of their arrival. Izmat Khan was in the fifth truck and heard the boom from a hundred yards away. One of the Arabs, gathering several Uzbeks around him, detonated his grenade, blowing himself and five Uzbeks to pemmican. Night was coming down. There were no lights. Dostum's men decided to do body searches the next morning. They herded the prisoners into the compound without food or water and left them, squatting on the ground surrounded by armed but already nervous guards.

At dawn the searches began. The prisoners, still docile in their battle-fatigue, allowed their hands to be tied behind them. As there were no ropes the Uzbeks used the prisoners' turbans. But turbans are not ropes.

One by one the prisoners were hauled upright

to be frisked. Out came handguns, grenades – and money. As the money piled up it was taken away to a side room by Sayid Kamel and his deputy. An Uzbek soldier, peering through the window a little later, saw the two men pocketing the lot. The soldier entered to protest and was told in no uncertain terms to get lost. But he came back with a rifle.

There were two prisoners who saw this and had worked their hands free. They entered the room after the soldier, seized the rifle and used its butt to beat all three Uzbeks to death. As there had been no shooting, nothing was noticed, but the compound was becoming a powder keg.

The Americans from the CIA, Johnny 'Mike' Spann and Dave Tyson, had entered the area and Mike Spann began a series of interrogations right out in the open. He was surrounded by six hundred fanatics whose only ambition before going to Allah was to kill an American. Then some Uzbek guard saw the armed Arab and yelled a warning. The Arab fired and killed him. The powder keg went up.

Izmat Khan was squatting on the dirt waiting for his turn. Like others he had worked his hands free. As the shot Uzbek soldier fell, others atop the walls opened up with machine guns. The slaughter had begun.

Over a hundred prisoners died in the dirt with bound hands and were found that way when it was finally safe for the UN observers to enter. Others untied their neighbours' hands so that they could fight. Izmat Khan led a group of others, including his eleven fellow Afghans, in a dodging, weaving run through the trees to the south wall where he knew the armoury was from a previous visit when the fort was in Taliban hands.

Twenty Arabs nearest to Mike Spann fell on him and beat him to death with fists and feet. Dave Tyson emptied his handgun into the mob, killed three, heard the click of hammer on empty chamber and was lucky to make the main gate just in time.

Within ten minutes the open compound was empty except for the corpses and the wounded, who lay and cried out until they died. The Uzbeks were now outside the wall, the main gate was slammed and the prisoners were inside. The siege had begun; it would last six days and no one was even interested in taking prisoners. Each side was convinced the other had broken the terms of surrender, but by then it did not matter any more.

The armoury door was quickly shattered and the treasure trove distributed. There was enough for a small army and masses of resupply for only five hundred men. They had rifles, grenades, launchers, RPGs and mortars. Taking what they could they fanned out through the tunnels and passages until they owned the fortress. Every time an Uzbek outside put his head over the parapet, an Arab, firing through a slit from across the compound, took a shot.

Dostum's men had no choice but to call for help, urgently. It came in the form of hundreds more Uzbeks sent by General Dostum, who hurried towards Qala-i-Jangi. Also on their way were American Green Berets in the form of four men from Fort Campbell, Kentucky, one US Air Force man to assist in air-coordination and six from the 10th Mountain Division. Basically their job was to observe, report and call in air strikes to break the resistance.

By mid-morning, coming up from Bagram base north of the recently captured capital of Kabul were two long-base Land-Rovers bearing six British Special Forces from the Special Boat Squadron (SBS) and an interpreter, Lieutenant Colonel Mike Martin of the SAS.

Tuesday saw the Uzbek counter-attack taking shape. Shielded by their single tank, they re-entered the compound and began to pound the rebel positions. Izmat Khan had been recognized as a senior commander and given charge of one wing of the south face. When the tank opened up he ordered his men into the cellars. When the bombardment stopped they came back up again.

He knew it was only a matter of time. There was no way out and no chance of mercy. Not that he wanted it. He had finally, at the age of twenty-nine, found the place he was going to die, and it was as good as any other.

Tuesday also saw the arrival of the US strike aircraft. The four Green Berets and the airman were lying just outside the parapet at the top of the external ramp, plotting targets for the fighter-bombers. Thirty strikes took place that day and twenty-eight of them slammed into the masonry inside which the rebels were hiding, killing about a hundred of them, largely by rockfalls. Two bombs were not so good.

Mike Martin was down the wall from the Green Berets, about a hundred yards from them, when the first bomb went amiss. It landed right in the middle of the circle formed by the five Americans. If it had been a contact-fused anti-personnel bomb they would have been shredded. The fact all survived with shattered eardrums and some bone-breaks was itself a miracle.

The bomb was a JDAM, a bunker-buster, designed to penetrate deep into masonry before exploding. Landing nose-down in gravel, it shot forty feet down before going off. The Americans found themselves on top of an earthquake, were hurled around, but survived.

The second mis-hit was even more unfortunate. It took out the Uzbek tank and their command post behind it.

By Wednesday the western media had arrived and were swarming all over the fort, or at least the outside of it. They may not have realized it, but their presence was the only factor that would eventually inhibit the Uzbeks from achieving a total wipe-out of the rebels to the last man.

In the course of the six days, twenty rebels tried to take their chances by escaping under cover of night and seeking escape across country. Every one was caught by the peasantry – the Hazaras who recalled the Taliban butchery of their people three years before – and lynched.

Mike Martin lay on top of the ramp, peering through the parapet and down into the open compound. The bodies from the first days still lay there and the stench was appalling. The Americans, with their black woolly hats, had uncovered faces and had already been well photographed by cameramen and TV film makers. The seven British preferred anonymity. All wore the shemagh, the cotton wraparound head-dress that keeps out flies, sand, dust and gawpers. By Wednesday it served another purpose, a filter against the stink.

Just before sundown the surviving CIA man, Dave Tyson, who had come back after a day in Mazar-e-Sharif, was bold enough to enter the compound with a TV crew desperate for an award-winning movie. Martin watched them creeping along the far wall. Marine J was lying beside him. As they watched, a snatch squad of rebels came out of an unseen door in the wall, seized the four westerners and dragged them inside.

'Someone ought to get them out of there,' remarked Marine J in a conversational tone. He looked round. Six pairs of eyes were staring at him without a sound.

He uttered two intensely sincere words, 'Oh shit', vaulted the wall, went down the inner ramp and raced across the open space. Three SBS men went with him. The other two and Martin gave sniper cover. The rebels were by now confined to the south wall only. The sheer daftness of what the four Marines had done caught the rebels by surprise. There were no shots until they reached the door in the far wall.

Marine J was first in. Hostage recovery is practised and practised by both SAS and SBS until it is second nature. At Hereford the SAS have 'the death house' for little else but; at their Poole HQ the SBS have the same.

The four SBS men came through the door

without ceremony, identified the three rebels by their clothes and beards and fired. The procedure is called 'double tap'; two bullets straight in the face. The three Arabs did not get off a shot; anyway, they were facing in the wrong direction. Dave Tyson and the British TV crew agreed then and there never to mention the incident, and they never have.

By Wednesday evening Izmat Khan realized he and his men could not stay above ground any longer. Artillery had arrived and down the length of the compound it was beginning to reduce the south face to rubble. The cellars were the last resort. The surviving rebels were down to under three hundred.

Some of these decided not to go below ground but to die under the sky. They staged a suicidal counter-attack which succeeded for a hundred yards, killing a number of unwary Uzbeks of short reaction time. But then the machine gun on the Uzbeks' replacement tank opened up and cut the Arabs to pieces. They were mostly Yemenis with some Chechens.

On Thursday, on American advice, the Uzbeks took barrels of diesel fuel brought for their tank and poured it down conduits into the cellars below. Then they set fire to it.

Izmat Khan was not in that section of the cellars and the stench of the bodies overrode the smell of the diesel, but he heard the 'whoomf' and felt the heat. More died but the survivors came staggering out of the smoke towards him. They were all choking and gagging. In the last cellar, with about a hundred and fifty men around him, Izmat Khan slammed and bolted the door to keep out the smoke. Beyond the door the hammering of the dying became fainter and finally stopped. Above them the shells slammed into the empty rooms.

The last cellar led to a passage and at the far end the men could smell fresh air. They tried to see if there was a way out, but it was only a gutter from above. That night the new Uzbek commander Din Muhammad hit upon the idea of diverting an irrigation ditch into that pipe. After the November rains the ditch was full and the water icy.

By midnight the remaining men were waist deep. Weakened by hunger and exhaustion, they began to slip beneath the surface and drown.

Up on the surface the United Nations was in charge, surrounded by media, and its instructions were to take prisoners. Through the rubble of the collapsed buildings above them the last rebels could hear the bullhorn ordering them to come out, unarmed and with hands up. After twenty hours the first began to stagger towards the stairs. Others followed. Defeated at last, Izmat Khan, with the six other Afghans left alive, went with them.

Up on the surface, stumbling over the broken stone blocks that had once been the south face, the last eighty-six rebels found themselves facing a forest of pointed guns and rockets. In the daylight of Saturday dawn they looked like scarecrows from a horror film. Filthy, stinking, black from cordite soot, ragged, matted, bearded and hypothermic, they tottered and some fell. One of these was Izmat Khan.

Coming down a rock pile he slipped, reached out to steady himself and grabbed a rock. A chunk came away in his hand. Thinking he was being attacked, a nervous young Uzbek fired his RPG.

The fiery grenade went past the Afghan's ear into a boulder behind him. The stone splintered and a piece the size of a baseball hit him with devastating force in the back of the head.

He was wearing no turban. It had been used to bind his hands six days earlier and never recovered. The rock would have pulped the skull if it had hit at ninety degrees. But it ricocheted off, slicing the scalp and knocking him into a near coma. He fell among the rubble, blood gushing from the gash. The rest were marched away to trucks waiting outside.

An hour later the seven British soldiers were

moving through the compound taking notes. Mike Martin, as senior officer, although technically the unit interpreter, would have a long report to make. He was counting the dead, though he knew there were scores, maybe up to two hundred, still underground. One body interested him; it was still bleeding. Corpses do not bleed.

He turned the scarecrow over. The clothing was wrong. This was Pashtun dress. There were not supposed to be any Pashtun present. He took his shemagh from his head and wiped the grime-smeared face. Something vaguely familiar.

When he took out his K-Bar, a watching Uzbek grinned. If the foreigner wanted to have some fun, why not? Martin cut into the pants leg of the right thigh.

It was still there, puckered by the six stitches, the scar where the Soviet shell fragment had gone in over thirteen years before. For the second time in his life he hoisted Izmat Khan over one shoulder in a fireman's lift and carried him. At the main gate he found a white Land-Rover with the sign of the United Nations on it.

'This man is alive but injured,' he said. 'He has a bad head wound.'

Duty done, he boarded the SBS Land-Rover for the drive back to Bagram.

The American trawl team found the Afghan in

Mazar hospital three days later and claimed him for interrogation. They trucked him to Bagram, but to their own side of this vast air base, and there he came to, slowly and groggily, on the floor of a makeshift cell, cold and shackled but just alive, two days after that.

On 14 January 2002 the first detainees arrived at Guantanamo Bay, Cuba, from Kandahar. They were blindfolded, shackled, hungry, thirsty and soiled. Izmat Khan was one of them.

Colonel Mike Martin returned to London in the spring of 2002 to spend three years as Deputy Chief of Staff, HQ Directorate of Special Forces, Duke of York Barracks, Chelsea. He retired in December 2005 after a party at which a group of friends including Jonathan Shaw, Mark Carleton-Smith, Jim Davidson and Mike Jackson tried, and failed, to drink him under the table. In January 2006 he bought a listed barn in the Meon valley, Hampshire, and started in the late summer to restore it into a country home.

United Nations records later showed that 514 Al-Qaeda fanatics died at Qala-i-Jangi and eighty-six survived, all injured. All went to Guantanamo Bay. Sixty Uzbek guards also died. General Rashid Dostum became Defence Minister in the new Afghan government.

PART THREE

Crowbar

CHAPTER EIGHT

Operation Crowbar's first task was to choose its cover story so that even those working inside it would not know anything about Mike Martin or even the concept of infiltrating a ringer inside Al-Qaeda.

The 'legend' chosen was that it would be an Anglo-American joint venture against a steadily growing opium threat coming out of the poppy fields of Afghanistan to the refinery/kitchens of the Middle East. Thence the refined heroin was infiltrating the West both to destroy lives and generate funds for further terrorism.

The 'script' continued to the effect that western efforts to shut off terrorism's supply of funds at the level of the world's banks had driven the fanatics to turn to drugs – a cash-only crime method.

And finally, even though the West already had powerful agencies like the US DEA and British Customs engaged in the fight against narcotics, Crowbar had been agreed by both governments as a specific, one-target operation prepared to use covert forces outside the niceties of diplomatic courtesy to raid and destroy any factories found in any foreign country turning a blind eye to the trade.

The modus operandi, Crowbar staff would be told as they were reassigned, involved using the highest tech known to man, both to listen and to watch, in order to identify high-ranking criminals, routes, stores, refineries, ships and air-craft that might be involved. As it happened, none of the new staff doubted a word of it.

This was just the cover story and it would remain in place until there was simply no further use for it, whenever that would be. But after the Fort Meade conference there was no way western intelligence was going to place all its eggs in the Crowbar basket. Frantic, though ultra-discreet, efforts would continue elsewhere to discover what Al-Isra could possibly refer to.

But the intelligence agencies were in a quandary. Between them they had scores of informants inside the world of Islamic funda-mentalism, some willing, some under duress.

The question was: how far can we go before

the real leaders realize that we know about Al-Isra? There were clear advantages to letting Al-Qaeda believe that nothing had been harvested from the laptop of the dead banker at Peshawar.

This was confirmed when the first mentions of the phrase in general conversation with Koranic scholars known to be sympathetic to extremism drew only courteous but blank responses.

Whoever knew about the real significance of the phrase, AQ had kept that circle extremely tight and it was quickly clear it did not include any western informants. So the decision was taken to match secrecy with secrecy. The West's counter-measure would be Crowbar and only Crowbar.

The project's second chore was to find and establish a new and remote headquarters. Both Marek Gumienny and Steve Hill agreed to get well away from London and Washington. Their second agreement was to base Crowbar somewhere in the British Isles.

After analysis of what would be needed in terms of size, lodgings, space and access the consensus came down firmly on the side of a decommissioned air base. Such places are usually well away from cities, contain mess halls, canteens, kitchens and accommodation in plenty. Add to that hangars for storage and a runway for the landing and departure of covert visitors. Unless the decommissioning had been too long ago, refurbishment back to operational requirements could be quickly accomplished by the property-maintenance division of one of the armed services – in this case the Royal Air Force.

When it came to which base, the choice fell on a former American base of which the Cold War had planted several dozen on British soil. Fifteen were listed and examined, including Chicksands, Alconbury, Lakenheath, Fairford, Molesworth, Bentwaters, Upper Heyford and Greenham Common. All were vetoed.

Some were operational, and service personnel still chatter. Others were in the hands of property developers; some had had their runways ploughed up and returned to agriculture. Two are still used as training sites for the intelligence services. Crowbar wanted a virgin site all to itself. Phillips and McDonald settled upon RAF Edzell and secured the approval of their respective superiors.

Although the sovereign ownership of Edzell base never left the RAF, it was for years leased to the US Navy, even though it is miles from the sea. It is actually situated in the Scottish county of Angus, due north of Brechin and north-west of Montrose, on the southern threshold of the Highlands.

It lies well off the main A90 highway from Forfar to Stonehaven. The village itself is one of a thinly scattered number spread over a large area of forest and heather with the North Esk flowing through it.

The base, when the two executive officers went up to visit it, served all their purposes. It was as remote from prying eyes as one could wish; it contained two good runways with control tower, and all the buildings they required for the resident staff. All they needed to do was add the golf-ball shaped white domes hiding listening antennae that could hear the click of a beetle half a world away and convert the former USN Ops block into the new communications or comms centre.

Into this complex would be diverted links to GCHQ Cheltenham and NSA Maryland; direct and secure lines to Vauxhall Cross and Langley to permit instant access to Marek Gumienny and Steve Hill; and a permanent 'feed' from eight more intel-gathering agencies from both nations, prime among them the yield from America's space satellites, run by the National Reconnaissance Office in Washington.

With permission granted, the 'works and bricks' people from the Royal Air Force went on a 'blitz' assignment to bring Edzell back into commission. The good folk of Edzell village noticed that something was afoot but with much winking and tapping of the sides of noses accepted that once again it would be hush-hush, just like the good old days. The local landlord laid in some extra supplies of ale and whisky, hoping that custom might revert to the level he had enjoyed before decommissioning. Otherwise, nobody said a thing.

While the painters were running their paintbrushes over the walls of the officers' quarters of a Scottish air base, the office of Siebart and Abercrombie, in a modest City of London street called Crutched Friars, received a visit.

Mr Ahmed Lampong had arrived by appointment following an exchange of e-mails between London and Jakarta, and was shown into the office of Mr Siebart, son of the founder. Had the London-based shipping broker known it, Lampong is simply one of the minor languages of the island of Sumatra whence his Indonesian visitor originally came. And it was an alias, though his passport would confirm the name and his passport was flawless.

So also was his English, and in response to Alex Siebart's compliments he admitted that he had perfected it while studying for his master's degree at the London School of Economics. He was fluent, urbane and charming; more to the point, he brought the prospect of business. There was nothing to suggest he was a fanatical member of the Islamist terrorist organization Jemaat Islamiya, responsible for a wave of bombings in Bali.

His credentials as senior partner of Sumatra Trading International were in order, as were his bank references. When he asked permission to outline his problem, Mr Siebart was all ears. As a preamble Mr Lampong solemnly laid a sheet of paper in front of the British ship broker.

The sheet had a long list. It began with Alderney, one of the British Channel Islands, and continued through Anguilla, Antigua and Aruba. Those were just the 'A's. There were forty-three names, ending with Uruguay, Vanuatu and Western Samoa.

'These are all tax-haven countries, Mr Siebart,' said the Indonesian, 'and all practise banking secrecy. Like it or not, some extremely dubious businesses, including criminal enterprises, shelter their financial secrets in places like these. And these' – he produced a second sheet – 'are just as dubious in their way. These are merchant shipping flags of convenience.'

Antigua was again up front, with Barbuda, Bahamas, Barbados, Belize, Bermuda, Bolivia, Burma and Cambodia to follow. There were twenty-seven in this list, ending with St Vincent, Sri Lanka, Tonga and Vanuatu.

There were African hellholes like Equatorial Guinea, flyspecks on the world map like Sao Tome and Principe, the Comoros and the coral atoll Vanuatu. Among the more enchanting were Luxembourg and Mongolia, which have no coast at all. Mr Siebart was perplexed though nothing he had seen was news to him.

'Put the two together and what do you come up with?' asked Mr Lampong in triumph. 'Fraud, my dear sir, fraud on a massive and increasing scale. And alas most prevalent of all in the part of the world where I and my partners trade. That is why we have decided in future to deal only with the institution renowned for its integrity. The City of London.'

'Very kind of you,' murmured Mr Siebart. 'Coffee?'

'Cargo theft, Mr Siebart. Constant and increasing. Thank you, no, I have just had breakfast. Cargos are assigned, valuable cargos, and then vanish. No trace of the ship, the charterers, the brokers, the crew, the cargo and least of all the owners. All hiding amidst this forest of different flags and banks. And far too many of them highly corrupt.'

'Dreadful,' agreed Siebart. 'How can I help?'

'My partners and I have agreed we will have

190

no more of it. True, it will cost a bit more. But we wish to deal in future only and solely with ships of the British merchant fleet flying the Red Ensign, out of British ports under a British skipper and vouched for by a London broker.'

'Excellent.' Siebart beamed. 'A wise choice, and of course we must not forget full insurance coverage for vessel and cargo by Lloyd's of London. What cargoes do you want shipped?'

Matching freighters to cargoes and cargoes to freighters is precisely what a shipping broker does, and Siebart and Abercrombie were long-standing pillars of the City of London's ancient partnership, the Baltic Exchange.

'I have done my research well,' said Mr Lampong, producing more letters of recommendation. 'We have been in discussion with this company: importers of high-value British limousines and sports cars into Singapore. For our part, we ship fine furniture timbers like rose-wood, tulipwood and padauk from Indonesia to the USA. This comes from North Borneo, but would be a part-cargo with the remainder being sea containers on deck with embroidered silks from Surabaya, Java, also bound for the USA. Here' – he laid down a final letter – 'are the details of our friends in Surabaya. We all agree we wish to trade British. Clearly, this would be a triangular voyage for any British freighter. Could you find us a suitable UK-registered freighter for this task? I have in mind a regular and ongoing partnership.'

Alex Siebart was confident he could find a dozen suitable Red Ensign vessels to pick up the charter. He would need to know vessel size, price and desired dates.

It was finally agreed that he would supply Mr Lampong with a 'menu' of vessels of the needed tonnage for the double-cargo and the charter price. Mr Lampong, when he had consulted his partners, would provide desired collection dates at the two Far Eastern ports and the US delivery port. They parted with mutual expressions of confidence and good will.

'How nice,' sighed Alex Siebart's father when he told him over lunch at Rules, 'to be dealing with old-fashioned and civilized gentlemen.'

If there was one place that Mike Martin could not show his face it was Edzell air base. Steve Hill was able to call into play the array of contacts that exists in every business called the 'old boys' network'.

'I won't be at home most of this winter,' said his guest at lunch in the Special Forces Club. 'I'm going to try and see a bit more of the Caribbean sun. So I suppose you could borrow the place.'

'There will be a rent, of course,' said Hill.

'As much as my modest budget can afford.'

'And you won't knock it about?' asked the guest. 'All right then. When can I have it back?'

'We hope to be there no longer than mid-February. It's just for some instructional seminars. Tutors coming and going, that sort of thing. Nothing . . . physical.'

Martin flew from London to Aberdeen and was met by a former SAS sergeant whom he knew well. He was a tough Scot who clearly had returned to his native heather in his retirement.

'How are you keeping, boss?' he asked, employing the old jargon for SAS men talking to an officer. He hefted Martin's kitbag into the rear and eased out of the airport car park. He turned north at the outskirts of Aberdeen and took the A96 road in the direction of Inverness. The mountains of the Scottish Highlands enveloped them within a few miles. Seven miles after the turn he pulled left off the main road.

The signpost said simply: 'Kemnay'. They went through the village of Monymusk and hit the Aberdeen–Alford road. Three miles later the Land-Rover turned right, ran through Whitehouse and headed for Keig. There was a river beside the road; Martin wondered whether it contained salmon or trout or neither.

Just before Keig the off-road turned across the river and up a long, winding private drive. Round two bends the stone bulk of an ancient castle sat on a slight eminence looking out over a stunning vista of wild hills and glens.

Two men emerged from the main entrance, came forward and introduced themselves.

'Gordon Phillips. Michael McDonald. Welcome to Castle Forbes, family seat of Lord Forbes. Good trip, Colonel?'

'It's Mike, and you were expecting me. How? Angus here made no phone call.'

'Well, actually we had a man on the plane. Just to be on the safe side,' said Phillips.

Mike Martin grunted. He had not spotted the tail. He was clearly out of practice.

'Not a problem, Mike,' said the CIA man McDonald. 'You're here. Now a range of tutors have your undivided attention for eighteen weeks. Why not freshen up and after lunch we'll start the first briefing.'

During the Cold War the CIA maintained a chain of 'safe houses' right across the USA. Some were inner-city apartments for the holding of discreet conferences whose participants were better not seen at head office. Others were rural retreats such as renovated farmhouses where agents back from a stressful mission could have a relaxed vacation while also being debriefed detail by detail on the time abroad.

And there were some chosen for their obscurity where a Soviet defector could be held in the kindliest of detention while checks were made on his authenticity, and where a vengeful KGB, working out of the Soviet Embassy or Consulate, could not get at him.

Agency veterans still wince at the memory of Colonel Yurchenko who defected in Rome and was amazingly allowed to dine out in Georgetown with his debriefing officer. He went to the men's room and never came back. In fact he had been contacted by the KGB who reminded him of his family back in Moscow. Full of remorse, he was daft enough to believe the promises of amnesty and redefected. He was never heard of again.

Marek Gumienny had one simple question for the small office inside Langley that runs and maintains the safe houses: 'What is the most remote, obscure and hard-to-get-into-or-out-of facility that we have?'

The answer from his real-estate colleague took no time at all.

'We call it the Cabin. It is lost to the human race, somewhere up in the Pasayten Wilderness of the Cascades Range.'

Gumienny asked for every detail and every

picture available. Within thirty minutes of receiving the file he had made his choice and given his orders.

East of Seattle, in the wilds of Washington State, is the range of steep, forested and, in winter, snow-clothed mountains known as the Cascades. Inside the borders of the Cascades are three zones: the National Park, the logging forest and the Pasayten Wilderness. The first two have access roads and some habitations.

Hundreds of thousands of visitors go to the Park every year while it is open, and it is riddled with tracks and trails; the former viable for rugged vehicles, the latter for hikers or horses. And the wardens know every inch of it.

The logging forest is off limits to the public for safety reasons, but it too has a network of tracks along which snarling trucks habitually haul the felled tree trunks to the delivery points for the sawmills. In deep winter both have to close down because the snow makes most movement almost impossible.

But east of them both, running up to the Canadian border, is the Wilderness. Here there are no tracks, one or two trails and only in the far south of the terrain, near Hart's Pass, a few log cabins.

Winter and summer the Wilderness teems with wildlife and game; the few cabin owners tend to summer in the Wilderness, then disconnect all systems, lock up and withdraw to their city mansions. There is probably nowhere in the USA as bleak or remote in winter, with the possible exception of the area of northern Vermont known simply as 'the Kingdom', where a man may vanish and be found rock-solid in the spring thaw.

Years earlier a remote log cabin had come up for sale and the CIA bought it. It was an impulse purchase, later regretted but occasionally used by senior officers for summer vacations. In October when Marek Gumienny made his enquiry it was closed and locked. Despite the looming winter and the costs, he demanded it be reopened and that its transformation begin.

'If that's what you want,' said the head of the real-estate office, 'why not use the North-west Detention Centre in Seattle?'

Despite the fact he was talking to a colleague, Gumienny had no choice but to lie.

'It is not just a question of keeping an ultra-high-value asset away from prying eyes, nor yet preventing him from escape. I have to consider his own safety. Even in supermax jails there have been fatalities.'

The head of safe houses got the point. At least, he thought he had. Utterly and completely invisible, utterly and completely escape-proof.

Totally self-contained for at least a six-month period. It was not really his speciality. He brought in the team who had devised the security at the fearsome Pelican Bay Supermax in California.

The Cabin was almost inaccessible to start with. A very basic road went a few miles north of the tiny town of Mazama and then ran out, still ten miles short. There was nothing for it but to use sky-hooks and use them extensively. With the power invested in him Marek Gumienny commandeered a Chinook heavy-lift helicopter from McChord Air Force Base south of Seattle to be used as a carthorse.

A build team from the Army's Corps of Engineers; raw materials were purchased locally with State Police advice. Everyone was on a need-to-know basis and the legend was that the Cabin was being converted into an ultra-high-security research centre. In truth it was to become a one-man jail.

At Castle Forbes the regime started intensive and became more so. Mike Martin was required to change out of western clothes into the robes and turban of a Pashtun tribesman. His beard and hair were to grow as long as the time allowed.

The housekeeper was allowed to stay on; she

had not the slightest interest in the laird's guests and nor did Hector the gardener. The third remaining resident was Angus, the former SAS sergeant who had become Lord Forbes's estate manager, or factor. Even if an interloper had wished to penetrate the estate, he would have been most unwise with Angus on the prowl.

For the rest, 'guests' came and went, save two whose residence had to be permanent. One was Najib Qureshi, a native Afghan and former teacher in Kandahar, once a refugee given asylum in Britain, now a naturalized citizen and translator at GCHQ Cheltenham. He had been detached from his duties and transferred to Castle Forbes. He was the language tutor and coach in all forms of behaviour that would be expected of a Pashtun. He taught body language, gestures, how to squat on the heels, how to eat, how to walk and the postures for prayer.

The other was Dr Tamian Godfrey: mid-sixties, iron-grey hair in a bun at the back; she had been married for years to a senior officer in the Security Service, MI5, until his death two years earlier. Being 'one of us', as Steve Hill put it, she was no stranger to security procedures, the cult of need-to-know, and had not the slightest intention of mentioning her presence in Scotland to anyone ever.

Moreover, she could work out without being

told that the man she was here to tutor would be going into harm's way and became determined he would never slip up because of something she had forgotten. Her expertise was the Koran; her knowledge of it was encyclopaedic and her Arabic impeccable.

'Have you heard of Muhammad Asad?' she asked Martin. He admitted he had not.

'Then we shall start with him. Born Leopold Weiss, a German Jew, he converted to Islam and became one of its greatest scholars. He wrote probably the best commentary ever on Al-Isra, the journey from Arabia to Jerusalem and thence to heaven. This was the experience that instituted the five daily prayers, keystone of the faith. You would have this at your *madrassah* as a boy, and your imam, being a Wahhabi, would have believed totally that it was a real, physical journey, and not just a vision in a dream. So you believe the same. And now, the daily prayers. Say after me . . .'

Najib Qureshi was impressed. She knows more about the Koran than I do, he mused.

For exercise they wrapped up warmly and went walking the hills, shadowed by Angus, quite legally equipped with his hunting rifle.

Even though he knew Arabic, Mike Martin realized what a staggering amount he had to learn. Najib Qureshi taught him to speak Arabic with a Pashtun accent, for Izmat Khan's voice, speaking Arabic to fellow prisoners in Camp Delta, had been recorded secretly in case he had secrets to divulge. He did not, but for Mr Qureshi the accent was invaluable because he could teach his pupil to imitate it.

Although Mike Martin had spent six months with the Muj in the mountains during the Soviet occupation, that was eighteen years earlier and he had forgotten much. Qureshi coached him in Pashto, even though it had been agreed from the start that Martin could never pass as a Pashtun among other Pashtun.

But mostly it was two things: the prayers and what had happened to him in Guantanamo Bay. The CIA was the principal provider of inter-rogators in Camp Delta; Marek Gumienny had discovered three or four who had had dealings with Izmat Khan from the moment of his arrival onwards.

Michael McDonald flew back to Langley to spend days with these men, draining them dry of every detail they could recall, plus the notes and tapes they had made. The cover story was that Izmat Khan was being considered for release under the NFD rules – no further danger – and Langley wanted to be sure.

All the interrogators were adamant that the Pashtun mountain warrior and Taliban commander was the hardest man in detention. He had vouchsafed very little, complained not at all, cooperated to the minimum, accepted all the privations and punishments with stoicism. But, they agreed, when you looked into those black eyes, you just knew he would love to tear your head off.

When McDonald had it all he flew back in the CIA Grumman and landed right at Edzell air base. Thence a car took him north to Forbes Castle and he briefed Mike Martin.

Tamian Godfrey and Najib Qureshi concentrated on the daily prayers. Martin would have to say them in front of others, and he had better get them right. There was one ray of hope, according to Najib. He was not a born Arab; the Koran was only in classical Arabic and no other language. A one-word slip could be put down to mispronunciation. But for a boy who had spent seven years in a *madrassah*, one entire phrase was too much. So, with Najib rising and bowing, forehead to the carpet, beside him, and Tamian Godfrey (due to her stiff knees) in a chair, they recited and recited and recited.

There was progress also at Edzell air base where an Anglo-American technical team was installing and linking all the British intelligence services and those of the USA into one nexus. The accommodation and facilities were up and running. When the US Navy were in residence the base had had, apart from housing and work stations, a bowling alley, beauty salon, delicatessen, post office, basketball court, gym and theatre. Gordon Phillips, aware of his budget and Steve Hill breathing down his neck, left the fripperies much as they were – defunct.

The RAF shipped in catering staff and the RAF Regiment took over perimeter security. No one doubted the base was becoming a listening post for opium-traffickers.

From the USA giant Galaxies and Starlifters flew in with listening monitors that could and would scan the world. Arabic translations were not imported because this would be handled by GCHQ Cheltenham and Fort Meade, both of whom would be in constant secure contact with Crowbar, as the new listening post had been coded.

Before Christmas the twelve computer work stations were established and brought on stream. These would be the nerve centre and six operators would hover over them day and night.

Crowbar Centre was never devised as a new intelligence agency of its own, but simply a short-term 'dedicated' (i.e. single purpose) operation, with whom all British and US agencies would, thanks to John Negroponte's blanket authority, cooperate without stint or delay.

To assist this, Crowbar's computers were fitted with ultra-secure ISDN BRENT lines with two BRENT keys for each station. Each had its own removable hard disk which would be taken out when not in use and stored in a guarded safe.

Crowbar's computers were then linked directly into the communications systems of Head Office, or HO, the term for SIS headquarters at Vauxhall Cross, and Grosvenor, the term employed for the CIA Station at the US Embassy in Grosvenor Square, London.

To seal the operation from any unwanted interference, the Crowbar address for its communications was hidden under a STRAP3 access code with a Bigot list limited to those in the know: a very few senior officers indeed.

Then Crowbar began to listen to every word spoken in the Middle East, in the Arabic language and in the world of Islam. By then it was only doing what was already being done by others, but the pretence had to be maintained.

When Crowbar went operational it had one other access. Apart from sound, it was interested in vision. Also piped into the obscure Scottish air base were the images the National Reconnaissance Office was picking up from its KH-11 Keyhole satellites over the Arab world and the yield of the increasingly popular

Predator drones whose high-definition images from twenty thousand feet went back to the American Army Central Command, or CENTCOM, headquarters at Tampa, Florida.

Some of the more penetrating minds at Edzell realized that Crowbar was ready and waiting for something but they were not quite sure what.

Shortly before Christmas 2006 Mr Alex Siebart recontacted Mr Lampong at his Indonesian company office to propose one of the two general-cargo freighters registered in Liverpool as suitable for his purpose. By chance both were owned by the same small shipping company and the firm of Siebart and Abercrombie had chartered them before on behalf of clients who had been amply satisfied. McKendrick Shipping was a family business; it had been in merchant marine for a century. The company chief was the patriarch, Liam McKendrick; he captained the *Countess of Richmond* and his son Sean captained the other ship.

The *Countess of Richmond* was eight thousand tons, flew the Red Ensign, was moderately priced and would be available for a fresh cargo out of a British port by 1 March.

What Alex Siebart did not add was that he had warmly recommended the contract to Liam McKendrick if it came his way, and the old skipper had concurred. If Siebart and Abercrombie could find him a cargo from the USA back to the UK, it would make a very nice and profitable triangular voyage for the spring.

Unbeknown to either man, Mr Lampong contacted someone in the British city of Birmingham, an academic at Aston University, who drove himself to Liverpool. With high-powered binoculars the *Countess of Richmond* was examined in detail and a long-range lens took over a hundred pictures of her from different angles. A week later Mr Lampong e-mailed back. He apologized for the delay, explaining that he had been up-country examining his sawmills, but that the *Countess of Richmond* sounded exactly right. His friends in Singapore would be in touch with details of the cargo of limousines to be brought from the UK to the Far East.

In truth the friends in Singapore were not Chinese but Malaysians; and not simply Muslims but ultra-fanatical Islamists. They had been put in funds out of a new account created in Bermuda by the late Mr Tewfik al-Qur, who had deposited the original moneys, before transfer, with a small private bank in Vienna that suspected nothing. They did not even intend to make a loss on the limousines, but to recoup their investment by selling them once their purpose had been served.

* * *

Marek Gumienny's explanation to the CIA
interrogators that Izmat Khan might be coming
up for trial was not untrue. He intended to
arrange exactly that, and to secure an acquittal
and release.

In 2005 a US Appeals Court had decreed that
the rights of prisoners of war did not apply to
members of Al-Qaeda. The Federal Court had
upheld President Bush's intention to order the
trials of terrorist suspects by special military
tribunals. That, for the first time in four years,
gave the detainees the chance of a defence
attorney. Gumienny intended that Izmat Khan's
defence would be that he had never been in
Al-Qaeda, but a serving Afghan army officer,
albeit under the Taliban, and had nothing whatever to do with 9/11 or Islamist terrorism. And
he intended that the court should accept that.

It would require the Director of National
Intelligence to request his colleague the Secretary
of Defense, to 'have a word' with the military
judges of the case.

Mike Martin's leg was healing nicely. He had
noted when he read Izmat Khan's slim file after
the concordat in the orchard that the man had
never described how he had acquired the scar on
the right thigh. Martin saw no reason to mention

it either. But when Michael McDonald arrived back from Langley with the more copious notes from Izmat Khan's numerous interrogations, he had been concerned that the questioners had pressed the Afghan for an explanation of the scar and never received one. If the existence of the scar was by any chance known to anyone inside Al-Qaeda and Mike Martin bore no such scar, he would be 'blown'.

Martin had no objection for he had something in mind. A surgeon was flown from London to Edzell and then by the newly acquired Bell Jetranger helicopter to the lawn of Forbes Castle. He was the Harley Street surgeon with full security clearance who could be relied on to remove the occasional bullet and say nothing more about it.

It was all done with a local anaesthetic. The incision was easy, for there was no bullet or fragment to be extracted. The problem was to make it heal in a few weeks but look much older than that.

The surgeon, James Newton, excised a quantity of flesh tissue beneath and around the incision to make it deeper, as if something had come out and created a concavity in the meat. His sutures were large, clumsy, unstraight stitches, drawing the edges of the wound together so that they would pucker as they healed. He sought to make it look like the work done in a field hospital in a cave, and there were six stitches.

'You must understand,' he said as he left, 'this scar is supposed to be over fifteen years old. A surgeon would probably spot that it cannot be, but a non-medical man should accept it. Especially if it has twelve weeks to settle down.'

That was in early November. By Christmas nature and the body of a very fit forty-four-year-old had done an excellent job. The puffiness and redness were gone.

CHAPTER NINE

'If you are going where I think you are going, young Mike,' said Tamian Godfrey on one of their daily hikes, 'you will have to master the various levels of aggressiveness and fanaticism that you will be likely to encounter. At the core is self-arrogated jihad or holy war, but various factions arrive at this via various routes and behave in various ways. They are not all the same by a long chalk.'

'It seems to start with Wahhabism,' said Martin.

'In a way, but let us not forget that Wahhabism is the state religion of Saudi Arabia and Osama bin Laden has declared war on the Saudi establishment for being heretics. There are many groups way out on the extremist wing beyond the teachings of Muhammad al-Wahhab.

'He was an eighteenth-century preacher who came out of the Nejd, the bleakest and harshest part of the interior of the Saudi peninsula. He left behind him the harshest and most intolerant of all the many, many interpretations of the Koran. That was then, this is now. He has been superseded. Saudi Wahhabism has not declared war on the West, or on Christianity; nor does it propose indiscriminate mass murder of anyone, let alone women and children. What Wahhab did was leave behind the seedbed of total intolerance in which today's terror-masters could plant the young seedlings before turning them into killers.'

'Then how come they are not still confined to the Arabian peninsula?' asked Martin.

'Because,' cut in Najib Qureshi, 'for thirty years Saudi Arabia has used its petrodollars to fund the internationalization of its state creed, and that includes every Muslim country in the world, including the place of my birth. There is no reason to think any of them realized what a monster was being set free or how it would be diverted to mass murder. Indeed there is ample reason to believe now, a bit late in the day, that Saudi Arabia is terrified of the creature it has funded for three decades.'

'Then why has Al-Qaeda declared war on the source of its creed and its funding?'

'Because other prophets have arisen, even more intolerant, even more extreme. These have preached the creed not simply of intolerance of anything not Islamic, but of the duty of attack and destruction. The Saudi government is denounced for dealing with the West, permitting US troops on its holy soil. And that applies to every secular Muslim government as well. For the fanatics they are all as guilty as Christians and Jews.'

'So who do you think I shall be meeting in my travels, Tamian?' asked Martin. The scholar found a stone the size of a chair and sat down to rest her legs.

'There are numerous groups but two are at the core. Do you know the word "Salafi"?'

'I have heard of it,' admitted Martin.

'These are the back-to-the-beginning brigade. They really want to restore the great golden age of Islam. Back to the first four Caliphates, over a thousand years ago. Wild beards; sandals; robes; Sharia'ah – the rigorous legal code; rejection of modernity and the West which brought it. There is no such earthly paradise, of course, but fanatics were never deterred by unreality. In pursuit of their manic dream Nazis, Communists, Maoists, followers of Pol Pot have slaughtered hundreds of millions, half of them their own kith and kin, for not being extreme enough. Think of Stalin's and Mao's purges – all fellow Communists but butchered for being backsliders.'

'When you described the Salafis, you were describing the Taliban,' said Martin.

'Among others. These are the suicide bombers, the simple believers; trusting their masters, following their spiritual guides, not very bright but completely obedient and believing that all their deranged hatred is going to please the mighty Allah.'

'There are worse?' asked Martin.

'Oh yes,' said Tamian Godfrey, resuming her walk but directing the party firmly back towards the castle whose tower could just be seen two short valleys away.

'The ultras, the real ultras, I would designate with one word. *Takfir*. Whatever it meant in Wahhab's day, it has changed. The true Salafi will not smoke, gamble, dance, accept music in his presence, drink alcohol or consort with western women. With his dress, appearance and religious devotion, he is immediately identifiable for what he is. From an internal security point of view, identifiability is half the battle.

'But some will adopt every single custom of the West, however much they may loathe them, in order to pass as fully westernized and there-fore harmless. All nineteen of the Nine/ Eleven bombers slipped through because they looked and acted the part. The same with the four London bombers: apparently normal young men, going to the gym, playing cricket, polite, helpful, one of them a special needs teacher, smiling constantly and planning mass murder. These are the ones to watch.

'Many are educated, barbered, clean-shaven, groomed, dressed in suits, with a good degree. These are the ultimate; prepared to become chameleons against their faith to achieve mass murder for their faith. Thank heavens, here we are, my old legs are giving out. Time for the midday prayers. Mike, you will utter the call, and then lead us in prayer. You may be asked to later. It is a great privilege.'

Just after the New Year an e-mail was sent from the office of Siebart and Abercrombie to Jakarta. The *Countess of Richmond,* with a full cargo of crated Jaguar saloon cars for Singapore, would sail from Liverpool on 1 March. After unloading at Singapore she would proceed in ballast to North Borneo to take aboard the hold cargo of timber before turning for Surabaya for the deck cargo of crated silks.

The construction crew working inside the Pasayten Wilderness was finally and deeply grateful when the job was done by the end of January. To keep up the work rate the men had chosen to overnight right on the site and until the central heating came on stream they had been extremely cold. But the bonus was large and tempting. They took the discomfort and completed on schedule.

To the naked eye the Cabin looked much the same but larger. In fact it had been transformed. To cope with a staff of two officers the bedrooms would suffice; for the extra eight guards to accomplish a twenty-four-hours-a-day surveillance regime, an extra bunkhouse had been added, and a refectory beside it.

. The spacious sitting room was retained as such, but a recreation room with pool table, library, plasma TV and ample DVD selection had created yet another extension. All the rooms were built of interior-insulated pine logs.

The third extension appeared to be of the usual rustic logs but its exterior walls were in fact only clad with split tree trunks; inside the walls were stressed concrete. The whole penitentiary wing was impregnable from without and escape-proof from within.

It was reached from the guards' quarters through a single steel door with food-service hatch and spyhole. Beyond this door was a single but spacious room. It contained a steel bed frame deeply embedded in the concrete floor. It could never be removed by bare hands. Nor could the wall shelving, which was integral to the concrete.

There were however carpets on the floor and heat came from skirting-level grills that could never be opened. The room also contained a door opposite the spyhole and this the detainee could open or close at will. It led only to the exercise yard.

This was bare save for a concrete bench in the centre out of reach of the walls. These were ten feet tall and smooth as a pool table. No man could get anywhere near the top, nor was there anything that could be detached, propped against the wall or stood on.

For sanitation there was a recess off the sitting room/bedroom containing a single hole in the floor for bodily functions and a shower whose controls were in the hands of the guards outside.

Because all the new materials had come in by helicopter, the only visible exterior addition was a landing pad under the snow. Otherwise the isolated Cabin stood in its five-hundred-acre tract, surrounded on all sides by the pines, larch and spruce even though the trees had been cut back to a hundred yards in every direction.

When they came, the ten guardians of probably the country's most expensive and exclusive prison were two middle-grade CIA men from

Langley and eight junior staffers who had completed all the mental and physical tests at the 'Farm' training school and were hoping for an exciting first assignment. Instead they got a forest in the snow. But they were all fit and eager to impress.

The military trial at Guantanamo Bay began just before the end of January and was held in one of the larger rooms in the interrogation block, decked out now for its judicial purpose. Anyone hoping for a half-mad Colonel Jessup or any of the histrionics portrayed in *A Few Good Men* would have been sorely disappointed. The proceedings were low in tone and orderly.

There were eight detainees being considered for release as of 'no further danger' and seven were vociferous in stating their harmlessness. Only one maintained a scornful silence. His case was heard last.

'Prisoner Khan, into what language would you like these proceedings to be translated?' asked the colonel presiding, flanked by a major and a female captain on the dais at the end of the room under the seal of the United States of America. All three were from the US Marines legal branch.

The prisoner was facing them; he was hauled to his feet by the Marine guards flanking him. Desks set facing each other had been allocated to prosecuting and defending attorneys, the former military, the latter civilian. The prisoner shrugged gently and stared at the female Marine captain for several seconds; then he let his gaze come to rest on the wall above the judges.

'This court is aware that the prisoner understands Arabic, so that is the language the court chooses. Any objection, counsellor?'

The question was to the defending attorney, who shook his head. He had been warned about his client when he took the case. From all he had heard he was convinced he had no chance. It was a civil-rights-based appearance and he knew what the surrounding Marines thought of white knights from the civil-rights movement. A helpful client would have been nice. Still, he reasoned, the Afghan's attitude at least got his counsel off the hook. He shook his head. No objection; Arabic would do.

The Arabic terp advanced and positioned himself close to the Marine guards. It was a wise choice; there was only one Pashtun interpreter and he had had a rough time with the Americans because he had coaxed nothing out of his fellow Afghan. Now he had nothing to do and saw the end of a quite comfortable lifestyle approaching.

There had only ever been seven Pashtun at 'Gitmo', the seven wrongly included among the foreign fighters at Kunduz five years earlier. Four had gone back, simple farm boys who had renounced all Muslim extremism with considerable enthusiasm; and the other two had had mental breakdowns so complete that they were still in psychiatric care. The Taliban commander was the last one.

The prosecuting counsel began and the terp uttered a stream of sibilant Arabic. The gist was that the Yankees are going to send you back to the slammer and throw away the keys, you arrogant Taliban shit. Izmat Khan slowly lowered his gaze and fixed the terp. The eyes said it all. The Lebanon-born American reverted to literal translation. The man might be dressed in a ludicrous orange jumpsuit, shackled hand and foot, but you never knew with this bastard.

The prosecutor did not take long. He stressed five years of virtual silence, a refusal to name collaborators in the war of terror against the USA and the fact the prisoner had been caught in a jail uprising in which an American had been brutally stomped to death. Then he sat down. He had no doubt of the outcome. The man would have to remain in custody for years to come.

The civil-rights attorney took a little longer. He was pleased that as an Afghan the prisoner had had absolutely nothing to do with the atrocity of 9/11. He had been fighting in an all-Afghan civil war at the time and had nothing to do with the

Arabs behind Al-Qaeda. As for Mullah Omar and the Afghan government sheltering Bin Laden and his cronies, that was a dictatorship of which Mr Khan was a serving officer but not a part.

'I really must urge this court to admit the reality,' he wound up. 'If this man is a problem, he is an Afghan problem. There is a new and democratically elected government there now. We should ship him back for them to deal with.'

The three judges withdrew. They were away for thirty minutes. When they returned the captain was pink with anger. She still could not believe what she had heard. Only the colonel and the major had had the interview with the Chairman, Joint Chiefs of Staff, and knew their orders.

'Prisoner Khan, be upstanding. This court has been made aware that the government of President Karzai has agreed that if you are returned to your native land, you will be sentenced to life imprisonment over there. That being so, this court intends to burden the American taxpayer with you no longer. Arrangements will therefore be made to ship you back to Kabul. You will return as you arrived – in shackles. That is all. Court rises.'

The captain was not the only one in shock. The prosecuting attorney wondered how this would look on his résumé. The defending counsel was feeling slightly light-headed. The terp had for one panicking moment thought the mad colonel would order the cuffs taken off in which case he, the good son of Beirut, was going straight out of the window.

The British Foreign & Commonwealth Office is situated in King Charles Street, just off Whitehall and within easy glancing distance of the window outside which King Charles I was decapitated. As the New Year holiday slipped into memory the small protocol team that had been set up the previous summer resumed its task.

This was to coordinate with the Americans the ever more complex details of the forthcoming 2007 G8 conference. The 2005 meeting of the governments of the eight richest states in the world had been at Gleneagles Hotel, Scotland, and it had been a success up to a point. The point, however, had as always been the roaring crowds of protesters. Each year they presented problems that grew steadily worse. At Gleneagles the Perthshire landscape had had to be disfigured by miles and miles of chain-link fencing to create a complete *cordon sanitaire* round the entire estate. The access road had had to be fenced and guarded.

Led by two ageing pop stars, the call had gone

out for a million protesters against world poverty to march through nearby Edinburgh. That was just the anti-poverty brigade. Then the anti-globalization cohorts had thrown their flour bombs and waved their placards.

'Don't these yo-yos realize that global trade generates the wealth with which to fight poverty?' asked one angry diplomat. The answer was: apparently not.

Genoa was remembered with a shudder. That was why the idea out of the White House, who would be hosting 2007, was acclaimed as simple, elegant, brilliant. A location sumptuous but utterly isolated; immune, unreachable, secure in total control. It was the mass of detail that concerned the protocol team; that and the advancement to mid-April. So the British team accepted what had been agreed and announced, and got on with their administrative task.

Far away to the south-east two huge USAF C-5 Galaxies began to drop towards the Sultanate of Oman. They came from the east coast of the USA with one mid-air refuelling by a tanker out of the Azores. The two aerial juggernauts came out of the sunset on the Dhofari hills, heading east and asking for landing instructions at the Anglo-American desert air base of Thumrait.

In their cavernous hulls the two giants

contained an entire military unit. One had the living accommodation: from flat-pack, skilled-assembly hutments, through generators, air conditioning, refrigeration plants and TV aerials, to the corkscrews for the fifteen-person technical team. The other carried what is called 'the sharp end': two pilotless reconnaissance drones called Predator, their guidance and imaging kit and the men and women who would operate them.

A week later they were set up. On the far side of the air base, out of bounds to non-unit personnel, the bungalows were up, the air conditioners hummed, the latrines were dug, the kitchen cooked; and under their hooped shelters the two Predators waited until their mission should be given to them. The aerial surveillance unit was also patched through to Tampa, Florida and Edzell, Scotland. Some day they would be told what they had to watch – day and night, rain and cloud – photograph and transmit back. Until then men and machines waited in the heat.

Mike Martin's final briefing took a full three days and it was important enough that Marek Gumienny flew over in the agency Grumman. Steve Hill came up from London and the two spymasters joined their executive officers McDonald and Phillips.

There were only five of them in the room, for

Gordon Phillips operated what he called 'the slide show' himself. Rather more developed than the old slide projectors of yesterday, the demonstrator threw up picture after picture on a high-definition plasma screen in perfect colour and detail. At a touch on the remote, it could close in on any detail and magnify to fill the screen.

The point of the briefing was to show Mike Martin every last piece of information in the possession of the entire gamut of western agencies concerning the faces he might meet.

The sources were not just the Anglo-American agencies. Over forty nations' agencies were pouring their discoveries into central databases. Apart from the rogue states, Iran, Syria, and the failed states like Somalia, governments across the planet were sharing information on terrorists of the ultra-aggressive Islamist creed.

Rabat was invaluable in targeting its own Moroccans; Aden fed in names and faces from South Yemen; Riyadh had swallowed its embarrassment and provided columns of faces from its own Saudi list.

Martin stared at them all as they flashed up. Some were face-on portraits taken in a police station; others were snatched with long lenses on streets or in hotels. The faces' possible variants were shown: with or without beard; in Arab or western dress; long hair, short or shaven.

There were mullahs and imams from various extremist mosques; youths believed to be simple message-carriers; faces of those known to help with support services like funds, transport, safe houses.

And there were the big players, the ones who controlled the various global divisions and had access to the very top.

Some were dead, like Muhammad Atef, first Director of Operations, killed by an American bomb in Afghanistan; his successor, serving life without parole; his successor, also dead; and the believed present one.

Somewhere in there was the doctorly face of Tewfik al-Qur, who had dived over a balcony in Peshawar five months earlier. A few faces down the line was Saud Hamud al-Utaibi, new head of AQ in Saudi Arabia and believed very much alive.

And there were the blanks, the outline of a head, black on white. These included the AQ chief from South-east Asia, successor to Hanbali and probably the man behind the latest bombings of tourist resorts in the Far East. And, surprisingly, the AQ chief for the United Kingdom.

'We knew who he was until about six months ago,' said Gordon Phillips. 'Then he quit just in time. He is back in Pakistan, hunted day and night. The ISI will get him eventually ...'

'And ship him up to us in Bagram,' grunted Marek Gumienny. They all knew that inside the US base north of Kabul was a very special facility where everyone 'sang' eventually.

'You will certainly seek out this one,' said Steve Hill as a grim-faced imam flashed on the screen. It was a snatched shot and came from Pakistan. 'And this one.'

It was an elderly man, looking mild and courtly; also a snatched shot, on a quayside somewhere with bright blue water in the background; it came from the Special Forces of the United Arab Emirates in Dubai.

They broke, ate, resumed, slept and started again. Only when the housekeeper was in the room with trays of food did Phillips switch off the TV screen. Tamian Godfrey and Najib Qureshi stayed in their rooms or walked the hills together. Finally it was over.

'Tomorrow we fly,' said Marek Gumienny.

Mrs Godfrey and the Afghan analyst came to the helipad to see him off. He was young enough to be the Koranic scholar's son.

'Take care of yourself, Mike,' she said, then swore. 'Damn, stupid me, I'm choking up. God go with you, lad.'

'And if all else fails, may Allah keep you in his care,' said Qureshi.

The Jetranger could only take the two senior controllers and Martin. The two executive officers would drive down to Edzell and resume their mission.

The Bell landed well away from prying eyes and the group of three ran across to the CIA Grumman V. A Scottish snow squall caused them all to shelter under waterproofs held over their heads, so no one saw that one of the men was not in western dress.

The crew of the Grumman had tended to some strange-looking passengers and knew better than to raise even an eyebrow at the heavily-bearded Afghan whom the Deputy Director (Operations) was escorting across the Atlantic with a British guest.

They did not fly to Washington but to a remote peninsula on the south-east coast of Cuba. Just after dawn on 14 February they touched down at Guantanamo and taxied straight into a hangar whose doors closed at once.

'I'm afraid you have to remain in the plane, Mike,' said Marek Gumienny. 'We'll get you out of here under cover of dark.'

Night comes fast in the tropics and it was pitch black by seven p.m. That was when four CIA men from 'special tasks' entered the cell of Izmat Khan. He rose, sensing something wrong. The regular guards had quit the corridor outside his cell half an hour earlier. That had never happened before.

The four men were not brutal but they were not taking no for an answer either. Two grabbed the Afghan, one round the torso pinioning his arms, the other round the thighs. The chloroform pad took only twenty seconds to work. The writhing stopped and the prisoner went limp.

He was put on a stretcher and thence on to a wheeled trolley. A cotton sheet went over the body and the prisoner was wheeled outside. The crate was waiting. The entire cell block was devoid of guard staff. No one saw a thing. A few seconds after the abduction the Afghan was inside the crate.

It was not badly equipped as crates go. From the outside it was just a large timber box such as are used for general freight purposes. Even the markings were totally authentic.

Inside it was insulated against any sound being able to emerge. In the roof there was a small removable panel to replenish fresh air, but that would not be taken down until the crate was safely airborne. There were two comfortable armchairs welded to the floor and a low-wattage amber light.

The recumbent Izmat Khan was placed in the chair that already had restrainer straps fitted.

Without cutting off circulation to the limbs, the prisoner was secured so that he could relax but not leave the chair. He was still asleep.

Finally satisfied, the fifth CIA man, the one who would travel in the crate, nodded to his colleagues and the end of it was closed off. A forklift hoisted the crate a foot off the ground and ran it out to the airfield where the Hercules was waiting. It was an AC-130 Talon from Special Forces fitted with extra-range tanks and could make its destination easily.

Unexplained flights into and out of Gitmo are regular as clockwork; the tower gave a quick 'clear take-off' in response to the staccato request and the Hercules was airborne for McChord Base, Washington State.

An hour later a closed car drove up to the Camp Echo block and another small group got out. Inside the empty cell a man was garbed in orange jumpsuit and soft slippers. The unconscious Afghan had been photographed before being covered and removed. With the use of the Polaroid print a few minor snips were made to the beard and hair of the replacement. Every fallen tuft was collected and removed.

When it was over there were a few gruff farewells and the party left, locking the cell door behind them. Twenty minutes later the soldiers were back, mystified but incurious. The poet

Tennyson had got it right: 'theirs not to reason why'.

They checked the familiar figure of their prize prisoner and waited for the dawn.

The morning sun was tipping the pinnacles of the Cascades when the AC-130 drifted down to its home base at McChord. The base commander had been told this was a CIA shipment, a last consignment for their new research facility up in the forests of the Wilderness. Even with his rank, he needed to know no more, so he asked no more. The paperwork was in order and the Chinook stood by.

In flight the Afghan had come round. The roof panel was open and the air inside the hull of the Hercules fully pressurized and fresh. The escort smiled encouragingly and offered food and drink. The prisoner settled for a soda through a straw.

To the escort's surprise the prisoner had a few phrases in English, clearly gleaned over five years listening in Guantanamo. He asked the time only twice in the journey, and once bowed his face as far as it would go and murmured his prayers. Otherwise he said nothing.

Just before touchdown the roof panel was replaced and the waiting forklift driver had not the slightest suspicion he was not lifting an ordinary load of freight from the rear ramp of the Hercules across to the Chinook.

Again the ramp doors closed. The small battery-powered pilot light inside the crate remained on, but invisible from outside, as all sounds were inaudible. But the prisoner was, as his escort would later report to Marek Gumienny, like a pussy-cat. No trouble at all, sir.

Given that it was mid-February, they were lucky with the weather. The skies were clear but freezing cold. At the helipad outside the Cabin the great twin-rotored Chinook landed and opened its rear doors. But the crate stayed inside. It was easier to disembark the two passengers straight from the crate to the snow.

Both men shivered as the rear wall of the crate came off. The snatch team from Guantanamo had flown with the Hercules and up front in the Chinook. They were waiting for the last formality.

The prisoner's hands and feet were shackled before the restraining straps were removed. Then he was bidden to rise and shuffled down the ramp into the snow. The resident staff, all ten of them, stood around in a semi-circle, guns pointing.

With an escort so heavy they could hardly get through the doors, the Taliban commander was walked across the helipad, through the cabin and into his own quarters. As the door closed, shutting out the bitter air, he stopped shivering.

Six guards stood round him in his large cell as the manacles were finally removed. Shuffling backwards, they left the cell and the steel door slammed shut. He looked around. It was a better cell, but it was still a cell. He recalled the courtroom. The colonel had told him he would return to Afghanistan. They had lied again.

It was mid-morning and the sun was blazing down on the Cuban landscape when another Hercules rolled in to land. This also was equipped for long-distance flying, but unlike the Talon it was not armed to the teeth and did not belong to Special Forces. It came from MATS, the Air Force transport division. It was to carry one single passenger across the globe.

The cell door swung open.

'Prisoner Khan, stand up. Face the wall. Adopt the position.'

The belt went round the midriff; chains fell from it to the ankle cuffs and another set to the wrists, held together and in front of the waist. The position permitted a shuffling walk, no more.

There was a short walk to the end of the block with six armed guards. The high-security truck had steps at the back, a mesh screen between the prisoners and the driver, and black windows.

When he was ordered out at the airfield, the prisoner blinked in the harsh sunlight.

He shook his shaggy head and looked bewildered. As his eyes grew accustomed to the glare, he gazed around and saw the waiting Hercules and a group of American officers staring at him. One of them advanced and beckoned.

Meekly he followed him across the scorching tarmac. Shackled though he was, six armed grunts surrounded him all the way. He turned to have one last look at the place that had held him for five miserable years. Then he shuffled up into the hull of the aircraft.

In a room one flight below the operations deck of the control tower two men stood and watched him.

'There goes your man,' said Marek Gumienny.

'If they ever find out who he really is,' replied Steve Hill, 'may Allah have mercy on him.'

PART FOUR

Journey

CHAPTER TEN

It was a long and wearisome flight. there were no in-flight refuelling facilities, which are expensive. This Hercules was just a prison ship, doing a favour for the Afghan government who ought to have picked up their man in Cuba but had no aircraft for the job.

They flew via American bases in the Azores and Ramstein, Germany, and it was late afternoon of the following day that the C-130 dropped towards the great air base of Bagram at the southern edge of the bleak Shomali Plain.

The flight crew had changed twice, but the escort squad had stayed the course, reading, playing cards, catnapping as the four sets of whirling blades outside the portholes drove them east and ever east. The prisoner remained shackled. He too slept as best he could.

As the Hercules taxied on to the apron beside the huge hangars that dominate the American zone within Bagram base, the reception group was waiting. The US Provost Major heading the escort party was gratified to see the Afghans were taking no chances. Apart from the prison van there were twenty Afghan Special Forces soldiers headed by the unit commander Brigadier Yusuf.

The major trotted down the ramp to clear the paperwork before handing over his charge. This took a few seconds. Then he nodded to his colleagues. They unchained the Afghan from the fuselage rib and led him shuffling out into a freezing Afghan winter.

The troops enveloped him, dragged him to the prison van and threw him inside. The door slammed shut. The US major decided he absolutely would not want to change places. He threw up a salute to the brigadier, who responded.

'You take good care of him, sir,' said the American, 'that is one very hard man.'

'Do not worry, major,' said the Afghan officer. 'He is going to Pul-i-Charki jail for the rest of his days.'

Minutes later the prison van drove off, followed by the truck with the Afghan SF soldiers. It took the road south to Kabul. It was not until the darkness was complete that the van and the truck became separated in what would later be officially described as an unfortunate accident. The van proceeded alone.

Pul-i-Charki is a fearsome, brooding block of a place to the east of Kabul, near the gorge at the eastern end of the Kabul plain. Under the Soviet occupation it was controlled by the Khad secret police and constantly rang with the screams of the tortured.

During the civil war several tens of thousands of prisoners failed to leave alive. Conditions had improved since the creation of the new, elected Republic of Afghanistan, but its stone battlements, corridors and dungeons still seemed to echo with the shrieks of its ghosts. Fortunately the prison van never made it.

Ten miles after losing the military escort a pick-up truck came out of a side road and took up station behind the van. When it flashed its lights, the van driver pulled over at the pre-reconnoitred flat area off the road and behind a clump of stunted trees. There the 'escape' took place.

The prisoner had been uncuffed as soon as the van left the last security check at Bagram's perimeter. Even as the van rolled, he had changed into the warm grey woollen shalwar kameez and boots provided. Just before the pullover he had wound round his head the feared black turban of the Talib.

Brigadier Yusuf, who had descended from the cabin of the truck to be taken on board by the pick-up, now took charge. There were four bodies in the open back of the utility.

All had come fresh from the city mortuary. Two were bearded, and they had been dressed in Talib clothing. They were actually construction workers who had been atop some very insecure scaffolding when it collapsed and killed them both.

The other two derived from separate car accidents. Afghan roads are so potholed that the smoothest place to drive is the crown at the centre. As it is considered rather effeminate to pull over just because someone is coming the other way, the harvest in fatalities is impressive. The two smooth-shaven bodies were in prison service uniform.

The prison officers would be found with handguns drawn, but dead; the bullets were fired into the bodies there and then. The ambushing Taliban were scattered at the roadside, also shot with slugs from the pistols of the guards. The van door was savaged with a pickaxe and left swinging open. That was how the van would be found sometime the next day.

When the theatre had been accomplished Brigadier Yusuf took the front seat of the pick-up beside the driver. The former prisoner climbed in the back with the two Special Forces men he had brought with him. All three wrapped the trailing end of their turbans round their faces to shelter from the cold.

The pick-up skirted Kabul City and cut across country until it intercepted the highway south to Ghazni and Kandahar. There waited, as each night, the long column of what all Asia knows as the 'jingly' trucks.

They all seem to have been built about a century ago. They snort and snarl along every road of the Middle and Far East, emitting their columns of choking black smoke. Often they are seen broken down by the roadside, the driver being prepared to trudge many miles to find and buy the needed part.

They seem to find their way over impossible mountain passes and along the sides of bare hillsides on crumbling tracks. Sometimes the gutted skeleton of one can be seen in the defile below the road. But they are the commercial lifeblood of a continent, carrying an amazing variety of supplies to the tiniest and most isolated settlements and the people who live in them.

The British named them jingly trucks many years ago because of their decorations. They are carefully painted on every available surface with scenes from religion and history. There are representations from Christianity, Islam, Hinduism, Sikhism and Buddhism, often gloriously mixed up. They are decorated and caparisoned with ribbons, tinsel and even bells. Hence, they jingle.

The line on the highway south of Kabul contained several hundred, their drivers sleeping in their cabs, waiting for the dawn. The pick-up slewed to a halt beside the line. Mike Martin jumped from the back and walked to the cab. The shrouded figure behind the wheel had his face hidden by a shemagh of checked cloth.

On the other side Brigadier Yusuf nodded but said nothing. End of the road. Start of the journey. As he turned away he heard the driver speak.

'Good luck, boss.'

That term again. Only the SAS called their officers 'boss'. What the American provost major at Bagram had not known as he made the handover was not only who his prisoner was, but that since the installation of President Hamid Karzai the Afghan Special Forces had been created and trained at his request by the SAS.

Martin turned away and started to walk down the line of trucks. Behind him the tail lights of the pick-up faded as it headed back to Kabul. In the cab the SAS sergeant made a cellphone call to a number in Kabul. It was taken by the Head of Station. The sergeant uttered two words and terminated.

The SIS chief for all Afghanistan also made a call on a secure line. It was three-thirty in the morning in Kabul, eleven at night in Scotland. A one-line message came up on one of the screens. Phillips and McDonald were already in the room, hoping to see what they then saw. 'Crowbar is running.'

On a freezing, pitted highway Mike Martin permitted himself one last glance behind him. The red lights of the pick-up were gone. He turned and walked on. Within a hundred yards he had become the Afghan.

He knew what he was looking for but he was a hundred trucks down the line until he found it. A licence plate from Karachi, Pakistan. The driver of such a truck would be unlikely to be Pashtun and so would not notice the imperfect command of Pashto. He would be likely to be a Baluchi heading home to Pakistan's Baluchistan province.

It was too early for the drivers to be rising, and unwise to rouse the driver of the chosen truck; tired men woken suddenly are not in the best of tempers and Martin needed him in a generous mood. For two hours he curled up beneath the truck and shivered.

Around six there was a stirring and a hint of pink in the east. By the roadside someone started a fire and set a billy on it to boil. In central Asia much of life is lived in and around the tea-house, the *chai-khana*, which can be created even with a fire, a brew of tea and a group of men. Martin rose, walked over to the fire and warmed his hands.

The tea-brewer was Pashtun but taciturn, which suited Martin fine. He had taken off his turban, unwound it and stowed it in the tote-bag hanging from his shoulder. It would be unwise to advertise being Talib until one knew the company was sympathetic. With a fistful of his Afghanis he bought a steaming cup and sipped gratefully. Minutes later the Baluchi clambered sleepily out of his cab and came over for tea.

Dawn rose. Some of the trucks began to kick into life with plumes of black smoke. The Baluchi walked back to his cab. Martin followed.

'Greetings, my brother.'

The Baluchi responded, but with some suspicion.

'Do you by any chance head south to the border and Spin Boldak?'

If the man was heading back to Pakistan, the small border town south of Kandahar would be where he would cross. By then Martin knew there would be a price on his head. He would have to skirt the border controls on foot.

'If it please Allah,' said the Baluchi.

'Then in the name of the all-merciful would you let a poor man trying to get home to his family ride with you?'

The Baluchi thought. His cousin normally came with him on these long hauls to Kabul, but he was sick in Karachi. This trip he had driven alone, and it was exhausting.

'Can you drive one of these?' he asked.

'In truth, I am a driver of many years.'

They drove south in companionable silence, listening to the eastern pop music on the old plastic radio propped above the dash. It screeched and whistled but Martin was not sure whether this was just the static or the tune.

The day wore on and they chugged through Ghazni and on towards Kandahar. On the road they paused for tea and food, the usual goat and rice, and filled the tank. Martin helped with the cost from his bundle of Afghanis and the Baluchi became much more friendly.

Though Martin spoke neither Urdu nor the Baluchi dialect and the man from Karachi only a smattering of Pashto, with sign language and some Arabic from the Koran they got along well.

There was a further overnight stop north of Kandahar, for the Baluchi would not drive in the darkness. This was Zabol province, wild country and peopled by wild men. It was safer to drive in the light with hundreds of other lorries in front, behind and yet more heading north. Bandits would prefer the night.

At the northern outskirts of Kandahar Martin claimed he needed a nap and curled up along the bench behind the seats which the Baluchi used as his bed. Kandahar had been the headquarters and stronghold of the Taliban and Martin wanted no reformed Talib to think he saw an old friend in a passing truck.

South of Kandahar he again spelled the Baluchi at the wheel. It was still mid-afternoon when they came to Spin Boldak; Martin claimed he lived in the northern outskirts, bade his host a grateful farewell and dropped off miles before the border checkpoint.

Because the Baluchi spoke no Pashto he had kept his radio tuned to a pop station and never heard the news. At the border the queues were longer even than usual and when he finally rolled to the barrier he was shown a picture. A black-bearded Talib face stared at him.

He was an honest and hard-working man. He wanted to get home to his wife and four children. Life was hard enough. Why spend days, even weeks, in an Afghan jail trying to explain that he had been totally ignorant?

'By the Prophet, I have never seen him,' he swore, and they let him go.

Never again, he thought as he trundled south on the Quetta road. He might hail from the most corrupt city in Asia, but at least you knew where you were in your own home town. Afghans were not his people; why get involved? He wondered what the Talib had done.

Martin had been warned the hijack of the prison van, the murder of its two warders and the escape of a returnee from Guantanamo Bay could not be covered up. To start with the American Embassy would make a fuss.

The 'murder' scene had been discovered by patrols sent up the Bagram road when the prison van failed to arrive at the jail. The separation of the van from its military escort was put down to incompetence. But the freeing of the prisoner was clearly by a criminal gang of Taliban leftovers. A hunt was put out for them.

Unfortunately the US Embassy offered the Karzai government a photograph, which could not be refused. The CIA and SIS Heads of Station tried to slow things down but there was only so much they could do. By the time all border posts received a faxed photograph, Martin was still north of Spin Boldak.

Though he knew nothing of this, Martin was determined there would be no chances taken at border crossings. In the hills above Spin Boldak he hunkered down and waited for night. From the position he had climbed to, he could see the lie of the land and the route he would take on the night march to come.

The small town was five miles ahead and half a mile below him. He could see the road snaking in and the trucks on it. He could see the massive old fort that had once been a stronghold of the British army.

He knew the capture of that fort in 1919 had been the last time the British army used medieval scaling ladders. They had approached secretly by night and apart from the bellowing of the mules, the clang of ladles on cauldrons and the swearing of the soldiers as they stubbed their toes, were silent as the grave so as not to wake the defenders.

The ladders were ten feet too short so they crashed into the dry moat with a hundred soldiers on them. Happily, the Pashtun defenders, crouching behind the walls, presumed the force attacking them must be enormous, so they quit through the back door and ran for the hills. The fort fell without a shot being fired.

Before midnight Martin stole quietly past its walls, through the town and into Pakistan. Sunrise found him ten miles down the Quetta road. Here he found a *chai-khana* and waited until a truck that accepted paying passengers came along and gave him passage to Quetta. At last the black Talib turban, instantly recognizable in those parts, became an asset and not a liability. So on it went.

If Peshawar is a fairly extreme Islamist city, Quetta is more so, only exceeded in its ferocity of sympathy for Al-Qaeda by Miram Shah. These are within the North-West Frontier Provinces where local tribal law prevails. Though technically across the border from Afghanistan the Pashtun people still prevail, as does the Pashto language and extreme devotion to ultra-traditional Islam. A Talib turban is the mark of a man to be reckoned with.

Though the main road south from Quetta heads for Karachi, Martin had been advised to take the smaller track of a highway south-west to the wretched port of Gwador.

This lies almost on the Iranian border at the extreme western end of Baluchistan. Once a sleepy and malodorous fishing village, it has developed into a major harbour and entrepôt, contentedly devoted to smuggling, especially opium. Islam may denounce the use of narcotics but that is for Muslims. If the infidels of the West wish to poison themselves and pay handsomely for the privilege, that has nothing to do with true servants and followers of the Prophet.

Thus the poppies are grown in Iran, Pakistan and most of all Afghanistan, refined to base morphine locally and hence smuggled further west to become heroin and death. In this holy trade Gwador plays its part.

In Quetta, seeking to avoid conversation with Pashto speakers who might unmask him, Martin had found another Baluchi truck driver heading for Gwador. It was only in Quetta that he learned there was a five-million Afghani price on his head – but only in Afghanistan.

It was on the third morning after he heard the words 'good luck, boss' that he dropped off the truck and settled gratefully for a cup of sweet green tea at a pavement café. He was expected, but not by locals.

The first of the two Predators had taken off from Thumrait twenty-four hours earlier. Flying in rotation, the UAVs would keep up a constant day-and-night patrol over their assigned surveillance area.

A product of General Atomics, the UAV-RQ 1 L Predator is not much to look at. It resembles something that might have come from the aero-modeller's doodling pad.

It is only twenty-seven feet long and pencil-slim. Its tapered seagull wings have a span of forty-eight feet. Right at the rear a single 113-hp Rotax engine drives the propellers that push it along, and the Rotax just sips petrol from its hundred-gallon fuel tank.

Yet from this puny impulsion it can speed up to 117 knots or loiter along at seventy-three. Its maximum endurance aloft is forty hours, but its more normal mission would be to fly up to a 400-nautical-mile radius from home base, spend twenty-four hours on the job and fly home again.

Being a rear-engined 'pusher' device, its directional controls are up front. They can be operated by its controller manually or switched to remote control from a computerized programme to do what is wanted and keep doing it until given fresh instructions.

The Predator's true genius lies in its bulbous nose: the detachable Skyball avionics pod.

All the communications kit faces upwards to talk to and listen to the satellites up in space. These receive all its photo-images and overheard conversations and pass them back to base.

What faces downwards is the Lynx synthetic-aperture radar and the L-3 Wescam photographic unit. More modern versions, such as the two used over Oman, can overcome night, cloud, rain, hail and snow with the multi-spectral targeting system.

After the invasion of Afghanistan, when the juiciest of targets were spotted but could not be attacked in time, the Predator went back to the makers and a new version emerged. It carried the Hellfire missile, giving the eye-in-the-sky a weaponized variant.

Two years later the head of Al-Qaeda from the Yemen left his compound far in the invisible interior with four chums in a Land Cruiser. He did not know it but several pairs of American eyes were watching him on a screen in Tampa.

On the word of command the Hellfire left the belly of the Predator and seconds later the Land Cruiser and its occupants were simply vaporized. It was all witnessed in full colour on a plasma screen in Florida.

The two Predators out of Thumrait were not weaponized. Their sole task was to patrol at twenty-thousand feet, out of sight, inaudible, radar-immune, and watch the ground and sea below.

There were four mosques in Gwador but discreet British enquiries of the Pakistani ISI extracted the information that the fourth and smallest was flagged as a hotbed of fundamentalist agitation. Like most of the smaller mosques in Islam, it was a one-imam place of worship, surviving on donations from the faithful. This one had been created and was run by Imam Abdullah Halabi.

He knew his congregation well and from his raised chair as he led the prayers he could spot a visiting newcomer at a glance. Even at the back, the black Talib turban caught his eye.

Later, before the black-bearded stranger could

replace his sandals and lose himself in the crowds of the street, the imam tugged at his sleeve.

'Greeting of our all-merciful Lord be upon you,' he murmured. He used the Arabic phrase, not Urdu.

'And upon you, imam,' said the stranger. He too spoke Arabic, but the imam noticed the Pashto accent. Suspicion confirmed; the man was from the tribal territories.

'My friends and I are adjourning to the *madafa*,' he said. 'Would you join us and take tea?'

The Pashtun considered for a second, then gravely inclined his head. Most mosques have a *madafa* attached, a more relaxed and private social club for prayers, gossip and religious schooling. In the West the indoctrination of teenagers into ultra-extremism is often accomplished there.

'I am Imam Halabi. Does our new worshipper have a name?' he asked.

Without hesitation Martin produced the first name of the Afghan President and the second of the Special Forces brigadier.

'I am Hamid Yusuf,' he said.

'Then welcome, Hamid Yusuf,' said the imam. 'I notice you dare to wear the turban of the Taliban. Were you one of them?'

'Since I joined Mullah Omar at Kandahar in nineteen ninety-five.'

There were a dozen in the *madafa*, a shabby shack behind the mosque. Tea was served. Martin noticed one of the men staring at him. The same man then excitedly drew the imam aside and whispered frantically. He would not, he explained, ever dream of watching television and its filthy images, but he had passed a TV shop and there was a set in the window.

'I am sure it is the man,' he hissed. 'He escaped from Kabul but three days ago.'

Martin did not understand Urdu, least of all in the Baluchi accent, but he knew he was being talked about. The imam may have deplored all things western and modern, but like most he found the cellphone damnably convenient, even if it was made by Nokia of Christian Finland. He asked three friends to engage the stranger in talk and not to let him leave. Then he retired to his own humble quarters and made several calls. He returned much impressed.

To have been a Talib from the start; to have lost his entire family and clan to the Americans; to have commanded half the northern front in the Yankee invasion; to have broken open the armoury at Qala-i-Jangi, to have survived five years in the American hellhole, to have escaped the clutches of the Washington-loving Kabul regime – this man was not a refugee, he was a hero.

Imam Halabi may have been a Pakistani, but he had a passionate loathing of the government of Islamabad for its collaboration with America. His sympathies were wholly with Al-Qaeda. To be fair to him, the five million Afghani reward, which would make him rich for life, did not tempt him in the slightest.

He returned to the hall and beckoned the stranger to him.

'I know who you are,' he hissed. 'You are the one they call the Afghan. You are safe with me but not in Gwador. Agents of the ISI are everywhere and you have a price on your head. Where are your lodgings?'

'I have none. I have only just arrived from the north,' said Martin.

'I know where you have come from; it is all over the news. You must stay here, but not for long. Somehow you must leave Gwador. You will need papers, a new identity, safe passage away from here. Perhaps I know a man.'

He sent a small boy from his *madrassah* running to the harbour. The boat he sought was not in port. It arrived twenty-four hours later. The boy was still patiently waiting at the berth where it always docked.

Faisal bin Selim was a Qatari by birth. He had been born to poor fisherfolk in a shack on the edge of a muddy creek near a village that

255

eventually became the bustling capital of Doha. But that was after the discovery of oil, the creation of the United Arab Emirates out of the Trucial States, the departure of the British, the arrival of the Americans and long before the money poured in like a roaring tide.

In his boyhood he had known poverty and automatic deference to the lordly white-skinned foreigners. But from his first days Bin Selim had determined he would rise in the world. The path he chose was what he knew: the sea. He became a deck hand on a coastal freighter, and as his ship plied the coast from Masirah Island and Salalah in the Dhofari province of Oman round to the ports of Kuwait and Bahrain at the head of the Persian Gulf, he learned many things with his agile mind.

He learned that there was always someone with something to sell and prepared to sell it cheap. And there was someone else, somewhere, prepared to buy that something and pay more. Between the two stood the institution called the Customs. Faisal bin Selim made himself prosperous by smuggling.

In his travels he saw many things that he came to admire: fine cloths and tapestries, Islamic art, true culture, ancient Korans, precious manuscripts and the beauty of the great mosques. And he saw other things he came to despise: rich westerners, porcine faces lobster-pink in the sun, disgusting women in tiny bikinis, drunken slobs, all that undeserved money.

The fact that the rulers of the Gulf States also benefited from money that simply poured in black streams from the desert sands did not escape him. As they also flaunted their western habits, drank the imported alcohol, slept with the golden whores, he came to despise them too.

By his mid-forties, twenty years before a small Baluchi boy waited for him at the dock in Gwador, two things had happened to Faisal bin Selim.

He had earned and saved enough money to commission, buy and own outright a superb timber trading dhow, constructed by the finest craftsmen at Sur in Oman and called *Rasha*, the *Pearl*. And he had become a fervent Wahhabi.

When the new prophets arose to follow the teachings of Maududi and Sayyid Qutb, they declared jihad against the forces of heresy and degeneracy, and he was with them. When young men went to fight the godless Soviets in Afghanistan his prayers went with them; when others flew airliners into the towers of the western god of money he knelt and prayed that they would indeed enter the gardens of Allah.

To the world he remained the courteous, frugally living, fastidious, devout master and owner of the *Rasha*. He plied his trade along the entire Gulf coast and round into the Arabian Sea. He did not seek trouble, but if a True Believer sought his help, whether in alms or a passage to safety, he would do what he could.

He had come to the attention of western security forces because a Saudi AQ activist, captured in the Hadramaut and confessing all in a cell in Riyadh, let slip that messages of the utmost secrecy destined for Bin Laden himself, so secret that they could only be confided verbally to a messenger who would memorize them verbatim and take his own life before capture, would occasionally leave the Saudi peninsula by boat. The emissary would be deposited on the Baluchi coast whence he would take his message north to the unknown caves of Waziristan where the Sheikh resided. The boat was the *Rasha*. With the agreement and assistance of the ISI it was not intercepted, just watched.

Faisal bin Selim arrived in Gwador with a cargo of white goods from the duty-free entrepôt of Dubai. Here the refrigerators, washing machines, microwave cookers and televisions were sold at a fraction of their retail price outside the free-port warehouses.

He was commissioned to take back with him to the Gulf a cargo of Pakistani carpets, knotted by the thin fingers of little boy slaves, destined for the feet of the rich westerners buying luxury villas on the sea islands being built off Dubai and Qatar.

He listened gravely to the small boy with the message, nodded, and two hours later, with his cargo safely inland without disturbing Pakistani Customs, left the *Rasha* in the charge of his Omani deck hand and walked sedately through Gwador to the mosque.

From years of trading with Pakistan, the courtly Arab spoke good Urdu and he and the imam conversed in that language. He sipped his tea, took sweet cakes and wiped his fingers on a small cambric handkerchief. The while, he nodded and glanced at the Afghan. When he heard of the break-out from the prison van he smiled in approval. Then he broke into Arabic.

'And you wish to leave Pakistan, my brother?'

'There is no place for me here,' said Martin. 'The imam is right. The secret police will find me and hand me back to the dogs of Kabul. I will end my life before that.'

'Such a pity,' murmured the Qatari, 'so far . . . such a life. And if I take you to the Gulf States, what will you do?'

'I will try to find other True Believers and offer what I can.'

'And what would that be? What can you do?'

'I can fight. And I am prepared to die in Allah's holy war.'

The courtly captain thought for a while.

'The loading of the carpets takes place at dawn,' he said. 'It will take several hours. They must be well below decks lest the sea-spray touch them. Then I shall depart, sails down. I shall cruise close past the end of the harbour mole. If a man were to leap from the concrete to the deck, no one would notice.'

After the ritual salutations he left. In the darkness Martin was led by the boy to the dock. Here he studied the *Rasha* so that he would recognize her in the morning. She came past the mole just before eleven. The gap was eight feet and Martin made it with inches to spare after a short run.

The Omani had the helm. Faisal bin Selim greeted Martin with a gentle smile. He offered his guest fresh water to wash his hands and delicious dates from the palms of Muscat.

At noon the elderly man spread two mats on the broad coaming about the cargo hold. Side by side the two men knelt for the midday prayers. For Martin it was the first occasion of prayer other than in a crowd where a single voice can be drowned by all the others. He was word perfect.

When an agent is way out there in the cold, on a 'black' and dangerous job, his controllers at home are avid for some sign that he is all right; still alive, still at liberty, still functioning. This indication may come from the agent himself, by a phone call, a message in the small ads column of a paper or a chalk mark on a wall, a pre-agreed drop. It may come from a watcher who makes no contact but observes and reports back. It is called 'sign of life'. After days of silence, controllers become very twitchy waiting for some sign of life.

It was midday in Thumrait; breakfast time in Scotland; the wee small hours in Tampa. The first and the third could see what the Predator could see but did not know its significance. Need to know; they had not been told. But Edzell air base knew.

Clear as crystal, alternately lowering the forehead to the deck and raising the face to the sky, the Afghan was saying his prayers on the deck of the *Rasha*. There was a roar from the terminal operators in the ops room. Seconds later Steve Hill took a call at his breakfast table and gave his wife a passionate and unexpected kiss.

Two minutes later Marek Gumienny took a call in bed in Old Alexandria. He woke up, listened, smiled, murmured 'way to go' and went back to sleep. The Afghan was still on course.

CHAPTER ELEVEN

With a good wind from the south, the *Rasha* hoisted sail, closed down her engine and the rumbling below was replaced by the calm sounds of the sea: the lapping of the water under the bow, the sigh of the wind in the sail, the creak of block and tackle.

The dhow, shadowed by the invisible Predator four miles above her, crept along the coast of southern Iran and into the Gulf of Oman. Here she bore away to starboard, reset her sail as the wind took her full astern and headed for the narrow gap between Iran and Arabia called the Strait of Hormuz.

Through this narrow gap, where the tip of Oman's Musandam Peninsula is only eight miles from the Persian shore, a constant stream of mighty tankers went past; some low in the water, full of crude oil for the energy-hungry West, others riding high, going up-Gulf to fill with Saudi or Kuwaiti crude.

The smaller boats like the dhow stayed closer to the shore to allow the leviathans the freedom of the deep channel. Supertankers, if there is something in their way, simply cannot stop.

The *Rasha*, being in no hurry, spent one night hove-to amid the islands east of the Omani naval base at Kumzar. Sitting on the raised poop deck in the balmy night, still clearly visible on a plasma screen in a Scottish air base, Martin caught sight of two 'cigarette boats' by the light of the moon and heard the roar of their huge outboards as they sped out of Omani waters to make the crossing to south Iran.

These were the smugglers he had heard about; owing allegiance to no country, their operators ran the smuggling trade. On some empty Iranian or Baluchi beach they would make rendezvous at dawn with the receivers, offload their cargo of cheap cigarettes and take on board, surprisingly, angora goats so valued in Oman.

On a flat sea their pencil-slim aluminium boats, with the cargo lashed midships and the crew clinging on for dear life, would be powered by two immense 250-hp outboards to over fifty knots. They are virtually uncatchable, know every creek and inlet, and are accustomed to driving without lights and in complete darkness right across the paths of the tankers to the shelter of the other side.

Faisal bin Selim smiled tolerantly. He too was a smuggler, but rather more dignified than these vagabonds of the Gulf whom he could hear in the distance.

'And when I have brought you to Arabia, my friend, what will you do?' he asked quietly. The Omani deck hand was at the bow, handline over the side, trying for a fine fish for breakfast. He had joined the other two for evening prayers. Now was the hour of pleasant conversation.

'I do not know,' admitted the Afghan. 'I know only that I am a dead man in my own country; Pakistan is closed to me for they are running-dogs of the Yankees. I hope to find other True Believers and ask to fight with them.'

'Fight? But there is no fighting in the United Arab Emirates. They too are wholly allied to the West. The interior is Saudi Arabia, where you will be found immediately and sent back. So . . .'

The Afghan shrugged.

'I ask only to serve Allah. I have lived my life. I will leave my fate in His care.'

'And you say you are prepared to die for Him,' said the courtly Qatari.

Mike Martin thought back to his boyhood and

his prep school in Baghdad. Most of the pupils were Iraqi boys but they were the sons of the cream of society and their fathers were keen that they would speak perfect English and rise to rule great corporations dealing with London and New York. The curriculum was in English, and that included the learning of traditional English poetry.

Martin had always had one favourite: the story of how Horatius of Rome defended the last bridge before the invading army of the House of Tarquin as the Romans hacked down the bridge behind him. There was a verse the boys used to chant together:

> To every man upon this earth
> Death cometh soon or late.
> And how can man die better
> Than facing fearful odds,
> For the ashes of his fathers
> And the temples of his Gods?

'If I can die *shahid*, in the service of His jihad, of course,' he replied.

The dhow master considered for a while and changed the subject.

'You are wearing the clothes of Afghanistan,' he said. 'You will be spotted in minutes. Wait.'

He went below and came back with a freshly

laundered dishdash, the white cotton robe that falls from shoulders to ankles in unbroken line.

'Change,' he ordered. 'Drop the shalwar kameez and the Talib turban over the side.'

When Martin was changed Bin Selim handed him a new headdress, the red-flecked keffiyeh of a Gulf Arab and the black cord circlet to hold it in place.

'Better,' said the old man when his guest had completed the transformation. 'You will pass for a Gulf Arab, save when you speak. But there is a colony of Afghans in the area of Jeddah. They have been in Saudi Arabia for generations, but they speak like you. Say that is where you come from, and strangers will believe you. Now let us sleep. We rise at dawn for the last day of cruising.'

The Predator saw them weigh anchor and leave the islands, sailing gently round the rocky tip of Al-Ghanam and turning south-west down the coast of the United Arab Emirates.

There are seven in the UAE but only the names of the biggest and richest – Dubai, Abu Dhabi and Sharjah – spring to mind. The other four are much smaller, much poorer and almost anonymous. Two of these, Ajman and Umm-al-Qaiwain, are cheek by jowl alongside Dubai, whose oil riches have made it the most developed of the seven. Fujairah alone lies on the other side of the peninsula, facing east on to the Gulf of Oman. The seventh is Ras-al-Khaimah.

Ras-al-Khaimah lies on the same coast as Dubai but far up along the shore towards the Strait of Hormuz. It is dirt poor and ultra-traditional. For that reason it has eagerly accepted the gifts of Saudi Arabia, including heavily financed mosques and schools – but all teaching Wahhabism. Ras-al-K, as westerners know it, is the local home of fundamentalism and sympathy for Al-Qaeda and jihad. On the port side of the slowly cruising dhow, it would be the first to be reached. This occurred at sundown.

'You have no papers,' said the captain to his guest, 'and I cannot provide them. No matter, they have always been a western impertinence. More important is money. Take these.'

He thrust a wad of UAE dirhams into Martin's hand. They were cruising in the fading light past the town, a mile away on the shore. The first lights began to flicker among the buildings.

'I will put you ashore further down the coast,' said Bin Selim. 'You will find the coast road and walk back. I know a small guest house in the Old Town. It is cheap, clean and discreet. Take lodgings there. Do not go out. You will be safe and, *inshallah*, I may have friends who can help you.'

It was fully dark when Martin saw the lights of

the hotel and the *Rasha* slipped towards the shore. Bin Selim knew it well: the converted Hamra Fort, which had a beach club for its foreign guests, and the club had a jetty. After dark it would be abandoned.

'He's leaving the dhow,' said a voice in the ops room at Edzell air base. Despite the darkness, the thermal imager of the Predator at twenty thousand feet saw the agile figure leap from the dhow to the jetty, and the trader reverse her engine and pull back to the deeper water and the sea.

'Never mind the boat, stay with the moving figure,' said Gordon Phillips, leaning over the console operator's shoulder. The instructions went to Thumrait and the Predator was instructed to follow the thermal image of a man walking along the coast road back towards Ras-al-K.

It was a five-mile hike but Martin reached the Old Town section around midnight. He asked twice and was directed to the address of the guest house. It was five hundred yards from the family home of the Al-Shehhi, whence had come Marwan al-Shehhi who flew the airliner into the South Tower of the World Trade Center on 9/11. He was still a local hero.

The proprietor was surly and suspicious until Martin mentioned Faisal bin Selim. That and the sight of a wad of dirhams cleared the air. He was bidden to enter and shown to a simple room. There were seemingly just two other paying guests and they had retired.

Unbending his attitude the room-keeper invited Martin to join him for a cup of tea before turning in. Over tea Martin had to explain that he was from Jeddah, but of Pashtun extraction.

With his dark looks, full black beard and the repeated references to Allah of the truly devout, Martin convinced his host that he also was a True Believer. They parted with mutual wishes for a good night's sleep.

The dhow master sailed on through the night. His destination was on the harbour known as the Creek in the heart of Dubai. Once simply that, a muddy creek smelling of dead fish, in which men mended their nets in the heat of the day, it has become the last 'picturesque' sight in the bustling capital, opposite the gold soukh, beneath the windows of the towering western hotels. Here the trading dhows are berthed side by side and the tourists come to stare at the last portion of 'old Arabia'.

Bin Selim hailed a taxi and instructed it to take him three miles up the coast to the Sultanate of Ajman, smallest and second-poorest of the seven. There he dismissed the taxi, ducked into a covered soukh of twisting alleys and clamouring stalls and lost himself to any following 'tail' – should there have been one.

There was not. The Predator was concentrating on a guest house in the heart of Ras-al-Khaimah. The dhow master slipped from the soukh into a small mosque and made a request of the imam. A boy was sent scurrying through the town and came back with a young man who genuinely was a student in the local technical college. He was also a graduate of the Darunta training camp owned and run by Al-Qaeda outside Jalalabad until 2001.

The old man whispered in the ear of the younger, who nodded and thanked him. Then the dhow captain went back through the covered market, emerged, hailed a taxi and returned to his freighter in the Creek. He had done all he could. It was up to the younger men now. *Inshallah*.

That same morning, but later due to the time difference, the *Countess of Richmond* eased out of the estuary of the Mersey and into the Irish Sea. Captain McKendrick had the conn and took his freighter south. In time she would, keeping Wales to her port side, clear the Irish Sea and Lizard Point to meet the Channel and the eastern Atlantic. Then her course lay south past Portugal, through the Mediterranean to the Suez Canal and thence to the Indian Ocean.

Below his decks, as the cold March seas flew up over the bow of the *Countess*, was a cargo of carefully protected and crated Jaguar saloons, destined for the showrooms of Singapore.

Four days passed before the Afghan sheltering in Ras-al-Khaimah received his visitors. Following his instructions he had not gone out, or at least not as far as the street. But he had taken the air in the closed courtyard at the rear of the house, screened from the streets by double gates eight feet high. Here various delivery vans came and went.

While in the courtyard he was seen by the Predator and his controllers in Scotland noted his change of dress.

His visitors, when they came, did not arrive to deliver food, drink or laundry, but to make a collection. They backed the van close to the rear door of the building. The driver stayed at the wheel; the other three entered the house.

The lodgers were both away at work, the room-keeper by agreement out at the shops. The team of three had their directions. They went swiftly to the appropriate door and entered without knocking. The seated figure, reading his Koran, rose to find himself facing a handgun in the grip of a man trained in Afghanistan. All three were hooded.

They were quiet and efficient. Martin knew enough of fighting men to recognize his visitors knew their business. The hood went over his head and fell to his shoulders. His hands came behind his back and the plastic cuffs went on. Then he was marching, or being marched, out of his door, down the tiled corridor and into the back of a van. He lay on his side, heard the door slam, felt the van lurch out of the gate and into the street.

The Predator saw it, but the controllers thought it was another laundry delivery. In minutes the van was out of sight. There are many miracles that modern spy technology can accomplish, but controllers and machines can still be fooled. The snatch squad had no idea there was a Predator above them but shrewdly choosing mid-morning for the snatch rather than midnight fooled the watchers at Edzell.

It took three more days before they realized that their man no longer appeared daily in the courtyard to give the sign of life. In short, he had disappeared. They were watching an empty house. And they had no idea which of the several vans had taken him.

In fact the van had not gone far. The hinterland behind the port and city of Ras-al-K is wild and rocky desert rising to the mountains of Rus-al-Jibal. Nothing can live here but goats and salamanders.

Just in case the man they had snatched was under surveillance, with or without his knowledge, the kidnappers were taking no chances. There were tracks leading up into the hills and they took one. In the rear, Martin felt the vehicle leave the tarred road and start to jolt over pitted track.

Had there been a tailing vehicle, it could not have avoided detection. Even staying out of sight, its plume of rising desert dust would have given it away. A surveillance helicopter would have been even more obvious.

The van stopped five miles up the track into the hills. The leader, the one with the handgun, took powerful binoculars and surveyed the valley and the coast, right back to the Old Town whence they had come. Nothing came towards them.

When he was satisfied, the van turned and went back down the hills. Its real destination was a villa standing in a walled compound in the outer suburbs of the town. With the gates relocked, the van reversed up to an open door and Martin was marched back out and down another tiled passage.

The plastic ties came off his wrists and a cool metal shackle went on to the left one. There would be a chain, he knew, and a bolt in the wall which could not be ripped free. When his hood came off, it was the kidnappers who had their heads covered. They withdrew backwards and the door slammed. He heard bolts go into sockets.

The cell was not a cell in the true meaning. It was a ground-floor room that had been fortified. The window had been bricked up and, though Martin could not see it, a painting of a window adorned the outside to fool even those with binoculars peering over the compound wall.

Considering what he had undergone years before in the SAS programme of interrogation resistance it was even comfortable. There was a single bulb in the ceiling protected against thrown objects by a wire frame. The light was subdued but adequate.

There was a camp bed and just enough slack in his chain to allow him to lie on it to sleep. The room also had an upright chair and a chemical toilet. All were in reach but in different directions.

His left wrist, however, was in a stainless-steel shackle that linked to a chain and the chain went to a wall bracket. He could not begin to reach the door through which his interrogators would enter, if at all, with food and water, and a spyhole in the door meant they could check on him any time and he would neither hear nor see them.

At Castle Forbes there had been lengthy and

passionate discussions over one problem: should he carry any tracking device on him?

There are now tracker transmitters so tiny they can be injected under the skin without cutting the epidermis at all. They are pinhead-sized. Warmed by the blood, they need no power source. But their range is limited. Worse, there are ultra-sensitive detectors that can spot them.

'These people are absolutely not stupid,' Phillips had stressed. His colleague from CIA Counter-Terrorism agreed.

'Among the best educated of them,' said McDonald, 'their mastery of very high technology, and especially the computer sciences, is awesome.'

No one at Forbes doubted that if Martin was subjected to a hyper-tech body search and something was discovered he would be dead within minutes.

Eventually the decision was: no planted bleeper. No signal-sender. The kidnappers came for him an hour later. They were hooded again.

The body search was lengthy and thorough. The clothes went first until he was naked, and they were taken away for searching in another room.

They did not even employ invasive throat and anal search. The scanner did it all. Inch by inch it was run over his body in case it gave the bleep that would mean it had discovered a non-body-tissue substance. Only at the mouth did it do that. They forced his mouth open and examined every filling. Otherwise – nothing.

They returned his clothing and prepared to leave.

'I left my Koran at the guest house,' said the prisoner. 'I have no watch or mat, but it must be the hour of prayer.'

The leader stared at him through the eyeholes. He said nothing, but two minutes later he returned with mat and Koran. Martin thanked him gravely.

Food and water was brought regularly. Each time he was waved back with the handgun as the tray was deposited where he could reach it when they had done. The chemical lavatory was replaced in the same way.

It was three days before his interrogation began, and for this he was masked, lest he look out of the windows, and led down two corridors. When his mask was removed he was astonished. The man in front of him, sitting calmly behind a carved refectory table, for all the world like a potential employer interviewing an applicant, was youthful, elegant, civilized, urbane and uncovered. He spoke in perfect Gulf Arabic.

'I see no point in masks,' he said, 'nor silly names. Mine, by the way, is Dr Al-Khattab. There is no mystery here. If I am satisfied you are who you say you are, you will be welcome to join us. In which case, you will not betray us. If not, then I am afraid you will be killed at once. So let us not pretend, Mr Izmat Khan. Are you really the one they call the Afghan?'

'They will be concerned about two things,' Gordon Phillips warned him during one of their interminable briefings at Forbes Castle. 'Are you truly Izmat Khan and are you the same Izmat Khan who fought at Qala-i-Jangi? Or have five years in Guantanamo turned you into something else?'

Martin stared back at the smiling Arab. He recalled the warnings of Tamian Godfrey. Never mind the wild-bearded screamers; watch out for the one who will be smooth-shaven, who will smoke, drink, consort with girls, pass for one of us. Wholly westernized. A human chameleon, hiding the hatred. Totally deadly. There was a word . . . *takfir*.

'There are many Afghans,' he said. 'Who calls me the Afghan?'

'Ah, you have been incommunicado for five years. After Qala-i-Jangi word spread about you. You do not know about me, but I know much about you. Some of our people have been released from Camp Delta. They spoke highly of you. They claim you never broke. True?'

'They asked me about myself. I told them that.'

'But you never denounced others? You mentioned no names? That is what the others say of you.'

'They wiped out my family. Most of me died then. How do you punish a man who is dead?'

'A good answer, my friend. So, let us talk about Guantanamo. Tell me about Gitmo.'

Martin had been briefed hour after hour about what had happened to him on the Cuban peninsula. The arrival on 14 January 2002, hungry, thirsty, soiled with urine, blindfolded, shackled so tightly the hands were numb for weeks. Beards and heads shaved, clothed in orange coveralls, stumbling and tripping in the darkness of the hoods . . .

Dr Al-Khattab took copious notes, writing on yellow legal notepaper with an old-fashioned fountain pen. When a passage was reached where he knew all the answers, he ceased and contemplated his prisoner with a gentle smile.

In the late afternoon he offered a photograph.

'Do you know this man?' he asked. 'Did you ever see him?'

Martin shook his head. The face looking up from the photo was General Geoffrey D. Miller, successor as camp commandant to General Rick Baccus. The latter had sat in on interrogations but General Miller left it to the CIA teams.

'Quite right,' said Al-Khattab. 'He saw you, according to one of our released friends, but you were always hooded as a punishment for non-cooperation. And when did the conditions start to improve?'

They talked until sundown, then the Arab rose. 'I have much to check on,' he said. 'If you are telling the truth, we will continue in a few days. If not, I'm afraid I shall have to issue Suleiman with the appropriate instructions.'

Martin went back to his cell. Dr Al-Khattab issued rapid orders to the guard team and left. He drove a modest rented car and he returned to the Hilton Hotel in Ras-al-Khaimah town, elegantly dominating the Al-Saqr deep-water harbour. He spent the night and left the next day. By then he was wearing a well-cut cream tropical suit. When he checked in with British Airways at Dubai International Airport his English was impeccable.

In fact Ali Aziz al-Khattab had been born a Kuwaiti, the son of a senior bank official. By Gulf standards that meant that his upbringing had been effortless and privileged. In 1989 his father had been posted to London as Deputy Manager of the Bank of Kuwait. The family had gone with him and avoided the invasion of their homeland by Saddam Hussein in 1990.

Ali Aziz, already a good English speaker, was

enrolled in a British school at age fifteen and emerged three years later with accentless English and excellent grades. When his family returned home, he elected to stay on and go for a degree at Loughborough Technical College. Four years later he emerged with a degree in chemical engineering and proceeded to a doctorate.

It was not in the Arabian Gulf but in London that he began to attend the mosque run by a firebrand preacher of anti-western hatred and became what the media like to call 'radicalized'. In truth, by twenty-one he was fully brainwashed and a fanatical supporter of Al-Qaeda.

A 'talent spotter' suggested he might like to visit Pakistan; he accepted and then went on, through the Khyber Pass, to spend six months at an Al-Qaeda terrorist training camp. He had already been marked out as a 'sleeper' who should lie low in England and never come to the attention of the authorities.

Back in London he did what they all do; he reported to his embassy that he had lost his passport and was issued a new one which did not carry the tell-tale Pakistan entry stamp. As far as anyone who asked was concerned, he had been visiting family and friends in the Gulf and had never been near Pakistan, let alone Afghanistan. He secured a post as lecturer at Aston University, Birmingham, in 1999. Two years later

Anglo-American forces invaded Afghanistan.

There were several weeks of panic in case any trace of him in the terror camps had been left lying around, but in his case AQ's head of personnel, Abu Zubaydah, had done his job. No traces were found of any Al-Khattab ever having been there. So he remained undiscovered and rose to be AQ's commanding agent in the UK.

As Dr Al-Khattab's London-bound airliner was taking off the *Java Star* eased away from her berth in the Sultanate of Brunei on the coast of Indonesian North Borneo and headed for the open sea.

Her destination was the Western Australian port of Fremantle, as usual, and her Norwegian skipper Knut Herrmann had no inkling his journey would be other than usual; which meant routine and eventless.

He knew that the seas in those parts remain the most dangerous waters in the world; but not from shoals, riptides, rocks, tempests, reefs or tsunamis. The danger here is pirate attacks.

Every year, between the Malacca Strait in the west and the Celebes Sea to the east, there are over five hundred pirate attacks on merchant shipping and up to a hundred hijackings. Occasionally the crew are ransomed back to the ship owners; sometimes they are all killed and never heard of again; in those cases the cargo is stolen and sold on the black market.

If Captain Herrmann sailed with an easy mind on the 'milk run' to Fremantle, it was because he was convinced his cargo was useless to the dacoits of the sea. But on this trip he was wrong.

The first leg of his course lay north, away from his eventual destination. It took him six hours to pass the ramshackle town of Kudat and come round the northernmost tip of Sabah and the island of Borneo. Only then could he run south-east for the Sulu Archipelago.

He intended to move through the coral and jungle islands by taking the deep-water strait between Tawitawi and Jolo Islands. South of the islands it was a clear run down the Celebes Sea to the south and eventually Australia.

His departure from Brunei had been watched, and a cellphone call made. Even if it had been intercepted, the call referred only to the recovery of a sick uncle who would be out of hospital in twelve days. That meant: twelve hours to intercept.

The call was taken in a creek on Jolo Island and the man who took it would have been recognized by Mr Alex Siebart of Crutched Friars, City of London. It was Mr Lampong, who no longer affected to be a businessman from Sumatra.

The twelve men he commanded in the velvety

tropical night were cut-throats but they were well paid and would stay obedient. Criminality apart, they were also Muslim extremists. The Abu Sayyaf movement of the southern Philippines, whose last peninsula is only a few miles from Indonesia on the Sulu Sea, has the reputation of including not only religious extremists but also killers for hire. The offer Mr Lampong had put to them enabled them to fulfil both functions.

The two speedboats they occupied put to sea at dawn, took up position between the two islands and waited. An hour later the *Java Star* bore down on them to pass from the Sulu Sea into the Celebes. Taking her over was a simple task and the gangsters were well practised.

Captain Herrmann had taken the helm through the night and as dawn came up over the Pacific away to his left he handed over to his Indonesian first officer and went below. His crew of ten Lascars were also in their bunks in the forecastle.

The first thing the Indonesian officer saw was a pair of speedboats racing up astern, one each side. Dark, barefoot, agile men leaped effortlessly from speedboat to deck and ran aft towards the superstructure and bridge where he stood. He just had time to press the emergency buzzer to his captain's cabin before the men burst through the door from the fly-bridge. Then there was a knife at his throat and a voice screaming 'Capitan, capitan . . .'

There was no need. A tired Knut Herrmann was coming topsides to see what was going on. He and Mr Lampong arrived on the bridge together. Lampong held a mini-Uzi. The Norwegian knew better than to begin to resist. The ransom would have to be sorted out between the pirates and his employer company HQ in Fremantle.

'Captain Herrmann . . .'

The bastard knew his name. This had been prepared.

'Please ask your first officer did he in any circumstances make a radio transmission in the past five minutes?'

There was no need to ask. Lampong was speaking in English. For the Norwegian and his Indonesian officer it was the common language. The first officer screamed that he had not touched the radio's transmit button.

'Excellent,' said Lampong and issued a stream of orders in the local dialect. This the first officer understood and opened his mouth to scream again. The Norwegian understood not a word, but he understood everything when the dacoit holding his Number Two jerked the seaman's head back and sliced his throat open with a single cut. The first officer kicked, jerked, slumped and died. Captain Herrmann had not been sick in forty years at sea, but he leaned against the wheel and emptied his stomach.

'Two pools of mess to be cleaned up,' said Lampong. 'Now, Captain, for every minute you refuse to obey my orders, that will happen to one of your men. Am I clear?'

The Norwegian was escorted to the tiny radio shack behind the bridge where he selected Channel 16, the international distress frequency. Lampong produced a written sheet.

'You will not just read this in a calm voice, Captain. When I press "transmit" and nod, you will shout this message with panic in your voice. Or your men die, one by one. Are you ready?'

Captain Herrmann nodded. He would not even have to act in order to affect extreme distress.

'Mayday, Mayday, Mayday. *Java Star*, *Java Star* . . . Catastrophic fire in engine room . . . I cannot save her . . . My position . . .'

He knew the position was wrong even as he read it out. It was a hundred miles south into the Celebes Sea. But he was not about to argue. Lampong cut the transmission. He brought the Norwegian at gunpoint back to the bridge.

Two of his own seamen had been put to work frenziedly scrubbing up the blood and the vomit on the floor of the bridge. The other eight he could see marshalled in a terrified group out on the hatch covers with six dacoits to watch them.

Two more of the hijackers stayed on the bridge. The other four were tossing liferafts, lifebelts and a pair of inflatable jackets down into one of the speedboats. It was the one with the extra fuel tanks stored amidships.

When they were ready the speedboat left the side of the *Java Star* and went south. On a calm tropical sea at an easy fifteen knots they would be a hundred miles south in seven hours and back in their pirate creeks ten hours after that.

'A new course, Captain,' said Lampong civilly. His tone was gentle but the implacable hatred in his eyes gave the lie to any humanity towards the Norwegian.

The new course was back towards the northeast, out of the cluster of islands that make up the Sulu Archipelago and across the national line into Filipino water.

The southern province of Mindanao Island is Zamboanga and parts of it are simply no-go areas for Filipino government forces. This is the terrain of Abu Sayyaf. Here they are safe to recruit, train and bring their booty. The *Java Star* was certainly booty, albeit unmarketable. Lampong conferred in the local lingo with the senior among the pirates. The man pointed ahead to the entrance to a narrow creek flanked by impenetrable jungle.

What he asked was: 'Can your men manage her from here?' The pirate nodded. Lampong called his orders to the group round the Lascar seamen at the bow. Without even replying they herded the sailors to the rail and opened fire. The men screamed and toppled into the warm sea. Somewhere below, shark turned to the blood smell.

Captain Herrmann was so taken by surprise he would have needed two or three seconds to react. He never got them. Lampong's bullet took him full in the chest and he too tumbled back from the fly-bridge into the sea. Half an hour later, towed by two small tugs, which had been stolen weeks earlier, and with much shrieking and shouting, the *Java Star* was at her new berth beside a stout teak jetty.

The jungle concealed her from all sides and from above. Also hidden were the two long, low, tin-roofed workshops that housed the steel plates, cutters, welders, power generator and paint.

The last despairing cry from the *Java Star* on Channel 16 had been heard by a dozen vessels but the nearest to the spot given as her position was a refrigerator ship loaded with fresh and highly perishable fruit for the American market across the Pacific. She was commanded by a Finnish skipper who diverted at once to the spot. There he found the bobbing liferafts, small tents on the ocean swell which had opened and inflated automatically as designed. He circled once and spotted the lifebelts and two inflated jackets. All were marked with the name: MV *Java Star*. According to the law of the sea, which he respected, Captain Raikkonen cut power and lowered a pinnace to look inside the rafts. They were empty so he ordered them sunk. He had lost several hours and could stay no longer. There was no point.

With a heavy heart he reported by radio that the *Java Star* was lost with all hands. Far away in London the news was noted by insurers Lloyd's International and at Ipswich, UK, *Lloyd's Register of Shipping* logged the loss. For the world the *Java Star* had simply ceased to exist.

CHAPTER TWELVE

In fact the interrogator was gone for a week. Martin remained in his cell with only the Koran for company. He would, he felt, soon be among that revered company who had memorized every one of the 6,666 verses in it. But years in special forces had finally given him a rare gift among humans: the ability to remain motionless for exceptionally long periods and defy boredom and the urge to fidget.

So he schooled himself again to adapt to the inner contemplative life that alone can stop a man in solitary confinement from going mad.

This talent did not prevent the operations room at Edzell air base becoming very tense. They had lost their man, and the enquiries from Marek Gumienny in Langley and Steve Hill in

London became more pressing. The Predator was double-assigned: to look down on Ras-al-Khaimah in case Crowbar appeared again, and to monitor the dhow *Rasha* when it appeared in the Gulf and docked somewhere in the UAE.

Dr Al-Khattab returned when he had confirmed every aspect of the story as it concerned Guantanamo Bay. It had not been easy. He had not the slightest intention of betraying himself to any of the four British inmates who had been sent home. They had all declared repeatedly that they were not extremists and had been swept up in the American net by accident. Whatever the Americans thought, Al-Qaeda could confirm they were telling the truth.

To make it harder, Izmat Khan had spent so long in solitary for non-cooperation that no other detainee had got to know him well. He admitted he had picked up fragmentary English, but that was from the endless interrogations when he had listened to the CIA man and then the translation by the one Pashto-speaking terp.

From what Al-Khattab could discover his prisoner had not slipped up once. What little could be gleaned from Afghanistan indicated that the break-out from the prison van between Bagram and Pul-i-Charki jail had indeed been genuine. What he could not know was that this episode had been accomplished by the very able

Head of Station of the SIS office inside the British Embassy. Brigadier Yusuf had acted out his rage most convincingly and the agents of the by now resurgent Taliban were convinced. And they said so to Al-Qaeda enquiries.

'Let us go back to your early days in the Tora Bora,' Al-Khattab proposed when the interrogation resumed. 'Tell me about your boyhood.'

Al-Khattab was a clever man but what he could not know was that, even though the man in front of him was a ringer, Martin knew the mountains of Afghanistan better than he. The Kuwaiti's six months in the terrorist training camps had been exclusively among fellow Arabs, not Pashtun mountain men. He noted copiously, even the names of the fruits in the orchards of Maloko-zai. His hand sped across the legal pad, covering page after page.

On the third day of the second session the narrative had reached the day which proved a crucial hinge in the life of Izmat Khan: 20 August 1998, the day the Tomahawk cruise missile crashed in the mountains.

'Ah, yes, truly tragic,' he murmured. 'And strange, for you must be the only Afghan for whom no family member remains alive to vouch for you. It is a remarkable coincidence, and as a scientist I hate coincidences. What was the effect on you?'

In fact Izmat Khan in Guantanamo had refused to talk about why he hated Americans with such a passion. It was information from the other fighters who had survived Qala-i-Jangi and reached Camp Delta that filled the gap. In the Taliban army Izmat Khan had become an iconic figure and his story was whispered round the camp fires as the man immune to fear. The other survivors had told the interrogators the story of the annihilated family.

Al-Khattab paused and gazed at his prisoner. He still had grave reservations, but of one thing he had become certain. The man truly was Izmat Khan; his doubts were over the second question: had he been 'turned' by the Americans?

'So you claim you declared a sort of private war? A very personal jihad? And you have never relented? But what did you actually do about it?'

'I fought against the Northern Alliance, the allies of the Americans.'

'But not until October and November two thousand and one,' said Al-Khattab.

'The Americans first came in the autumn of two thousand and one,' said Martin.

'True. So you fought for Afghanistan ... and lost. Now you wish to fight for Allah.'

Martin nodded.

'As the Sheikh predicted,' he said.

For the first time Dr Al-Khattab's urbanity

completely forsook him. He stared at the black-bearded face across the table for a full thirty seconds, mouth agape, pen poised but un-moving. Finally he spoke in a whisper: 'You . . . have actually met the Sheikh?'

In all his weeks in the camp Al-Khattab had never actually met Osama bin Laden. Just once he had seen a black-windowed Land Cruiser passing by but it had not stopped. But he would, quite literally, have taken a meat cleaver and severed his left wrist for the chance of meeting, let alone conversing with, the man he venerated more than any other on earth. Martin met his gaze and nodded. Al-Khattab recovered his poise.

'You will start at the beginning of this episode and describe exactly what happened. Leave out nothing, no tiny detail.'

So Martin told him. He told him of serving in his father's *lashkar* as a teenager freshly back from the *madrassah* outside Peshawar. He told of the patrol with others and how they had been caught on a mountainside with only a group of boulders to shelter in.

He made no mention of any British officer, nor any Blowpipe missile, nor the destruction of the Hind gunship. He told only of the roaring chain gun in the nose; of the fragments of bullet and rock flying around until the Hind, eternal praise be to Allah, ran out of ammunition and flew away.

He told of feeling a blow like a punch or a hit from a hammer in the thigh, and being carried by his comrades across the valleys until they found a man with a mule and took it from him.

And he told of being carried to a complex of caves at Jaji and being handed over to Saudis who lived and worked there.

'But the Sheikh, tell me of the Sheikh,' insisted Al-Khattab. So Martin told him. The Kuwaiti took down the dialogue word for word.

'Say that again, please.'

'He said to me: "The day will come when Afghanistan will no longer have need of you, but the all-merciful Allah will always have need of a warrior like you."'

'Then what happened?'

'He changed the dressing on the leg.'

'The Sheikh did that?'

'No, the doctor who was with him. The Egyptian.'

Dr Al-Khattab sat back and let out a long breath. Of course, the doctor, Ayman al-Zawahiri, companion and confidant, the man who had brought Egyptian Islamic Jihad to join the Sheikh to create Al-Qaeda. He began to tidy up his papers.

'I have to leave you again. It will take a week,

maybe more. You will have to stay here. Chained, I am afraid. You have seen too much; you know too much. But if you are indeed a True Believer, and truly the Afghan, you will join us as an honoured recruit. If not . . .'

Martin was back in his cell when the Kuwaiti left. This time Al-Khattab did not return straight to London. He went to the Hilton and wrote steadily and carefully for a day and a night. When he had done he made several calls on a new and lily-white cellphone which then went into the deep-water harbour. In fact he was not being listened to, but even if he had been, his words would have meant little. But Dr Al-Khattab was still free because he was a very careful man.

The calls he made arranged a meeting with Faisal bin Selim, master of the *Rasha*, which was moored in Dubai. That afternoon he drove his cheap rental car to Dubai and conversed with the elderly captain who took a long personal letter and hid it deep in his robes. And the Predator kept circling at twenty thousand feet.

Islamist terror groups have already lost far too many senior operatives not to have realized that for them, however careful they are, cellphone and satphone calls are dangerous. The West's interception, eavesdrop and decryption technology is simply too good. Their other weakness is the transferring of sums of money through the normal banking system.

To overcome the latter danger they use the *hundi* system which, with variations, is as old as the first Caliphate. *Hundi* is based on the total-trust concept, which any lawyer will advise against. But it works because any money-launderer who cheated his customer would soon be out of business – or worse.

The payer hands over his money in cash to the *hundi* man in place A and asks that his friend in place B shall receive the equivalent minus the *hundi* man's cut.

The *hundi* man has a trusted partner, usually a relative in place B. He informs his partner, and instructs him to make the money available, all in cash, to the payer's friend who will identify himself in a described manner.

Given the tens of millions of Muslims who send money back to families in the old home country, and given that there are neither computers nor even checkable dockets; given that it is all in cash and both payers and receivers can use pseudonyms, the money movements are virtually impossible to intercept or trace.

For communications the solution lies in hiding the terrorist messages in three-figure codes which can be e-mailed or texted across the world. Only the recipient with the decipher list of up to three hundred such number-groups can work out the message. This works for brief instructions and warnings. Occasionally a lengthy and exact text must travel halfway across the world.

Only the West is always in a hurry. The East has patience. If it takes so long, then it takes that long. The *Rasha* sailed that night and made her way back to Gwador. There a loyal emissary alerted in Karachi down the coast by a text message had arrived on his motorcycle. He took the letter and rode north across Pakistan to the small but fanatic town of Miram Shah.

There the man trusted enough to go into the high peaks of South Waziristan was waiting at the named *chai-khana* and the sealed package changed hands again. The reply came back the same way. It took ten days.

But Dr Al-Khattab did not stay in the Arabian Gulf. He flew to Cairo and then due west to Morocco. There he interviewed and selected the four North Africans who would become part of the second crew. Because he was still not under surveillance, his journey appeared on no one's radar.

When the handsome cards were dealt, Mr Wei Wing Li received a pair of twos. Short, squat and toad-like, his shoulders were surmounted by a football of a head and a face deeply pitted with smallpox scars. But he was good at his job.

He and his crew had arrived at the hidden creek on the Zamboanga Peninsula two days before the *Java Star*. Their journey from China, where they featured in the criminal underworld of Guangdong, had not involved the inconvenience of passports or visas. They had simply boarded a freighter whose captain had been amply rewarded and had thus arrived off Jolo Island where two speedboats out of the Filipino creeks had taken them off.

Mr Wei had greeted his host, Mr Lampong, and the local Abu Sayyaf chieftain who had recommended him, inspected the living quarters for his dozen crewmen, taken the fifty per cent of his fee 'up front' and asked to see the workshops. After a lengthy inspection he counted the tanks of oxygen and acetylene and pronounced himself satisfied. Then he studied the photos taken in Liverpool. When the *Java Star* was finally in the creek, he knew what had to be done and set about it.

Ship transformation was his speciality and over fifty cargo vessels plying the seas of South-East Asia with false names and papers also had false shapes thanks to Mr Wei. He had said he needed two weeks and had been given three, but not an hour longer. In that time the *Java Star* was going to become the *Countess of Richmond*. Mr Wei did not know that. He did not need to know.

In the photos he studied the actual name of the vessel had been airbrushed out. Mr Wei was not bothered with names or papers. It was shapes that concerned him.

There would be parts of the *Java Star* to cut out and others to cut off. There would be features to be fashioned from welded steel. But most of all he would create six long steel sea containers that would occupy the deck from below the bridge to the bow in three pairs.

Yet they would not be real. From all sides and from above they would appear authentic, down to the Hapag-Lloyd markings. They would pass inspection at a range of a few feet. Yet inside they would have no interior walls; they would constitute a long gallery with a hinged removable roof and access through a new door to be cut in the bulkhead below the bridge and then disguised to become invisible unless one knew the release catch.

What Mr Wei and his team would not do was the painting. The Filipino terrorists would do that, and the ship's new name would be painted after he had left.

The day he fired up his oxy-acetylene cutters the *Countess of Richmond* was passing through the Suez Canal.

* * *

When Ali Aziz al-Khattab returned to the villa he was a changed man. He ordered the shackles removed from his prisoner and invited him to share his table at lunch. His eyes glittered with a deep excitement.

'I have communicated with the Sheikh himself,' he purred. Clearly the honour consumed him. The reply had not been written. It had been confided in the mountains to the messenger verbally and he had memorized it. This is also a practice common in the higher reaches of Al-Qaeda.

The messenger had been brought all the way to the Arabian Gulf and when the *Rasha* docked the message had been given word for word to Dr Al-Khattab.

'There is one last formality,' he said. 'Would you please raise the hem of your dishdash to mid-thigh?'

Martin did so. He knew nothing of Al-Khattab's scientific discipline; only that he had a doctorate. He prayed it was not in dermatology. The Kuwaiti examined the puckered scar with keen attention. It was exactly where he was told it would be. It had the six stitches sutured into place in a Jaji cave nineteen years earlier by a man he revered.

'Thank you, my friend. The Sheikh himself

300

sends his personal greetings. What an incredible honour. He and the doctor remembered the young warrior and the words spoken.

'He has authorized me to include you in a mission that will inflict on the Great Satan a blow so terrible that even the destruction of the Towers will seem minor.

'You have offered your life to Allah. The offer is accepted. You will die gloriously, a true *shahid*. You and your fellow martyrs will be spoken of a thousand years from now.'

After three weeks of wasted time Dr Al-Khattab was now in a hurry. The resources of Al-Qaeda down the entire coast were called upon. A barber came to trim the shaggy mane to a western-style haircut. He also prepared to shave off the beard. Martin protested. As a Muslim and an Afghan he wanted his beard. Al-Khattab conceded it could be clipped to a neat Vandyke around the point of the chin, but no longer.

Suleiman himself took full-face photos and twenty-four hours later appeared with a perfect passport showing the owner to be a marine engineer from Bahrain, known to be a staunchly pro-western sultanate.

A tailor came, took measurements and re-appeared with shoes, socks, shirt, tie and dark grey suit, along with a small valise to contain them.

The travelling party prepared to leave the next day. Suleiman, who turned out to be from Abu Dhabi, would be going all the way, accompanying the Afghan. The other two guards were 'muscle', locally recruited and dispensable. The villa had served its purpose; it would be scoured and abandoned.

As he prepared to leave before them, Dr Al-Khattab turned to Martin.

'I envy you, Afghan. You can never know how much. You have fought for Allah, bled for Him, taken pain and the foulness of the infidel for Him. And now you will die for Him. If only I could be with you.'

He held out his hand, English-style, then recalled that he was an Arab and embraced the Afghan. At the door he turned one final time.

'You will be in paradise before me, Afghan. Save a place for me there. *Inshallah.'*

Then he was gone. He always parked his hire car several hundred yards away and round two corners. Outside the villa gates he crouched, as always, adjusting a shoe so he could glance up and down the road. There was nothing but some chit of a girl two hundred yards up, trying to start a scooter that refused to fire. But she was local, in jilbab, covering the hair and half the face. Still, it offended him that a woman would have any motorized vehicle at all.

He turned and walked away towards his car. The girl with the spluttering engine leaned forward and spoke into something inside the basket above the front mudguard. Her clipped English spoke of Cheltenham Ladies' College.

'Mongoose One, on the move,' she said.

Anyone who has ever been involved in what Kipling called 'the Great Game' and what James Jesus Angleton of the CIA referred to as 'a wilderness of mirrors' will surely agree the greatest enemy is the UCU.

The Unforeseen Cock-Up has probably wrecked more covert missions than treachery or brilliant counter-intelligence by the other side. It almost put an end to Operation Crowbar. And it all started because everyone consumed by the new atmosphere of cooperation was trying to be helpful.

The pictures from the two Predators which were 'spelling' each other over the UAE and the Arabian Sea were going back from Thumrait to Edzell air base, which knew exactly why, and American army CENTCOM at Tampa, Florida, which thought the British had simply asked for some routine aerial surveillance. Martin had insisted that no more than twelve should ever know he was out in the cold, and the number was still only at ten. And they were not in Tampa.

Whenever the Predators were over the Emirates, their images contained a teeming mass of Arabs, non-Arabs, cars, cabs, docksides and houses. There were far too many to begin checking out everyone. But the dhow called the *Rasha* and her elderly master *were* known about. So when she was in dock anyone visiting her was also of possible interest.

But there were scores. She had to be loaded and unloaded, refuelled and victualled. The Omani crewman scrubbing her down exchanged pleasantries with passers-by on the quayside. Tourists wandered by to gawp at a real trading dhow of traditional teak. Her skipper was visited on board by his local agents and personal friends. When a single clean-shaven young Gulf Arab in white dishdash and white filigree 'thub' skullcap conferred with Faisal bin Selim, he was just one of many.

Edzell's operations room had a menu of a thousand faces of confirmed and suspected AQ members and sympathizers and every image from the Predators was electronically compared. Dr Al-Khattab did not trigger red flags because he was not known. So Edzell missed him. These things happen.

The slim young Arab visiting the *Rasha* rang no bells in Tampa either, but the army sent the images as a courtesy to the National Security

Agency at Fort Meade, Maryland, and the National Reconnaissance Office (Spy Satellites) in Washington. The NSA provided them as a service to their British partners at GCHQ Cheltenham who had a good, long look, missed Al-Khattab and sent the images to the British Security Service (Counter-intelligence), more commonly known as MI5, at Thames House, just down the embankment from the Houses of Parliament.

Here a young probationer, keen to impress, ran the faces of all the visitors to the *Rasha* through the Face Recognition database.

It is not all that long ago that the recognition of human faces relied on talented agents who worked in half-darkness poring with magnifying glasses over grainy images to try to answer two questions: who is the man/woman in this photo and have we ever seen them before? It was always a lonely quest and took years before a dedicated scrutineer developed the sixth sense that could recall that the 'Chummy' in the photo had been at a Vietnamese diplomatic cocktail party in Delhi five years earlier and was certainly for that reason from the KGB.

Then came the computer. Software was prepared that reduced the human face to over six hundred tiny measurements and stored them. It seems every human face in the world can be broken down by measurement. It may be the exact (to the micron) distance between the pupils of the eyes, the width of the nose at seven points between eyebrows and tip, twenty-two measurements for the lips alone, and the ears . . .

Ah, the ears. Face analysts love the ears. Every crease and furrow, wrinkle and curve, fold and lobe, is different. They are like fingerprints. Even the ones on the left and right side of the head are not quite the same. Plastic surgeons ignore them, but give a skilled face-watcher both ears in good definition and he will get his 'match'.

The computer software had a memory bank far bigger than a thousand faces stored at Edzell. It had convicted criminals of apparently no political persuasion at all, because even they can work for terrorists if the price is right. It had immigrants, legal and illegal, and not necessarily Muslim converts. It had thousands and thousands of faces taken from demonstrations, as the protesters rolled by the hidden cameras, waving their placards and chanting their slogans. And it did not confine its database to the United Kingdom. In short it had over three million human faces from all over the world.

The computer broke down the face talking to the master of the *Rasha*, compensated for the oblique angle of shot by picking the single image where the man raised his head to look at a jet taking off from Abu Dhabi airport, secured its six hundred measurements and began to compare. It could even adjust for added or shaved facial hair.

Fast though it worked, the computer still took an hour. But it found him.

He was a face in a crowd outside a mosque just after 9/11 cheering enthusiastically whatever the orator was saying. This orator was known as Abu Qatada, fanatical Al-Qaeda supporter in Britain, and the crowd he was addressing that late September day of 2001 was from Al-Muhajiroun, a jihad-supporting extremist group.

Abstracting the face of the student from the file, the probationer took it to his superior. From there it went up to the formidable lady running MI5, Eliza Manningham-Buller. She ordered that the man be traced. No one then knew the probationer had uncovered the chieftain of Al-Qaeda in Britain.

It took a bit more time, but another match came up; he was receiving his doctorate at an academic ceremony. His name was Ali Aziz al-Khattab, a highly anglicized academic with a post at Aston University, Birmingham.

With what the authorities had, he was either a highly successful long-term sleeper or a foolish man who in his student days had dabbled with extreme politics. If every citizen in the second category were arrested there would be more detainees than policemen.

For sure, he had apparently never been anywhere near extremists since that day outside the mosque. But a fully reformed foolish boy is not spotted conferring with the captain of the *Rasha* in Abu Dhabi port. So ... he was in the first category: an AQ sleeper until proven otherwise.

Further discreet checks revealed he was back in Britain, resuming his laboratory work at Aston. The question was: arrest him or watch him? The problem was: one aerial photograph that could not be revealed would not secure a conviction. It was decided to put the academic under surveillance, costly though it was.

The quandary was solved a week later when Dr Al-Khattab booked a flight back to the Arabian Gulf. That was when the SRR was brought in.

Britain has for years possessed one of the best 'tracker' units in the world. It was known as the 14th Intelligence Company, or the Detachment, or more simply 'the Det'. And it was extremely covert. Unlike the SAS and the SBS it was not designed as a unit of ultra-hard fighters. Its talents were extreme stealth and skill at planting bugs, taking long-range photos, eavesdropping and tracking. It was particularly effective against the IRA in Northern Ireland.

In several cases it was the information provided by the Det that enabled the SAS to set an ambush for a terrorist attack unit and wipe them out. Unlike the hard units, the Det used women extensively. As trackers they were more likely to pass as harmless and not to be feared. The information they were able to bring back was indeed very much to be feared.

In 2005 the British government decided to expand and upgrade the Det. It became the Special Reconnaissance Regiment. It had an inaugural parade in which everyone, including the presiding general, was only photographed from the waist down. Its headquarters remain secret and if the SAS and SBS are discreet, the SRR is invisible. But Dame Eliza asked for them and got them.

When Dr Al-Khattab boarded the airliner from Heathrow to Dubai there were six from the SRR on board, scattered invisibly among three hundred passengers. One was the young accountant in the row behind the Kuwaiti.

Because this was just a shadowing operation, no reason could be seen not to ask the Special Forces of the UAE for cooperation. Ever since World Trade Center bomber Marwan al-Shehhi was discovered to have come from the UAE, and even more since the leak that the White House was tempted to bomb the Al-Jazeera TV station at Qatar, the UAE had been extremely sensitive about Islamist extremism, and nowhere more than in Dubai, headquarters of the Special Forces.

Thus two hired cars and two rented scooters were available for the SRR team when it landed, just in case Dr Al-Khattab was being picked up. It was noted he had carry-on baggage only. They need not have bothered; he rented a small Japanese compact which gave them time to move into position.

He was tailed first from the airport to the Creek in Dubai where once again the *Rasha* was moored after her return from Gwador. This time he did not approach the vessel but stood by his car a hundred yards away until Bin Selim spotted him.

Minutes later a young man known to no one emerged from below decks on the *Rasha*, moved through the crowd and whispered in the ear of the Kuwaiti. It was the answer coming back from the man in the mountains of Waziristan. Al-Khattab's face registered amazement.

He then drove along the traffic-teeming road up the coast, through Ajman and Umm-al-Qaiwain and into Ras-al-Khaimah. There he went to the Hilton to check in and change. It was considerate of him, because the three young women in the SRR team could use the female washroom to change into the all-covering jilbab and get back to their vehicles.

Dr Al-Khattab emerged in his white dishdash and drove away through the town. He adopted several manoeuvres designed to shake off a 'tail' but he had no luck. In the Arabian Gulf the motor scooter is everywhere, ridden by both sexes and, the clothes being the same, one rider is much like another. Since being assigned to the job, the team had been studying road maps of all seven emirates until they had memorized every high-way. That was how he was tailed to the villa.

If ever there had been any residual doubt that he was up to no good, his tail-shaking antics dispelled it. Innocent men do not behave like that. He never spent the night at the villa and the SRR women followed him back to the Hilton. The three men found a position on a hilltop that commanded a view of the target villa and kept vigil through the night. No one came or left.

The second day was different. There were visitors. The watchers could not know it but they brought the new passport and the new clothes. Their car numbers were noted and one would be traced and arrested later. The third was the barber, also later traced.

At the end of the second day Al-Khattab emerged for the last time. That was when Katy Sexton, tinkering with her scooter up the road, alerted her colleagues that the target was on the move.

At the Hilton the Kuwaiti academic revealed his plans when, speaking from his room, which had been bugged in his absence, he booked passage on the morning flight out of Dubai for London. He was escorted all the way home to Birmingham and never saw a thing.

MI5 had done a cracking job and knew it. The coup was circulated on a 'your eyes only' basis to just four men in the British intelligence community. One of them was Steve Hill. He nearly went into orbit.

The Predator was reassigned to survey the villa in the far desert-side suburbs of Ras-al-Khaimah. But it was mid-morning in London, afternoon in the Gulf. All the bird saw were the cleaners going in. And the raid.

It was too late to stop the Special Forces of the UAE sending in their close-down squad commanded by a former British officer, Dave de Forest. The SIS Head of Station in Dubai, a personal friend anyway, was on to him like a shot. Word was immediately put out on the jungle telegraph that the 'hit' had stemmed from an anonymous tip from a neighbour with a grudge.

The two cleaners knew nothing; they came from an agency, they had been pre-paid and the keys had been delivered to them. However, they had not finished and swept up in a pile was a

312

quantity of black hair, some evidently from a scalp and some from a beard – the texture is different. Other than that there were no traces of the men who had lived there.

Neighbours reported a closed van, but no one could recall the number. It was eventually discovered abandoned, and revealed to have been stolen, but much too late to be of help.

The tailor and the barber were a better harvest. They did not hesitate to talk, but they could only describe the five men in the house. Al-Khattab was already known. Suleiman was described and then identified from mug-shots because he was on a suspect list locally. The two underlings were described but rang no bells of recognition.

It was the fifth man that De Forest, with his perfect Arabic, concentrated on. The SIS Station Chief sat in. The two Gulf Arabs who had done the tailoring and the barbering came from Ajman and were simply workers at their trade.

No one in that room knew about any Afghan; they simply took a complete description and passed it to London. No one knew about any passport because Suleiman had done it all himself. No one knew why London was becoming hysterical about a big man with shaggy black hair and a full beard. All they could report was that he was now neatly barbered and possibly in a dark mohair two-piece suit.

But it was the final snippet that came from the barber and the tailor that delighted Steve Hill, Marek Gumienny and the team at Edzell.

The Gulf Arabs had been treating their man like an honoured guest. He was clearly being prepared for departure. He was not a dead body on a tiled floor in the Arabian Gulf.

At Edzell Michael McDonald and Gordon Phillips shared the same joy, but a puzzle. They knew their agent had passed all the tests and been accepted as a True Jihadi. After weeks of worry they had had their second sign of life. But had their agent discovered a single thing about Stingray, the object of the whole exercise? Where had he gone? Was there any way he could contact them?

Even if they could have spoken to their agent, he could not have helped. He did not know either.

And no one knew that the *Countess of Richmond* was unloading her Jaguars at Singapore.

CHAPTER THIRTEEN

Even though the travelling party could not know there were pursuers a few hours behind them, their escape was, for them, a lucky chance.

Had they turned towards the coast housing the six emirates they would probably have been caught. In fact they headed east, over the mountainous isthmus towards the seventh emirate, Fujairah, on the Gulf of Oman.

They soon left the last metalled road and took to rutted tracks which lost themselves among the baking brown hills of Jebel Yibir. From the col at the height of the range they descended towards the small port of Dibbah.

Well to the south on the same coast the police at Fujairah city received a request and a full description from Dubai, and mounted a roadblock at the entrance to their town on the mountain road. Many vans were stopped, but none contained the four terrorists.

There is not much to Dibbah: just a cluster of white houses, a green-domed mosque, a small port for fishing vessels and the occasional charter boat for western scuba divers. Two creeks away an aluminium boat waited, drawn up on the shingle, its huge outboards out of the water. Its cargo space amidships was occupied by chained-down tanks of extra fuel. Its two-man crew was sheltering in the shade of a single camelthorn among the rocks.

For the two local youths this was the end of their road. They would take the stolen van high into the hills and abandon it. Then they would simply disappear into the same streets that had produced Marwan al-Shehhi. Suleiman and the Afghan, their western clothes still in bags to shield them from the flying salt water, helped push the cigarette boat backwards into waist-deep water.

With both passengers and the crew aboard, the smuggler craft idled its way up the coast almost to the tip of the Musandam Peninsula. The smugglers would only make the high-speed dash across the Strait in darkness.

Within twenty minutes of the sun setting the helmsman bade his passengers hold on, and opened up the power. The smuggler erupted out of the rocky waters of the last tip of Arabia and hurled itself towards Iran. With 500-hp behind it, the nose rose and the craft began to skim. Martin judged they were covering the water at almost fifty knots. The slightest ripple on the sea was like hitting a log, and the spray flayed them. All four had wrapped their keffiyehs round their faces as a shield from the sun; now they kept them there as protection from the spray.

In less than thirty minutes the first scattered lights of the Persian coast were visible to port and the smuggler raced east towards Gwador and Pakistan. This was the route Martin had covered under the sedate sails of the *Rasha* a month before. Now he was returning at ten times her speed.

Opposite the lights of Gwador the crew slowed and stopped. It was a welcome relief. With funnels and muscles they hoisted the drums to the stern and refilled each engine to the brim. Where they were going to fill up again for the return journey was their business.

Faisal bin Selim had told Martin these smugglers could get from Omani waters to Gwador in a single night and be back with a fresh cargo by dawn. This time they were clearly going further and would have to travel in daylight as well.

Dawn found them well inside Pakistani waters

but close enough inshore to be taken for a fishing boat going about its business, save that no fish can swim that fast. However, there was no sign of officialdom and the bare brown coast sped past. By midday Martin realized their destination must be Karachi. As to why, he had no idea.

They refuelled at sea one more time and as the sun dipped to the west behind them were deposited at a reeking fishing village outside the sprawl of Pakistan's biggest port and harbour.

Suleiman may not have been there before, but his briefing must have been by someone who had done a recce. Martin knew that Al-Qaeda did meticulous research, regardless of time and expense; it was one of the few things he could admire.

The Gulf Arab sought out the only vehicle for hire in the village and negotiated a price. The fact that two strangers had come ashore from a smuggler craft with no suggestion of legality raised not an eyebrow. This was Baluchistan; the rules of Karachi were for idiots.

The interior stank of fish and body odour, and the misfiring engine could manage no more than forty miles per hour. Neither could the roads. But they found the highway and reached the airport with time to spare.

The Afghan was appropriately bewildered and clumsy. He had only twice travelled by air, each time in an American C-130 Hercules and each time as a prisoner in shackles. He knew nothing of check-in desks, flight tickets, passport controls. With a mocking smile, Suleiman showed him.

Somewhere in the vast sprawling mass of pushing and shoving humanity that comprises the main concourse of Karachi International Airport, the Gulf Arab found the ticket desk of Malaysian Airlines and bought two single tickets in economy class to Kuala Lumpur. There were lengthy visa application forms to fill out, which Suleiman did, in English. He paid in cash, in American dollars, the world's common currency.

The flight was on a European Airbus A330 and took six hours, plus three for time-zone changes. It landed at nine-thirty, after the serving of a snack breakfast. For the second time, Martin offered his new Bahraini passport and wondered if it would pass muster. It did; it was perfect.

From international arrivals Suleiman led the way to domestic departures and bought two single tickets. Only when Martin had to proffer his boarding pass did he see where they were heading: the island of Labuan.

He had heard of Labuan, but only vaguely. Situated off the northern coast of Borneo, it belonged to Malaysia. Though its tourist publicity spoke of a bustling cosmopolitan island with stunning coral in the surrounding waters, western briefings on the criminal underworld mentioned another and darker reputation.

It was once part of the Sultanate of Brunei, twenty miles across the water on the Borneo coast. The British took it in 1846 and kept it for 117 years barring three under Japanese occupation in World War II. Labuan was handed by the British to the state of Sabah in 1963 as part of decolonization, then ceded to Malaysia in 1984.

It is one of those oddities that has no visible economy within its fifty-square-mile oval territory, so it has created one. With a status of international offshore financial centre, tax free port, flag of convenience and smuggling mecca, Labuan has attracted some extremely dubious clientele.

Martin realized he was being flown into the heart of the world's most ferocious ship-hijacking, cargo-stealing and crew-murdering industry. He needed to make contact with base to give a sign of life, and he needed to work out how. Fast.

There was a brief stopover at Kuching, first port of call on the island of Borneo but non-alighting travellers did not leave the aeroplane.

Forty minutes later it took off to the west, circled over the sea and turned north-east for Labuan. Far below the turning aircraft the

Countess of Richmond, in ballast, was steaming for Kota Kinabalu to pick up her cargo of padauk and rosewood.

After take-off the stewardess distributed landing cards. Suleiman took them both and began to fill them in. Martin had to pretend he neither understood nor wrote English and could speak it only haltingly. He could hear it all around him. Besides, though he and Suleiman had changed into shirts and suits at Kuala Lumpur, he had no pen and no excuse for asking for the loan of one. Ostensibly they were a Bahraini engineer and an Omani accountant heading for Labuan on contract to the natural gas industry, and that was what Suleiman was filling in.

Martin muttered that he needed to go to the lavatory. He rose and went aft where there were two. One was vacant, but he pretended both were in use, turned and went forward. There was a point. The Boeing 737 had a two-cabin service: economy and business. Dividing the two was a curtain and Martin needed to get beyond it.

Standing outside the door of the business-class toilet, he beamed at the stewardess who had distributed the landing cards, uttered an apology and plucked from her top pocket a fresh landing card and her pen. The lavatory door clicked open and he went in. There was only time to scrawl a brief message on the reverse of the landing card, fold it into his breast pocket, emerge and return the pen. Then he went back to his seat.

Suleiman may have been told the Afghan was trustworthy, but he stuck like a clam. Perhaps he wanted his charge to avoid making any mistakes through naivety or inexperience; perhaps it was the years of training in the ways of Al-Qaeda, but his watchfulness never faltered, even during prayers.

Labuan airport was a contrast to Karachi: small and trim. Martin still had no idea exactly where they were headed, but suspected the airport might be the last chance to get rid of his message and hoped for a stroke of luck.

It was only a fleeting moment and it came on the pavement outside the concourse. Suleiman's memorized instructions must have been extraordinarily precise. He had brought them halfway across the world and was clearly a seasoned traveller. Martin could not know that the Gulf Arab had been with Al-Qaeda for ten years and had served the Movement in Iraq and the Far East, notably Indonesia. Nor could he know what Suleiman's speciality was.

Suleiman was scouring the access road to the concourse building which served both arrivals and departures on one level: he was looking for a taxi when one appeared heading towards them.

It was occupied but clearly about to deposit its cargo on the pavement.

Two men alighted and Martin caught the English accents immediately. Both were big and muscular; both wore khaki shorts and flowered beach shirts. Both were damp in the blazing sun and moist, thirty-degree pre-monsoon heat. One produced Malaysian currency to pay the driver, the other emptied the boot of their luggage. There were two hard-framed suitcases and two scuba diver's kitbags. Both had been diving the offshore reefs on behalf of the British magazine *Sport Diver*.

The man by the boot could not handle all four bags, one each for clothes, one each for diving tackle. Before Suleiman could utter a word, Martin helped the diver by hefting one of the kitbags from the road to the pavement. As he did so the folded landing card went into one of the side pockets of which all divebags have an array.

'Thanks, mate,' said the diver, and the pair of them headed for departure check-in to find their flight to Kuala Lumpur with a connection to London.

Suleiman's instructions to the Malay driver were in English; a shipping agency in the heart of the docks. Here at last the travellers met someone waiting to receive them. Like the newcomers he excited no interest by the wearing of ostentatious clothing or facial hair. Like them he was *takfir*. He introduced himself as Mr Lampong and took them to a fifty-foot cabin cruiser, tricked out as a game-fisherman, by the harbour wall. Within minutes they were out of the harbour.

The cruiser steadied her speed at ten knots and turned north-east for Kudat, the access to the Sulu Sea and the terrorist hideout in Zamboanga Province of the Philippines.

It had been a gruelling journey, with only cat-naps on the aeroplanes. The rocking of the sea was seductive, the breeze after the sauna-heat of Labuan refreshing. Both passengers fell asleep. The helmsman was from the Abu Sayyaf terror group; he knew his way; he was going home. The sun dropped and the tropical darkness was not long behind. The cruiser motored on through the night, past the lights of Kudat, through the Balabac Strait and over the invisible border into Filipino waters.

Mr Wei had finished his commission before schedule and was already heading home to his native China. For him it could not have come too quickly. But at least he was on a Chinese vessel, eating good Chinese food rather than the rubbish the sea dacoits served in their camp up the creek.

What he had left behind he neither knew nor cared. Unlike the Abu Sayyaf killers or the two or three Indonesian fanatics who prayed on their knees, foreheads to the matting, five times a day, Wei Wing Li was a member of a Snakehead triad and prayed to nothing.

In fact the results of his work were a to-the-rivet replica of the *Countess of Richmond*, fashioned from a ship of similar size, tonnage and dimensions. He never knew what the original ship had been called, nor what the new one would be. All that concerned him was the bulbous roll of high-denomination dollar bills drawn from a Labuan bank against a line of credit arranged by the late Mr Tewfik al-Qur, formerly of Cairo, Peshawar and the morgue.

Unlike Mr Wei, Captain McKendrick prayed. Not as often, he knew, as he ought, but he had been raised a good Liverpool–Irish Catholic; there was a figurine of the Blessed Virgin on the bridge just forward of the wheel, and a crucifix on the wall of his cabin. Before sailing he always prayed for a good voyage and on returning thanked his Lord for a safe return.

He did not need to pray as the Sabah pilot eased the *Countess* past the shoals and into her assigned berth by the quay at Kota Kinabalu, formerly the colonial port of Jesselton where British traders, in the days before refrigeration, and if they had acquired tinned butter in the monthly drop-off, had to pour it on to the bread from a small jug.

Captain McKendrick ran his bandanna kerchief round his wet neck once again and thanked the pilot. At last he could close up all the doors and portholes and take relief in the air conditioning. That, he reckoned, and a cold beer would do him nicely. The water ballast would be evacuated in the morning and he could see his log-cargo under the lights of the dock. With a good loading crew he could be back at sea the evening of the next day.

The two young divers, having changed planes at Kuala Lumpur, were on a British Airways jet for London and, it not being a 'dry' airline, had consumed enough beer to send them into a deep sleep. The flight might be twelve hours but they would be gaining eight on the time zones and touching down at Heathrow at dawn. The hard-frame suitcases were in the hold but the divebags were above their heads as they slept.

They contained fins, masks, wetsuits, regulators and buoyancy control jackets, with only the diving knives in the suitcases in the hold. One of the divebags also contained an as yet undiscovered Malaysian landing card.

In a creek off the Zamboanga Peninsula, working by floodlights from a platform hung over the stern, a skilled painter was affixing the last 'D' to the name of the moored ship. From her mast fluttered a limp Red Ensign. On either side of her bow and round her stern were the words 'Countess of Richmond' and, at the stern only, the word 'Liverpool' beneath. As the painter descended and the lights flickered out, the transformation was complete.

At dawn a cruiser disguised as a game-fisherman motored slowly up the creek. It brought the last two members of the new crew of the former *Java Star*, the ones who would take the ship on her, and their, last voyage.

The loading of the *Countess of Richmond* began at dawn when the air was still cool and agreeable. Within three hours it would return to its habitual sauna heat. The dockside cranes were not exactly ultra-modern but the stevedores knew their business and chained logs of rare timber swung inboard and were stowed in the hold below by the crew that toiled and sweated down there.

In the heat of midday even the local Borneans had to stop and for four hours the old logging port slumbered in whatever shade it could find. The spring monsoon was only a month away and already the humidity, never much less than ninety per cent, was edging towards a hundred.

Captain McKendrick would have been happier at sea, but loading and the replacement of the deck covers was achieved at sundown and the pilot would come aboard only in the morning to guide the freighter back to the open sea. It meant another night in the hothouse so McKendrick sighed and again found refuge in the air conditioning below decks.

The local agent came bustling aboard with the pilot at six in the morning and the last paperwork was signed. Then the *Countess* eased away into the South China Sea.

Like the *Java Star* before her, she turned northeast to round the tip of Borneo, then south through the Sulu Archipelago for Java, where the skipper believed six sea containers full of eastern silks awaited him at Surabaya. He was not to know that there were not, nor ever had been, any silks at Surabaya.

The cruiser deposited its cargo of three at a ramshackle jetty halfway up the creek. Mr Lampong led the way to a longhouse on stilts above the water that served as a sleeping area and mess hall for the men who would depart on the mission that Martin knew as Stingray and Lampong as Al-Isra. Others in the longhouse would be staying behind. It was their labours that had prepared the hijacked *Java Star* for sea.

These were a mix of Indonesians from Jemaat Islamiya, the group who had planted the Bali bombs and others up the island chain, and Filipinos from Abu Sayyaf. The languages varied from local Tagalog to Javanese dialect with an occasional muttered aside in Arabic from those further west. One by one Martin was able to identify the crew and the special task of each of them.

The engineer, navigator and radio operator were all Indonesians. Suleiman revealed that his expertise was photography. Whatever was going to happen his job, before dying a martyr, would be to photograph the climax on a digital radio camera and transmit via a laptop computer and satphone the entire datastream for transmission on the Al-Jazeera TV network.

There was a teenager who looked Pakistani, yet Lampong addressed him in English. When he replied the boy revealed he could only have been British-born and -raised but of Pakistani parentage. His accent was broad English north country; Martin put it as coming from the Leeds/Bradford area. Martin could not work out what he was for, except possibly as cook.

That left three: Martin himself clearly granted his presence as the personal gift of Osama bin Laden; a genuine chemical engineer and presumably explosives expert; and the mission commander. But he was not present. They would all meet him later.

In the mid-morning the local commander Lampong took a call on his satellite phone. It was brief and guarded, but enough. The *Countess of Richmond* had left Kota Kinabalu and was at sea. She should be coming between Tawitawi and Jolo Islands around sundown. The speedboat crews that would intercept her still had four hours before they need leave. Suleiman and Martin had changed from their western suits into trousers, flowered local shirts and sandals that had been provided. They were allowed down the steps into the shallow water of the creek to wash before prayers and a dinner of rice and fish.

All Martin could do was watch, understanding very little, and wait.

The two divers were lucky. Most of their fellow passengers were from Malaysia and were diverted to the non-UK passport channel, leaving the few British easy access to immigration control. Being among the first down to the luggage carousel, they could grab their valises and head for the nothing-to-declare Customs hall.

It might have been the shaven skulls, the stubble on the chins or the brawny arms emerging from short-sleeved flowered shirts on a bitter British March morning, but one of the customs officers beckoned them to the examination bench.

'May I see your passports, please?'

It was a formality. They were in order.

'And where have you just arrived from?'

'Malaysia.'

'Purpose of visit?'

One of the young men pointed at his divebag. His expression indicated it was a pretty daft question, given that the divebags bore the logo of a famous scuba-equipment company. It is, however, a mistake to mock a customs officer. The official's face remained impassive but he had in a long career intercepted quantities of exotic smoking or injecting material coming in from the Far East. He gestured to one of the divebags.

There was nothing inside but the usual scuba gear. As he was zipping the bag back up, he ran his fingers into the side pockets. From one he drew a folded card, looked and read it.

'Where did you get this, sir?'

The diver was genuinely puzzled.

'I don't know. I've never seen it before.'

A few yards away another customs man caught the rising tension, indicated by the exemplary courtesy, and moved closer.

'Would you remain here, please?' said the first, and walked through a door behind him. Those ample mirrors in customs halls are not for the vain to touch up their make-up. They have one-way vision and behind them are the duty shift of one of the arms of British internal security – in this case Scotland Yard's Special Branch.

Within minutes both divers, with their luggage, were in separate interview rooms. The customs men went through the luggage fin by fin, mask by mask and shirt by shirt. There was nothing illegal.

The man in plain clothes studied the now unfolded card.

'It must have been put there by someone, but not by me,' protested the diver.

By now it was nine-thirty. Steve Hill was at his desk in Vauxhall Cross when his private and very unlisted phone rang.

'To whom am I speaking?' asked a voice. Hill bristled.

'Perhaps I should ask the same question. I think you may have a wrong number,' he replied.

The MI5 officer had read the text of the message stuffed into the diver's kitbag. He tended to believe the man's explanation. In which case . . .

'I am speaking from Heathrow, Terminal Three. The internal security office. We have intercepted a passenger from the Far East. Stuffed into his divebag was a short handwritten message. Does Crowbar mean anything to you?'

To Steve Hill it was like a punch in the stomach. This was no wrong number; this was no crossed line. He identified himself by service and rank, asked that both men be detained and said that he was on his way. Within five minutes his car swept out of the underground car park, crossed Vauxhall Bridge and turned down the Cromwell Road to Heathrow.

It was bad luck on the divers to have lost their whole morning, but after an hour's interrogation Steve Hill was sure they were just innocent dupes. He secured for them a full with-trimmings breakfast from the staff canteen and asked them to rack their brains for a clue as to who had stuffed the folded note into the side pocket.

They went over everyone they had met since packing the bags. Finally one said: 'Mark, do you remember that Arab-looking fella who helped you unload at the airport?'

'What Arab-looking fellow?' asked Hill.

They described the man as best they could. Black hair, black beard. Neatly trimmed. Dark eyes, olive skin. About forty-five, fit-looking. Dark suit. Hill had had the descriptions from the barber and the tailor of Ras-al-Khaimah. It was Crowbar. He thanked them sincerely and asked that they be given a chauffeured ride back to their Essex home.

When he called Gordon Phillips at Edzell and Marek Gumienny over breakfast in Washington, he could reveal the scrawl in his hand. It said simply: 'IF YOU LOVE YOUR COUNTRY, GET HOME AND RING XXXXXXXXXXX. JUST TELL THEM CROWBAR SAYS IT WILL BE SOME KIND OF SHIP.'

'Pull out all the stops,' he told Edzell. 'Just scour the world for a missing ship.'

As with Captain Herrmann of the *Java Star*, Liam McKendrick had chosen to bring his vessel round the various headlands himself and hand over after clearing the strait between the islands of Tawitawi and Jolo. Ahead was the great expanse of the Celebes Sea, and the course directly south for the Strait of the Makassar.

He had a crew of six: five Indians from Kerala, all Christians, loyal and efficient, and his first officer, a Gibraltarian. He had handed over the helm and gone below when the speedboats swept up from astern. As with the *Java Star*, the crew had no chance. Ten dacoits were over the rails in seconds and running for the bridge. Mr Lampong, in charge of the hijack, came at a more leisurely pace.

This time there was no need for ceremony or threats of violence unless instructions were obeyed. The only task the *Countess of Richmond* had to perform was to disappear, with her crew and for ever. What had lured her to these waters in the first place – her valuable cargo – would be a total write-off, which was a pity but could not be helped.

The crew were simply marched to the taffrail and machine-gunned. Their bodies, jerking in protest at the unfairness of death, went straight over the rail. There was not even any need for weights or ballast to send them to the bottom. Lampong knew his sharks.

Liam McKendrick was the last to go, roaring his rage at the killers, calling Lampong a heathen pig. The Muslim fanatic did not like being called a pig and made sure the Liverpudlian mariner was riddled but still alive when he hit the sea.

The Abu Sayyaf pirates had sunk enough ships to know where the seacocks were. As the bilges began to flood below the cargo the raiders left the *Countess* and bobbed on the water a few cables away until she reared on her stern, bow in the air, and slid backwards to tumble slowly to the bottom of the Celebes Sea. When she was gone the killers turned and raced for home.

For the party in the longhouse in the Filipino creek it was another brief call on a satphone from Lampong out at sea that triggered the hour of departure. They filed down to the cruiser moored at the foot of the steps. As they went Martin realized that the ones being left behind were not showing any sense of relief, but only a deep envy.

In a career in special forces he had never actually met a suicide bomber before the act. Now he was surrounded by them, had become one of them.

At Forbes Castle he had read copiously of their state of mind; of their total conviction that the deed is being done in a truly holy cause; that it is automatically blessed by Allah himself; that a guaranteed and immediate passage to paradise will ensue; and that this vastly outweighs any residual love of life.

He had also come to realize the depth of hatred that must be imbued in the *shahid* alongside the love of Allah. One of the two alone will not work. The hatred must be like a corrosive acid inside the soul, and he was surrounded by it.

He had seen it in the faces of the dacoits of Abu Sayyaf who relished every chance to kill a westerner; he had seen it in the hearts of the Arabs as they prayed for a chance to kill as many Christians, Jews and secular or insufficient Muslims as possible in the act of death; most of all he had seen the hatred in the eyes of Al-Khattab and Lampong, precisely because they sullied themselves in order to pass unnoticed among the enemy.

As they chugged slowly further up the creek, the jungle closing in on every side and beginning to shut out the sky above them, he studied his companions. They all shared the hate and the fanaticism. They all counted themselves more blessed than any other True Believers on earth.

Martin was convinced that the men around him had no more clue than he exactly what the sacrifice would entail; where they would be going, to target what, and with what.

They only knew, because they had offered themselves to die, and been accepted and carefully selected, that they were going to strike at the Great Satan in a manner that would be spoken of for a hundred years. They, like the Prophet so long ago, were going on a great journey to heaven itself; the journey called Al-Isra.

Up ahead the creek split. The chugging cruiser took the wider branch and round a corner a moored vessel came into sight. She was facing downstream, ready to depart for the open sea. Her deck cargo was apparently stored in the six sea containers that occupied her foredeck. And she was called the *Countess of Richmond*.

For a moment Martin toyed with the thought of escaping into the surrounding jungle. He had had weeks of jungle training in Brunei, the SAS's tropical training school. But he realized as soon as the thought crossed his mind that it was hopeless. He would not make a mile without compass or machete and the hunting party would have him within the hour. Then would come days of unspeakable agony as his mission details were wrenched out of him. There was no point. He would have to wait for a better opportunity if one ever came.

One by one they climbed the ladder to the deck of the freighter: the engineer, navigator and radio man, all Indonesians; the chemist and photographer, both Arabs; the Pakistani from the UK with the flat northern accent, who it turned out was there in case anyone should insist on speaking to the *Countess* by radio; and the Afghan, who could be taught to hold the wheel and steer a course. In all his training at Forbes, in all the hours of studying faces of known suspects, he had never seen any of them. When he reached the deck the man who would command them all on their mission to eternal glory was there to meet them. Him the ex-SAS man did recognize. From the rogues' gallery he had been shown at Castle Forbes he knew he was staring at Yusuf Ibrahim, deputy and right-hand man of Al-Zarqawi, his homicidal fellow-Jordanian.

The face had been one of the 'first division' in the gallery he had been shown at Castle Forbes. The man was short and stocky, as expected, and the stunted left arm hung by his side. He had fought in Afghanistan against the Soviets and his left arm had stopped several shards of shrapnel during an air attack. Rather than accept a clean amputation he preferred to let it hang, useless.

There had been rumours that he had died there: not true. He had been patched up in the caves, then smuggled into Pakistan for more advanced surgery. After the Soviet evacuation he had disappeared.

The man with the withered left arm reappeared after the 2003 Coalition invasion of Iraq, having spent the missing time as chief of security in one of the AQ camps under Taliban rule.

For Mike Martin there was a heart-stopping moment in case the man recognized Izmat Khan from those Afghan days and wished to discuss it. But the mission commander just stared at him with black-pebble expressionless eyes.

For twenty years this man had killed and killed, and he loved it. In Iraq, as aide to Musab al-Zarqawi, he had hacked off heads on camera and loved it. He loved to hear them plead and scream. Martin gazed into the blank, manic eyes and gave the habitual greeting. Peace be unto you, Yusuf Ibrahim, Butcher of Karbala.

CHAPTER FOURTEEN

The former *Java Star* emerged from the hidden
Filipino creek twelve hours after the destruction
of the *Countess of Richmond*. She cleared the Moro
Gulf and headed into the Celebes Sea, heading
south by south-west to join the sea-track
the *Countess* would have taken through the
Makassar Strait.

The Indonesian helmsman had the wheel but
beside him stood the British/Pakistani teenager
and the Afghan, to whom he gave instruction on
the keeping of a true course at sea.

Though neither of his pupils could be aware of
it, counter-terrorist agencies within the world
of merchant marine had for years known and
been perplexed by the times a ship in these
waters had been hijacked, steered round in

circles for several hours with her crew in the chain locker, then abandoned.

The reason was simply that just as the hijackers of 9/11 had achieved their practice in US flying schools, the marine hijackers of the Far East had been practising the handling of a large ship at sea. The Indonesian at the helm of the new *Countess* was one of these.

The engineer down below really had been a marine engineer before the ship he worked on had been hijacked by Abu Sayyaf. Rather than die, he had agreed to join the terrorists and become one of them.

The third Indonesian had learned all about ship-to-shore radio procedures while working in the harbour master's office of a North Borneo trading port until he was radicalized within Islam and accepted into the ranks of Jemaat Islamiya, later helping to plant the Bali disco bombs.

These were the only three of eight who needed technical knowledge of ships. The Arab chemist would eventually be in charge of cargo-detonation; the man from the UAE, Suleiman, would take the datastream images that would rock the world; the Pakistani youth would, if need be, emulate the North Country voice of Captain McKendrick, and the Afghan would spell the helmsman at the wheel through the days of cruising that lay ahead.

* * *

By the end of March spring had not even attempted to touch the Cascades mountain range. It was still bitterly cold and snow lay thick in the forest beyond the walls of the Cabin.

Inside, it was snug and warm. The enemy, despite TV day and night, movies on DVD, music and board games, was boredom. As with lighthouse-keepers, the men had not much to do and the six-month term was a great test of their capacity for internal solitude and self-sufficiency.

Nevertheless the guard detail could don skis or snowshoes and slog through the forest to keep fit and get a break from the bunkhouse, eatery and games room. For the prisoner, immune to fraternization, the strain was that much greater.

Izmat Khan had listened to the president of the military court at Guantanamo pronounce him free to go and was convinced Pul-i-Charki jail would not have held him for more than a year. When he was brought to this lonely wilderness, so far as he knew for ever, it was hard to hide the screaming rage inside.

So he donned the kapok-lined jacket they had issued him, let himself outside and paced up and down the walled enclosure. Ten paces long, five paces wide. He could do it with eyes shut and never bump into the concrete. The only variety was occasionally in the sky above.

Mostly it was of heavy leaden-grey cloud, from which the snow drifted down. But earlier, in that period when the Christians decorated trees and sang songs, the skies had been freezing cold but blue.

Then he had seen eagles and ravens wheeling overhead. Smaller birds had fluttered to the top of the wall and looked down at him, perhaps wondering why he could not come and join them in freedom. But what he liked most to watch were the aeroplanes.

Some he knew were warplanes, though he had never heard of either the Cascades Range where he was, nor McChord Air Force Base fifty miles to the west. But he had seen American combat aircraft turning into their bombing runs over northern Afghanistan, and he knew these were the same.

And there were the airliners. They were in different liveries, with varying designs on their tailfins, but he knew enough to know these were not national but company insignia. Except for the maple leaf. Some always had that leaf on the fin, they were always climbing and they always came from the north.

North was easy to work out; to the west he could see the sun set, and he prayed the opposite way, towards Mecca far to the east. He suspected he was in the USA because the voices of his guards were clearly American. So why did air-liners with a different national emblem come from the north? It could only be because there was another land up there somewhere, a land where people prayed to a red leaf on a white ground. So he paced up and down, up and down, and wondered about the land of the red leaf. In fact he was watching the Air Canada flights out of Vancouver.

In a sleazy dockside bar in Port of Spain, Trinidad, two merchant seamen were attacked by a local gang and left dead. Both had been skilfully knifed.

By the time the Trinidadian police arrived the witnesses had acquired amnesia and could recall only that there had been five attackers who had provoked the bar fight and that they were islanders. The police would never get further than that, and no arrests were ever made.

In fact the killers were local low-life and they had nothing to do with Islamist terrorism. But the man who had paid them was a senior terrorist in the Jamaat-al-Muslimeen, the principal Trinidadian group on the side of Al-Qaeda.

Though still low profile across the western media, JaM has been growing steadily for years, as have other groups right across the Caribbean basin. In an area known for its down-home Christian worship, Islam has been quietly growing with wholesale immigration from the Middle East, Central Asia and the Indian subcontinent.

The money paid out by JaM for the killings came from a line of credit set up by the late Mr Tewfik al-Qur, and the specific orders had come from an emissary of Dr Al-Khattab who was still on the island.

No attempt had been made to steal the wallets of the dead men, so the Port of Spain police could quickly identify them as Venezuelan citizens and deck crew from a Venezuelan ship then in port.

Her master, Captain Pablo Montalban, was shocked and saddened to be informed of the loss of his crewmen, but he could not wait for too long in harbour.

The details of shipping the bodies back to Caracas fell to the Venezuelan Embassy and Consulate while Captain Montalban contacted his local agent for replacement sailors. The man asked around and struck lucky. He came up with two polite and eager young Indians from Kerala who had worked their passage across the world and who, even if they lacked naturalization papers, had perfectly good seamen's tickets.

They were taken on, joined the other four seamen who made up the crew and the *Doña Maria* sailed only a day late.

Captain Montalban knew vaguely that most of India is Hindu but he had no idea that there are also a hundred and fifty million Muslims. He was not aware that the radicalization of Indian Muslims has been just as vigorous as in Pakistan, or that Kerala, once the hotbed of Communism, has been particularly receptive territory for Islamist extremism.

His two new crewmen had indeed worked their way from India as deck hands, but on orders and to gain experience. And finally the Catholic Venezuelan had no idea that, though neither had suicide in mind, they were working with and for Jamaat-al-Muslimeen. The two unfortunates in the bar had been killed precisely to put the two Indian matelots on his ship.

Marek Gumienny chose to fly the Atlantic when he heard the report from the Far East. But he brought with him a specialist in a different discipline.

'Arab experts have served their purpose, Steve,' he told Hill before he flew. 'Now we need people who know the world's merchant marine.'

The man he brought was from America's Bureau of Customs and Border Protection, merchant-marine division. Steve Hill came north from London accompanied by another of his colleagues, who came from the SIS's anti-terrorism desk, maritime section.

At Edzell the two younger men met: Chuck Hemingway from New York and Sam Seymour from London. Both had heard of the other from the reading of papers and briefings within the West's anti-terror community. They were told they had twelve hours to go into a huddle and come up with an evaluation of the threat and game plan for coping with it. When they addressed Gumienny, Hill, Phillips and McDonald, Chuck Hemingway went first.

'This is not just a hunt, this is a search for a needle in a haystack. A hunt has a known target; all we have is something that floats. Maybe. Let me lay this on the line.

'There are forty-six thousand merchant ships plying their trade on the world's oceans as of now. Half of them are flying flags of convenience, which can be switched almost at the whim of the captain.

'Six-sevenths of the world's surface is covered by ocean, giving an area so vast that literally thousands of ships are out of sight of land or any other vessel all the time.

'Eighty per cent of the world's trade is still carried out by sea, and that means just under six billion tonnes. And there are four thousand viable merchant ports around the world.

'Finally, you want to find a vessel; but you do not know her type, size, tonnage, contours, age, ownership, stern-flag, captain or name. To have a hope of tracing this vessel – we call them ghost ships – we will need more than that; or a large dose of luck. Can you offer us either?'

There was a depressed silence.

'That's damn downbeat,' said Marek Gumienny. 'Sam, can you suggest a ray of hope?'

'Chuck and I agree there might be a way if we identify the kind of target the terrorists could be aiming at, then check out any ship heading towards that target and demand a gunpoint inspection of ship and cargo,' said Seymour.

'We're all listening,' said Hill. 'What kind of target could they be most likely heading for?'

'People in our line of business have been worried for years and filing reports for years. The oceans are a terrorists' playground. The fact that Al-Qaeda chose for its first huge spectacular an attack from the air was actually illogical. They only hoped to take out four floors of the Trade Center towers, and even then they were incredibly lucky. All that time the sea has been beckoning to them.'

'Security of ports and harbours has been massively tightened,' snapped Marek Gumienny. 'I know, I have seen the budgets.'

'With respect, sir, not enough. We know shiphijacking in the waters around Indonesia – that is, in all directions – has been steadily increasing since the turn of the millennium. Some has simply been to make money to fund terrorism's coffers. Other events at sea defy logic.'

'Such as?'

'There have been ten cases of sea dacoits stealing tugs. Some have never been recovered. They have no value as resales because they are pretty noticeable and hard to disguise. What are they for? We think they could be used to tow a captured supertanker right into a busy international port like Singapore.'

'And blow her up?' asked Hill.

'No need. Just sink her with her cargo hatches open. The port is closed for a decade.'

'OK,' said Marek Gumienny, 'so . . . possible target number one. Take over a supertanker and use her to close down a commercial port. This is a spectacular? Sounds pretty mundane, except for the port in question . . . no casualties.'

'It gets worse,' said Chuck Hemingway. 'There are other things that can be destroyed with a blocking ship with vast damage to the world's economy. In his October two thousand and four video Bin Laden himself said he was switching to economic damage.

'Nobody out there in the shopping malls or the gas stations realizes how the whole of world trade is now geared to just-in-time delivery. No one wants to store or stockpile any more. The

T-shirt made in China sold in Dallas on Monday probably arrived at the docks the previous Friday. Same with gasoline.

'What about the Panama Canal? Or the Suez? Close them down and the whole global economy spins into chaos. You are talking damage in the hundreds of billions of dollars. There are ten other straits so narrow and so vital that sinking a really big freighter or tanker broadside-on would close them.'

'All right,' said Marek Gumienny. 'Look, I have a president and the other five principals to report to. You, Steve, have a prime minister. We cannot just sit on this message from Crowbar. Nor can we simply burst into tears. We have to propose concrete measures. They will want to be active, to be seen to be doing something. So list the likelihoods and suggest some counter-measures. Dammit, we are not without resources of self-defence.'

Chuck Hemingway produced a paper he and Seymour had worked on earlier.

'OK, sir, we feel probability one is likely to be the taking-over of a very large vessel – tanker, freighter, ore-carrier – and sinking her in a narrow but vital marine bottleneck. Measures to counter? Identify all such bottlenecks and post warships at either end. All entering vessels to be boarded by Marines.'

'Christ,' said Steve Hill, 'that will cause chaos.

It will be claimed we are acting as pirates. What about the owners of the host waters? Don't they have a say?'

'If the terrorists succeed, both the other ships and the coastal countries will be ruined. There need be no delays – the Marines can board without the freighter slowing down. And, frankly, the terrorists on board any ghost ship cannot permit boarding. They have to fire back, expose themselves and scuttle prematurely. I think the ship owners will see it our way.'

'Probability two?' queried Steve Hill.

'Running the ghost ship, crammed with explosives, into a major facility like a sea island of oil pipes or an oil rig and blowing it to pieces. It causes astronomical eco-damage and economic ruin for years. Saddam Hussein did it to Kuwait, torching all their oil wells as the Coalition moved in, so that he would leave them living off scorched earth. Counter-measure: same again. Identify and intercept every vessel even approaching the facility. Secure positive identification outside the ten-mile *cordon sanitaire*.'

'We don't have enough warships,' protested Steve Hill. 'Every sea island, every seashore oil refiner, every offshore rig?'

'That is why the national owners have to share the cost burden. And it need not be a warship. If any interceptor vessel is fired on, the ghost ship is exposed and may be sunk from the air, sir.'

Marek Gumienny ran his hand over his forehead.

'Anything else?'

'There is a possible third,' said Seymour. 'The use of explosives to cause a terrible massacre of humans. In that case the target would likely be a tourist facility crammed with holidaymakers by the seaside. It's a horrible prospect, reminiscent of the destruction of Halifax, Nova Scotia, in 1917 when an ammunition ship blew up in the heart of the inner harbour. It wiped the city off the map. It still rates as the biggest non-nuclear explosion in history.'

'I am going to have to report all this to the principals, Steve, and they are not going to like it,' Gumienny said as they shook hands on the tarmac. 'By the way, if counter-measures are taken, and they will have to be, there is no way we can keep the media out of this. We can devise the best cover story we can to divert the bad guys' attention away from Colonel Martin. But, as you know, much as I take my hat off to him, you have to accept the reality. Chances are he's history.'

Major Larry Duval glanced out of the flight dispersal hut in the Arizona sunshine and marvelled as he always did at the sight of the F-15 Strike Eagle that awaited him. He had flown the F-15E version for ten years and reckoned it had to be the love of his life.

His career postings included the F-111 Aardvark and the F-4G Wild Weasel and they were both serious pieces of machinery that the US Air Force granted him the privilege to fly, but the Eagle was for him, after twenty years as a USAF flier, the ace of them all.

The fighter he would be flying that day from Luke Air Force Base right up to Washington State was still being worked on. Immune to love or lust, hate or fear, it crouched silently amid the teeming swarm of men and women in coveralls who crawled over its burly frame. Larry Duval envied his Eagle; for all its myriad complexities, it could not feel anything. It could never be afraid.

The aeroplane being readied for this morning's air test had been at Luke AFB for fundamental overhaul and ground-up servicing. After such a period in the workshops the rules stated she had to be given a proving flight.

So it waited in the bright spring sunshine of an Arizona morning; 63 feet long, 18 high and 42 across, weighing in at 40,000 lb bone dry and 81,000 at maximum take-off weight. Larry Duval turned as his Weapons Systems Officer, Captain

Nicky Johns, strolled in from his own equipment checks. In the Eagle the WSO, or wizzo, rides in tandem behind the pilot, surrounded by millions of dollars' worth of avionics. On the long flight to McChord AFB he would test them all.

The open utility drove up to the windows and the two aircrew were driven the half-mile to the waiting fighter. They spent ten minutes on their pre-flight checks, even though the chances their ground crew had missed something were extremely slim.

Once on board they strapped themselves in, gave one last nod to the ground crew, who clambered down, headed back and left them in peace.

Larry Duval started the two powerful F-100 engines, the canopy hissed down into its seals and the Eagle began to roll. It turned into the light breeze down the runway, paused, received clearance and crouched for one last testing of the brakes. Then thirty-foot flames leapt back from its twin afterburners and Major Duval unleashed its full power.

A mile down the runway, at 185 knots, the wheels left the tarmac and the Eagle was airborne. Wheels up, flaps up, throttles back to pull the engines out of gas-drinking afterburn mode and into military power setting. Duval set a climb rate of five thousand feet per minute and from behind him his wizzo gave him a compass heading for their destination. At thirty thousand feet in a pure blue sky the Eagle levelled out and pointed her nose north-west towards Seattle. Below, the Rockies were clothed in snow and would stay with them all the way.

In the British Foreign Office the final details for the transfer of the British government and its advisers to the April G8 were almost complete. The entire delegation would fly in a chartered airliner from Heathrow to JFK, New York, there to be formally met by the US Secretary of State.

The other six non-American delegations would fly in from six different capitals to the same Kennedy International.

All the delegations would remain 'airside' within the airport, a mile away from the nearest demonstrators and protesters outside the perimeter. The President was simply not going to allow those whom he called 'loony-toons' to scream insults at his guests or harass them in any way. Repeats of Seattle and Genoa were not to be entertained.

Transfer out of JFK would be by an air bridge of helicopters which would deposit their cargoes into a second totally sealed environment. From there they would simply stroll into the venue of the five-day conference and be enclosed in luxury and privacy. It was simple and flawless.

'No one had ever thought of it before, but when you think about it, it's brilliant,' said one of the British diplomats. 'Perhaps we should do it ourselves one day.'

'The even better news,' muttered an older and more experienced colleague, 'is that after Gleneagles it won't be our turn for ages. Let the others cope with the security headaches for a few years.'

Marek Gumienny was not long getting back to Steve Hill. He had been escorted by the Director of his own Agency to the White House, and had explained to the six principals the deductions that had followed the receipt of a bizarre message from the unheard-of island of Labuan.

'They said much the same as before,' Gumienny reported. 'Whatever it is, wherever it is, find it and destroy it.'

'The same with my government,' said Steve Hill. 'No holds barred, destroy on sight. And they want us to work together on this.'

'No problem. But, Steve, my people are convinced the USA is likely to be the target, so our coastal protection takes precedence over everything else – Mideast, Asia, Europe. We have total priority on all our assets – satellites, warships, the lot. If we locate the ghost ship anywhere away from our shores, OK, we'll divert assets to destroy it.'

The American Director of National Intelligence, John Negroponte, authorized the CIA to inform their British counterparts on an 'eyes-only' basis of the measures the States intended to take.

The defence strategy would be based on three stages: aerial surveillance, identification of vessel and 'check-it-out'. Any unsatisfactory explanation, any unexplained diversion from course and track, would generate a physical intercept. Any resistance would entail destruction at sea.

To establish a sea territory, a line was drawn to create a complete circle of three hundred miles' radius round the island of Labuan. From the northern curve of this circle a line was drawn right across the Pacific to Anchorage on the south coast of Alaska. A second was drawn from the southern arc of the Indonesian circle heading south-east across the Pacific to the coast of Ecuador.

The enclosed area was most of the Pacific Ocean. It included the entire western seaboard of Canada and the USA and Mexico down to Ecuador, including the Panama Canal.

There was no need to announce it yet, the White House had decided, but it was intended to monitor every ship in that triangle steaming east to the American coast. Anything leaving the triangle or heading to Asia would be left alone. The rest would be identified and checked out.

Thanks to years of pressure by a few bodies often dubbed cranky, there was one procedural ally. Major merchant-marine shipping lines had agreed to file destination plans, as airliners file flight plans, as a matter of routine. Seventy per cent of the vessels in the check-it-out zone would be on file and their owning companies could contact their captains. Under the new rules there was also an agreement that sea captains would always use a certain word, known only to their owners, if they were secure. Failure to use the agreed word could mean the captain was under duress.

It was seventy-two hours after the White House conference when the first KH-11 Keyhole satellite rolled on to its track in space and began to photograph the Indonesian circle. Its computers had been instructed to photograph, regardless of steaming direction, any merchant-marine vessel within a three-hundred-mile radius of Labuan Island. Computers obey instructions, so it did. As they began to photograph, the *Countess of Richmond*, heading due south through the Strait of Makassar, was 310 miles south of Labuan. It was not photographed.

* * *

358

From London the White House obsession with an attack from the Pacific was only half the picture. The warnings from the Edzell conference had been submitted in the UK and the USA to further scrutiny but the findings were broadly endorsed.

It took a long personal call on the hotline between Downing Street and the White House to conclude a concordat on the two most vital narrows east of Malta. The agreement provided that the Royal Navy, in partnership with the Egyptians, would monitor the southern end of the Suez Canal to intercept all ships save the very smallest coming up from Asia.

The US Navy's warships in the Persian Gulf, Arabian Sea and Indian Ocean would patrol the Strait of Hormuz. Here the threat would only be from a huge vessel capable of sinking itself in the deep-water channel running down the centre of the Strait. The principal traffic here was super-tankers, entering empty from the south, coming back low in the water and full of crude after loading at any of the score of sea islands scattered off Iran, the UAE, Qatar, Bahrain, Saudi Arabia and Kuwait.

The good news for the Americans was that the owning companies of such vessels are relatively few altogether, and ready to cooperate to prevent a disaster for all of them. Landing a party of US

Marines by Sea Stallion helicopter on the deck of a supertanker heading for the Strait but still three hundred miles short, and having a quick tour of the bridge, took very little time and did not slow the vessel at all.

As for threats two and three, every government in Europe with a major sea port was warned of the possible existence of a ghost ship under the command of terrorists. It was up to Denmark to protect Copenhagen; Sweden to look after Stockholm and Göteborg; Germany to watch out for anything entering Hamburg or Kiel; France was warned to defend Brest and Marseille. British navy aeroplanes out of Gibraltar started to patrol the narrows between the Pillars of Hercules, between the Rock and Morocco, to identify anything coming in from the Atlantic.

All the way over the Rockies Major Duval had put the Eagle through its paces and it had performed perfectly. Below him the weather had changed.

The cloudless blue skies of Arizona betrayed first a few wisps of mares' tail cloud lines, which thickened as he left Nevada for Oregon. When he crossed the Columbia River into Washington the cloud below him was solid from treetop height to twenty thousand feet and moving down from the Canadian border to the north. At thirty thousand feet he was still in clear blue sky, but the descent would involve a long haul through dense vapour. Two hundred miles out he called McChord AFB and asked for a ground-controlled descent to landing.

McChord asked him to stay out to the east, turn inbound over Spokane and descend on instructions. The Eagle was in the left-hand turn towards McChord when what was about to become the USAF's most expensive spanner slipped out of where it had lain jammed between two hydraulic lines in the starboard engine. When the Eagle levelled out, it fell into the blade of the turbofan.

The first result was a massive bang from somewhere deep in the guts of the starboard F-100 as the compressor blades, sharp as cleavers and spinning close to the speed of sound, began to shear off. Each sheared blade jammed among the rest. In both cockpits a blazing red light answered the yell from Nicky Johns of 'What the fuck was that?'

In front of him Larry Duval was listening to something inside his head screaming: 'Close it down.'

After years of flying Duval's fingers were doing the job almost unbidden: flicking off one switch after another, fuel, electric circuits, hydraulic lines. But the starboard engine was

361

blazing. The in-housing fire extinguishers operated automatically but were too late. The starboard F-100 was tearing itself to pieces in what is known as 'catastrophic engine failure'.

Behind Duval, the wizzo was telling McChord, 'Mayday, Mayday, Mayday, starboard engine on fire—'

He was interrupted by another roar from behind him. Far from shutting down, fragments of the starboard engine had torn through the fire-wall and were attacking the port side. More red lights blazed. The second had caught fire also. With reduced fuel, which he had, and one functioning engine, Larry Duval could have made it down. But with both of its engines dead, a modern fighter does not glide like those of long ago; it plunges like a bullet.

Captain Johns would tell the inquiry later that his pilot's voice remained calm and level. He had switched the radio to 'transmit' so that the air-traffic controller at McChord did not need to be informed; he was hearing it in real time.

'I have lost both engines,' said the major. 'Stand by to eject.'

The wizzo looked one last time at his instruments. Height: twenty-four thousand feet. Diving; dive steepening. Outside the sun still shone but the cloud bank was seething towards them. He glanced around, over his shoulder. The

Eagle was a torch, flaming from end to end. He heard the same calm voice up front.

'Eject. Eject.'

Both men reached down for the handle beside the seat and pulled. That was all they needed to do. Modern ejector seats are so automated that even if the airman is unconscious they will do everything for him.

Neither Larry Duval nor Nicky Johns actually saw their plane die. With seconds to spare their bodies were hurled upwards through the shattering canopy and into the freezing stratosphere. The seat retained their legs and arms so they would not flail and snap off. The seat protected their faces from the blast that could push their cheekbones through the skull.

Both falling ejectors stabilized with tiny drogues and plunged towards the ground. In a second they were lost in the cloud bank. Even when they were able to see through their visors, the two aircrew could only watch the wet grey cloud rushing past them.

The seats sensed when they were near enough to the ground to release their charges from their 'chutes'. The restraining straps just flicked open and the men, now separated by a mile from each other, fell out of the seats, which dropped into the landscape below.

The men's parachutes were also automatic. They

too deployed first with a small drogue to steady the falling men in the air, then with the main canopy. Each man felt the heaving jerk as a terminal velocity of 120 mph slowed to around fourteen.

They began to feel the intense cold through their light nylon flying suits and G-suits. They seemed to be in a weird wet, grey limbo between heaven and hell until they crashed into the topmost branches of pine and spruce.

In half darkness beneath the cloud base the major landed in a form of clearing, his fall cushioned by springy conifer branches lying flat on the ground. After several seconds dazed and winded, he released the main chute buckle at his midriff and stood up. Then he began to broadcast so the rescuers could get a fix on him.

Nicky Johns had also come down in trees, but not in a clearing; he was right in the thick of them. As he hit the branches he was drenched in the snow that fell off. He waited for the 'hit' of the ground, but it never came. Above him in the freezing gloom he could see that his canopy was caught in the trees. Below, he could make out the ground. Snow and pine needles, he thought, about fifteen feet down. He took a deep breath, hit the release buckle and fell.

With luck he would have landed and stood up. In fact he felt the left leg snap neatly at the shin as it slid between two stout branches under the snow. That told him that cold and shock would start to eat into his reserve without mercy. He too unhooked his transmitter and began to broadcast.

The Eagle had attempted to fly for a few seconds after its crew had left it. It turned its nose up, wallowed, tilted over, resumed its dive and, as it entered the cloud bank, simply blew up. The flames had reached the fuel tanks.

As it disintegrated both its engines tore themselves from their fixtures and fell away. Twenty thousand feet below, each engine, five tons of blazing metal roaring down at five hundred mph, hit the Cascades wilderness. One destroyed twenty trees. The other did more.

The CIA special ops officer who commanded the garrison on the Cabin took over two minutes to regain consciousness and pull himself off the floor of the chow room where he had been eating lunch. He was dazed and felt sick. He leaned against the wall of the log cabin amid the swirling dust and called names. He was answered by groans. Twenty minutes later he had made his inventory. The two men playing pool in the games room were dead. Three others were injured. The lucky ones had been those outside on a hiking break. They had been a hundred yards away when the meteorite, as they thought, hit the Cabin. When they had confirmed that of twelve CIA staffers two were dead, three needed emergency hospitalization, the two hikers were fine and the other five badly shaken, they checked on the prisoner.

They would later be accused of being slow on the uptake, but the inquiry found in the end that they were justified in looking out for themselves first. A glance through the peephole of the Afghan's room revealed there was too much light in there. When they burst in, the door from the living area to the walled exercise court was open. The room itself, being of reinforced concrete, had survived intact.

The wall of the compound was not so lucky. Concrete or not, the falling F-100 jet engine had taken a five-foot chunk out of the wall before ricocheting into the garrison quarters. And the Afghan was gone.

CHAPTER FIFTEEN

As the great American sea-trap closed around the Philippines, Borneo and eastern Indonesia, all the way across the Pacific to the US coast, the *Countess of Richmond* slipped out of the Flores Sea, through the Lombok Strait between Bali and Lombok, and into the Indian Ocean. Then she turned due west for Africa.

The distress call from the dying Eagle had been heard by at least three listeners. McChord AFB of course had it all on tape because they had actually been talking to the crew. The Naval Air Station at Whidbey Island, north of McChord, also kept a listening watch on Channel 16, and so did the US Coastguard unit up at Bellingham. Within seconds of the call they were in contact, to say they were standing by to triangulate on the positions of the downed aircrew.

The days of pilots bobbing helplessly in a dinghy or lying in a forest waiting to be found are long gone. Modern aircrew have a lifejacket with a state-of-the-art beacon, small but powerful, and a transmitter that permits in-voice communication.

The beacons were picked up at once and the three listening posts had the men located to a few yards. Major Duval was down in the heart of the state park and Captain Johns had fallen in the logging forest. Both were still closed for access owing to the winter.

The cloud cover right on top of the trees would prevent extraction by helicopter, the fastest and the favoured way. The cloud base would force an old-fashioned rescue. Off-road vehicles or half-tracked vehicles would take the rescue parties to the nearest point along one of the tracks; from there to the downed airmen it would be muscle and sweat all the way.

The enemy now was hypothermia, and in the case of Johns with his broken leg, trauma. The sheriff of Whatcom County radioed to say he had deputies ready to move and they would rendezvous in the small town of Glacier on the edge of the forest within thirty minutes. They were nearest to the wizzo, Nicky Johns, with his broken leg. A number of the loggers lived around Glacier and knew every logging road through the forest. The sheriff was given Johns's exact position to a few yards and set off.

To keep up the injured man's morale McChord patched the sheriff right through to the communicator on the wizzo's lifevest so that the sheriff could encourage the airman as they came nearer and nearer.

The Washington National Park Service opted for Major Duval. They had experience and to spare; every year they had to pull out the occasional camper who slipped and fell. They knew every road through the Park and, where the roads ran out, every trail. They went in with snowmobiles and quad bikes. As their man was not injured, a full stretcher service would hopefully not be necessary.

But as the minutes ticked by the body temperature of the airmen started to drop slowly for Duval but faster for Johns who could not move. The race was on to bring the two men gloves, boots, space blankets and piping hot soup before the cold beat them to it.

Nobody told the rescue parties, because nobody knew, that there was another man out in the Wilderness that day, and he was very dangerous indeed.

* * *

The saving grace for the CIA team at the shattered Cabin was that their communications had survived the hit. The commander only had one number to call but it was a good one. It went on a secure line to the desk of DDO Marek Gumienny at Langley. Three time zones east, just after four p.m., he took the call.

As he listened he went very quiet. He did not rant or rave, even though he was being told of a major Company disaster. Before his junior colleague in the Cascades Wilderness had finished, he was analysing the catastrophe. In freezing temperatures the two corpses might have to wait a while. The three injured needed urgent casevac. And the fugitive had to be hunted down.

'Can a helo get in there to reach you?' he asked.

'No, sir, we have cloud right to the treetops and threatening more snow.'

'What is your nearest town with a track leading to it?'

'It's called Mazama. It's outside the Wilderness but there is a fair-weather track from the town to Hart's Pass. That's a mile away. No track from there to here.'

'You are a covert research facility, understand? You have had a major accident. You need urgent help. Raise the sheriff at Mazama and get him to come in there for you with anything he has got.

Half-tracks, snowmobiles, off-roads as near as possible. Skis, snowshoes and sleds for the last mile. Get those men to hospital. Meanwhile, can you stay warm?'

'Yes, sir. Two rooms are shattered, but we have three sealed off. The central heating is down but we are piling logs on the fire.'

'Right. When the rescue party reaches you, lock everything down, smash all covert comms equipment, bring all codes with you and come out with the injured.'

'Sir?'

'Yes.'

'What about the Afghan?'

'Leave him to me.'

Marek Gumienny thought of the original letter John Negroponte had given him at the start of Operation Crowbar. Powers plenipotentiary. No limits. Time the army earned its tax dollars. He rang the Pentagon.

Thanks to years in the Company and the new spirit of information-sharing, he had close contacts with the Defense Intelligence Agency, and they in turn were best buddies with Special Forces. Twenty minutes later he learned he might have had his first break of a very bad day.

No more than four miles from McChord Air Force Base is the army's Fort Lewis. Though a huge army camp, there is a corner off-limits to

371

non-authorized personnel and this is the home of the First Special Forces Group, known to its few friends as Operational Detachment Group (OD) Alpha 143. The terminal '3' means a mountain company, or 'A' team. Its Ops Commander was Senior Captain Michael Linnett.

When the unit adjutant took the call from the Pentagon he could not be very helpful, even though he was speaking to a two-star general.

'Right now, sir, they are not on base. They are involved in a tactical exercise on the slopes of Mount Rainer.'

The Washington-based general had never heard of this bleak pinnacle way down south of Tacoma in Pierce County.

'Can you get them back to base by helicopter, Lieutenant?'

'Yessir, I believe so. The cloud base is just high enough.'

'Can you airlift them to a place called Mazama, close to Hart's Pass on the edge of the Wilderness?'

'I'll have to check that, sir.'

He was back on the line in three minutes. The general held on.

'No, sir. The cloud up there is right on the tree-tops and snow pending. To get up there means going by truck.'

'Well, get them there by the fastest possible route. You say they are on manoeuvre?'

'Yessir.'

'Do they have with them all they need to operate in the Pasayten Wilderness?'

'Everything for sub-zero rough-terrain operating, General.'

'Live ammunition?'

'Yessir. This was for a simulated terrorist hunt in Rainer National Park.'

'Well, it ain't simulated any more, Lieutenant. Get the whole unit to Mazama sheriff's office. Check with a CIA spook called Olsen. Stay in contact with Alpha at all times and report to me on progress.'

To save time Captain Linnett, apprised of some kind of emergency while he was descending Mount Rainer, asked for exfiltration by air. Fort Lewis had its own Chinook troop-carrier helicopter, which picked up the Alpha team from the empty visitor car park at the foot of the mountain thirty minutes later.

The Chinook took the team as far north as the snow clouds would allow and set them down on a small airfield west of Burlington. The truck had been heading there for an hour and they arrived almost at the same time.

From Burlington the Interstate 20 wound its bleak path along the Skagit River and into the Cascades. It is closed in winter to all but official and specially equipped traffic; the SF truck was equipped for every kind of terrain and a few not yet invented. But progress was slow. It took four hours until the exhausted driver crunched into the townlet of Mazama.

The CIA team was also exhausted, but at least their injured colleagues, doped with morphine, were in real ambulances heading south for a helicopter pick-up and a final transfer to Tacoma Memorial Hospital.

Olsen told Captain Linnett what he thought was enough. Linnett snapped that he was security cleared and insisted on more.

'This fugitive, has he got arctic clothing and footwear?'

'No. Hiking boots, warm trousers, a light quilted jacket.'

'No skis, snowshoes? Is he armed?'

'No, nothing like that.'

'It's dark already. Does he have night-vision goggles? Anything to help him move?'

'No, certainly not. He was a prisoner in close confinement.'

'He's toast,' said Linnett. 'In these temperatures, ploughing through a metre of snow with no compass, going round in circles. We'll get him.'

'There is just one thing. He's a mountain man. Born and raised in them.'

'Round here?'

'No. In the Tora Bora. He's an Afghan.'

Linnett stared in dumb amazement. He had fought in the Tora Bora. He had been in the first Afghan invasion when Coalition Special Forces, American and British, ranged through the Spin Ghar looking for a runaway party of Saudi Arabs, one of them six feet four inches tall. And he had been back to take part in Operation Anaconda. That had not gone well either. Some good men had been lost on Anaconda. Linnett had a score to settle with Pashtun from the Tora Bora.

'Saddle up,' he shouted and the ODA climbed back in their truck. It would take them up the remainder of the track to Hart's Pass. After that their transportation would go back three thousand years to the ski and the snowshoe.

As they left, the sheriff's radio brought the news that both airmen had been found and brought out, very cold but alive. Both were in hospital in Seattle. The news was good but a bit too late for a man called Lemuel Wilson.

The Anglo-American investigators of merchant marine who had taken over Operation Crowbar were still concentrating on threat one, the idea that Al-Qaeda might be planning to close down a vital world highway in the form of a narrow strait.

375

In that contingency the size of the vessel was paramount. The cargo was immaterial, save only that venting oil would make the job of demolition divers almost impossible. Enquiries were flying across the world to identify every vessel on the seas of huge tonnage.

Clearly the bigger the ship, the fewer there would be of them, and most would belong to respectable and gigantic companies. The principal five hundred ultra-large and very large crude carriers, the ULCCs and VLCCs, known to the public as supertankers, were checked and found to be unattacked. Then the tonnages were lowered in modules of ten thousand tonnes fully loaded. When all vessels of fifty thousand tonnes and up were accounted for, the 'strait blockage' panic began to subside.

Lloyd's Register is probably still the world's most comprehensive archive and the Edzell team set up a direct line to Lloyd's, which was constantly in use. On Lloyd's advice, they concentrated on vessels flying flags of convenience and those registered in 'dodgy' ports or owned by suspect proprietors. Both Lloyd's, and the Secret Intelligence Service's Anti-Terrorist (Marine) desk joined with the American CIA and Coastguard in slapping a 'no approach to coast' label on over two hundred vessels without their captains or owners being aware of it. But still nothing showed up to set the storm cones flying in the breeze.

Captain Linnett knew his mountains and was aware that a man with no specialist footwear, trying to progress through snow over ground riddled with unseen trees, roots, cracks, ditches, gullies and streams, would be lucky to make a heart-breaking half a mile per hour across country.

Such a man would probably stumble through the snow crust into a trickling rivulet and, with wet feet, start to lose body core temperature at an alarming rate, leading to hypothermia and frost-bite in the frozen toes.

Olsen's message from Langley had left no room for doubt; under no circumstances must the fugitive reach Canada, nor must he reach a functioning telephone. Just in case.

Linnett had few doubts. His target would wander in circles without a compass. He would stumble and fall at every second step. He could not see in the blackness under the trees where even the moon, had it not been hidden by twenty thousand feet of freezing cloud, could not penetrate.

True, the man had a five-hour head start; but even in a straight line, that would give him under three miles of ground covered. Special Forces men on skis could treble that, and if rocks and tree trunks forced the use of snowshoes, he could still double the speed of the fugitive.

He was right about the skis. From the drop-off point of the truck at the end of the track, he reached the wrecked CIA Cabin in under an hour. He and his men examined it briefly to see if the fugitive had come back to rifle it for better equipment. There was no sign of that. The two bodies, rigid in the cold, were laid out, hands crossed on chests in the now freezing refectory, safe from roaming animals. They would have to wait for the cloud to lift and a helicopter to land.

There are twelve men in an 'A' team; Linnett was the only officer and his Number Two was a chief warrant officer. The other ten were all senior enlisted men, the lowest rank being a staff sergeant. They broke down into two engineers (for demolition), two radio operators, two 'medics', a team sergeant (not one but two specialities), an intelligence sergeant and two snipers. While Linnett was inside the wrecked Cabin his team sergeant, who was an expert tracker, scouted the ground outside.

The threatening snow had not fallen; the area around the helipad and the front door, where the rescue team from Mazama had arrived, was a mush of snowshoe marks. But from the shattered compound wall a single trail of footprints led away due north.

Coincidental? thought Linnett. It was the one direction the fugitive must not take. It led to Canada, twenty-two miles away. But, for the Afghan, forty-four hours of hiking. He would never make it, even if he could keep in a straight line. Anyway, the Alpha team would get him halfway there.

It took another hour to cover the next mile, on snowshoes. That was when they found the other cabin. No one had mentioned the other two or three cabins that were permitted in the Pasayten Wilderness because they pre-dated the building prohibition. And this one had been broken into. The shattered triple-glazing and the rock beside the gaping hole left no doubt.

Captain Linnett went in first, carbine forward, safety catch off. Round the edges of the shattered glass two men gave cover. It took them less than a minute to ensure there was no one present, either in the cabin, the adjacent log store or the empty garage. But the signs were everywhere. Linnett tried the light switch, but the power clearly came from a generator when the owner was in residence, and that was closed down behind the garage. They relied on their flashlights.

Beside the deep fireplace in the main sitting area was a box of matches and several long tapers, clearly for lighting the logs in the grate;

also a bundle of candles in case the generator failed. The intruder had used both to find his way around. Captain Linnett turned to one of his comms sergeants.

'Raise the county sheriff and find out who owns this place,' he said. He began to explore. Nothing seemed to be smashed, but everything had been rifled.

'It's a surgeon from Seattle,' reported the sergeant. 'Vacations up here in the summer, closes it all down in the fall.'

'Name and phone number. He must have left them with the sheriff's office.' When the sergeant had them he was told to contact Fort Lewis, have them call the surgeon at his Seattle home and put him on a direct patch-through. A surgeon was a lucky break; surgeons have pagers in case of an emergency. This situation definitely rated.

The ghost ship never went near Surabaya. There was no consignment of expensive oriental silks to be taken aboard, and the six apparent sea containers on the *Countess of Richmond*'s foredeck were in place anyway.

She took the route south of Java, passed Christmas Island and headed out into the Indian Ocean. For Mike Martin the onboard routines became a ritual.

The psychopath Ibrahim remained mainly in

his cabin and the good news was that most of the time he was violently ill. Of the remaining seven men, the engineer tended his engines, set at maximum speed regardless of fuel use. Where the *Countess* was going she would need no fuel for a return journey.

For Martin the twin enigmas remained unanswered. Where was she going, and what explosive power lay beneath her decks? No one seemed to know, with the possible exception of the chemical engineer. But he never spoke and the subject was never raised.

The radio expert kept a listening watch and must have learned of a sea search taking place right across the Pacific and at the entrances to the Strait of Hormuz and the Suez Canal. He may have reported this to Ibrahim but made no mention of it to the rest.

The other five men took turns in the galley to turn out plate after plate of cold tinned food, and also took turns at the wheel. The navigator set the heading – always west, then south of due west to the Cape of Good Hope.

For the rest, they prayed five times a day according to scripture, read the Koran yet again and stared at the sea.

Martin considered attempting to take over the ship. He had no weapon other than the chance to steal a kitchen knife, and he would have to kill seven men, one of whom, Ibrahim, he had to presume had one or more firearms. And they were scattered from the engine room to the radio shack to the forecastle at the bow. If and when they came close to a clear target on shore he knew he would have to do it. But across the Indian Ocean he bided his time.

He did not know whether his message in the divebag had ever been found or was tossed into some attic unread; and he did not know he had triggered a global ship-hunt.

'This is Dr Berenson, whom am I talking with?'

Michael Linnett took the speaker from the set on the sergeant's back and lied.

'I am with the sheriff's office at Mazama,' he said. 'Right now I am in your cabin in the Wilderness. I'm sorry to have to tell you there has been a break-in.'

'Hell, no. Dammit, is there damage done?' the tinny voice speaking from Seattle asked.

'He broke in by smashing the main front window with a rock, doctor. That seems to be the only structural damage. I just want to check on theft. Did you have any firearms here?'

'Absolutely not. I keep two hunting rifles and a scatter gun, but I bring them out with me in the fall.'

'OK, now, clothing. Do you have a closet with heavy winter clothing?'

'Sure. It's a walk-in right beside the bedroom door.'

Captain Linnett nodded to his team sergeant who led the way by flashlight. The closet was spacious, full of winter kit.

'There should be my pair of arctic snow boots, quilted pants and a parka with zippered hood.'

All gone.

'Any skis or snowshoes, doctor?'

'Sure, both. In the same cupboard.'

Also gone.

'Any weapons at all? Compass?'

The big Bowie knife in its sheath should have been hanging inside the closet door and the compass and flashlight should have been in the drawers of the desk. They were all taken. That apart, the fugitive had ransacked the kitchen, but there had been no fresh food left there to rot. A newly opened, and emptied, tin of baked beans and the can opener lay on the worktop with two empty cans of soda. There was also an empty pickle jar that had been full of quarters but no one knew that.

'Thanks, doc. I'd get up here when the weather clears with a team for a new window, and file a loss claim.'

The Alpha leader cut the connection and looked round at his unit.

'Let's go,' was all he said. He knew the cabin and what the Afghan had taken shortened the odds and they could even now be against him. He put the fugitive, who must have spent over an hour in the cabin to Linnett's thirty minutes, at two to three hours ahead, but now moving much faster.

Swallowing his pride he decided to bring up some cavalry. He called a pause and spoke to Fort Lewis again.

'Tell McChord I want a Spectre and I want it now. Engage all the authority you need; Pentagon if you have to. I want it over the Cascades and talking to me direct.'

While waiting for their new ally to show up, the twelve men of Alpha 143 pressed on hard, pushing the pace. The sergeant-tracker was at point, his flashlight picking up the marks of the snowshoes of the fugitive in the frozen snow. They were pushing the pace, but they were carrying much more equipment than the man ahead of them. Linnett estimated they had to be keeping up, but were they gaining? Then the snow started. It was a blessing and a curse. As the deceptively gentle flakes drifted down from the conifers around them, they covered the rocks and stumps, permitting another quick pause to switch from shoes to the faster skis. They also wiped out the trail.

Linnett needed a guiding hand from heaven and it came just after midnight in the form of a Lockheed Martin AC-130 Hercules gunship, circling at twenty thousand feet, above the cloud layer but looking straight through it.

Among the many toys that Special Forces are given to play with the Spectre gunship is, from the viewpoint of the enemy on the ground, about as nasty as it gets.

The original Hercules transport plane has been gutted and her innards replaced with a cockpit-to-tail array of technology designed to locate, target and kill an opponent on the ground. It is seventy-two million dollars' worth of pure bad news.

In its first 'locate' role it does not depend on daylight or dark, wind or rain, snow or hail. Mr Raytheon has been kind enough to provide a synthetic-aperture radar and infra-red thermal imager which can pick out any figure in a land-scape that emits body heat. Nor is the image a vague blur; it is clear enough to differentiate between a four-legged beast and a two-legged one. But it still could not work out the weirdness of Mr Lemuel Wilson.

He too had a cabin, just outside the Pasayten Wilderness on the lower slopes of Mount

Robinson. Unlike the Seattle surgeon, he prided himself on his capacity to over-winter up there, for he had no alternative metropolitan home.

So he survived without electricity, using a roaring log fire for heat and kerosene lamps for lighting. Each summer he hunted game and air-dried the meat strips for winter. He cut his own logs and gathered in forage for his tough mountain pony. But he had another hobby.

He had enough CB equipment, powered by a tiny generator, to spend his winter hours scanning the wavebands of the sheriff, the emergency services and the public utilities. That was how he heard the reports of a two-man aircrew down in the Wilderness and professional teams struggling towards the spot.

Lemuel Wilson was proud to call himself a concerned citizen. As so often, the authorities preferred the term 'interfering busybody'. Hardly had the two airmen broadcast their plight, and the authorities had replied with their exact positions, than Lemuel Wilson had saddled up and ridden out. He intended to cross the southern half of the Wilderness to reach the Park and rescue Major Duval.

His band-scanning equipment was too cumbersome to bring along, so he never heard the two aviators were rescued anyway. But he did make human contact.

He did not see the man come at him. One second he was urging his horse through a deeper than usual snowdrift, the next a bank of snow came up to meet him. But the snow bank was a man in a silver space-age-material quilted two-piece.

There was nothing space age about the Bowie knife, invented around the time of the siege of the Alamo and still very efficient. One arm round his neck dragged him off his horse; as he crashed down the blade entered his rib cage from the back and sliced open his heart.

A thermal imager is fine for detecting body heat, but Lemuel Wilson's corpse, dropped into a crevasse ten yards from where he died, lost its heat fast. By the time the AC-130 Spectre began its circling mission high above the Cascades thirty minutes later, Lemuel Wilson did not show up at all.

'This is Spectre Echo Foxtrot, calling Team Alpha, do you read me, Alpha?'

'Strength five,' reported Captain Linnett. 'We are twelve on skis down here; can you see us?'

'Smile nicely and I'll take your picture,' said the infra-red operator four miles above them.

'Comedy comes later,' said Linnett. 'About three miles due north of us is a fugitive. Single man, heading north on skis. Confirm?'

There was a pause, a long pause.

'Negative. No such image,' said the voice in the sky.

'There must be,' argued Linnett. 'He is up ahead of us somewhere.'

The last of the maple and tamarack was well behind them. They emerged from the forest to a bare scree, always climbing north, and the snow fell straight on them without being filtered by branches. Way behind in the darkness stood Lake Mountain and Monument Peak. His men were looking like spectral figures, white zombies in a white landscape. If he was having trouble, so was the Afghan. There was only one explanation for the no-image scenario: the Afghan had taken shelter in a cave or snow hole. The overhang would mask the heat escape. So he was closing on the fugitive. The skis were running easily across the shoulder of the mountain and there was more forest up ahead.

The Spectre fixed Linnett's position to the yard. Twelve miles to the Canadian border. Five hours to dawn or what passed for dawn in this land of snow, peaks, rocks and trees.

Linnett gave it another hour. The Spectre circled and watched but saw nothing to report.

'Check again,' asked Captain Linnett. He was beginning to think something had gone wrong. Had the Afghan died up here? Possible, and that would explain the absence of heat signature. Crouching in a cave? Possible too, but he would die in there or come out and run. And then . . .

Izmat Khan, urging the feisty but tired horse off the scree and into the forest, had actually lengthened his lead. The compass told him he was still going north, the angle of the horse beneath him that he was climbing.

'I am scanning an arc subtending ninety degrees with you at the point,' said the imager-operator. 'Right up to the border. In that arc I can see eight animals. Four deer, two black bear that are very faint because they are hibernating in deep cover, what looks like a marauding mountain lion and a single moose ambling north. About four miles ahead of you.'

The surgeon's arctic clothing was simply too good. The horse was sweating as it neared exhaustion and showed up clearly, but the man on top of it, leaning forward along its neck to urge it onwards, was so well muffled he blended with the animal.

'Sir,' said one of the engineer sergeants, 'I'm from Minnesota.'

'Save your problems for the chaplain,' snapped Linnett.

'What I mean, sir,' said the snow-caked face beside him, 'is that moose do not move up into the mountains in weather like this. They come down to the valley to forage for lichen. It cannot be a moose.'

Linnett called a halt. It was welcome. He stared at the falling snow ahead. He had not the faintest idea how the man had done it. Another isolated cabin, maybe, with an over-wintering idiot with a stable. Somehow the Afghan had got himself a horse and was riding away from him.

Four miles ahead, back in deep forest, Izmat Khan, who had ambushed Lemuel Wilson, was himself ambushed. The cougar was old, a bit slow for deer, but cunning and very hungry. It came down from a ledge between two trees, and the pony would have smelled it but for its own exhaustion.

The first the Afghan knew, something fast and tawny had hit the horse and it was going down sideways. The rider had time to grab Wilson's rifle from the sleeve alongside the pommel and go backwards over the rump. He landed, turned, aimed and fired.

He had been lucky the mountain lion had gone for the horse and not himself, but he had lost his mount. The animal was still alive, but ripped around the head and shoulders by claws with 135 pounds of angry muscle behind them. It was not going to get up. He used a second bullet to finish its misery. The horse crumpled, lying half across the body of the cougar. It did not matter to the Afghan, but the torso and front legs of the cougar were under the horse.

He unhitched the snowshoes from behind the saddle, fitted them over his boots, shouldered the rifle, checked the compass and moved forward. A hundred yards from him was a large rock overhang. He paused under it for a brief respite from the snow. He did not know it, but it masked his heat-source.

'Take out the moose,' said Captain Linnett. 'I think it's a horse with the fugitive on it.'

The operator studied his image again.

'You're right,' he said. 'I can see six legs. He's paused for a rest. Next circuit, down he goes.'

The 'destroy' section of the Spectre's role is provided by three systems. Heaviest is the M102 105-mm howitzer which is so powerful that to use it on a single human being would be a tad excessive.

Next down comes the 40-mm Bofors cannon, derived, long ago, from the Swedish anti-aircraft weapon, a fast repeater with enough muscle to rip buildings or tanks to fragments. The Spectre crew, told their target was a man on a horse, chose the Gau-12/U Gatling gun. This horror fires 1,800 rounds per minute and each round is a 25-mm (one-inch diameter) slug, a single one of which will pull a human body apart. So intense is the fire of the rotating five-barrel gun that if used on a football pitch for thirty seconds nothing much bigger than a dormouse will be left alive. And the mouse will die of shock.

The maximum altitude for the gun is twelve thousand feet so in the circling turn the Spectre dropped to ten thousand, locked on and fired for ten seconds, loosing off three hundred rounds at the body of the horse in the forest.

'There's nothing left,' remarked the imager-operator. 'Man and beast, both gone.'

'Thank you, Echo Foxtrot,' said Linnett. 'We'll take over now.' The Spectre, mission accomplished, returned to McChord AFB.

The snow stopped, the skis hissed over the new powder, making the sort of progress that skis ought to make with a skilled athlete on them, and the Alpha team came across the remains of the horse. Few fragments were bigger than a man's arm but they were definitely horse, not human. Except the bits with tawny fur.

Linnett spent ten minutes looking for pieces of arctic clothing, boots, femurs, skull, Bowie knife, beard or snowshoes.

The skis were lying there, but one was broken. That had been done by the falling horse. There was a sheepskin sleeve but no rifle. No snowshoes, no Afghan.

Two hours to dawn and it had become a race. One man on snowshoes, twelve on skis. All exhausted, all desperate. The Alpha team had their GPS positioning system. As the sky lightened fractionally in the east the team sergeant murmured: 'Border half a mile.'

They arrived twenty minutes later on a bluff overlooking a valley running from their left to right. Below was a logging road that formed the Canadian border. Right across from them was another bluff with a cleared area containing a cluster of log cabins, a facility for Canadian lumberjacks when the timber concessions resumed after the snows.

Linnett crouched, steadied his forearms and studied the landscape through binoculars. Nothing moved. The light factor increased.

Unbidden, his snipers eased their weapons from the sleeves that had contained them throughout the mission, fixed their scopes, inserted one shell each and lay down to stare across the gulf through their telescopes.

By the norms of soldiering snipers are a strange breed. They never get near the men they kill, yet they see them with a clarity and an apparent proximity greater than anyone else today. With hand-to-hand combat almost extinct, most men die not by the hand of their enemy but by his computer. They are blown away by a missile fired a continent away or from somewhere under the sea. They are destroyed by a smart bomb loosed by an aircraft so high they neither see nor hear it. They die because someone fires a shell from two counties away. At the nearest, their killers, crouching behind a machine gun in a swooping helicopter, see them only as vague shapes, running, hiding, trying to fire back. But not as real humans.

That is how the sniper sees them. Lying in total silence, utterly immobile, he sees his target as a man with three days' stubble, a man who stretches and yawns, who spoons beans out of a can, unzips his fly or simply stands and stares at a lens a mile away that he cannot see. And then he dies. Snipers are special – inside the head.

They also live in a private world. So total does the obsession with accuracy become that they lapse into a silence peopled only by the weights of projectile heads, the power of various powder loads, how much a bullet will wind-drift, how far it will drop over various distances, whether yet another tiny improvement can be made to the rifle.

Like all specialists they have their passions for rival pieces of equipment. Some snipers like a really tiny bullet like the M700 round out of the Remington .308, a slug so small that it has to be sheathed in a detachable sleeve to go down the barrel at all.

Others stay with the M21, the sniper version of

the M14 standard combat rifle. Heaviest of all is the Barrett Light Fifty, a monster that sends a bullet like a human forefinger over a mile with enough speed times weight to cause a human body to explode.

Lying prone at Captain Linnett's feet was his leading sniper, Master Sergeant Peter Bearpaw. He was a half-blood Santee Sioux with a Hispanic mother. He came from the slums of Detroit and the army was his life. He had high cheekbones and eyes that sloped like a wolf. And he was the best marksman in the Green Berets.

What he cradled as he squinted across the valley was the Cheyenne .408 by CheyTac of Idaho. It was a more recent development than the others, but over three thousand rounds on the range it had become his weapon of choice. It was a bolt-action rifle, which he appreciated because the total lock-down of a closed bolt give that tiny extra stability at the moment of detonation.

He had inserted the single slug, very long and slim, and he had burnished and buffed the nose tip to eradicate the tiniest vibration in flight. Along the top of the breech ran a Jim Leatherwood ×24 scope sight.

'I have him, Captain,' he whispered.

The binoculars had missed the fugitive, but the scope sight had found him. Set among the cabins across the valley, encased on three sides by timber, with one single glass-panelled door, was a phone booth.

'Tall, long shaggy hair, bushy black beard?'

'Roger that.'

'What's he doing?'

'He is in a phone booth, sir.'

Izmat Khan had had little communication with his fellow inmates at Guantanamo, but one with whom he had spent many months in the same 'solitary' block had been a Jordanian who had fought in Bosnia in the mid-nineties before returning to become a trainer in the AQ camps. He was hardline.

As security slackened around the Christmas period, they found they could whisper from one cell to another. If you ever get out of here, the Jordanian told him, I have a friend. We were in the camps together. He is safe; he will help a True Believer. Mention my name.

There was a name. And a phone number. Izmat Khan did not know where it was. He was not quite sure of the complexities of Subscriber Trunk Dial, for which he actually had enough quarters, but, worse, he did not know the overseas dial code out of Canada. So he punched in a quarter and asked for the operator.

'What number are you trying, caller?' said the unseen Canadian telephonist. Slowly, in halting

English, he pronounced the figures he had so painstakingly memorized.

'That is a UK number,' said the operator. 'Are you using US quarters?'

'Yes.'

'That's acceptable. Put in eight of them and I will connect you. When you hear the pips put in more if you wish to continue the call.'

'Have you acquired the target?' asked Linnett.

'Yes, sir.'

'Take the shot.'

'He's in Canada, sir.'

'Take the shot, sergeant.'

Peter Bearpaw took a slow, calm breath, held it inside, and squeezed. The range was a still-air 2,100 yards on his range-meter, well over a mile.

Izmat Khan was pushing quarters into the slot. He was not looking up. The glass front of the booth disintegrated into pinpricks of perspex and the bullet took away the occiput from the rest of his head.

The operator was as patient as she could be. The man down in the logging camp had inserted only two quarters, then left the handset hanging and apparently left the booth. Finally she had no choice but to hang up on him and cancel the call.

Because of the sensitivity of the cross-border shot, no official report was ever made.

Captain Linnett reported to his commanding

officer who told Marek Gumienny in Washington. Nothing more was heard.

The body was found in the thaw when the lumberjacks returned. The hanging phone was disconnected. The coroner could do little but record an open verdict. The man wore US clothing but in the border country that was not odd. He had no ID; no one recognized him locally.

Unofficially most people around the coroner's office presumed the man had been the victim of a tragic stray shot from a deer hunter, another death from careless shooting or ricochet. He was buried in an unmarked grave.

Because no one south of the border wanted to make waves, it was never thought to ask what number the fugitive had asked for. Even to make the enquiry would give away the source of the shot. So it was not made.

In fact the number he wanted was that of a small apartment off-campus near Aston University in Birmingham. It was the home of Dr Ali Aziz al-Khattab, and the phone was on intercept by Britain's MI5. All they were waiting for was enough evidence to justify a raid and arrest. They would get it a month later. But that morning the Afghan was trying to call the only man west of Suez who knew the name of the ghost ship.

CHAPTER SIXTEEN

After two weeks enthusiasm for the hunt for a seemingly non-existent ghost ship was starting to fade and the mood came from Washington.

How much time, trouble and treasure could be expended on a vague scrawl on a boarding card stuffed into a divebag on an island no one had ever heard of? Marek Gumienny had flown to London to confer with Steve Hill when the SIS expert in maritime terrorism, Sam Seymour, called up from the Ipswich HQ of *Lloyd's Register* and made matters worse. He had changed his mind. Hill ordered him to London to explain.

'With hindsight,' said Seymour, 'the option of Al-Qaeda seeking to use a huge blocking ship to close down a vital sea highway to wreck global trade was always the likeliest option. But it was never the only one.'

'What makes you think it was the wrong path to go?' asked Marek Gumienny.

'Because, sir, every single vessel in the world big enough to achieve that has been checked out. They are all safe. That leaves options two and three which are almost interchangeable but with different targets. I think we should now look at three: mass murder in a seashore city. Bin Laden's public switch to economic targets could have been a hoax, or he has changed his mind.'

'OK, Sam, convince me. Steve and I both have political masters demanding results or our heads. What kind of ship if not a blocking vessel?'

'For threat number three we do not look at the ship so much as the cargo. It need not be large so long as it is absolutely deadly. Lloyd's have a hazardous cargo division – obviously, it changes the premium.'

'Ammunition ship?' asked Hill. 'Another Halifax wipe-out?'

'According to the boffins, military ordnance simply does not explode like that any more. The modern stuff needs huge provocation to go off inside the hull. You'd get worse from an exploding firework factory, but it would not begin to deserve the word "spectacular" as in Nine/Eleven. The Bhopal chemical leak was far worse and that was dioxin, a deadly weedkiller.'

'So, a tanker-truck driving dioxin into Park Avenue and completing the job with Semtex,' suggested Hill.

'But these chemicals are closely guarded inside their manufacturing and storage base,' objected Gumienny. 'How do they get the cargo with no one noticing?'

'And we were specifically told a ship would be the carrier,' said Seymour. 'Any hijacking of such a cargo would create immediate retaliation.'

'Except in some parts of the Third World that are virtually lawless,' said Gumienny.

'But these ultra-lethal toxins are not made in such places any more, not even for labour-cost savings, sir.'

'So, we are back to a ship?' said Hill. 'Another exploding oil tanker?'

'Crude oil does not explode,' Seymour pointed out. 'When the *Torrey Canyon* was ripped open southwest of the English coast it took phosphorus bombs to persuade the oil to ignite and burn off. A vented oil tanker will only cause eco-damage, not mass murder. But a quite small gas tanker could do it. Liquid gas, massively concentrated for transportation.'

'Natural gas, liquid form?' asked Gumienny. He was trying to think how many ports in the USA imported concentrates of gas for industrial power, and the number was becoming unsettling. But surely these docking facilities were miles from massed humanity?

'Liquid natural gas, known as LNG, is hard to ignite,' Seymour countered. 'It is stored at minus two hundred and fifty-six degrees Fahrenheit in special double-hulled vessels. Even if you took one over, the stuff would have to leak into the atmosphere for hours before it became combustible. But according to the eggheads there is one that frightens the hell out of them. LPG. Liquid Petroleum Gas.

'It is so awful that a quite small tanker, if torched within ten minutes of catastrophic rupture, would unleash the power of thirty Hiroshima bombs. It would be the biggest non-nuclear explosion on this planet.'

There was total silence in the room above the Thames. Steve Hill rose, strolled to the window and looked down at the river flowing past in the April sunshine.

'In layman's language, what have you come here to say, Sam?'

'I think we have been looking for the wrong ship in the wrong ocean. Our only break is that this is a tiny and very specialist market. But the biggest importer of LPG is the USA. I know there is a mood in Washington that all this may be a wild-goose chase. I think we should go the last mile. The USA can check out every LPG tanker expected in her waters, and not just from the Far East. And stop them until boarded. From Lloyd's I can check out every other LPG cargo world-wide; from any point in the compass.'

Marek Gumienny took the next flight back to Washington. He had conferences to attend and work to do. As he flew out of Heathrow the *Countess of Richmond* came round Cape Agulhas, South Africa, and entered the Atlantic.

She had made good speed and her navigator, one of the three Indonesians, estimated the Agulhas Current and the north-running Benguela Current would give her an extra day and plenty of time to reach her intended destination.

Further out into the seas off the Cape, and on into the Atlantic, other ships were moving from the Indian Ocean to head for Europe or North America. Some were huge ore carriers; others general cargo ships bringing the ever-increasing amount of Asian goods to both western continents as marketers 'outsourced' their manu-facturing bases to the low-cost workshops of the East. Others still were supertankers too big even for the Suez Canal, their computers following the hundred-fathom line from the east to the west while their crews played cards.

They were all noted. High above, out of sight

and mind, the satellites drifted across inner space, their cameras passing back to Washington every line of their structure and the names on their sterns. More, under recent legislation they all carried transponders emitting their individual call-sign to the listening ears. Each identification was checked out, and that included the *Countess of Richmond*, vouched for by Lloyd's and Siebart and Abercrombie as being a Liverpool-registered small freighter bringing a legitimate cargo on a foreseen route from Surabaya to Baltimore. For the USA there was no point in probing deeper; she was thousands of miles from the American coast.

Within hours of the return of Marek Gumienny to Washington changes were made to the US precautions. In the Pacific the check-out-and-examine cordon was brought to a thousand-mile band off the coast. A similar cordon was established in the Atlantic from Labrador to Puerto Rico and across the Caribbean Sea to the Yucatan Peninsula in Mexico.

Without fuss or announcement the emphasis abandoned the giant tankers and freighters (which by then had all been checked) and looked hard at the scores of smaller tankers that ply the seas from Venezuela to the St Lawrence River. Every P-3 Orion available was pressed into coastal patrol, flying over hundreds of thousands of square miles of tropical and subtropical sea looking for small tankers, and especially for those bearing gas.

American industry cooperated to the full, supplying details of every cargo expected, where and when due. The data from industry was cross-indexed with the sightings at sea and they all checked out. Gas tankers were permitted to arrive and dock, but only after taking on board a posse of US Navy, Marines or Coast Guards to escort them in under guard, from a point two hundred miles out.

The *Doña Maria* was back in Port of Spain when the two terrorists she harboured in her crew saw the signal they had been briefed to expect. As instructed, when they saw the signal they acted.

The Republic of Trinidad and Tobago is a major supplier of petrochemical products across a wide spectrum to the United States. The *Doña Maria* was berthed at the offshore sea island, the tank farm where tankers large and small could approach, take cargo on board and leave without ever approaching the city itself.

Doña Maria was one of the smaller tankers, a member of that fleet of vessels that service the islands whose facilities neither need nor can accommodate the giants. The big vessels are wont to bring in the Venezuelan crude, which is refined down to its various 'fractions' at the onshore refinery, then piped out to the sea island for loading into the onward handlers.

Along with two other small tankers, the *Doña Maria* was at a specially remote section of the tank farm. Her cargo after all was liquefied petroleum gas, and no one wanted to be too close during the loading. It was late afternoon when she was finished and Captain Montalban prepared her for sea.

There were still two hours of tropical daylight left when she slipped her mooring lines and eased away from the jetty. A mile offshore she passed close to a rigid inflatable launch in which four men sat with fishing rods. It was the awaited sign.

The two Indians left their posts, ran below to their lockers and returned with handguns. One went to the waist of the tanker, where the scuppers were closest to the water and the men would board. The other went to the bridge and pointed his gun straight at the temple of Captain Montalban.

'Do nothing, please, Captain,' he said with great courtesy. 'There is no need to slow down. My friends will board in a few minutes. Do not attempt to broadcast or I will have to shoot you.'

The captain was simply too amazed to fail to

obey. As he recovered he glanced at the radio at one side of the bridge but the Indian caught his glance and shook his head. At that, all resistance was snuffed out. Minutes later the four terrorists were aboard and opposition became futile.

The last man out of the inflatable slashed it with a carving knife and it sank in the wake when the painter was released. The other three men had already hefted their canvas grips and stepped over the spaghetti-mix of pipes, tubes and tank hatches that define a tanker's foredeck as they made their way aft.

They appeared on the bridge seconds later: two Algerians and two Moroccans, the ones Dr Al-Khattab had sent over a month earlier. They spoke only Moorish Arabic but the two Indians, still courteous, translated. The four South American crewmen were to be summoned to the foredeck and would wait there. A new sea course would be calculated and adhered to.

An hour after dark the four crewmen were coldly murdered and tossed overboard after a length of chain from the forward locker had been wired to each body's ankle. If Captain Montalban had had any spirit to resist left in him, that was the end of it. The executions were very mechanical; the two Algerians had, back at home, been in the AIG, the Armed Islamic Group, and had slaughtered hundreds of helpless *fellagha*, outback farmers whose mass murder was simply a way of sending a message to the government in Algiers. Men, women, children, sick and old, they had killed them all many times, so four sailors was a formality.

Through the night the *Doña Maria* steamed north, but no longer towards her scheduled destination of Puerto Rico. To her port side was the expanse of the Caribbean basin, unbroken all the way to Mexico. To starboard, quite close, were the two chains called the Windward and Leeward Islands, whose warm seas are often thought of only as vacation targets but are alive with hundreds of small tramps and tankers who keep the islands victualled and alive for the tourists.

Into this blizzard of coastal freighters and islands the *Doña Maria* would disappear and remain disappeared until she was logged overdue at Puerto Rico.

When the *Countess of Richmond* reached the doldrums the sea calmed and Yusuf Ibrahim emerged from his cabin. He was pale and drained by nausea but the hate-filled black eyes were the same as he gave his orders. The crew brought out from its storage place in the engine room a twenty-foot inflatable speedboat. When it was fully rigid, it was suspended from the two davits above the stern.

It took six men, sweating and grunting, to bring up the 100-hp outboard engine from below and fix it to the rear of the speedboat. Then it was winched down into the gentle swell beneath the stern.

Fuel tanks were lowered and hooked up. After several false starts the engine coughed into life. The Indonesian navigator was at the helm and took the speedboat away for a fast circle round the *Countess*.

Finally the other six men descended a ship's ladder over the gunwales to join him, leaving only the crippled killer at the helm. It was evident this was a dress rehearsal.

The point of the exercise was to allow the cameraman, Suleiman, to be taken three hundred yards from the freighter, turn and photograph her with his fully digital equipment. When linked through his laptop to the Mini-M sat-phone, his images could be transmitted to another website on the other side of the world for recording and broadcast.

Mike Martin knew what he was watching. For terrorism the internet and cyberspace have become must-have propaganda weapons. Every atrocity that can be read about in a newscast is good; every atrocity that can be seen by millions of Muslim youths in seventy countries is gold dust. This is where the recruits come from – actually seeing it happen and lusting to imitate.

At Forbes Castle Martin had watched the video recordings out of Iraq, with the suicide bombers grinning into the lens before driving away to die on camera. In such cases the cameraman survived; in the case of the circling speedboat it was clear that the target would have to be in vision as well, and photography would continue until the boat and its seven men were wiped out. Only Ibrahim, it seemed, would stay at the helm.

But he could not know when and where, or what horror lay inside the sea containers. He considered one possibility: being first back on the *Countess*, casting the inflatable adrift, killing Ibrahim and taking over the freighter. But there would be no such chance. The speedboat was so fast that the six men would be swarming over the rail in seconds.

When the exercise was over the speedboat was swung empty from the davits where it looked like any other ship's dinghy, the engineer increased power and the *Countess* headed northwest to skirt the coast of Senegal.

Recovered from his nausea, Yusuf Ibrahim spent more time on the bridge or in the wardroom where the crew ate together. The atmosphere was already hyper-tense and his presence made it more so.

All eight men on board had made their decision to die *shahid*, a martyr. But that did not prevent the waiting and the boredom tearing at their nerves. Only constant prayer and the obsessive reading of the Holy Koran enabled them to stay calm and true to the belief in what they were doing.

No one but the explosives engineer and Ibrahim knew what lay beneath the steel containers that covered the foredeck of the *Countess of Richmond* from just in front of the bridge almost to the bow. And only Ibrahim appeared to know their eventual destination and planned target. The other seven had to take on trust the pledges that their glory would be everlasting.

Martin had realized within hours of the mission commander joining them that he was constantly the object of Ibrahim's blank and crazy stare. He would not have been human if the phenomenon had not rattled him.

Disquieting questions began to haunt him. Had Ibrahim after all seen Izmat Khan in Afghanistan? Was he about to be asked some questions he simply could not answer? Had he slipped up, even by a few words, in the relentless reciting of the prayers? Would Ibrahim test him by asking for the recital of passages he had not studied?

He was in fact part-right, part-wrong. The Jordanian psychopath across the mess table had never seen Izmat Khan though he had heard of the legendary Taliban fighter. And there had been no mistakes in his prayers. He simply hated the Pashtun for his reputation in combat, something he had never acquired. Out of his hatred was born a desire that the Afghan should after all be a traitor, so that he could be unmasked and killed.

But he kept his rage under control for one of the oldest reasons in the world. He was afraid of the mountain man; and even though he carried a handgun in a sash under his robe, and was sworn to die, he could not suppress his awe of the man from the Tora Bora. So he brooded, stared, waited and kept his counsel.

For a second time the West's search for the ghost ship, even if it existed, had run into complete frustration. Steve Hill was being bombarded with requirements for information, anything, to appease the frustration that went right up to Downing Street.

The Controller Middle East could offer no resolution to the four questions that were raining upon him from the British prime minister and the

US presidency. Does this ship exist at all? If so, what is it, where is it and which city is its target? The daily conferences were becoming purgatory.

The Chief of the SIS, never known or greeted by any term other than 'C', was steely in his silences. After Peshawar all the superior authorities had agreed there was a terrorist spectacular in preparation. But the world created by a 'wilderness of mirrors' is not a forgiving place for those who fail their political masters.

Since the discovery at Customs of the scrawled message on the folded landing card there had been no sign of life from Crowbar. Was he dead or alive? No one knew and some were ceasing to care. It had been nearly four weeks and with each passing day the mood was swinging to the view he was something now in the past tense.

Some muttered that he had done his job, been caught and killed, but had been the cause of the plot being abandoned. Only Hill counselled caution and a continuation of the search for the source of a still unfound threat. In some gloom he motored to Ipswich to talk to Sam Seymour and the two eggheads in the hazardous cargo office of *Lloyd's Register* who were helping him go through every possibility, however bizarre.

'You used a pretty hair-raising phrase in London, Sam. Thirty times the Hiroshima bomb.

How on earth can a small tanker be worse than the entire Manhattan project?'

Sam Seymour was exhausted. At thirty-two he could see a promising career in British Intelligence ending in a polite side-lining to the archives of Central Registry, even though he had been saddled with a job that was looking every day more impossible to fulfil.

'With an atomic bomb, Steve, the damage comes in four waves. The flash is so searingly bright it can cauterize the cornea of a watcher unless he has black lens shields. Then comes the heat, so bad it causes everything in its path to self-incinerate. The shock wave knocks down buildings miles away and the gamma-ray radiation is long term, causing carcinoma and malformations. With the LPG explosion forget three – this explosion is all heat.

'But it is a heat so fierce that it will cause steel to run like honey and concrete to crumble to dust. You've heard of the fuel-air bomb? It is so powerful it makes napalm seem mild, yet they both have the same source: petroleum.

'LPG is heavier than air. In transportation it is not, like LNG, at an amazingly low temperature; it is under pressure. Hence the double-hulled skins of LPG tankers. When ruptured the LPG will gush out, quite invisible, and mix with the air. It is heavier than air so it will swirl around the place it came from, forming one enormous fuel-air bomb. Ignite that, and the entire cargo will explode in flame, terrible flame, rising quickly to five thousand degrees Centigrade. Then it will start to roll.

'Now it creates its own wind. It will roll outwards from the source, a roaring tide of flame, consuming everything in its path until it has consumed itself. Then it gutters like a fading candle and dies.'

'How far will the fireball roll?'

'Well, according to my new-found boffin friends a small tanker of, say, eight thousand tonnes, fully vented and ignited, would consume everything and extinguish all human life within a five-kilometre radius.

'One last thing, I said it creates its own wind. It sucks in the air from periphery to centre, to feed itself, so even humans in a protective shell five clicks away from the epicentre will die of asphyxia.'

Steve Hill had a mental image of a city clustered round its harbour and port after such a horror exploded within it. Not even the outer suburbs would survive.

'Are these tankers being checked out?'

'Every one. Large and small, right down to tiny. The hazardous cargo team here is only two guys but they're good. As a matter of fact they are down to the last handful of LPG tankers.

'As for the general freighters, the sheer numbers mean that we had to cut off at those under ten thousand tonnes. Except when they enter the American forbidden zone along each seaboard. Then the Yanks spot them and investigate.

'For the rest, every major port in the world has been apprised that western intelligence thinks there may be a hijacked ghost ship on the high seas and they must take their own precautions. But frankly any port likely to be targeted by Al-Qaeda for a human-carnage massacre would be in a western, developed country; not Lagos, Dakar; not Muslim, Hindu, Buddhist. That leaves our non-American list of possible ports at under three hundred.'

There was a tap on the door and a head came round. Pink-cheeked, very young, name of Conrad Phipps.

'Just got the last one in, Sam. *Wilhelmina Santos*, out of Caracas, bringing LPG to Galveston, confirms she is OK, Americans prepared to board her.'

'That's it?' asked Hill. 'Every LPG tanker in the world accounted for?'

'It's a small menu, Steve,' said Seymour.

'Still, it looks as if the LPG tanker idea was a blind alley,' said Hill. He rose to leave and return to London.

'There is one thing that worries me, Mr Hill,' said the cargo egghead.

'It's Steve,' said Hill. The SIS has always maintained the tradition of first names, from the highest to the humblest, with the sole exception of the Chief himself. The informality underwrites the one-team ethos.

'Well, three months ago an LPG tanker was lost with all hands.'

'So?'

'No one actually saw her go down. Her captain came on the radio in high distress to say he had a catastrophic engine-room fire and did not think he could save his ship. Then . . . nothing. She was the *Java Star*.'

'Any traces?' asked Seymour.

'Well, yes. Traces. Before he went off the air he gave his exact position. First on the scene was a refrigerator ship coming up from the south. Her captain reported self-inflating dinghies, lifebelts, and various flotsam at the spot. No sign of survivors. Captain and crew have never been heard of since.'

'Tragic, but so what?' asked Hill.

'It was where it happened, sir . . . er . . . Steve. In the Celebes Sea. Two hundred miles from a place called Labuan Island.'

'Oh, shit,' said Steve Hill and left for London.

* * *

While Martin was driving, the *Countess of Richmond* crossed the Equator. She was heading north by north-west, and only her navigator knew exactly where. He was going for a spot eight hundred miles west of the Azores and twelve hundred miles east of the American coast. If extended due west, her track would bring her to Baltimore at the top of the vastly populated Chesapeake Bay.

Some of those on board the *Countess* began their early preparations for the entry into paradise. This involved the shaving of all body hair and the writing of the last testaments of faith. These were done into the camera lens and the last wills were read out by each writer.

The Afghan did his as well, but he chose to speak in Pashto. Yusuf Ibrahim, from his time in Afghanistan, had a few words of the language, and strained to understand, but even if he had been fluent he could not have faulted the testament.

The man from the Tora Bora spoke of the destruction of his family by an American rocket and his joy that he would soon see them again while bringing justice at last to the Great Satan. As he spoke, he realized that none of this was ever going to reach any shore in physical form. It would all have to be transmitted by Suleiman in datastream before he too died and his equipment with him. What no one seemed to know was how they would die and what justice would be visited upon the USA – the exceptions being the explosives expert and Ibrahim himself. But they revealed nothing.

Given that the entire crew was surviving on cold tinned food, no one noticed that a steel carving knife with a seven-inch blade was missing from the galley.

When he was unobserved Martin was quietly honing its blade to a razor edge with the whetstone in the knife drawer. He thought of using the dead of night to drop over the stern to slash the dinghy, but rejected the idea.

He was with the four men who slept in bunks in the forecastle up in the bow. There was always a helmsman at the wheel, which was right next to the access point for going over the stern on a rope. The radio expert practically lived in his tiny communications shack behind the bridge and the engineer was always down in his engine room, below the bridge at the stern. Any of them could put a head outside and see him.

And the damage would be spotted. A saboteur would be known about at once. The loss of the dinghy would be a setback but not enough to abort the mission. And there might be time to patch the damage. He dropped the idea but kept the rag-sheathed knife strapped to the small of his back. Each spell at the bridge he tried to work out which port they were going for and what lay inside the sea containers that he might be able to sabotage to destruction. Neither answer appeared, and the *Countess* steamed north by north-west.

The global hunt switched and narrowed. All the marine giants, all the tankers and all the gas ships had been checked and verified. All the ID transponders conformed to their required transmissions; all the course and tracks conformed to their predicted journeys; three thousand captains had spoken in voice to their head offices and agents, giving personal birth and background details so that, even if they were under duress, no hijacker could know whether they were lying or not.

The USA, her Navy, Marines and Coast Guards, stretched to the limits without furlough or time off, was boarding and escorting in every cargo vessel seeking berth in a major port. This was causing economic inconvenience, but nothing big enough to inflict real damage to the biggest economy on earth.

After the tip from Ipswich the origins and ownership of the *Java Star* were checked with a toothcomb. Because she was small, her owning company concealed itself behind a 'shell' company lodged with a bank that turned out to be a brass plate in a Far-Eastern tax haven. The Borneo refinery that had provided the cargo was legitimate but knew little about the ship itself. Her builders were traced – she had had six owners in her life – and provided plans. A sister ship was found and swarmed over by Americans with measuring tapes. Computer imaging produced an exact replica of the *Java Star*, but not the ship itself.

The government of the flag of convenience she flew when last seen was visited in force. But it was a Polynesian atoll republic and the checkers were soon satisfied that the gas tanker had never even been there.

The western world needed answers to three questions: was she really dead? If not, where was she now? And what was her new name? The KH-11 satellites were instructed to narrow their search to something resembling the *Java Star*.

In the first week of April the joint operation at Edzell air base in Scotland was stood down. There was no more it could do that was not now being done far more officially by the main western intel-gathering agencies.

Michael McDonald returned with relief to his native Washington. He stayed with the hunt for the ghost ship, but out of Langley. Part of the

CIA's mission was to reinterrogate any detainee in any of its covert detention centres who might, before capture, have heard a whisper of a project called Al-Isra. And they called in every source they had out in the shadowy world of Islamist terrorism. There were no takers. The very phrase referring to the magical journey through the night to great enlightenment seemed to have been born and died with an Egyptian terror-financier who went off a balcony in Peshawar in September.

With regret Colonel Mike Martin was presumed to have been lost on mission. He had clearly done what he could, and if the *Java Star* or another floating bomb were discovered heading for the USA, he would be deemed to have succeeded. But no one expected to see him again. It had simply been too long since his last sign of life in a diver's kitbag on Labuan.

Three days before the G8 meeting patience finally ran out, and at the highest level, with the global search based on the British tip-off. Marek Gumienny, at his desk in Langley, called Steve Hill on a secure line with the news.

'Steve, I'm sorry. I'm sorry for you and even more so for your man Mike Martin. But the conviction here is that he's gone and with the biggest trawl of global shipping ever attempted, he must have been wrong.'

'And Sam Seymour's theory?' asked Hill.

'Same thing. No dice. We have checked out just about every goddam tanker on the planet, all categories. About fifty left to locate and identify, then it's over. Whatever this Al-Isra phrase meant, either we'll never find out or it means nothing or it has been long discontinued. Hold on . . . I'll kill the other line.'

In a moment, he came back on. 'There's a ship overdue. Left Trinidad for Puerto Rico four days ago. Due yesterday. Never showed. Won't answer.'

'What kind of ship?' asked Hill.

'A tanker. Three thousand tonnes. Look, she may have foundered. But we're checking now.'

'What was she carrying?' asked Hill.

'Liquefied petroleum gas,' was the answer.

It was a Keyhole KH-11 satellite that found her, six hours after the complaint from Puerto Rico to the head office of the oil-company owners of the refinery, based in Houston, was turned into a major alarm situation.

Sweeping through the eastern Caribbean with its cameras and listening sensors checking on a five-hundred-mile wide swathe of sea and islands, the Keyhole heard a transponder signal from far below and its computer confirmed it was from the missing *Doña Maria*.

The knowledge went instantly to a variety of agencies, which was why Marek Gumienny was interrupted in his phone call to London. Others in the loop were SOCOM headquarters at Tampa, Florida, the US Navy and the Coast Guards. All were given the exact grid reference of the missing vessel.

In not switching off the transponder, the hijackers were either being very stupid or hoping to get very lucky. But they were only following their orders. With the transponder emitting, they gave away their name and position. With it switched off, they became immediately suspect as a possible rogue ship.

The small LPG tanker was still being navigated and steered by a terrified Captain Montalban, four days without sleep, save only a few catnaps before he was kicked awake again. She had slipped past Puerto Rico in the darkness, passed west of the Turks and Caicos Islands and lost herself for a while in the cluster of seven hundred islands that make up the Bahamas.

When the Keyhole found her she was steaming due west just south of Bimini, the westernmost island of the whole archipelago.

At Tampa her course was plotted and extended forward. It went straight into the open mouth of the Port of Miami, a waterway that leads into the heart of the city.

Within ten minutes the small tanker was attracting real company. A P-3 Orion sub-hunter, aloft from the naval air station at Key West, found her, dropped to a few thousand feet and began to circle, filming her from every angle. She appeared on a wall-sized plasma screen in the near-darkness of the ops room at Tampa, almost life-size.

'Jesus, would you look at that,' murmured an operator to no one in particular.

While at sea someone had gone over the stern of the tanker with a brush and white paint to daub a cross-bar over the letter 'i' in Maria. It attempted to rechristen her the *Doña Marta* but the white smear was simply too crude to dupe any onlooker for more than a few seconds.

There are two coastguard cutters operating out of Charleston, South Carolina, both Hamilton class and both were at sea. They are the 717 USCG *Mellon* and her sister ship the *Morgenthau*. The *Mellon* was closer and turned towards the hijacked fugitive, moved from optimum cruise revolutions to flank speed. Her navigator rapidly plotted her intercept at ninety minutes, just before sundown.

The word 'cutter' hardly does the *Mellon* justice; she can perform like a small destroyer at 150 metres in length and 3,300 tons deadweight. As she raced through the Atlantic swell of early

April her crew ran to prepare her armament – just in case. The missing tanker was already rated as 'likely hostile'.

The *Mellon*'s weaponry is not to be trifled with. Lightest of her three systems is the six-barrel 20-mm Gatling gun which pumps out such a blizzard of ordnance that it is used as an anti-missile weapon. In theory even an incoming rocket would be torn apart by flying through such a hail of bullets. But the Phalanx gun does not have to be used against missiles; it can tear almost anything apart but it needs to be fairly close.

She also carried two Bushmaster 25-mm cannon, not as rapid but heavier and enough to give a small tanker a completely spoiled day. And she has her deck-mounted Oto Melara 76-mm rapid-fire cannon. By the time the *Doña Maria* became a speck on the horizon all three systems were crewed and ready, and the men crouching over what so far they had only used in training would have been more than saintly if they did not harbour a sneaking lust to use them in real action.

With the Orion above them, filming everything in real time and passing the images to Tampa, the *Mellon* curved round the stern of the tanker and came abreast of her, throttling back to format just two hundred yards off the beam. Then the *Mellon* called on the *Doña Maria* with her loudhailer.

'Unidentified tanker, this is United States Coast Guard vessel *Mellon*. Heave to. I say again, heave to. We are coming aboard.'

Powerful field glasses could pick up the figure at the helm holding the wheel, and two other figures flanking the man. There was no response. The tanker did not slow down. The message was repeated.

After the third message the captain gave the order for a single shell to be fired into the sea ahead of the tanker's bow. As the water spout erupted over the bow, soaking the tarpaulins with which someone had vainly tried to hide the network of pipes and tubes that betray any tanker's real purpose, those on the bridge of the *Doña Maria* must have got the message. Still she did not slow down.

Then two figures appeared from the door of the sterncastle, just behind the bridge. One had an M60 machine gun slung round his neck. It was a futile gesture and sealed the tanker's fate. His North African features were clearly visible in the setting sun. He loosed off a short burst that went over the top of the *Mellon*, then took a bullet in the chest from one of the four M16 carbines being aimed at him from the deck of the *Mellon*.

That was the end of negotiations. As the Algerian's body slumped backwards and the steel door through which he had stepped slammed shut, the captain of the *Mellon* asked for permission to sink the runaway. But permission was denied. The message from base was unequivocal.

'Pull away from her. Make distance now and make it fast. She's a floating bomb. Resume station a mile from the tanker.'

Regretfully the *Mellon* turned away, powered up to maximum speed and left the tanker alone to her fate. The two F-16 Falcons were already airborne and three minutes distant.

There is a squadron at Pensacola Air Force Base in the Florida panhandle that maintains a five-minute-to-scramble standby readiness round the clock. Its primary use is against drug smugglers, airborne and sometimes seaborne, trying to slip into Florida and neighbouring states with (mainly) cocaine.

They came out of the sunset in a clear darkling sky, locked on to the tanker west of Bimini and armed their Maverick missiles. Each pilot's visual display showed him the smart missiles' lock on the target and the death of the tanker was very mechanical, very precise, very devoid of emotion.

There was a clipped command from the element leader and both Mavericks left their racks beneath the fighters and followed their noses. Seconds later two warheads involving 135 kilograms of unpleasantness hit the tanker.

Even though her cargo was not air-mixed for maximum power the detonations of the Mavericks deep inside the petrol jelly were enough.

From a mile away the crew of the *Mellon* watched her torch and were duly impressed. They felt the heat wash over their faces and smelled the stench of concentrated gasoline on fire. It was quick. There was nothing left to smoulder on the surface. The forward and stern ends of the tanker went down as two separate pieces of molten junk. The last of her heavier fuel oil flickered for five minutes, then the sea claimed it all.

Just as Ali Aziz al-Khattab had intended.

Within an hour the President of the USA was interrupted at a state banquet with a brief whispered message. He nodded, demanded a full verbal report at eight the next morning in the Oval Office, and returned to his soup.

At five minutes before eight the Director of the CIA with Marek Gumienny at his side were shown into the Oval Office. Gumienny had been in that room twice before and it still impressed the hell out of him. The President and the other five of the six principals were there.

The formalities were brief. Marek Gumienny was bidden to report on the progress and termination of a lengthy exercise in counter-terrorism known as Crowbar.

He kept it short, aware that the man sitting under the round window giving on to the Rose Garden, with its six-inch bullet-proof glass, loathed long explanations. The rule of thumb was always 'fifteen minutes and then shut up'. Marek Gumienny telescoped the complexities of Crowbar into twelve.

There was silence when he stopped.

'So the tip from the Brits turned out to be right?' said the Vice-President.

'Yes, sir. The agent they slipped inside Al-Qaeda, a very brave officer whom I had the privilege of meeting last fall, must be presumed dead. If not he would have shown sign of life by now. But he got the message out. The terror weapon was indeed a ship.'

'I had no idea cargoes that dangerous were being carried around the world on a daily basis,' marvelled the Secretary of State in the ensuing silence.

'Nor I,' said the President. 'Now, regarding the G8 Conference, what is your advice to me?'

The Secretary of Defense glanced at the Director of National Intelligence and nodded. They had clearly prepared their go-ahead.

'Mr President, we have every reason to believe the terrorist threat to this country, notably to the city of Miami, was destroyed last night. The peril is over. Regarding the G8, during the entire conference you will be under the protection of the US Navy, and the Navy has pledged its word that no harm will come to you. Our advice therefore is that you go ahead to your G8 with an easy mind!'

'Why then, that's what I shall surely do,' said the President of the USA.

CHAPTER SEVENTEEN

David Gundlach reckoned he had the best job in the world. Second-best, anyway. To have that fourth gold ring on the sleeve or epaulette and be the captain of the vessel would be even better, but he happily settled for First Officer.

On an April evening he stood at the starboard wing of the huge bridge and looked down at the swarming humanity on the dock of the new Brooklyn Terminal two hundred feet below him. The borough of Brooklyn was not above him; at the height of a twenty-three-storey building, he was looking down on most of it.

Pier Twelve on Buttermilk Channel, which was being inaugurated that very evening, is not a small dock but this liner took up all of it. At 1,132 feet long, 135 feet in the beam and drawing

432

39 feet so that the whole channel had had to be deepened for her, she was the biggest passenger liner afloat by a big margin. The more First Officer Gundlach, on his first crossing since his promotion, looked at her, the more magnificent she seemed.

Far below and away in the direction of the streets beyond the terminal buildings he could make out the banners of the frustrated and angry demonstrators. New York's police had with great effectiveness simply cordoned off the entire terminal. Harbour Police boats skimmed and swerved round the terminal at sea level to ensure that no protesters in boats could come near.

Even if they had been able to approach at sea level it would have done them no good. The steel hull of the liner simply towered above the waterline, its lowest ports more than fifty feet up. So those boarding that evening could do so in complete privacy.

Not that they were of interest to the protesters. So far the liner was simply taking on board the lowly ones: stenographers, secretaries, junior diplomats, special advisers and all the human ants without whom the great and good of the world could apparently not discuss hunger, poverty, security, trade barriers, defence and alliances.

As the notion of security crossed his mind,

David Gundlach frowned. He and his fellow officers had spent the day escorting scores of American Secret Servicemen over every inch of the ship. They all looked the same; they all scowled in concentration; they all jabbered into their sleeves where the mikes were hidden and they all got their answers in earpieces without which they felt naked. Gundlach finally concluded they were professionally paranoid – and they found nothing amiss.

The backgrounds of the 1,200 crew had been vetted and checked and not a shred of evidence had been found against any of them. The Grand Duplex Apartment set aside for the US President and First Lady was already sealed and guarded by the Secret Service, having been given an inch-by-inch search. Only having seen it for the first time did David Gundlach realize the enveloping cocoon that must surround this President at all times.

He checked his watch. Two hours to completion of boarding of the three thousand passengers before the eight heads of state or government were due to arrive. Like the diplomats in London he was admiring of the simplicity of chartering the biggest and most luxurious liner in the world to host the biggest and most prestigious conference in the world; and to do so during a five-day crossing of the Atlantic from New York to Southampton.

The ruse confounded all the forces that habitually sought to bring chaos to the G8 Conference every year. Better than a mountain, better than an island, with accommodation for 4,200 souls, the *Queen Mary 2* was untouchable.

Gundlach would stand beside his captain as the Typhoon hooters sounded their deep bass 'A' note to bid farewell to New York. He would give the required power settings from her four Mermaid pod motors and the captain, using only a tiny joystick on the control console, would ease her out into the East River and turn her towards the roads and the waiting Atlantic. So delicate were her controls and so versatile her two aft pods that swivel through 360 degrees that she needed no tugs to bring her out of the terminal.

Far to the east the *Countess of Richmond* was passing the Canary Islands, away to her starboard. The holiday islands for so many Europeans seeking to leave the snow and sleet of their winter homes to find December sunshine off the African coast were out of view. But the tip of Mount Tiede could be seen on the horizon with field glasses.

She had two days in hand before her rendezvous with history. The Indonesian navigator had instructed his compatriot in the engine room to cut power to 'slow ahead' and she was moving at a walking pace through the gentle swell of an April evening.

The peak of Mount Tiede dropped out of sight and the helmsman eased her a few more degrees to port where, 1,600 miles away, lay the American coast. From high in space she was spotted yet again; and again, when consulted, the computers read her transponder, checked the records, noted her harmless position so far out at sea and repeated her clearance: 'Legitimate trader, no danger.'

The first government party to arrive was the Prime Minister of Japan and his entourage. As agreed they had flown into Kennedy direct from Tokyo. Staying airside out of sight and sound of the demonstrators, the party had transferred to the passenger cabins of a small fleet of helicopters which lifted them straight out of Jamaica Bay and brought them to Brooklyn.

The landing zone was inside the perimeter of the great halls and sheds which made up the new terminal. From the Japanese passengers' point of view, the protesters beyond the barriers, mouthing silently whatever point it was they wished to make, simply dropped out of sight. As the rotor blades slowed to a gentle twirl, the delegation was greeted by ship's officers and conducted along the covered tunnel to the entrance in the side of the hull; and from thence to one of the Royal Suites.

The helicopters left for Kennedy to collect the Canadians who had just arrived.

David Gundlach remained on the bridge, fifty yards from side to side with huge panoramic windows looking forward to the sea. Even though the bridge was two hundred feet in the air, the wipers in front of each window revealed that when the bow of the *Queen Mary 2* hit the sixty-foot Atlantic waves of midwinter, spray would still drench the bridge.

But this crossing, so ran the forecasts, would be gentle, with a slow swell and light winds. The liner would be taking the southern Great Circle route, always more popular with guests for its milder weather and sea. This would bring her in an arc sweeping across the Atlantic at its shortest point and, at its southernmost, just north of the Azores.

The Russians, French, Germans and Italians succeeded each other in smooth sequence and dusk fell as the British, owners of the *Queen Mary 2*, used the last flights of the helicopter shuttle.

The US President, who would be hosting the inaugural dinner just after eight p.m., came in his customary dark blue White House helicopter on the dot of six. A marine band on the quay struck up 'Hail to the Chief' as he strode into the hull and the steel doors closed to shut away the outside world. At six-thirty the last mooring ropes were cast off and the *Queen Mary*, dressed overall and lit like a floating city, eased out into the East River.

Those on smaller vessels in the river and the outer roads watched her go and waved. High above them, behind toughened plate glass, the state and government heads of the eight richest nations in the world waved back. The brilliantly illuminated Statue of Liberty slid by, the islands dropped away and the *Queen Mary* sedately increased her power.

Either side, her two escorting missile cruisers of the US Navy's Atlantic fleet took up position several cables away and announced themselves to the captain. To port was the USS *Leyte Gulf* and to starboard the USS *Monterey*. In accordance with the courtesies of the sea, he acknowledged their presence and thanked them. Then he left the bridge to change for dinner. David Gundlach had the helm and the command.

There would be no escorting submarine, for this was not a carrier group. The submarine was absent for two reasons. No nation possessing the kind of submarine that could evade the missile cruisers' detect-and-sink capacity existed, and the *Queen Mary* was so fast that no submarine could keep up.

As the convoy cleared the roads and the lights of Long Island dropped away, First Officer Gundlach increased the power to optimum cruise. The four mermaid pods, pounding out 157,000 horsepower between them, could push the *Queen Mary* to thirty knots if needed. Normal cruise is twenty-five knots, and the cruiser escorts had to move to maximum cruise to keep up.

Overhead the aerial escort appeared: one US Navy E-2C Hawkeye with radar scopes that would illuminate the surface of the Atlantic for five hundred miles in any direction around the convoy. And an EA-6B Prowler capable of jamming any offensive weapons system that might dare to lock on to the convoy and destroying that source with its HARM missiles.

The air cover would be refuelled and replaced at end of shift out of the USA until its mission could be relieved by identical cover coming out of the US-leased base in the Azores. That in turn would continue until it could be replaced by cover out of the UK. Nothing had been unforeseen.

The dinner was a triumphal success. The statesmen beamed, the wives sparkled, the cuisine was agreed to be superb and the crystal glittered as it was filled with vintage wines.

Following the example of the American President – the more so as the other delegations had long flights behind them – the diners broke up early and retired for the night.

The conference met in full plenum the following morning. The Royal Court Theatre had been transformed to accommodate all eight delegations with, sitting behind the principals, the small army of minions that each seemed to need.

The second night was as the first, save that the host was the British Prime Minister in the two-hundred-seat Queen's Grill. Those less eminent spread themselves through the huge Britannia Restaurant or the various pubs and bars that also serve food. The younger element, freed from their diplomatic labours, favoured the Queen's Ballroom after dinner or the G32 nightclub/disco.

High above them all the lights were dimmed on the sweeping bridge where David Gundlach presided through the night hours. Spread out in front of him, just below the forward windows, was the array of plasma screens that depicted every system in the ship.

Foremost among these was the ship's radar, casting its gaze twenty-five miles in all directions. He could see the blips made by the cruisers either side of him and beyond them those of other vessels going about their business.

He also had at his disposal an Automatic Identification System which would read the transponder of any ship for miles around and a cross-checking computer based on Lloyd's records that would identify not just who she was but her known route and cargo, and her radio channel.

Either side of the *Queen Mary*, also on darkened bridges, the radar men of the two cruisers pored over their screens with the same task. Their duty was to ensure nothing remotely threatening got near the huge monster thundering along between them. Even for a harmless and checked-out freighter the closeness limit was three kilometres. On the second night there was nothing nearer than ten.

The picture created by the E2C Hawkeye was inevitably bigger because of its altitude. The image was like an immense circular torch beam moving across the Atlantic from west to east. But the great majority of what it saw was miles away and nowhere near the convoy. What it could do was create a ten-mile-wide corridor thrusting forward of the moving ships, and tell the cruisers what lay ahead of them. Being realistic, it put a limit on this projection as well. The limit was twenty-five miles or one hour's cruising.

Just before eleven on the third night the Hawkeye posted a low-level warning.

'There is a small freighter twenty-five miles ahead, two miles south of intended track. It seems to be motionless in the water.'

* * *

The *Countess of Richmond* was not quite motionless. Her engines were set to 'midships' so that
her propellers idled in the water. But there was a
four-knot current which gave her just enough
way to keep her nose into the flow, and that
meant towards the west.

The inflatable speedboat was in the water,
tethered to her port side with a rope-and-plank
ladder running down from the rail to the sea.
Four men were already in it, bobbing on
the current beside the hull of the freighter.

The other four were on the bridge. Ibrahim
held the wheel, staring at the horizon, seeking
the first glimmer of the approaching lights.

The Indonesian radio expert was adjusting the
transmitting microphone for strength and clarity.
Beside him stood the teenager of Pakistani
parents born and raised in a suburb of the
Yorkshire city of Leeds. The fourth was
the Afghan. When the radio man was satisfied he
nodded at the boy who nodded back and took a
stool beside the ship's console, waiting for the
call.

It came from the cruiser plunging through the sea
six cables to the starboard of the *Queen Mary*.
David Gundlach heard it loud and clear, as did
all on the night watch. The channel used was the

common wavelength for ships in the North Atlantic. The voice had the drawl of the Deep South.

'*Countess of Richmond, Countess of Richmond,* this is US Navy cruiser *Monterey.* Do you read me?'

The voice that came back was slightly distorted by less than state-of-the-art radio equipment aboard the old freighter. And the voice had the flat vowels of Lancashire or maybe Yorkshire.

'Oh, aye, *Monterey, Countess* 'ere.'

'You appear to be hove to. State your situation.'

'*Countess o' Richmond.* 'Aving a bit of overheating . . .' Click, click. '. . . prop shaft . . .' Static. '. . . repairing as fast as we can . . .'

There was a brief silence from the bridge of the cruiser. Then . . .

'Say again, *Countess of Richmond,* I repeat, say again.'

The reply came back and the accent was thicker than ever. On the bridge of the *Queen Mary* the First Officer had the blip entering his radar screen slightly south of dead ahead and fifty minutes cruising away. Another display gave all the details of the *Countess of Richmond,* including confirmation that her transponder was genuine and the signal from it accurate. He cut into the radio exchange.

'*Monterey*, this is *Queen Mary Two. Let me try.*'

David Gundlach was born and raised in the Wirral county of Cheshire, not fifty miles from Liverpool. The voice from the *Countess* he put at either Yorkshire or Lancashire, next door to his native Cheshire.

'*Countess of Richmond*, this is *Queen Mary Two*. I read you have an overheat of main bearing in the prop shaft and you are carrying out repairs at sea. Confirm.'

'Aye, that's reet. 'Ope to be finished in another hour,' said the voice on the speaker.

'*Countess*, give your details please. Port of registry, port of departure, destination, cargo.'

'*Queen Moory*. Registered in Liverpool, eight thousand tonnes, general cargo freighter, coming from Java with brocades and oriental timber, heading for Baltimore.'

Gundlach ran his eye down the screened information provided by the head office of McKendrick Shipping in Liverpool, brokers Siebart and Abercrombie in London and insurers Lloyd's. All accurate.

'Who am I speaking to, please?' he asked.

'This is Captain McKendrick. 'Oo are you?'

'First Officer David Gundlach speaking.'

The *Monterey*, following the exchange with difficulty, came back.

'*Monterey*, *Queen*. Do you want to alter course?'

Gundlach consulted the displays. The bridge computer was guiding the *Queen Mary 2* along the pre-planned track and would adjust for any change in the sea, wind, current or waves. To divert would mean going to manual or resetting the programme and then returning to their original course. He would pass the hove-to freighter in forty-one minutes and it would be two miles or three kilometres to his starboard.

'No need, *Monterey*. We'll be past her in forty minutes. Over two miles of sea between us.'

Formatting on the *Queen Mary*, the *Monterey* would be less than that, but there was still ample room. High above, the Hawkeye and the EA-6B scanned the helpless freighter for any sign of missile lock-on, or any electronic activity at all. There was none, but they would keep watching until the *Countess* was well behind the convoy. Two other ships were also in the no-entry alley, but much further ahead and would be asked to divert, left and right.

'Roger that,' said the *Monterey*.

It had all been heard on the bridge of the *Countess*. Ibrahim nodded that they should leave him. The radio engineer and the youth scuttled down the ladder to the speedboat and all six in the inflatable waited for the Afghan.

Still convinced that the crazed Jordanian

would re-engage the engine and attempt to ram
one of the oncoming vessels, Martin knew he
could not leave the *Countess of Richmond*. His
only hope was to take her over after killing the
crew.

He went down the rope ladder backwards.
Behind the thwarts Suleiman was setting up his
digital photography equipment. A rope trailed
from the rail of the *Countess*; one of the
Indonesians stood near the speedboat's bow,
gripping the rope and holding her against the
flow of the current running past the ship's side.

Martin held the ladder fast, turned, reached
down and slashed the grey rock-hard fabric over
a six-foot length. The act was so fast and so unexpected that for two or three seconds no one
reacted, save the sea itself. The escaping air made
a low roar and with six on board that side of the
inflatable dipped downwards and began to ship
water.

Leaning further out, Martin slashed at the
retaining rope. He missed but cut open the fore-
arm of the Indonesian. Then the men reacted. But
the Indonesian released his grip and the sea took
them.

There were vengeful hands reaching out at him
but the sinking speedboat dropped astern. The
weight of the great outboard pulled down the aft
end and more salt water rushed in. The wreckage

cleared the stern of the freighter and went away into the blackness of the Atlantic night. Somewhere down current it simply sank, dragged down by the outboard. In the gleam of the ship's sternlight Martin saw waving hands on the water, and then they too were gone. No one can swim against four knots. He went back up the ladder.

At that moment Ibrahim jerked one of the three controls the explosives expert had left him. As Martin climbed, there was a series of sharp cracks as tiny charges went off.

When Mr Wei had built the gallery masquerading as six sea containers along the deck of the *Java Star* from bridge to bow, he had created the roof or 'lid' of the empty space beneath as one single piece of steel held down by four strongpoints.

To these the explosives man had fitted shaped charges and linked all four to wires taking power from the ship's engines. When they blew, the sheet-metal lid of the cavern beneath lifted upwards several feet. The power of the charges was asymmetric so that one side of the sheet rose higher than the other.

Martin was at the top of the rope ladder, knife in teeth, when the charges blew. He crouched there as the huge sheet of steel slid sideways into the sea. He put the knife away and entered the bridge.

The Al-Qaeda killer was standing at the wheel staring forward through the glass. On the horizon, bearing down at twenty-five knots, was a floating city, seventeen decks and 150,000 tonnes of lights, steel and people. Right under the bridge the gallery was open to the stars. For the first time Martin realized its purpose. Not to contain something: to hide something.

The clouds moved away from the half-moon and the entire foredeck of the once-*Java Star* gleamed in its light. For the first time Martin realized this was not a general freighter containing explosives; it was a tanker. Running away from the bridge was the cat's cradle of pipes, tubes, spigots and hydrant-wheels that gave away her purpose in life.

Evenly spaced down the deck towards the bow were six circular steel discs – the venting hatches – above each of the cargo tanks beneath the deck.

'You should have stayed on the boat, Afghan,' said Ibrahim.

'There was no room, my brother. Suleiman almost fell overboard. I stayed on the ladder. Then they were gone. Now I will die here with you, *inshallah*.'

Ibrahim seemed appeased. He glanced at the ship's clock and pulled his second lever. The flexes ran from the control down to the ship's batteries, took their power and went forward into the gallery where the explosives man, entering through the secret door, had worked during his month at sea.

Six more charges detonated. The six hatches blew away from above the tanks. What followed was invisible to the naked eye: six vertical columns rose like volcanoes from the domes as the cargo began to vent. The rising vapour cloud reached a hundred feet, lost its impetus and gravity took over. The unseen cloud, mixing furiously with the night air, fell back to the sea and began to roll outwards, away from the source in all directions.

Martin had lost and he knew it. He was too late and he knew that too. He knew enough to realize he had been riding a floating bomb since the Philippines, and that what was pouring out of the six missing hatches was invisible death that could not now be controlled.

He had always presumed the *Countess of Richmond*, now become again the *Java Star*, was going to drive herself into some inner harbour and detonate what lay below her decks.

He had presumed she was going to ram something of value as she blew herself up. For thirty days he had waited in vain for a chance to kill seven men and take over her command. No such chance had appeared.

Now, too late, he realized the *Java Star* was not

going to deliver a bomb; she *was* the bomb. And with her cargo venting fast, she did not need to move an inch. The oncoming liner had only to pass within three kilometres of her to be consumed.

He had heard the interchange on the bridge between the Pakistani boy and the Deck Officer of the *Queen Mary 2*. He knew too late the *Java Star* would not engage engines. The escorting cruisers would never allow that, but she did not need to.

There was a third control by Ibrahim's right hand, a button to be hammered downward. Martin followed the flexes to a Very pistol, a flare-gun mounted just forward of the bridge windows. One flare, one single spark . . .

Through the windows the city of lights was over the horizon. Fifteen miles, thirty minutes' cruising, optimum time for maximum fuel–air mixture.

Martin's glance flicked to the radio speaker on the console. A last chance to shout a warning. His right hand slid down towards the slit in his robe inside which was his knife, strapped to his thigh.

The Jordanian caught the glance and the movement. He had not survived Afghanistan, a Jordanian jail and the relentless American hunt for him in Iraq without developing the instincts of a wild animal.

Something told him that despite the fraternal language, the Afghan was not his friend. The raw hatred charged the atmosphere on the tiny bridge like a silent scream.

Martin's hand slipped inside his robe for the knife. Ibrahim was first; the gun had been underneath the map on the chart table. It was pointing straight at Martin's chest. The distance to cross was twelve feet. Ten too many.

A soldier is trained to estimate chances and do it fast. Martin had spent much of his life doing that. On the bridge of the *Countess of Richmond*, enveloped in her own death cloud, there were only two: go for the man; go for the button. There would be no surviving either.

Some words came into his mind, words from long ago, in a schoolboy's poem, ' To every man upon this earth Death cometh soon or late . . .' And he recalled Ahmad Shah Massoud, the Lion of the Panjshir, talking by the camp fire. 'We are all sentenced to die, Angleez. But only a warrior blessed of Allah may be allowed to choose how!' Colonel Mike Martin made his choice . . .

Ibrahim saw him coming; he knew the flicker in the eyes of a man about to die. The killer screamed and fired. The charging man took the bullet in the chest and began to die. But beyond pain and shock there is always willpower, just enough for another second of life.

At the end of that second both men and ship were consumed in a rose-pink eternity.

David Gundlach stared in stunned amazement. Fifteen miles ahead, where the world's largest liner would have been in thirty-five minutes, a huge volcano of flame erupted out of the sea. From the other three men on the night watch came cries of 'What the hell was that?'

'*Monterey* to *Queen Mary 2*. Divert to port, I say divert to port. We are investigating.'

To his right Gundlach saw the US cruiser move up to attack speed and head for the flames. It was clear the *Countess of Richmond* had sustained some terrible accident. His job was to stay clear; if there were men in the water the *Monterey* would find them. But it was still wise to summon his captain. When the ship's master arrived on the bridge his First Officer explained what he had seen. They were now a full eighteen miles from the estimated spot and heading away fast.

To port the USS *Leyte Gulf* stayed with them. The *Monterey* was heading straight for the fireball miles up ahead. The captain agreed that in the unlikely event of survivors the *Monterey* should search for them.

As the two men watched from the safety of their bridge, the flames began to flicker and die. The last blotches of flame upon the sea would be the remnants of the vanished ship's fuel oil. All the hyper-volatile cargo was gone before the *Monterey* reached the spot.

The captain of the Cunarder ordered that the computers resume course for Southampton.

EPILOGUE

There was an inquiry. of course. It took almost two years. These things are never done in a few hours, except on television.

One team took the real *Java Star*: from the laying of her keel to the moment she steamed out of Brunei loaded with LPG, destination Fremantle, Western Australia.

It was confirmed by independent witnesses with no reason to lie that Captain Herrmann was in charge and that all was well. She was seen by two other captains rounding the north-eastern tip of Borneo Island shortly after that. Precisely because of her cargo, both ships' masters noted she was well away from them, and logged her name.

The single recording of her captain's last

Mayday message was played to a Norwegian psychiatrist who confirmed that the voice was a fellow-Norwegian speaking good English, but that he appeared to be speaking under duress.

The captain of the fruit ship that had noted her given position and diverted to the spot was traced and interviewed. He repeated what he had heard and seen. But experts in fire at sea reckoned that if the fire in the *Java Star*'s engine room was so catastrophic that Captain Herrmann could not save her, it must have ignited her cargo eventually. In which case there would be no fabric-tented life-rafts left floating on the water where she sank.

Filipino commandos carried out a raid, supported by US helicopter gunships, on the Zamboanga Peninsula, ostensibly on Abu Sayyaf bases. They trawled and brought back two jungle-dwelling Huq trackers who occasionally worked for the terrorists but were not prepared to face a firing squad for them.

They reported they had seen a small tanker in a narrow creek in the heart of the jungle being worked on by men with oxyacetylene torches.

The *Java Star* team entered its report within a year. It declared the *Java Star* had not been sunk by an onboard fire, but had been hijacked intact; and, further, that a lot of trouble had been gone to in order to persuade the marine world that she no longer existed when in fact she did. The entire crew was presumed dead already, and this had to be confirmed.

Owing to need-to-know, all the arms of the inquiry were working on the various facets without knowing why. They were told, and believed, that it was an insurance investigation.

Another team followed the fortunes of the real *Countess of Richmond*. They proceeded from the office of Alex Siebart in Crutched Friars, City of London, to Liverpool and checked out the family and crew. They confirmed all was in good order when the *Countess* unloaded her Jaguars at Singapore. Captain McKendrick had run into a friend from Liverpool on the docks and they shared a few beers before he sailed. And he telephoned home.

Independent witnesses confirmed she was still in the command of her lawful captain when she took on valuable timber at Kinabalu.

But an on-the-spot visit to Surabaya, Java, revealed she never even stopped there to take on her second part-cargo of Asian silks. Yet Siebart and Abercrombie in London had received confirmation from the shippers that she had. So it was forged.

A likeness of 'Mr Lampong' was created and Indonesian Homeland Security recognized a suspected but never-proven financial supporter of Jemaat Islamiya. A search was mounted but the terrorist had vanished into the human tides of South-East Asia.

The team concluded that the *Countess of Richmond* had been boarded and hijacked in the Celebes Sea. With all her papers, ID radio codes and transponder stolen, she would have been sunk with all hands. Next of kin were advised.

The clincher came from Dr Ali Aziz al-Khattab. The wiretaps on his phones revealed he was booking a departure to the Middle East. After a conference at Thames House, home of MI5, it was decided that enough was enough. Birmingham police and Special Branch took down the apartment door of the Kuwaiti academic when the listeners confirmed he was in the bath, and he was escorted away in a towelling robe.

But Al-Khattab was clever. A total strip search of his apartment, car and office, cellphone and laptop revealed not one incriminating detail about him.

He smiled blandly, and his lawyer protested, through the statutory twenty-eight days allowed to the British police for holding a suspect without preferring a formal charge. His smile faded when, as he stepped out of Her Majesty's Prison Belmarsh, he was rearrested, this time on an extradition warrant lodged by the government of the United Arab Emirates.

Under this legislation there is no limit of time. Al-Khattab went straight back to his cell. This time, his lawyer lodged a vigorous appeal against extradition. As a Kuwaiti he was not even a citizen of the UAE but that was not the point.

The Counter-Terrorist Centre at Dubai had amazingly come into possession of a sheaf of photos. These showed Al-Khattab conferring closely with a known Al-Qaeda courier, a dhow captain already under surveillance. Others showed him arriving at, and leaving, a villa in the outback of Ras-al-Khaimah, known to be a terrorist hideaway. The London judge was impressed and granted the extradition.

Al-Khattab appealed . . . and lost again. Faced with the dubious charms of HMP Belmarsh or an athletic interrogation by UAE Special Forces at their desert base in the Gulf, he asked to stay as a guest of Queen Elizabeth.

That posed a problem. The British explained they had nothing to hold him on, let alone try and convict him. He was halfway to Heathrow airport when he struck his deal and began to talk.

Once started, he caused CIA guests who sat in on the sessions to report back that it was like watching the Boulder Dam give way. He blew away over one hundred AQ agents who until then had been lily-whites, unknown to Anglo-American intelligence, and twenty-four sleeping bank accounts.

When the interrogators mentioned the AQ project code-named Al-Isra, the Kuwaiti was stunned into silence. He had no idea anyone knew. Then he started to talk again.

He confirmed everything London and Washington already knew or suspected, then added more. He could identify all the eight men aboard the *Countess of Richmond* on her final voyage except the three Indonesians.

He knew the origins and parentage of the teenager of Pakistani derivation who, born and raised in the English county of Yorkshire, could speak in place of Captain McKendrick on the ship's radio and fool First Officer David Gundlach.

And he admitted the *Doña Maria* and the men on board her had been a deliberate sacrifice, though unaware of it themselves; a mere diversion lest there be any hesitation for any reason in sending the American President to sea in a liner.

Gently the interrogators brought the subject round to an Afghan whom they knew Al-Khattab had interrogated in the UAE villa. In fact they did not know it at all: they suspected it, but Al-Khattab hardly hesitated.

He confirmed the arrival of the mysterious Taliban commander in Ras-al-Khaimah after a daring and bloody escape from custody outside Kabul. He claimed these details had been carefully checked by AQ sympathizers in Kabul and authenticated.

He admitted he had been instructed by Ayman al-Zawahiri himself to go to the Gulf and question the fugitive for as long as it took. And he revealed that it was the Sheikh, no less, who had verified the Afghan's identity on the basis of a conversation years earlier in a hospital cave in the Tora Bora.

It was the Sheikh who permitted the Afghan the privilege of joining Al-Isra, and he, Al-Khattab, had despatched the man to Malaysia with others.

It gave his Anglo-American interrogators exquisite pleasure to wreck what was left of his life by telling him who the Afghan really was.

In a final detail a handwriting expert confirmed that the hand of the missing colonel and the person who had scrawled the message thrust into the divebag at Labuan Island were one and the same.

The Crowbar Committee finally agreed that Mike Martin had boarded the *Countess of Richmond*, still posing as a terrorist, somewhere after Labuan and that there was not a shred of evidence that he had been able to get off in time.

Theories as to why the *Countess* blew up forty minutes prematurely were left open on the file.

It is customary in the UK for seven years to be required to elapse before a person missing without trace can legally be presumed dead and a certificate issued.

But when the interrogation of Dr Al-Khattab reached its conclusion the coroner for the City of Westminster, London, was entertained to a very discreet dinner in a private room at Brooks's Club, St James's Street. There were only three others present and they explained many things to the coroner when the stewards had left them alone.

The following week the coroner issued a certificate of death to an academic from the School of Oriental and African Studies, a Dr Terry Martin, in respect of his late brother, Colonel Mike Martin of the Parachute Regiment, who had vanished without trace eighteen months earlier.

In the grounds of the headquarters of the SAS Regiment outside the town of Hereford stands a rather odd-looking structure known simply as the Clock Tower. The tower was dismantled piece by piece when the regiment moved several years ago from its old base to the newer premises. Then it was reconstructed.

Predictably, it has a clock at the top, but the points of interest are the four faces of the tower on which are inscribed the names of all SAS men killed in combat.

Shortly after the issue of the death certificate a memorial service was held at the foot of the Clock Tower. There were a dozen men in uniform and ten in civilian clothes, and two women. One of these was the Director-General of MI5, the Security Service, and the other the dead man's ex-wife.

The missing-in-action status had needed a bit of persuasion but the pressure came from very high indeed. When apprised of all the known facts the Director, Special Forces, and the Commanding Officer of the Regiment had agreed that the status was justified. Colonel Mike Martin was certainly not the first, nor would be the last SAS man to be lost in a faraway place and never recovered.

Across the border to the west the sun was dipping across the Black Mountains of Wales on a bleak February day when the brief ceremony was held. At the end the chaplain spoke the habitual words from the Gospel of St John: 'Greater love hath no man than this, that a man lay down his life for his friends.'

Only those grouped round the Clock Tower knew that Mike Martin, Parachute Regiment and SAS Colonel, retired, had done this for four thousand complete strangers, none of whom ever knew he existed.

THE END

AVENGER
By Frederick Forsyth

A young American aid volunteer, Ricky Colenso,
is brutally murdered in the former Yugoslavia. His
billionaire grandfather is bent on revenge. Cal Dexter,
ex-Vietnam Special Forces, is the one man who could
bring the killers to justice. But what starts as a personal
tragedy explodes into a terrifying drama on the centre
stage of world terrorism

From the battlefield of Vietnam via war-torn Bosnia to the
jungles of Central America, *Avenger* is packed with
breathtaking action and political suspense, while in Cal
Dexter we meet an unforgettable hero in the most
dynamic Forsyth tradition.

'Forsyth's storytelling mastery goes from strength to
strength. Don't imagine you know what's going to happen
next. Forsyth delivers a brilliant finale and a twist that'll
make your head spin'
Daily Mirror

'This action-injected tale races from Vietnam to Bosnia to
Washington and on to the jungles of Central America with
a taut showdown and an ingenious twist at the end'
Daily Mail

'Highly readable and with that trademark of impressive
detail'
Mail on Sunday

'Orchestrated into a steady ratcheting-up of tension that
pays great dividends'
Sunday Express

'Vintage Forsyth'
Sunday Times

9780552150446

CORGI BOOKS